THE
LAST ONE
AT THE
WEDDING

Also by Jason Rekulak

Hidden Pictures
The Impossible Fortress

THE
LAST ONE
AT THE
WEDDING

A Novel

JASON REKULAK

FLATIRON
BOOKS
NEW YORK

THE LAST ONE AT THE WEDDING. Copyright © 2024 by Jason Rekulak. All rights reserved. Printed in the United States of America. For information, address Flatiron Books, 120 Broadway, New York, NY 10271.

www.flatironbooks.com

Floral bouquets by Alweina Design, with the blood of Will Staehle
Map illustration by Virginia Allyn

Library of Congress Cataloging-in-Publication Data

Names: Rekulak, Jason, author.
Title: The last one at the wedding : a novel / Jason Rekulak.
Description: First U.S. Edition. | New York : Flatiron Books, 2024.
Identifiers: LCCN 2024020006 | ISBN 9781250895783 (hardcover) |
  ISBN 9781250374615 (international, sold outside the U.S., subject to rights availability) |
  ISBN 9781250895790 (ebook)
Subjects: LCGFT: Thrillers (Fiction) | Novels.
Classification: LCC PS3618.E57275 L37 2024 | DDC 813/.6—dc23/eng/20240510
LC record available at https://lccn.loc.gov/2024020006

Our books may be purchased in bulk for promotional, educational, or business use. Please contact your local bookseller or the Macmillan Corporate and Premium Sales Department at 1-800-221-7945, extension 5442, or by email at MacmillanSpecialMarkets@macmillan.com.

First U.S. Edition: 2024

First International Edition: 2024

10 9 8 7 6 5 4 3 2 1

For great teachers everywhere—especially Ed Logue, John Balaban,
Charlotte Holmes, Robert C. S. Downs, Shelby Hearon,
T. R. Smith, and Charles Cantalupo

CONTENTS

WELCOME TO

OSPREY COVE

HOPPS FERRY, NEW HAMPSHIRE

THE GLOBE

6

OC

OSPREY LODGE

IMAGINATION GROVE

BIG BEN

14

13

12

B

CORMORANT POINT

GUARD STATION

SPA

LEGEND

1. KINGFISHER
2. LOON
3. WOODPECKER
4. PUFFIN
5. CARDINAL
6. GRACKLE
7. CRANE
8. HUMMINGBIRD
9. NUTHATCH
10. IBIS
11. WARBLER
12. BLACKBIRD
13. FALCON
14. BALD EAGLE
B BOATHOUSE
G GAME ROOM
+ FIRST AID
S STAFF

LAKE WYNDHAM

I.

THE INVITATION

1.

My phone lit up with the words UNKNOWN CALLER, which usually meant some kind of scam, but I guess I felt like talking because I answered anyway: "Hello?"

"Dad?"

I shot up so fast my knees banged against the kitchen table, sloshing coffee all over my bacon and eggs. "Maggie? Is that you?"

She answered but I couldn't make out the words. Her voice was faint. The line hissed and crackled, like I was gonna lose her at any moment.

"Hang on, hon. I can barely hear you."

The kitchen is the worst room in my house for taking calls. You never get more than a bar or two of signal strength. I carried the phone into my living room and tripped over some lumber I'd been trimming and sanding and staining. Just a little carpentry project to kill the time at night; it would all turn into a coffee table, eventually. But I could never motivate myself to finish the job, so there were screws and sawdust all over my rug.

I hopscotched through the mess and rushed down the hall to Maggie's childhood bedroom. She had a tiny window overlooking our backyard and the old Lackawanna rail lines—and when I leaned against the glass, the signal popped up to three bars.

"Maggie? Is this better?"

"Hello?" She still sounded a million miles away. Like she was calling from overseas. Or from a cabin deep in a remote wilderness. Or from the trunk of an abandoned car, buried at the bottom of an underground garage. "Dad, can you hear me?"

"Are you okay?"

"Dad? Hello? Can you hear me?"

I mashed the phone to my ear and shouted yes, YES, I could hear her. "Where are you? Do you need help?"

And the line went dead.

CALL FAILED.

Our first conversation in three years, and it hadn't lasted even a minute.

2.

But now I had her number. Now I finally, *finally* had a way to reach her. I pressed CALL BACK and got a busy signal. I tried again, two-three-four times: busy-busy-busy. Because *she* was calling *me*. I was so excited, my hands were shaking. I forced myself to stop dialing and waited for the phone to ring. I sat at the foot of the bed and glanced impatiently around my daughter's bedroom.

All her old stuff was still here. I never had houseguests, never had any reason to get rid of it. All her posters from high school were still taped up: One Direction and the Jonas Brothers and a goofy grinning sloth hanging from a tree. There was a big shelf of sports trophies and a big wicker basket filled with stuffed animals. Most days I kept the door closed and tried to ignore the room's existence. But every so often (more than I care to admit) I'd come inside and sit on her giant bean-bag chair and let myself remember when we were all still here and still acting like a family. I'd remember how Colleen and I used to squeeze into the little twin bed and Maggie would plop between us and we'd laugh ourselves silly reading *Good Night, Gorilla*.

My phone buzzed again.

The same UNKNOWN CALLER.

"Dad? Is this better?"

Now her voice was clear. Now she could have been sitting right beside me, changed into her *Lion King* pajamas and ready for bed.

"Maggie, are you okay?"

"I'm fine, Dad. Everything's fine."

"Where are you?"

"I'm home. I mean, my apartment. In Boston. And everything is fine."

I waited for her to continue, but she didn't say anything. Maybe she didn't know where to start. And neither did I, really. How many times had I imagined this moment? How many times had I rehearsed this conversation while standing in the shower? Now it was finally happening, and all I could think to blurt out was: "Did you get my cards?"

Because God I sent this kid so many cards: birthday cards, Halloween cards, just-because cards. Always with ten or twenty dollars of pocket money and a little note.

"I got them," she said. "I've been meaning to call for a while now, actually."

"I'm so sorry, Maggie. This whole situation—"

"I don't want to talk about it."

"Okay. All right." I felt like one of those hostage negotiators on *Rescue 911*. My number one objective was keeping Maggie on the phone, keeping her talking, so I pivoted to a safer topic: "Are you still at Capaciti?"

"Yeah, I just had my three-year anniversary."

Maggie was so damn proud of that job. She was hired by Capaciti right around the time our troubles started—and long before anyone had ever heard of the place. Back then it was just one of a thousand Cambridge start-ups promising to change the world with a new top secret technology. Now they have eight hundred employees spread across three continents, and they'd just run a Super Bowl commercial with George Clooney and Matt Damon. I read everything I could find about the company, always searching for a glimpse of my daughter's name, or at least some insights into her life and career.

"Those new Chevys look amazing," I told her. "As soon as the prices come down—"

She cut me off midsentence: "Dad, I've got some news. I'm getting married."

She didn't pause to let the information sink in. She just started spilling the details like she couldn't hold them back anymore. Her fiancé's name was Aidan. He was twenty-six years old. His family was hosting the reception at their home in New Hampshire. And all the while I was stuck on the first bombshell.

She was getting married?

". . . And in spite of everything that's happened," Maggie continued, "I'd really like you to be there."

3.

My name is Frank Szatowski and I am fifty-two years old. I've spent most of my adult life driving a package car for the United Parcel Service. You know those big brown trucks rumbling around your neighborhood full of goodies from the internet? UPS calls them package cars, even though they're technically large step vans. I started driving young, straight out of the army, and I was recently inducted into the Circle of Honor, an elite group of UPS drivers who've worked twenty-five years without an accident.

I make a decent living and I've always liked the work, even though it keeps getting harder and harder. When I started, back in the late nineties, most of the parcels were still boxes. The heaviest thing you'd lift might be a Gateway computer. These days, forget it. Any given shift, we're hauling futons, file cabinets, artificial Christmas trees, flat-screens, even Ping-Pong tables. And car tires, holy mother of God, those are the worst. Did you know you can buy car tires online? They ship in packs of four, strapped together and bundled in cardboard, so we can't even roll the damn things.

Still, if I pulled enough overtime, I could usually clear a hundred grand. My Jeep was all paid off; my mortgage was close, and I didn't owe a penny to Visa or Mastercard. I was three years away from early retirement with a decent pension and comprehensive healthcare. Not bad for a guy who never went to college, right? Up until my wife passed, and all my troubles with Maggie started, I used to say I was blessed. I used to feel like the luckiest bastard on earth.

So now listen to what happened:

"The wedding's in three months," Maggie told me. "July twenty-third. I know I'm calling super last-minute but—"

"I'll be there," I said, and my voice cracked because I was starting to cry. "Of course I'll be there."

"Okay, good. Because we're mailing the invites tomorrow and—I wanted to call first."

And then the conversation sputtered out. Like she was expecting me to say something, but I was too choked up to answer. I made a fist and thumped my breastbone, three hard whacks to keep myself from blubbering. *Come on, Frankie. Keep it together! Don't be such a baby!*

"Dad? Are you still there?"

"Tell me about Aidan," I suggested. "My future son-in-law. Where did you meet him?"

"At a costume party. Back on Halloween. I went as Pam, from *The Office*? And Aidan came as Jim. So as soon as he showed up, everyone wanted us to stand together. We started doing scenes from the show, and his impression was totally spot-on."

I had trouble focusing on her story because I was too busy doing the math. "You met *last* Halloween? Six months ago?"

"But it feels like I've known him forever. Sometimes we're talking and I swear he can read my mind. Like we have a telepathic connection. Did you and Mom ever feel that way?"

"Sure, I guess? When we first met?" But then we got older and wiser and realized these were just signs of youthful infatuation. I didn't bother pointing this out. I loved hearing the happiness in Maggie's voice, the sweet music of hope and optimism.

"What's Aidan do for a living?"

"He's a painter."

"In the union?"

"No, not a housepainter. He makes art."

I was determined to sound supportive, but you have to admit this was a curveball.

"He makes art for a living?"

"Well, he has a couple things in galleries? But right now he's building up his name. Growing his reputation. That's how it works. Plus he teaches a class, at MassArt."

"What does he get for that?"

"I'm sorry?"

"How much does he make?"

"I'm not going to tell you."

I couldn't understand why not, but I heard her taking a deep breath and getting annoyed so I decided not to push it. Maybe Maggie was right. Maybe her future artist-husband's salary was none of my business. Besides, I still had plenty of other questions:

"First marriage?"

"Yes."

"Any kids?"

"Zero kids and zero debt, don't worry."

"What about his mother?"

"I love her. She's got some health issues right now? Lots of migraines. But she's started a new medicine and it's really helping."

"And his dad?"

"Fantastic. Amazing."

"What's he do?"

Maggie hesitated. "That part's a little complicated."

"How is it complicated?"

"It's not *complicated*. It's just more of a conversation than I want to have right now."

What the hell was that supposed to mean?

"It's a straightforward question, Maggie. How does he make a living?"

"The headline is: I'm getting married and I want you to come to the wedding. July twenty-third in New Hampshire."

"But you can't tell me what his father does?"

"I could tell you, but you'll have more questions and I need to go. I have a dress fitting at ten and the seamstress is a total psycho. If I'm a single minute late, she'll make me reschedule the whole appointment."

Clearly she just wanted to get off the phone, but I couldn't resist making one more push: "Is Aidan's father in jail?"

"No, it's nothing bad."

"Is he famous? Is he an actor?"

"He's not an actor."

"But he's famous?"

"I told you: I don't want to get into it."

"Just give me his name, Maggie. I'll google him."

The line seemed to go dead for a moment. Like the call had been dropped, or perhaps she'd muted the phone to confer with someone. And then she was back.

"I think we should talk about it over dinner. Me and you and Aidan. Could you maybe drive up to Boston?"

And of course I could drive up to Boston. I could drive all the way to the North Pole, if that was what Maggie wanted. She suggested Saturday night at seven o'clock, and she gave me the name of an Irish pub on Fleet Street, near the Old State House. Then she insisted she had to end the conversation and get to her dress fitting. "I'll see you this weekend. I'm really looking forward to it."

I said, "Me, too," but I couldn't end the call without one more attempt at an apology: "And listen, Maggie, I am so sorry for everything, okay? I've felt so awful these past few years. I know I screwed up. I should have handled things better, and I wish—"

And then I was interrupted by a soft click.

She'd already hung up.

4.

My wife died from a brain aneurysm, one of these ticking time bomb things. Colleen used to work at Michaels, the arts and crafts store. One minute she's helping a schoolteacher look for glitter glue. Next thing you know, she's down on the floor, lights out. Died in the ambulance on the way to Holy Redeemer. Thirty-six years old. A tragedy on multiple levels, when you consider all the awful stuff I'm going to tell you about. Because my wife could spot a bullshitter from a mile away. She would have seen this trouble coming long before I did.

Maggie was only ten years old when her mother passed. Right on the cusp of puberty and womanhood and at pretty much the worst age to lose a parent. I remember wishing that I had gotten the aneurysm instead of Colleen, because my wife could have raised Maggie just fine and my Teamsters pension would have provided for them. Instead I had to make do with help from my sister, Tammy. She lived six miles away and gave me a ton of help; she was always driving Maggie to doctors' appointments and dentist visits and contact lens fittings and ob-gyn screenings and dermatology checkups and a million other things so I could pay the bills and keep food on our table. It was a stressful time of life, and I am first to admit that I made a shit ton of mistakes. You know you've messed up pretty bad when your only daughter stops speaking to you, when she gives you the silent treatment for three whole years. But I'll talk about that whole situation later. Before I tell you the story of Maggie's previous so-called boyfriend, I want to tell you about her new fiancé, and why I was instantly suspicious.

The day after her big surprise announcement, Maggie called me back with a change of plans: "We think you should come to our apartment instead. We'll just eat here."

She hadn't mentioned that she and Aidan were already living together, but I wasn't too surprised. Boston rents were brutally expensive, and Aidan probably saved a fortune by gaining a roommate. Plus, Maggie always hated her old apartment, anyway. It was a tiny, damp studio in the basement of a Victorian brownstone, and the place was overrun with silverfish—long hairy insects that looked like giant eyebrows. They fell into Maggie's bathtub every time she took a shower, and she'd have to tap-dance around their bloated drowning bodies. My daughter claimed to spend all her weekends in the Capaciti offices just to steer clear of the dank, damp apartment. I'm sure she was thrilled to break her lease and move to Aidan's place.

But I pushed to meet at a restaurant, anyway. "This is a special occasion. I don't want you to cook."

"I'm not cooking."

"Aidan's cooking?"

"We worked it out, Dad. You just need to show up."

I thought I understood what was happening. I figured that with a big wedding on the horizon, the kids were looking at their checkbooks and cutting expenses. I'd already googled "How much do they pay art teachers?" and let me tell you something, it is not good. The median salary was forty grand, and that won't go far in a city like Boston. Forty grand won't get you more than a couple of cans of baked beans.

I assured Maggie that I wanted to pay for the entire meal at the restaurant of their choice. "Chinese, Italian, anything you want. Let's splurge."

But she insisted I come to their apartment. "It's right off Route 93. By the Zakim Bridge."

"You live next to a bridge?"

"Not literally next to it. But you can see it from our window."

"And it's safe there? My Jeep will be okay?"

"It'll be fine, Dad. Aidan's lived here three years and he's never had any problems."

She seemed to think my questions were silly, but let's be honest: these days, you can't turn on the radio without hearing about another homicide or carjacking or random bursts of gunfire. And "right off Route 93" didn't sound like the best of neighborhoods. That highway was choked with traffic all day long and no one with any money would choose to live near it.

Still, I kept these concerns to myself and asked Maggie to text me the address. I was keeping an open mind. I was ready to meet my daughter anywhere.

5.

Apart from a four-year stint in the United States Army, I've lived my whole life in Stroudsburg, Pennsylvania, a small borough of six thousand people in the Pocono Mountains. We're popular with tourists because we've got skiing, swimming, horseback riding, and miles of hiking trails, plus a nice downtown with restaurants and shops. In the winter, we dress it all up with twinkle lights and it looks like a Lifetime Christmas movie. March brings the annual St. Patty's Day parade with fire trucks and bagpipes and the high school marching band. And every July we have Stroudfest, which is a giant outdoor music festival with live bands and dancing in the streets. I'm not trying to suggest we're any kind of world-class travel destination—I know Wolfgang Puck won't be opening a restaurant here anytime soon— but Stroudsburg is clean and affordable, and the schools are pretty good. You keep hearing about all these other small towns going broke, but somehow we're still getting by.

Boston was a long drive from home and I left early, anxious to get on the road. Halfway through Connecticut, I started seeing billboards for the new Chrysler Reactor and the Miracle Battery, which is the product that put Capaciti on the map. It's got the best range of any EV sold in the United States—well over eight hundred miles on a single charge, even with the music loud and the AC blasting. Every billboard had the same slogan—THE FUTURE OF DRIVING IS CLEAN—and I felt a little shiver of pride whenever I passed one. Because Maggie worked in the marketing department and I liked to believe that she'd helped with the signs, or at least knew the people who did. All these giant expensive advertisements seen by millions of drivers every day, and my daughter had played a part in them. I wished her mother was alive to see it.

A little after two o'clock I stopped in Worcester, about an hour west of Boston, to look around for a cheap hotel. There was a Super 8 right off the highway advertising vacancies for sixty-nine dollars and the manager was happy to grant me an early check-in, so I didn't bother to shop around. The room was on the shabby side, with water stains on the ceiling and cigarette burns on the furniture, but the mattress was firm and the bathroom was clean so I felt like I got a good deal.

On my way into the city, I stopped at a Sam's Club to pick up some flowers. They always have these nice little bouquets right by the registers. And then once I got in the store I had to buy Pepperidge Farm Milano cookies, because they were always Maggie's favorite. And two small fire extinguishers because they were on sale for ten dollars and you can always use some extras.

Were all these gifts a little excessive? Maybe. But I still remembered what it was like to be young and starting out, and I thought Maggie and Aidan would appreciate the help.

By six o'clock I'd made it to the Charles River and found myself snarled in Boston gridlock. It was a long, painful crawl over the Zakim Bridge, but traffic got better on the other side. I took the first exit and then followed the river for a mile or so until the road dead-ended at an enormous tower of steel and glass: Beacon Plaza. The GPS said I'd arrived at my destination, but I knew right away there'd been a mistake. It looked like the skyscraper in *Die Hard*. My headlights pointed at a sign listing all the major tenants: Accenture, Liberty Mutual, Santander Bank, and a bunch of names that sounded like law firms. It was Saturday night, so most of the floors were dark. But I saw a woman through the windows of the lobby, so I left my Jeep in a loading zone and went inside to ask for directions.

I felt like I was entering a cathedral—a vast cavernous space built of glass and polished stone. On a normal day, I imagined that thousands of commuters passed through this lobby on their way to work. But now it was just me and a lone young woman in the center of the room, standing at a high desk that resembled an altar.

"Mr. Szatowski?" she asked.

I couldn't believe it. "How do you know my name?"

"Margaret told us you were coming. I just need a quick peek at a photo ID, sir. A driver's license will be fine."

She was blond and petite and very pretty, dressed in a trim blue suit. I reached for my wallet, a worn leather billfold frayed at the seams, on the verge of falling apart. "This is an apartment building?"

"It's mixed use. Mostly commercial. But the top floors, where Aidan and Margaret live, they're all residential."

I offered my Pennsylvania driver's license, and Olivia (up close I could see her name tag) handled it with tremendous reverence. Like I'd just shared an original parchment copy of the Declaration of Independence. "Thank you, Mr. Szatowski. Elevator D is to your right, and that'll take you upstairs."

"My car's in the loading zone," I explained. "Is there—"

A young man materialized on my left, as if conjured out of thin air. "I'll take care of your vehicle, Mr. Szatowski. There's a garage beneath the building."

I didn't know what was more incredible—that everyone in the lobby already knew my name, or that they were all pronouncing it flawlessly. If you've got any Polish blood, you know the *s* is silent and it's pronounced *Zuh-TOW-skee*. But your average person tries to pronounce the *s* anyway. They call me Mr. *Sizza-TOO-skee* or worse. You would not believe all the different ways people butcher it.

He held out his hand, requesting the keys—but I still had all my gifts waiting in the Jeep, so I followed him outside to retrieve them. The young man gave me a paper tag with his phone number, and he instructed me to call it when I was ready to leave, so he could have the vehicle waiting for me. I reached into my wallet for a dollar and tried to give it to him, but he backed away like my money was radioactive.

"It's my pleasure, sir. Enjoy your evening."

I returned to the lobby and Olivia welcomed me back with another heart-melting smile. I didn't know what this woman was doing stuck behind a reception desk on a Saturday night. She could have been cheerleading for the NFL or modeling for Victoria's Secret. "Enjoy your evening, sir."

"Thank you."

I stepped aboard elevator D, a narrow black box with sleek metal walls. It was my first time in an elevator without buttons—there was no control panel, so I couldn't discern how to make it "go." Then the doors slid closed and the elevator started going anyway, seemingly of its own free will. Above the doors, a small screen flickered to life and tallied the numbers of the passing floors: 2–3–5–10–20–30–PH1–PH2–PH3. Then the elevator slowed to a stop and the door parted and there was Maggie with the setting sun at her back, dressed in a black turtleneck and black pants, holding a long-stemmed glass of white wine and standing on top of the world.

"Dad!"

Was this a mirage? I'd expected to arrive in a hallway of numbered doors and potted plants. Instead I had teleported right into someone's living room, bright and lavishly furnished with giant glass walls over-looking the city skyline. It felt dizzying and disorienting and also a tiny bit fake, like I'd arrived on the set of a TV show.

"Where's the apartment?"

She laughed. "This *is* the apartment."

"You live here?"

"Since February. After we got engaged, Aidan invited me to move in." The elevator door started to close and she blocked it with her hand. "Come on, Dad. You need to step off."

I took a careful step forward, disoriented, not completely sure the floor would support me. I almost didn't recognize my daughter. As a little girl, Maggie was what people used to call a tomboy. She favored overalls, sports jerseys, and flannel shirts from my closet, knotted at the waist so they didn't flap around. But then in high school she veered hard in the opposite direction, pivoting to swishy skirts and floral sundresses and crazy thrift-store discoveries. Now she'd adopted another new look, and this one was pure Cambridge Ivy League—smart and chic, urban and sophisticated. She'd grown out her hair—it fell halfway down her back, fuller with more layers, like she'd invested real money in it. And there was a light in her eyes that I hadn't seen since childhood. She looked like a Disney princess ready to burst into song. Or to put it more simply: my daughter looked head over heels in love.

"Maggie, you look amazing."

She waved off the compliment. "Aw, come on."

"I'm serious! What did you do to yourself?"

"It's just the lighting in the apartment. This building makes everyone look like a supermodel. Let me give you a hug."

She put her arms around my waist and pressed her face to my chest, and I was so happy I thought I might start to cry. Because this kid used to hug me every day. When she was six years old, we used to play this game called Hug Monster where she'd crawl around on the rug, snarling and growling and biting my ankles, and the only thing that would turn her back into a little girl was a monster hug that swooped her off the floor, arms and legs flailing. I probably hadn't thought about the game in ten years, but the memory came bubbling up out of nowhere.

"I'm glad you're here," she said, speaking softly into my shoulder. "Thank you for coming."

And I could feel myself getting choked up again. I worried that if I said anything, my voice would break and I'd start blubbering like a big baby. So I just broke away and gave her my bag of gifts. She seemed confused by the fire extinguishers but clearly loved the flowers.

"They're beautiful," she said. "Let's get them in water."

I'd never entered an apartment through an elevator so I needed a minute to orient myself and get my bearings. The "living room" was just one part of a sprawling open floor plan that wrapped the corner of the tower. The exterior walls were all glass and offered a panoramic view of the city skyline. And the interior walls were covered with faces—men and women of all different ages, all photographed in black and white and staring at the viewer. None of these people would ever be mistaken for supermodels, because their faces had too many flaws: wrinkles and blotches and drooping eyelids, crooked teeth and thinning hair and pointy chins. In other words, they looked like regular everyday people, the kind you'd see shopping for groceries or riding the bus after work.

"These are Aidan's," Maggie said proudly. I looked closer and realized that each photograph was actually a painting, expertly rendered in black and white and shades of silver and gray. "He's sold a couple but these are his favorites so we're hanging on to them. What do you think?"

I thought they were a little creepy, if I'm being honest. All these faces staring out with their cold expressions, looking like they'd been photographed against their will. But then again, if a couple of creepy faces paid the rent for a luxury penthouse apartment, I bet I could learn to live with them. "They're incredible, Maggie. He's very talented."

She led me around a corner, through a formal dining area, and into a very modern chef's kitchen with two sinks, marble countertops, stainless steel appliances, and lots of tiny computer screens. A short, dark-haired woman stood over the range, stirring a saucepan, but she interrupted her work to welcome me. "Hello, Mr. Szatowski. I'm Lucia."

"Please, call me Frank. It's great to meet you."

"Lucia's an amazing cook," Maggie said. "I've learned so much from watching her."

Lucia blushed easily—she was still fairly young—and I couldn't figure out how she was related to the family.

"Are you Aidan's sister?"

She blushed even more, like I'd paid her a compliment. "Oh, no, I just have the pleasure of cooking for you all tonight."

Maggie explained that Lucia trained at Cariño, one of the few restaurants in Boston to receive a prestigious Michelin star, and now she'd launched a new career as a private chef, preparing meals for guests in the privacy of their homes. And only then did I understand that Aidan had hired this woman to make our dinner.

"May I bring you something to drink? We have beer, wine, cocktails, sparkling water—"

"Whatever's easiest," I told her.

Lucia smiled patiently, not quite sure how to proceed, and I realized I was making her job harder.

"How about a beer?" Maggie suggested.

"Perfect," I said.

Lucia encouraged us to make ourselves comfortable; she said she would care for the flowers and bring the beer in a minute. Maggie steered me back to the living room and suggested we wait for Aidan outside, on the patio. "He's stuck in traffic, but he'll be home soon."

One of the big windows facing the skyline was actually a door, and with the slightest touch from Maggie's hand it slid sideways, creating an opening that we stepped through. Like the apartment itself, the patio wrapped around the corner of the building, and it was outfitted with all kinds of lounges, sofas, tables, and firepits. But of course my eyes went right to the view. I'd never seen the city from such spectacular heights. It was a whole new way of looking at Boston, a God's-eye view of Fenway Park, Faneuil Hall, the three-masted ships docked in the harbor; I could see everything laid out before me like a miniature model.

"Jesus, Maggie," I said. "You didn't tell me Aidan was—" I stopped short of using the word *rich*. I didn't want to jump to conclusions. "What kind of rent are you paying?"

"Aidan thinks rent is a waste of money. He bought the unit as an investment property."

"How does a twenty-six-year-old art teacher get an investment property?"

"Well, see, this is why I wanted to meet in person. Aidan's last name is Gardner. His father's Errol Gardner. Do you know who that is?"

I'd spent the last three years reading everything I could find about Capaciti, so of course I knew all about Errol Gardner. He was the man behind the Miracle Battery, the company's CEO and "Chief Miracle Worker." In the past year alone, he'd been profiled in the *Wall Street Journal* and the *Washington Post*, and he'd even visited the White House as a guest of President Biden. Maybe he didn't have the name recognition of a Jeff Bezos or an Elon Musk—but to anyone watching the American auto industry, Errol Gardner was a big deal.

"You're marrying Errol Gardner's son?"

"You're going to love him. He's really down-to-earth."

"Errol? Or his son?"

She laughed. "Both! They're both terrific."

I gripped the handrail to steady myself. Up until this moment, I'd thought I had a clear understanding of Maggie's future. I imagined she would face the traditional climb up the corporate ladder while juggling day care, childcare, homework, carpools, dance lessons, sports practice, and endless bills, bills, bills. I figured I'd help Maggie and Aidan as much as I could; I'd mail them an extra hundred bucks now and then, just to pitch in. But now here I was, forty stories above the Charles River, seeing her future from a brand-new perspective. I felt like I was standing on Mars, a hundred million miles from home.

"This is incredible, Maggie. Why didn't you tell me sooner?"

She gestured at the skyline, at its hundreds of high-rises and thousands of people and all the tiny blinking lights. "It's hard to describe this over the phone. You need to see it firsthand."

I thought back to her previous apartment, the dank clammy basement studio with the bathtub full of silverfish. "It's a nice change from that dump on Talmadge Street."

I only meant it as a joke, but something about the remark made her uncomfortable.

"It wasn't a dump. Just a little small."

"You hated it," I reminded her. "You called it a prison cell."

"I was just being dramatic," she said with a shrug. "It wasn't that bad."

Lucia brought me a frosted pint glass full of beer and then vanished as fast as she'd arrived. Maggie raised her white wine in a toast.

"To new beginnings," she said.

We clinked glasses and drank, and I couldn't hold back my apologies any longer. "I'm so glad you called me, Maggie. All those problems we had—I want you to know, I take the blame for everything."

She cut me off with a wave of her hand. "Dad, I'm going to make this easy on you. Let's just wipe the slate clean, okay? We both made mistakes. But I don't want to spend all night relitigating what happened."

"I'm trying to apologize."

"And I accept your apology. We don't need to dwell on it. Everything's settled."

It didn't feel settled to me. I thought it would be good to discuss what happened and put everything on the table, but Maggie wanted to talk about the future. "I'd much rather just tell you about the wedding. Could we have that conversation instead? Would that be all right with you?"

And of course it was all right with me. I was eager to hear all the details. Maggie said the Gardners insisted on paying for everything, because they wanted to host the reception at their "summer camp" in New Hampshire, and the guest list was fast approaching three hundred people. Aidan's mother had hired a wedding planner to orchestrate the logistics, but she'd left all the creative choices to Maggie: invitations, place settings, table linens, centerpieces—there were a thousand small decisions that required Maggie's attention, and she felt more over-whelmed than ever.

"Is there something I can do?"

She smiled like the offer was appreciated but utterly impractical. "Not really. You just need to show up." Then she must have glimpsed her fiancé through the windows of the apartment because she leaned closer to me and lowered her voice. "Here he comes. He's nervous about meeting you, so be nice, okay?"

"Of course I'll be nice—"

"And don't mention the bruises. He just got mugged, but he doesn't want to talk about it."

"He just got *mugged?*"

There was no time for her to elaborate because the glass door opened and Aidan Gardner stepped outside to join us. My immedi-ate thought was that he looked too young to be living in such a nice apartment. Aidan had the broad chest and shoulders of an adult, but his face still showed traces of a teenage boy. His hair was a messy brown mop that he probably combed with his fingers. His clothes were casual but looked expensive—a blue sports coat over a white V-neck. The sort of outfit favored by the boy band singers on my daughter's bedroom wall.

And he was undoubtedly handsome, if you ignored the dark ring around his left eye.

"Finally!" Maggie said, and she greeted her fiancé with a hug and a kiss. "We've been waiting forever."

Aidan and I shook hands. His grip was rock-solid. If this kid was nervous, I certainly didn't feel it.

"Mr. Szatowski. It's a pleasure to meet you, sir."

"Call me Frank, please."

"I'm sorry I'm late. There was an accident on the turnpike and—actually, you can still see it." Aidan pointed out across the city to a rib-bon of highway; we could see a short trail of red brake lights blinking on and off. "I just fought my way through that mess."

"Don't worry about it, Aidan. I've been enjoying your view. It's amazing."

"We can have dinner outside, if you like?" Aidan turned to Maggie. "Unless you think you'll be cold?"

Maggie loved this idea, so Aidan turned and rapped on the window glass, signaling for Lucia. She hurried outside. "Yes?"

"We'll take our dinner here," Aidan said.

"Of course."

"And I'll have an Old Forester Manhattan with dry vermouth." He pointed to me. "Frank, would you like another beer?"

In all the excitement, it seemed that I had already finished my first. "Sure, but I can grab it myself, if that's easier."

"Lucia will bring it. Let's sit down."

We moved to a table for four at the edge of the balcony. As we all took our seats, I stole another look at his face. There was a cut I hadn't noticed earlier, at the edge of his hairline, and Aidan noticed me noticing.

"Sorry about this," he said, gesturing to his bruises. "I know I'm a mess."

Maggie rested a sympathetic hand on his arm. "It's fine, hon. We don't have to talk about it."

"I'm meeting your dad for the first time and I look like I've come from a cage fight. We *have* to talk about it."

"Only if you're comfortable," I told him. "Maggie said there was some kind of mugging?"

Aidan explained that a gallery in Chicago was exhibiting five of his paintings, and he stayed too late at the opening-night reception. It was past midnight when he left for his hotel, and he'd found himself on a dark and desolate street. Three men crossed the road to approach him; one of them had been carrying a gun. They demanded his wallet and Aidan immediately turned it over, no questions asked. Then one of the guys decked him anyway, knocking him to the sidewalk, and the others started kicking him.

"That's terrible, Aidan. I'm so sorry."

Lucia arrived with our drinks, and Aidan paused to take a long sip of his Manhattan. The alcohol seemed to steady his nerves. "It could have been a lot worse. Because while I was down on the pavement, trying to shield my head, I could hear a car coming. A taxi driver. He saw what was happening and started honking his horn, and the guys ran off."

"Did the cops catch them?"

He looked sheepish. "I didn't call the police. I know I should have. But by that point it was really late and I had an early flight. I just wanted to go home."

"How'd you fly home without your wallet?"

"Oh, I had my passport back at the hotel. And I used my phone for everything else. Thank God for Apple Pay."

Maggie took his hand and pulled it into her lap and turned to me. "And now you know the whole story, so let's talk about something else, okay? Something a little more cheerful?"

I was happy to change the subject. I complimented Aidan's paintings and asked where he found his inspiration. He described his subjects as "characters" he spotted while walking around the city of Boston—schoolteachers, Uber drivers, bartenders, bouncers, nurses, and cashiers. He claimed to have an extraordinary memory for faces. He explained that a minute of careful observation was enough to "lock" a face in his mind, and then he'd spend days transferring the likeness to canvas.

"They're incredible, Aidan."

He raised his glass in a salute. "Thank you."

"I really mean it. They're so good, they could be photographs."

He smiled through pursed lips while Maggie shifted uncomfortably. "Dad, that's actually *not* a compliment."

"Sure it is."

"It's actually one of Aidan's biggest pet peeves. He hates when people say his paintings look like photographs."

"But they do!"

"No, they don't. You could never get these images with a camera. And think about your compliment from Aidan's point of view. Why did he waste all these hours painting if he could just snap an iPhone and get the same image?"

"It's fine," Aidan told her.

I tried to correct my mistake: "I just meant that they're very realistic, Aidan. I feel like you captured the souls of all these people."

"I appreciate it, Frank. And no offense taken. I totally understand."

Aidan drained the last of his Manhattan and signaled to Lucia through the windows, calling for another. After his second drink, he seemed a bit more relaxed, though I was a bit surprised when he asked for a third. I couldn't tell if he was nervous or simply annoyed by the prospect of having to eat with me.

6.

At seven o'clock, Lucia started carrying out many small plates of food, serving the meal family style. There were so many courses I couldn't keep track of them all. Maggie and Aidan were experimenting with a vegan diet so there was no actual meat on the table, just mushrooms, eggplants, beets, roasted squash, carrots, and more, all prepared in ways I'd never tasted before. You wouldn't think that a big plate of vegetables could fill a person up, but after the sixth or seventh course I was maxed out.

"Lucia, you're a magician," I told her. "If you cooked for me every night, I'd turn vegan in a heartbeat."

"Thank you, Frank," she said, blushing again. "Make sure you save room for dessert."

Throughout the meal, my daughter did most of the talking. She showed me her engagement ring, an enormous pear-cut diamond on an ornate gold band, and explained it was a family heirloom that had belonged to Aidan's grandmother. And she spoke with tremendous excitement about their wedding reception. It would be "rustic" and "country style" with lots of wildflowers and outdoor activities. From time to time I'd glance at Aidan to gauge his feelings, but he seemed happy to let his fiancée do all the talking. Clearly Maggie was calling the shots and he was simply along for the ride. I suppose a lot of young men feel the same way about their weddings, but I wanted to draw him into the conversation.

"How about a honeymoon?" I asked. "Are you taking a trip any-where?"

"Undecided," he said. "Do you have any suggestions?"

I told him that Colleen and I were always big fans of Carnival Cruises. As newlyweds we took a six-night excursion to the Baha-mas and the whole crew treated us like VIPs. I tried to describe all the incredible amenities—the waterslides, the couples massages, the Broadway-quality theater productions—but I must have prattled on too long because I realized Maggie had stopped listening. She was looking at a message on her Apple Watch. The stupid thing had been pinging and dinging all through dinner.

"I'm sorry," she said, abruptly standing up. "I need to call someone. There's a thing at work."

"It's eight-thirty," I said. "Who's still working at eight-thirty?"

"'Capaciti never stops moving,'" Aidan said, and I realized he was quoting the company tagline from the Super Bowl commercial. "Go ahead, Margaret. Don't worry about us. Your dad and I will hang out."

"Five minutes," she promised, and then she gave him a quick kiss on the forehead before darting into the apartment. Aidan finished the last of his Manhattan and then signaled to Lucia for another. His fourth, if I was counting correctly.

"Is she like this all the time?" I asked.

"Only seven days a week," he said with a good-natured shrug, like he'd already made his peace with her work habits.

And then the conversation sputtered out. I tried a couple of polite prompts just to get Aidan talking. I asked about his family and his teaching at MassArt, but his answers were short and perfunctory; he seemed happy to sit in silence and sip his cocktail. I remember feeling disappointed that he didn't ask me any questions; I'd hoped he might want to get to know me a little bit, or at least ask about Maggie's childhood.

Instead we just looked at the skyline in silence until Maggie returned to the balcony with a fresh glass of wine. "Last interruption, I promise." Aidan asked if everything was okay and she just sank into her chair. "Everything will be fine."

"Maybe you should tell your father the good news."

There was a quick flash of panic in her eyes—and then she shook her head very deliberately. "It's too early."

"But he's your dad—"

"I know, but we already agreed not to say anything."

And by this point I had a pretty good idea of what Maggie's good news might be. Anytime a man and woman hurry to the altar after six months of dating, there's usually just one reason. I crossed my finger over my heart and promised I wouldn't tell a soul, and then I leaned forward so Maggie could whisper her news. "What's the secret?"

She took a deep breath. "Well, Capaciti's starting a new division for the aerospace sector? And I'm going to be on the team."

"Not just *on* the team," Aidan said. "It's a huge promotion. She'll have her own staff and everything."

I must have looked bewildered because Maggie started explaining what it all meant. She said that the biggest obstacle to all-electric air travel was the enormous mass of traditional lithium batteries. The true miracle of the Miracle Battery was not its incredible capacity but its extremely low weight. The plan was to start with smaller planes for cargo flights before expanding to larger passenger airlines. "And you're going to love this next part," she said. "We're already in discussions with UPS. Last month we met with Armando Castado, and he's totally on board."

Holy mother of God. In a night full of surprises, this was the biggest bombshell of all. Armando Castado started working at UPS in 1990 as a preloader and package car driver before rising through the ranks to become chief executive officer. I'd never known anyone who'd actually met him in person. "Are you saying you *spoke* with Armando Castado? You were in the same room together?"

"Yes, and I told him you were a driver in the Circle of Honor. He was really impressed by that. He said he would remember your name." She snapped her fingers. "You know what, we took a picture!" She reached for her phone and poked at the screen until she summoned the image and then showed it to me. And yes, there was my daughter with Armando Castado and a dozen grinning executives.

"I can't believe this, Maggie." Suddenly all the alcohol was hitting me and I got kind of overwhelmed. "I don't even know what to say."

"Say you're happy for me," she said. "Because I am very, very happy, Dad. And I am so glad you're coming to our wedding."

She walked around to my side of the table and gave me a hug, and I couldn't help it, I might have leaked out a couple more tears. Aidan politely looked the other way while I dabbed my eyes, and then Lucia brought out coffee, and of course it was the best coffee I'd ever tasted.

And the night would have ended on a high note if I hadn't stopped to use the restroom on my way out the door. Lucia was in the powder room, so Maggie led me down a short hallway to the master bath, which could be accessed from either the hallway or the adjoining bedroom. "I'll box you up some leftovers," she offered. "Meet me back in the kitchen."

The bathroom was ridiculously large, like something you'd see in a *Real Housewives* McMansion, with two sinks, an enormous shower stall, and a bathtub big enough for LeBron James. I used the toilet and then went over to the sinks to wash my hands. There were all kinds of beauty and cosmetic products spread across the counter. Aztec healing clay. Charcoal-flavored toothpaste. Bamboo fiber dental floss. I spent a minute or two browsing through everything, trying to decipher why someone might pay extra for Acqua di Parma Italian shave gel over good old-fashioned Barbasol. But I decided that much of Maggie's new life was going to feel strange and unfamiliar to me—like her state-of-the-art electric toothbrush, charging on the edge of the sink via USB cable.

I'd finished snooping around and was ready to leave when I noticed the toilet was still running. I waited another minute for the water to turn off, and I suppose I'd fixed enough toilets in my lifetime to know something was wrong. Either the flapper was rotted out and needed to be replaced, or maybe (hopefully) the float ball just needed to be lowered, because that was an easy fix. I pulled off the porcelain lid, set it aside, and realized the problem was actually the refill tube—that tiny rubber hose that feeds into the overflow valve. Something had knocked it loose, so I just clipped it back into place and saved the kids a hundred-dollar house call from a plumber.

Then I went to replace the lid, and that's when I noticed a black plastic bag attached to its bottom, held fast by many strips of duct tape. It was the same type of plastic bag you'd find in a kitchen trash can, trimmed and cut into a kind of small pouch. I poked it with my finger and felt something hard inside, with the same size and dimensions of my checkbook.

Then came a knock at the door, loud and insistent.

"Dad?" Maggie asked. "Is everything all right?"

7.

Sunday morning I drove home to Pennsylvania and found Saturday's mail waiting on my porch. The highlight was a small cream-colored envelope with my name and address handwritten in elegant black calligraphy. Inside was a card with the following message:

Errol and Catherine Gardner
joyfully invite you to the wedding
of their son, Aidan Gardner, to
Margaret Szatowski,
daughter of Frank and Colleen Szatowski.

Saturday, July 23rd at 3 p.m.
Osprey Cove
1 State Road
Hopps Ferry, New Hampshire
Reception to follow

I had scarcely finished reading the invitation when my cell phone beeped. It was my sister, Tammy, and she was singing in a warbly, off-key voice: "We're gooooo-ing to the chapel, and she's gonnnnna get mar-ar-ar-ied! I can't believe it, Frankie! You must be so excited!"

"Did you get your invitation?"

"Yes, and Maggie just called me. She said you two have patched things up and you're finally speaking again."

Tammy wanted to hear all about my dinner in Boston, but I didn't know where to begin. I was still hung up on the black bag hidden in Aidan's toilet tank. I couldn't have looked inside the pouch without destroying it, so I'd just left everything alone, put the porcelain lid back on the toilet, and made a quick exit.

But I spent most of the drive home obsessing over the bag and its contents. I figured it had to be money. I think it's good common sense to keep a supply of cash on hand, so you'll be prepared in the event of an emergency. But why in the world would Aidan keep money in his toilet tank? It was so much easier to hide cash inside a book. Or a canister of flour. Or the pocket of an old, never-worn sports coat. A toilet tank didn't make any sense—unless he was trying to keep it hidden from Maggie. Because if you knew anything about my daughter, you knew she was never going to open a toilet tank and stick her fingers inside it.

"So what's the verdict?" Tammy asked. "Do we like this guy?"

"Sure, Tam, he seems fine."

She laughed. "Frankie, a frozen pizza from ShopRite 'seems fine.' This is Maggie's future husband!"

"He calls her Margaret."

"She likes the name Margaret. It sounds more professional. She works in a very male-dominated industry."

"I had a hard time getting a read on him. He was polite, but very quiet. I'm not sure I met the real Aidan."

"Or maybe you did. Maybe the real Aidan is polite but very quiet. You could do a lot worse, Frankie. He's certainly better than Dr. Cell Phone."

Dr. Cell Phone (aka Oliver Dingham) was a sore subject for me and my sister because we still couldn't agree on what that relationship had actually meant to Maggie. "She was never going to marry Oliver Dingham."

"Exactly! All the more reason to appreciate Aidan. I bet he was just nervous to meet you. Physically, you're a very intimidating figure—and the poor boy wants to marry your daughter. Put yourself in his shoes."

"He wasn't afraid of me, Tammy. He was just . . . disinterested. I tried to tell him about Maggie's mother and he couldn't have cared less."

"Or you're just misreading him," she said.

Tammy married at nineteen and divorced at twenty-one and she's never had children of her own. But she's spent the last decade hosting dozens of foster children, so she considers herself an expert on parent-child psychology. None of her placements have ever lasted more than a year or two, and she has certainly never parented a twenty-five-year-old woman. But my sister feels qualified to give me unsolicited advice.

"Frankie, let me tell you something. You've *always* been tough on Maggie's boyfriends. Ever since she was a teenager, since she started dating. No one's ever been good enough for your little girl. But I don't see how we top this guy. He's handsome, he's smart, he's artistic, *and* he owns eighty thousand shares of Capaciti stock."

"Maggie told you that?"

"I read it online. I've been Google-stalking the whole family. Ask me anything you want about Errol Gardner."

"She's marrying *Aidan* Gardner."

"But the apple doesn't fall far from the tree. And Errol Gardner looks after his whole family. He's supporting all his sisters plus ten nieces and nephews. Private high schools, fancy clothes, vacations in the Caribbean. These kids are like Kardashians!"

"You shouldn't spy on them."

"They're all on TikTok."

"I don't care what you call it. If you get caught, it's going to be really embarrassing."

"Please, Frankie. I have so many aliases I would never get caught. I'm just making sure our girl's protected. For example, do you know if she's signing a prenuptial agreement?"

I had to admit, this question had certainly crossed my mind, but I never mustered the courage to bring it up.

"I don't know."

"Well, I *do* know, because I asked her."

"And?"

"I have a simple rule for living, little brother: if you don't ask, you don't get. So when Maggie called me, I put all my cards on the table. I said, 'Sweetie, I'm sure Aidan's a great guy, but your interests need to be protected. Are you signing any kind of prenuptial agreement?'"

"And?"

Tammy paused for dramatic effect. There was nothing my sister loved more than a big, fat, tantalizing shred of gossip. She could savor it for hours, pulling apart every detail and examining it from various angles, like a dog working all night on a turkey leg. "Do you want to guess?"

"I'm guessing there isn't—and that's why you're so excited."

Tammy made a loud buzzing sound, like I'd just lost on a TV quiz show. "Wrong! They *did* sign a prenup, but it's the best possible kind of prenup. In the event of a divorce, regardless of the circumstances, they're splitting all their assets fifty-fifty."

"That can't be true, Tammy." I didn't know what eighty thousand shares of Capaciti stock were worth, but the value had to be astronomical. "Why would he agree to that?"

"Because he's in love! Completely smitten! Head over heels!"

She spoke like this was wonderful, fantastic news, but I didn't like it at all. I reminded her that they'd only been dating for six months. "What's the big rush to get married?"

"Bite your tongue, Frankie! No father in the history of the world has ever asked that question. She's getting married at the perfect age to the perfect guy and you don't even have to pay for the wedding! Do you know how many parents would *kill* to be in your situation?"

A short while after our call, Tammy sent me a long email with research supporting her claims—links to all kinds of tech websites, newspaper articles, social media posts, and YouTube videos. I read enough about the Gardners to write their family history. Catherine Gardner (née Riggins) was born in Houston, the granddaughter of a prominent Texas oilman. She'd grown up in the white-gloved world of cotillions and debutante balls, then attended Wellesley College to study art history. There she fell in love with Errol Gardner—and New England—and she'd been a prominent Bostonian ever since, showering her inheritance on a variety of philanthropic causes. She sat on the boards of a dozen different charities and nonprofits, everything from Boston Children's Hospital to the New England Aquarium.

Errol Gardner was born and raised in "blue-collar Lowell, Massachusetts" (according to his bio on the Capaciti website) and spent two years at Harvard before dropping out in 1987 to start Apollo, one of the earliest internet service providers. All his early funding came from his young wife, and within seven years the company was bought by AOL for an undisclosed sum rumored to be $100 million. Errol had been dabbling in new technologies ever since, everything from e-commerce sites to medical devices. Of course, Capaciti was his biggest success by far, and he was now CEO and the company's largest shareholder.

It was impossible to read all this stuff without feeling intimidated. Clearly Errol and Catherine were very smart and successful people, and I worried they would dismiss me as some kind of freeloader because I wasn't paying for any part of the reception. There was no way I could afford to host a party for three hundred people—but I felt more and more convinced that I needed to do *something*, just to arrive at the wedding with my pride intact.

So the next day, I called Maggie and asked for Errol Gardner's phone number. She was instantly suspicious. "Why do you want his number?"

"I'd like to introduce myself. Since you're marrying his son. Is that unreasonable?"

"No, but—"

"*And* I want to contribute to the wedding. I think I should pay for the alcohol."

Tammy wasn't the only one doing internet research. I'd started looking at bridal websites and they all warned that alcohol was the single largest expense of any wedding reception. I found an online calculator that let me input a number of guests (three hundred) and it gave me a predicted budget of $5,600 to $8,000. Which was a real kick in the balls, but I hadn't taken a vacation in a long time, so I could easily afford it. I knew it would be worth $8,000 to attend my daughter's wedding with my head held high. *Hey, everybody. The drinks are on Frank Szatowski, so let's give the guy a hand.*

"Dad, you can't pay for the alcohol."

"I have to pay for *something.* Traditionally, the father of the bride pays for everything."

"It's not the 1800s anymore. Errol Gardner won't take a dime from you."

"Why not?"

"Because he knows your financial situation."

"What's that mean?"

"Don't get sensitive. He just knows, when I was growing up, we didn't have money."

"I took you to Disney World!"

"Okay, sure—"

"We stayed on Disney property, Maggie. Do you have any idea what those character breakfasts cost?"

"Dad—"

"*And* I paid for your college. You don't have a dime of student debt. Why would you tell him I didn't have money?"

"Because money is relative, Dad. *Compared to Errol Gardner,* you don't have money. That's all I meant."

"I *do* have money, and I want to spend some on this wedding. And now I would like this man's phone number. Please."

"Well, see, that's the other thing. You don't just call Errol Gardner on the phone. The man is booked 24-7. Even his assistants have assistants. And he's traveling this week. He's in Yokohama. He's meeting with Isuzu."

I sensed that if I didn't interrupt her, she would offer another thousand explanations for why contacting Errol Gardner was simply impossible.

"Maggie, I just want ten minutes of the man's time. Because his son is marrying my daughter. Now, if you don't give me his number, I'm going to call Capaciti and explain the situation and ask for him myself."

She sounded terrified by this alternative and promised to have Errol call me within forty-eight hours. The very next night, I was sitting in the dark in my living room, drinking a Coors Light and watching the Phillies lose to the Diamondbacks, when my telephone rang with a private number. Errol Gardner apologized for the late hour; he was calling from an airport in Osaka. Then he must have heard my television in the background, because he asked if Zac Gallen was pitching. I said that he was, but he wasn't doing his team any favors. Turns out Errol was a baseball fan, so right away we had something in common, and that made me feel more comfortable.

He was very complimentary of "Margaret." He described her as smart and confident and "a real rising star" at Capaciti. "I keep telling Aidan he hit the jackpot. The girl's a total catch. I'm sure there were boys knocking on your door all through high school."

"The worst ones didn't even knock," I told him. "They'd just show up in their cars and text her to come outside."

Errol laughed. "Oh, I would have hated that, Frank! That must have been really hard for you!"

I figured I needed to return all of his compliments and say something nice about my future son-in-law, so I called Aidan a talented artist with a bright future. His father just laughed. "He's picked a brutal way to make a living, I'll tell you that much. Name the five most important painters working in America. Hell, name just one." I confessed that I was the wrong person to ask, that I hadn't been to an art museum since middle school. "But that's exactly my point, Frank. If you read the *New York Times*, you'll see hundreds of stories about artificial intelligence, gene therapy, nanotech, all these big world-changing innovations. Painting pictures is not one of them. I hate to say this but: nobody cares! It's a fruitless endeavor. But Aidan calls it his life's passion, so what can I do?"

I thought Errol was being unnecessarily tough on his son. I pointed out that it was brave of Aidan to blaze his own trail, to pursue a career outside his father's shadow.

"I'll tell you the hardest part of having kids, Frank. Eventually they reach an age where you can't control them anymore. They're going to take drugs or rob banks or paint weird face portraits and we can't do a goddamn thing about it. We either accept who they are or there's not going to be a relationship. Isn't that true?"

I wondered how much Maggie had told him about our three-year estrangement. I couldn't tell if Errol was tactfully broaching the subject or if I was simply being paranoid. "How's Mrs. Gardner feeling? Maggie mentioned some health problems."

"Most days, she's fine. But once or twice a month she gets terrible migraines. Feels like she's been hit by a truck. All she can do is lie down in a dark room and wait for them to pass. But next week we're seeing a new specialist, at Mount Sinai, and I think she's going to beat this thing before the big wedding."

The entire call lasted just fifteen minutes, but it was long enough to give me an impression of the man. Errol was smart, funny, plain-spoken, and unfailingly generous. When the conversation turned to the wedding, he encouraged me to invite as many guests as I wanted. He said that Osprey Cove (the name of their camp in New Hampshire) could accommodate about a hundred visitors, and there were motels nearby for everyone else. This seemed like the perfect moment to introduce my proposal: I said it was very generous of him to host the wedding, but I insisted on contributing to the cost.

"I'd like to cover the bar tab."

"Oh, no, no, no, Frank, I couldn't let you. My family's full of alcoholics. My sisters will bankrupt you."

"I want to do it, Errol. Beer, wine, Long Island iced teas, anything your sisters want."

"It's too much money—"

"I insist—"

"Absolutely not—"

"Please—"

"Never—"

We went around and around like that for a couple of minutes, two middle-aged men with their pride and dignity on the line. Errol argued there was "no way to fathom" how much alcohol might be consumed, so I told him about the calculator I'd found online. I offered to send him the full $8,000 as a deposit and then settle up the difference after the wedding. Eventually we compromised on "eight thousand dollars but not a penny more" and the next morning I mailed a check to his office in Cambridge. It was a huge sum, my biggest purchase in years, and I felt a shiver of pride as I signed my name to the check. I knew it was money well spent. It felt like a sound investment in my daughter's future.

8.

The weeks passed quickly. Even with Maggie and the Gardners shouldering all of the planning, I still had plenty of items on my to-do list. I went upstairs to my attic and pulled out my old tuxedo, last worn on my wedding day some twenty-eight years ago. It no longer fit me, but I enjoyed trying it on and going through all the pockets. I found a cocktail napkin smudged with Colleen's lipstick and moved it into my wallet for good luck.

I went to Men's Wearhouse and rented a light-gray summer tuxedo with a matching vest and bow tie. The salesman was a young and hungry kid with pink hair and pierced eyebrows. He was clearly working on commission, so I listened to all his patter and allowed him to sell me a deluxe nine-piece accessory package with shoes, cuff links, and pocket square. My little girl was getting married, and I was feeling goodwill toward the entire world.

I worked on my toast for the reception, which was my only real responsibility for the weekend. All the bridal websites said that the ideal speech would be ninety seconds in length. "Just speak from the heart," they advised me, "and the toast will write itself." So I tried writing from the heart and ended up with eighteen pages of notes. There was just so much I wanted to say, and I couldn't find a way to whittle it down to ninety seconds. Every time I sat down to work on it, the damned thing just got longer.

Meanwhile, I tried making overtures to my future son-in-law, hoping to get to know him a little better. I wanted to buy us tickets for a Red Sox game, but Maggie warned that Aidan wasn't big on sports, so I suggested we go to Boston's Museum of Fine Arts instead. "You can walk me around and show me your favorites." And Aidan seemed to appreciate the invitation, but we never managed to agree on a date. Every time I'd propose a weekend, he'd manufacture some conflict or excuse, and after my third or fourth attempt I realized he just didn't want to go. I tried not to take it personally. Aidan already had a great father and he didn't need another. And given the difference in our backgrounds, I suppose it was unlikely that we'd ever be friends.

But Maggie didn't make time for me, either, and this really bothered me. Now that we were back on speaking terms, I was anxious to make up for lost time. I'd call her at random moments just to catch up, but most of my calls went straight to voice mail. And on the few occasions we actually connected, our conversations never lasted more than a few minutes. Between planning the wedding and all her new job responsibilities at Capaciti, she said she felt overwhelmed.

"But we'll have lots of time together in New Hampshire," she promised. "You're still coming Thursday, right?"

This was the plan. Even though the ceremony wasn't until Saturday afternoon, family and close friends were invited to arrive at Osprey Cove on Thursday for three days of food, fun, and lakefront activities. Maggie seemed eager to show me everything the camp had to offer.

"We can even go canoeing!" she said. "It'll be like our Girl Scout camping trips all over again."

I told her that sounded great, and then I made an excuse to end the call so she could get back to work. By this point, it was mid-July, and I knew I'd be seeing her soon enough. I promised myself that I would stay out of her hair until the wedding—and I nearly met my goal.

9.

The night before I left for New Hampshire, I went over to Supercuts so Vicky could give me a trim. I kept my hair pretty short, so there was never much to cut, but Vicky worked carefully and methodically so that we always had plenty of time to chat.

She and I were about the same age, but I swear this woman didn't look a day over forty. She had long dark hair, warm brown eyes, and a smile that lit up the salon. Vicky always kept a library book in her workstation and she loved to discuss whatever she was reading. Her favorites were the historical romances, so she could tell you all about the Tudors and the Vikings and Queen Cleopatra. Most of these books were like eight hundred pages, but every time I saw her she always had a new one.

Vicky had been married twice and divorced twice, and her workstation mirror was decorated with snapshots of two smiling children. Todd, the boy, was her pride and joy. He lived in Brooklyn with his husband and wrote for the *Wall Street Journal*. Janet, the daughter, was the heartbreaker. Janet died a couple of years ago from a drug overdose. But she was still up on the mirror with her brother, posing for Halloween and prom night and Christmas morning, because she was a big part of Vicky's life and always would be.

Over the past few months, I'd told Vicky all about my estrangement from Maggie and our surprise reconciliation and the upcoming wedding. She was a really good listener. She didn't judge other people and she always asked smart, thoughtful questions. And to be honest, I'd briefly considered inviting Vicky to the wedding—until I reminded myself that I'd never seen her outside the salon, so the idea felt a little ridiculous.

That night, she spent an extra-long time on my hair, because she knew I was leaving for New Hampshire in the morning and she said she wanted me to look perfect. After she finished with the cut, she went over to the steamer to get a hot towel and pressed it to the back of my neck, and I just about melted. Vicky was supposed to charge me an extra dollar for this service but she never, ever did, and sometimes I wondered if this meant anything.

She smiled at my reflection in the mirror. "You look good, Frank. You're going to have a great time at this wedding, and I am so, so happy for you."

I hated to get out of the chair, but I knew she had customers waiting, so I followed her to the register to settle the bill. The normal rate was eighteen and I tried to give her my usual twenty-five, but she waved it off. "On the house."

"Oh, come on—"

"It's a wedding gift. Congratulations."

I put the bills on the counter and Vicky just pushed them back into my hand. This was such an incredibly sweet thing for her to do. I thanked her again and went outside to the strip mall parking lot. Next door was a Chipotle restaurant and there were two teenaged skateboarders, girls in knit hats and flannel shirts, doing kickflips off the curb. I watched them for a minute, thinking, then walked back inside.

Vicky's next customer was already in her chair—a little red-haired boy, seven or eight years old, propped up on a booster seat and covered by a cape of UFOs and flying saucers. Vicky saw me walking up in her mirror and turned in surprise. "What did you forget?"

"Do you want to come with me?"

"Where?"

"To New Hampshire."

"Tomorrow?"

"I'm sorry, Vicky. I know it's last-minute. I meant to ask you earlier, but I didn't want to put you on the spot."

"So you're asking me *now?*"

"The Gardners have a huge house, and I'm sure you'd get your own room. Maggie says there's tons of space. And I bet you'd love these people; I bet they all read like crazy."

The little boy in the barbershop cape watched Vicky's reaction in the mirror, suddenly very interested in her response. She opened a drawer of toys and pushed a plastic dinosaur into his hands. "Listen, Frank. I know this wedding is important to you. And I am very, very flattered to be invited. But I'm already scheduled to work—"

"Right—"

"And we're crazy busy all weekend—"

"Sure, sure, sure—"

"I can't leave the other girls in the lurch."

"Of course not. I should have asked you sooner. I'm sorry to be so weird about this."

"You're not being weird. I'm *glad* you invited me. And I swear to you, Frank, I would probably say yes if I had the weekend off." She thought for a moment and added, "And if I had the right dress. And shoes. And a gift for the couple—"

"I understand."

"But I'll tell you what. After you get back, let's go out for lunch. You could show me the photos, because I want to hear all about it." Vicky reached for her tray of business cards and pressed one into my hand. "My number's right here, okay?"

I already had five of her business cards at home, pinned to my refrigerator with magnets, but I took the extra one, anyway. I promised to call her, and she said she'd be waiting.

10.

That night, I pulled into my driveway around eight o'clock. On my way into the house, I stopped at my mailbox and pulled out the usual junk—a ShopRite circular, an invitation to join AARP, and pleas for money from a host of charities. But when I got inside and tossed the mail onto my kitchen counter, I noticed a white business-size envelope with no return address. My name and address looked like they'd been typed on an old-fashioned manual typewriter with a worn-out ribbon. There was nothing to identify the sender. Just a US flag stamp and a postmark of Hopps Ferry, New Hampshire.

I opened the refrigerator, grabbed a bottle of Coors Light, and sat down to open the envelope. Inside was a sheet of paper with a five-by-seven photograph printed in its center. Printed at home is what I mean, on one of those cheap Inkjets you get for free when you buy a new computer. The colors were dull and washed-out but the image was clear. A man and woman, both young, standing in front of a lake. I almost didn't recognize my future son-in-law, because Aidan was fifteen pounds heavier in the picture, with an easy, relaxed smile that he never shared at our dinner. It looked like the photographer had caught him telling a funny story. And the woman was completely un-familiar. She was young, Maggie's age, dressed in tight denim cutoffs and a black top with a low neckline. She was laughing at something off camera and leaning into Aidan's side; he had his arm around her waist and a hand on her hip. Scrawled across the bottom of the page was a handwritten message: **WHERE IS DAWN TAGGART???**

That was it. Four words printed in black Sharpie. I reached back into the envelope, spreading it wide with my fingers, checking to see if it contained anything else.

It didn't.

I uncapped the beer, took a long pull, and studied the photograph. Up until this moment, I might have had one or two small reservations about Aidan; I'd never really believed his bullshit story about the black eye, and I didn't like the secrets hiding in his toilet tank. But it'd been easy to give him the benefit of the doubt. I'd put all my faith in my daughter's good judgment. Maggie was a smart, mature, responsible woman who didn't need me second-guessing her decisions.

Only now—

WHERE IS DAWN TAGGART???

I gathered Dawn Taggart was the very shapely girl laughing in the photograph. But what was Aidan doing next to her?

And who sent me this picture?

I reached for my phone and called my daughter. Normally all my calls went right to her voice mail, but this night, for whatever reason, she answered.

"Hey, Dad. What's up?"

"How are you doing, Maggie?"

"Well, it's three days before the wedding," she said with a bit of an exasperated tone, as if I should have known better. "Are you all right?"

"I'm fine. But I just got a weird letter in the mail. Or not a letter, actually. Someone sent me a photo."

"What kind of photo?"

"It's a picture of Aidan. He's standing next to this girl. In front of a lake. And on the bottom somebody wrote 'Where is Dawn Taggart?'"

There was a long pause—so long, I started to think we'd been disconnected.

"Maggie? Are you still there?"

"What else does it say?"

"That's it. 'Where is Dawn Taggart?' I don't know who sent it, but the postmark says Hopps Ferry."

Maggie sighed. "Unbelievable."

"Who's Dawn Taggart?"

"Dad, I need you to do something for me. I need you to take the letter and the envelope, take the whole thing, and put them in a plastic bag. Like a Ziploc bag. And bring it to New Hampshire tomorrow. Can you do that for me?"

"Why?"

She took a deep breath. "All right, look. I should have told you this sooner. Because you'll probably hear about it at the wedding? And it sounds like a big deal? But it's *not* a big deal, okay? Because Aidan wasn't involved. He had nothing to do with this."

I forced myself to stay quiet. It's a tactic I learned from my wife, Colleen: she used to say that if you wanted a kid to share things, you couldn't interrupt them with lots of questions. You had to shut up and let them talk.

"Last year, Aidan dated a girl who went missing. Her name is Dawn Taggart. Back in November, she went for a hike and never came back. And no one knows where she went."

Maggie said there wasn't a lot of additional information. Dawn was a lifelong resident of Hopps Ferry and twenty-three years old at the time of her disappearance. Police officers discovered her car in the parking lot of a New Hampshire state forest, next to some public restrooms and a trailhead. Heavy rains had soaked the topsoil, hindering the efforts of the search and rescue teams. No one could determine if Dawn had hiked into the woods or if she simply got inside another vehicle and drove away.

"So how does Aidan factor in?"

"He doesn't. That's what I'm saying. The police cleared him immediately. The day Dawn disappeared, Aidan was two hundred miles away. In Boston. But Dawn's mother blames him, anyway."

"Why?"

"Because she's psycho! He barely knew the girl."

"You just said they dated."

"Once! They had one date. They never got serious."

I looked at the photograph on the table. Aidan had an arm around Dawn's waist, and he was resting his hand on her hip. They seemed comfortable with each other, like a boyfriend and girlfriend who had moved past the awkward preliminaries of early courtship.

"So who sent this to me?"

"Dawn's mother, most likely. She's already harassing the Gardners, so now it's your turn. That's why you need to bring it with you tomorrow. It's evidence the Gardners can give to the lawyers."

"There's lawyers involved?"

"Of course, Dad. This whole thing's just a ploy for money. Dawn's mother wants the Gardners to pay her to go away."

"She said that? She actually asked for money?"

"Not yet. But the lawyers say it's her endgame. Trust me, Dad, if you saw this woman, you'd understand. She's drunk all the time; she spends the whole day in her nightgown. And she wears this horrible orange pancake makeup. Like the people you see on *Dr. Phil.*"

"Who?"

"The talk show? With all the crazies fighting onstage? This woman would fit right in. She lives in a forest. In a trailer."

It's a funny thing about Maggie: I think she often forgets that I grew up in a trailer myself, that many of my friends grew up in trailers, and our parents were nothing like the crazies you see on reality TV shows. Most of our neighbors were decent hardworking people who lived modestly and paid their bills on time.

"The point is," Maggie said, "all she cares about is money. So you need to bring the photo and give it to Errol, okay?"

"Sure," I told her. I didn't ask too many questions because I wanted to sound supportive. If people were taking sides, I didn't want to end up on the wrong one. "How's Aidan dealing with this?"

"It's hard for him. The whole family feels terrible. They even hired their own private investigator. To find Dawn and put this whole thing to rest. But guess what? The detective thinks Dawn ran away on purpose. To get away from her mother. He says every year, six hundred thousand people go missing in the United States and a lot of them don't want to be found. He thinks Dawn's probably a waitress in Las Vegas. Or Key West. A million miles from home but perfectly safe."

She spoke with tremendous confidence, as if this was the definitive version of events—a theory I should accept as fact. But I still remembered how it felt to be young and in love, and how passion blinded me to my wife's worst flaws. For example, I always used to brag about Colleen's ability to finish sentences that I'd started—but after we married, it just felt like she was interrupting me all the time. So I worried that Maggie might not be seeing her fiancé clearly, but of course I didn't want to contradict her, so I kept these concerns to myself.

After the phone call, I went to my computer, opened Google, and searched for "Dawn Taggart" plus "New Hampshire." I found a small article in something called the *Hopps Ferry Messenger* detailing her disappearance more or less as Maggie described it. Dawn's Toyota Corolla was recovered from a parking lot in a state forest, but her whereabouts remained unknown. There was no mention of Aidan Gardner in the newspaper article—or anywhere else on the internet, as far as I could tell.

So I put the photograph and the envelope in a Ziploc bag, per my daughter's instructions. Then I carried the bag up to my bedroom and put it in my suitcase. I was so excited for the trip, I'd already packed most of my things. My black oxford shoes were polished to a shine, my tuxedo was sealed in a garment bag, and I'd even bought new swim trunks because Maggie said the lake had a beach. I was excited to get to New Hampshire and meet my new in-laws. I was excited to walk my daughter down the aisle, to make champagne toasts and dance with the bride. I wanted to celebrate her marriage and wish the newlyweds a happily ever after. So I willed myself to accept Maggie's explanation of Dawn Taggart, and I ignored the quiet voice in my brain saying something felt wrong.

II.

THE ARRIVAL

1.

I'd set my alarm for 5 a.m. Thursday morning, then woke in the dark at three-thirty. Ever since Maggie and I had our big blowup, I've had trouble sleeping—and anytime I'm lying awake at night, my thoughts turn to worries, and I start cataloging all the ways I've failed my daughter. Sometimes I wonder if other parents do this, too. Have you ever spent the night tossing and turning and reliving all your worst parenting screwups? Because I've got a couple hundred of them.

Like the time we drove to Busch Gardens for Maggie's seventh birthday and she left Mr. Panda Pal in a highway rest stop. We were two hours down the interstate before she realized he was missing, so turning around would have added an extra four hours to our trip. My wife and daughter pleaded with me to go back anyway and we all ended up in a shouting match. I wasn't going to ruin our whole day over a six-dollar stuffed animal. I promised Maggie that I would buy her a new panda—a bigger panda!—when we arrived at Busch Gardens. I thought she'd forget about the stuffed animal as soon as she saw the enormous roller coasters. Instead she spent the whole weekend sick with worry, convinced that poor Mr. Panda Pal had been discarded in a trash can, that he was suffocating under greasy napkins and ketchup-smeared hamburger wrappers. My daughter barely spoke to me for the rest of the weekend, and the whole trip was a bust. I don't think she ever forgave me for the episode, and I certainly never forgave myself.

But for every awful story like Mr. Panda Pal, I could tell you a dozen stories where I did something right. I helped Maggie paint her bedroom five times, because she was always discovering fresh colors and bold new looks. I taught her how to tape up the windows and use a roller and keep the paint from dripping on the trim. I showed her the basics of self-defense; I taught her how to make a fist and throw a punch, and I made sure she understood the devastating power of kicking a man in his coin purse. And since I drove for a living, you better believe that I coached Maggie on getting her license. She aced her test on her first try, and the lady at the DMV joked that Maggie was ready to work for UPS.

I tried focusing on these happier memories, thinking they would soothe me back to sleep. Believe it or not, there was a time when Maggie actually confided in me, when she felt comfortable sharing her hopes and dreams and even her secrets. I'll give you a perfect example. There was a time back in ninth grade when Maggie's mood seemed to plummet. She sulked all through dinner, and after we cleaned up, she just went to her bedroom, closed the door, and blasted Lana Del Rey songs about death and dying and heartbreak. I asked if anything was bothering her and she refused to fess up. So the next morning I brought her to Waffle House to coax some answers out of her.

Breakfast at Waffle House was a little tradition we had together. My wife, Colleen, used to work there and all the older waitresses still remembered her, so I always got the VIP treatment and everyone doted on Maggie. They'd bring her free refills and extra crayons and just about anything else she could wish for.

That morning we ordered our usuals—hot coffee and the farmer's omelet for me, and strawberry pancakes with whipped cream for Maggie. Neither of us said very much until our food arrived, and then I gently started grilling her.

"How's school?"

"Fine."

"Classes okay?"

"Yeah."

"Anyone giving you trouble?"

"Nope."

"'Cause you seem a little off."

Shrug.

"Are you sure no one's bothering you?"

"You are," she said. "Can you please stop hounding me?"

Well, I certainly didn't see that coming. I raised both hands in a show of surrender and stopped interrogating her—but my abrupt silence seemed to make her feel worse.

"Dad, everything's fine. You can relax." She leaned across the table and whispered, "It's just my period."

Until that moment, I didn't know she *had* a period.

"Since when?"

"I don't know. Christmas?"

I couldn't believe it. Christmas had been nearly four months ago. And I'd spent the last two years preparing for this occasion. I even bought her a picture book that showed why all this stuff was coming out of her.

"Why didn't you tell me?"

She gestured for me to keep my voice down. "I didn't want to make a big deal."

"But it is a big deal! Did you tell Aunt Tammy?"

"Just my friends."

"What about the equipment? How did you get it?"

"I went to CVS like a normal person. All my friends already have theirs, so I knew what to do."

This was such a classic Maggie moment. Over the years, I'd watched her grow more and more independent and now here she was, tackling this huge milestone with no help from me or my sister. I was surprised but also very, very proud.

"You should let me pay for the equipment," I told her. "Don't buy it with your allowance. Just tell me what it costs."

"Fine, but you have to stop calling it 'the equipment.' They're pads."

"I'll take you to Walmart," I promised. "We'll get you the biggest box of pads in the store."

After we'd finished eating, I waved to the waitress and called for the check. Maggie watched me calculate the tip and count out my money. Now that she was getting older, she was more keenly aware of the prices of things, and maybe buying her own pads had something to do with that.

"Isn't twenty-five percent too much?"

"Yeah, but your mother always did it. She said these waitresses deserved it. I used to complain she was throwing our money away."

"So why are you doing it now?"

I shrugged. "In case she's watching us. I think it would make her happy." I pointed the pen at her. "And you with your big news, *you* would definitely make her happy. She'd be so proud of you, Maggie."

2.

I'd told my sister that I wanted to get an early start, and she'd agreed to be ready at six in the morning. Tammy lived in a big complex of condos called the Preserve at Saddle Brook Crossing. The units were clean and quiet and full of people who worked for a living and went to bed at a decent hour. She had a two-bedroom apartment with an entrance at ground level, right off the parking lot.

I rang the bell and her door was opened by a little girl dressed in a T-shirt and shorts. She was maybe nine or ten years old with an army-style crew cut, like she'd just completed her basic training at Fort Jackson. "Hi, Mister Frank."

A lot of my sister's foster kids struggle with my last name, so Tammy tells them to call me Mister Frank. But I was certain I'd never seen this one before. She was kind of weird-looking, with a round, flat face and eyes that were too far apart. Like someone smooshed her features with a rolling pin.

"Who are you?"

"Abigail Grimm, with two *m*'s." She unlatched the screen door and pushed it open. "Miss Tammy says you better come inside. She says she's not quite ready."

My sister's condo has the vibe of an overly cluttered Hallmark store. She's always burning candles that smell like vanilla or pumpkin spice, and her walls are decorated with lots of framed quotations: "You Are Special." "When You're Here, You're Home." "There's Always Room at MY Table." Little cutesy sayings to help her foster kids feel like part of a family. But Tammy wasn't supposed to be hosting anyone all summer; she'd been keeping her schedule clear in anticipation of Maggie's wedding.

Abigail sank into the sofa and returned her attention to the television. She was watching the local news station out of Allentown. At her feet was a small black suitcase identical to mine. The bag used to belong to my wife, but after Colleen passed away I gave it to my sister. And now it seemed like Tammy had given it to Abigail Grimm.

"Are you waiting for a ride?" I asked.

"How do you mean?"

"Is someone coming to get you? To take you to another foster home?"

She scratched the side of her head, like a puzzled character in a comic strip. "Miss Tammy didn't say anything about that. She said we were waiting for you."

The girl kept scratching her scalp and then studying the tips of her fingers, like she was searching for traces of something. I crossed the living room and called upstairs to the second floor. "Hey, Miss Tammy? Can you come down here, please?"

Heavy footsteps shook the ceiling. It sounded like my sister was rearranging her furniture. "I just need five minutes," she called back. "Why are you here so early?"

"I'm not early."

"Yes, you are."

"Tammy, I told you I wanted to leave at six o'clock. But I took my time because I *knew* you'd be late, and now it's six-fifteen and you're *still* not ready."

Over on the sofa, Abigail smiled, revealing a mouthful of crooked yellow teeth.

"Have some coffee," Tammy said. "It's in the kitchen."

I didn't want coffee. We had a three-hundred-mile drive ahead of us, and I didn't want to make a ton of bathroom stops. So I just sat on the sofa and watched the local news with Abigail Grimm. There'd been a house fire in Allentown and two brothers had died from smoke inhalation. A news anchor explained that nine Americans died every day in accidental fires. He was interviewing the lone survivor, a middle-aged woman wrapped in an emergency blanket. The poor woman's face was covered with soot and ash and dirt, like she'd just clawed herself out of the wreckage, and her voice was shaking. "This is the worst day of my life," she said between great shuddering sobs. "A horrible, horrible day."

I looked around for the remote control and discovered that Abigail was holding it. "Could you turn this off?"

"Why?"

"Because it's awful. I don't want to watch it."

The woman on the television turned to face the camera and stared helplessly into my eyes. "From this day forward," she said, "nothing will ever be the same."

Abigail switched off the TV and the screen went dark, and then the kid looked expectantly to me. Like it was now *my* responsibility to entertain her. But I was happy to just sit and wait.

"Mister Frank, do you want some pie?"

"No, thank you."

"It's funnier if you say yes."

"What?"

"It's a joke. It's funnier if you say yes."

"Yes?"

Abigail shook her head, like I was still missing her point. "We need to start over from the beginning, okay? Now listen: Mister Frank, do you want some pie?"

"Yes."

"Three-point-one-four-one-five-nine!" She was laughing before she even finished her joke, falling back on the couch and hugging her knees and shuddering with delight. "Is that enough pi, or do you want some more?"

I shouted upstairs to my sister. "Tammy! Can you please come down here?"

"I memorized pi to the first thirty digits," Abigail explained. "But the joke is funnier if you only say five. I'm gonna tell Maggie, when we get to New Hampshire."

"You are?"

"Miss Tammy says Maggie has a great sense of humor."

My sister's suitcase came cartwheeling down the stairs, tumbling end over end before crashing into a wall, and then Tammy came hurrying after it. "Careful," she called, a little too late. She was short and pear-shaped with curly black hair, and she was easily the nicest, kindest person I'd ever known. Tammy worked as a home health care aide with a full roster of elderly and infirm patients, and she was paid to prepare their meals, change their clothes, sharpen their minds, test their memories, exercise their tired muscles, and clean their privates after they soiled themselves. It was a tough, tough job; I wouldn't last a week doing it and neither would you. And frankly, I didn't know how much longer Tammy could *keep* doing it. Since turning fifty, she'd seemed increasingly tired, like the work was finally catching up with her.

But that morning she was all smiles and sunshine. "Good morning, little brother!" She wore a blue blouse with a white butterfly pattern, khaki cargo pants, and pristine white Keds—all new clothes that she'd purchased for this weekend. She'd always been self-conscious about her appearance, so I made sure to tell her she looked great.

"Thank you, Frankie. Now, have you met Abigail? And did you hear the good news? She's coming with us!"

"We should talk about that. It's pretty late to start adding guests."

"I would have told you sooner but she just got here. And the kicker is, DHS left her without a suitcase! No coat, no sneakers, just the clothes on her back. So last night we spent three hours shopping in

Walmart—" She was interrupted by a gentle *ding!* from the kitchen. "Oh! That's the muffins."

"What muffins?"

"I made us breakfast. Come on, you can help."

I followed her into the kitchen. Tammy pulled on a pair of oversize mitts before reaching inside her oven. The muffins were baked to perfection—crispy golden crowns studded with fat, juicy blueberries. Tammy poked one with a toothpick and beamed when it came out clean. "These little babies are ready," she declared. "Would you like one or two?"

I ignored her question and closed the pocket door that separated her kitchen from the living room. "Tammy, listen to me. You cannot bring that kid to the wedding."

"I don't have a choice, Frankie. Hortensia was stuck and she begged me. She had another family all set to take her, but then they flaked at the last minute."

"Why?"

"Because people are stupid, Frankie. There's nothing wrong with Abigail. She's just a sweet kid in a tough situation."

My sister says the same thing about every foster kid who walks through her door, even the toughest cases. Like Emmalou, the little girl who pooped in my bathtub because she was afraid of "man toilets." Or Michael Jackson (seriously, the genius parents named their kid Michael Jackson), a sixth-grade boy who couldn't be trusted with sharp objects. One night he got into Tammy's thumbtacks and we had to call an ambulance. My point being, Tammy never brings home little orphan Annie singing "the sun'll come out tomorrow." She specializes in emergency short-term foster care, which means a lot of her kids are fleeing seriously dangerous situations. They're the children of drug addicts, criminals, white supremacists, and worse. Many were raised in poverty, and an appalling number have been sexually abused. Yet Tammy always maintains there is nothing wrong with any of them.

And I understood what she meant, but you have to understand my side, too, right? This wedding was a big deal for me, and I didn't want Tammy's big dumb heart to ruin it.

"Please be honest with me," I told her. "Why didn't the other family take her?"

"She's got a very small touch of pediculosis." I stared at my sister until she clarified what this meant. "Head lice."

"Oh, Jesus! Tammy!"

"She's already been treated."

"I don't care. These are my in-laws!"

"The eggs are completely dehydrated. If anything new hatches, I'll see it right away and put mayonnaise on it."

I pressed both hands to the sides of my head to keep it from exploding. "Please, Tammy, listen to yourself. We're not bringing mayonnaise to the wedding. We can't do this."

"How many times can I say it? I don't have a choice. She's already in my custody. So I bring her, or I miss the wedding, and I am *not* missing this wedding. Maggie's my niece. She's my family, too."

I was struck by a flash of inspiration—a last-minute Hail Mary loophole. "But the wedding's in New Hampshire," I reminded her. "Isn't it illegal to take your foster kids out of state?"

"Normally yes, but Hortensia got us a special dispensation. Her boss signed off on it. As long as we're back by Sunday, everyone's willing to look the other way."

"But if anything goes wrong, you'll never foster again. You'll lose your certification. I can't believe you're willing to take that risk."

She wrapped a muffin in a paper towel and placed the bundle in my hand. "If you knew Abigail's story, you'd understand. This poor kid's been through the wringer—"

I held up my hands, cutting her off. "I don't want to hear the story. We're already late."

"Then let me save you some time, Frankie. I was there for you when Colleen passed, remember? I helped you with Maggie all through high school. While you were busy making money, I got that kid everywhere

THE LAST ONE AT THE WEDDING   65

she needed to be. And when you guys had your big blowup, I never questioned you. I never left your side. So now *I* need something from you. This is important to me. Can you *please* be okay with this?"

And I felt like a real jerk for making her ask. Of course I could be okay with it. I was never going to say no to my sister. After all the ways she'd helped me, I would be repaying the debt for the rest of my life.

"It's fine, Tammy. I'm sorry. I didn't get a lot of sleep last night."

"I can see that. You look really tired." Then she opened her refrigerator and passed me a jar of mayonnaise. "Now put this in my bag, okay?"

3.

We had all the ingredients of a perfect road trip: clear blue skies, puffy white clouds, three lanes of swiftly moving traffic, and a newly serviced Jeep Wrangler with a full tank of gas. Tammy was a good traveling companion; she knew how to read a map, she chose radio stations she knew I could tolerate, and she'd packed a small insulated cooler with sodas, snacks, energy bars, Tylenol, breath mints, Kleenex, Handi Wipes, and just about anything else we might need.

The problem was Little Miss Chatterbox in the back seat. Generally speaking, my sister cared for two different types of foster kids. The first type never said a word. Through some combination of bad luck, bad parenting, and various forms of trauma, they'd learned to keep their mouths shut, and they spoke only when spoken to. They asked no questions and volunteered zero information. As if they feared the slightest wrong syllable might result in disaster.

Abigail clearly fell into the second category. These were the kids who couldn't *stop* talking. They were always on, always sharing, always making bids for your attention and affection. These kids seemed happier than the silent ones, but Tammy warned me that looks could be deceiving. She maintained that the chatty kids were equally traumatized and sometimes a lot worse. They just did a better job of hiding their pain.

Abigail had a thousand questions about Maggie and Aidan: How old were they? Where did they meet? When did they know they were destined to spend the rest of their lives together? After an hour of Q&A, I sighed long and loud, trying to suggest that enough was enough, but the kid kept going: How many guests were invited? What kind of cake were they serving? Would the reception have live music? She cross-referenced our answers against the enormous book in her lap: *Lady Evelyn's Complete Guide to Wedding Etiquette*. My sister had found a used copy at a library book sale for a dollar, and she'd encouraged Abigail to study it so she'd know how to behave at the ceremony. The bride on the cover was straight out of 1965, and the pages were brittle and yellow and stank of sour milk.

"Are you walking Maggie down the aisle?"

"Yes."

"You have to stay on her left side, Mister Frank. If you walk on her right side, it's bad luck."

I glanced at my sister. "Is that true?"

She shrugged. "If Lady Evelyn says so."

Abigail leaned over the book with a sharpened pencil and underlined a key passage. "You should read all of Chapter Seven. There's a whole list of Daddy Dos and Daddy Don'ts. Would you like to hear one?"

"No, thank you."

I reached to turn up the radio but Tammy pushed my hand away. "I'd like to hear one," she said. "I bet there are some good tips."

"*Do* tell your daughter she looks beautiful," Abigail read. "*Don't* criticize your future son-in-law. Try to focus on his positive qualities."

I said, "I'm already doing that," but Tammy went, "Hmmph," like she wasn't so sure.

"*Do* make friendly and intelligent conversation with your new in-laws. *Don't* introduce controversial topics, such as the plight of the Negro."

"Jesus, Tammy, how old is this book?"

"Honey, we don't use that word anymore. It's offensive." Then Tammy proceeded to explain that the advice was nevertheless on point. "We want to discuss safe topics, like recipes and horoscopes."

"Here's something I don't understand," Abigail said. "If the bride's family hosts the wedding, why are *we* going to New Hampshire? Why isn't Aidan's family coming to us?"

"Maggie wants it this way," Tammy said. "She planned the wedding without our input."

"Why?"

"It's a long story, honey. The bottom line is, the Gardners are paying for everything."

I glanced at Abigail through the rearview mirror. "I'm paying for the alcohol," I told her. "It's eight thousand dollars."

"Eight *thousand*? Seriously?"

"That's a lot of money, right? Alcohol is the most expensive part of the wedding. But I took care of it."

"You must be rich, Mister Frank."

Tammy snorted. "He's not rich."

"I do all right."

"Honey, listen," Tammy said. "Aidan is rich. And Aidan's father is mega rich. But me and Mister Frank, we're just middle-class."

"Like average?"

"Exactly. Some people have more. Some people have less. We're right in the middle."

"I want to be mega rich," Abigail said. "How did Aidan's father get mega rich?"

"He worked very hard in school," Tammy said. "He got good grades in science and math, and then he went to Harvard, and then he started his own business."

"With his wife's money," I added.

"Why does that matter, Frankie? Why would you say that?"

"Because it's true. Everyone carries on like he's this incredible self-made zillionaire, but the truth is he used her money to get started. Her family is crazy wealthy. Her grandfather built oil rigs."

"Fine, Frankie, you're right. Like most married couples, Errol and Catherine *shared* their money, and then Errol turned it into more money."

"How much more?" Abigail asked.

"Ooodles and oodles," Tammy said. "They're worth more than everyone you know combined. But my point is, if you work hard enough, you can have everything they have. Don't goof off in school like me and Frankie here."

God, she was really getting on my nerves. "I never goofed off in school, Tammy. Why would you say that?"

"I just meant you were never Harvard material."

"Can I be Harvard material?" Abigail asked.

"Yes! That's what I'm saying. All you have to do is work for it." Tammy reached into her cooler for a bag of Goldfish crackers and tossed it back to Abigail. "And then make sure you visit me after you're rich and famous. Remember how I took care of you. And then take me for drives in your stretch limousine, okay?"

4.

Maggie had suggested we arrive at twelve-thirty for lunch, but we didn't cross into New Hampshire until eleven o'clock, so I knew I had to pick up the pace. We followed Interstate 93 through the lakes region and then exited onto a smaller, two-lane highway. The road passed through long beautiful stretches of forest—miles of white pines, red maples, and hemlock trees—interrupted every ten minutes or so by a town. Gas stations, sports bars, vape shops, bait shops, and roadside produce stands. Many of the residents kept stacks of firewood on their front lawns, available for purchase on the honor system at five dollars a bundle.

Soon, the GPS said we were forty-five minutes from our destination. I was tired of driving and ready to stretch my legs. But also nervous about reaching Osprey Cove and grateful for the long miles still ahead. We passed a broken-down minivan on the shoulder of the road; its hood was popped open, venting white smoke, but there was no evidence of a driver or passengers. As if the occupants had simply vanished into thin air. It reminded me of the woman I'd seen on the news that morning, the lady wrapped in the emergency blanket who'd lost everything in a fire.

Tammy put a hand on my arm. "Don't be nervous."

"I'm not nervous."

"You're picking at your nails, Frankie. You only do that when you're nervous."

Fine, maybe I was a *little* nervous. For the past couple of months, the idea of meeting Errol and Catherine and their three hundred friends was an abstract concept—but now it was really happening and I felt unprepared.

"There was a fire on the news this morning," I told her. "This woman's house burned down to the foundation. She was standing in this pile of rubble and saying all these awful things."

This is the worst day of my life.

A horrible, horrible day.

From this day forward, nothing will ever be the same.

"And the way she looked at the camera, I felt like she was talking to me. Like a kind of omen."

"It's called the pre-wedding jitters," Tammy said, "and they're totally normal. I've got them, too, Frankie. I've never been to a summer camp before. I have no idea how the sleeping arrangements will work. And I'm sure my hair won't do well with all this humidity. But we just gotta show up and be ourselves. What's the worst that can happen?"

My biggest fear was doing or saying something that would embarrass Maggie—something that would tarnish her special weekend and ruin our chances of reconciliation. I worried about fitting in, about making a good impression on her new friends and family. I worried about bringing a foster kid with crooked yellow teeth and head lice.

But then I glanced in the rearview mirror and saw that Abigail was waiting for me to explain myself.

"I don't want to talk about this anymore."

"You're going to be fine," Tammy said. "Everybody loves the father of the bride. You're an automatic VIP and you don't even have to do anything. Just smile at your daughter and get a little misty-eyed."

Right before twelve-thirty, we crested a large hill with a view of the surrounding countryside. The White Mountains were on the horizon, and there was a bright blue lake speckled with sailboats and kayaks and canoes. Then an old wooden sign welcomed us to the historic village of Hopps Ferry, established 1903. We passed a post office, a barbershop, and several vacant storefronts with dirty windows. FOR LEASE. FOR RENT. AVAILABLE NOW. Unlike the previous towns, this one had seen better days.

Tammy lowered her window to look around. "Can we stop for a bathroom?"

"We're ten minutes away."

"That's why I want to stop. I don't want to show up at their house and run to the toilet. It's embarrassing."

But all the stores looked empty. We passed a fire station advertising a Wednesday Night Ham and Bean Supper (FREE FOR VETERANS; ALL OTHERS $6) and a shop repairing outboard motors, and then at last we arrived at a roadside restaurant with a porch full of rocking chairs and checkerboards. Like a Cracker Barrel but for real. The name of the place was Mom and Dad's and the sign promised cold beer and fresh sandwiches. I pulled into the crowded parking lot and turned off my engine.

"Be right back," Tammy said, and Abigail sprang from the back seat to follow her. I watched the two of them cross the parking lot, then got out to stretch my legs. I started toward the covered porch but noticed a man in one of the rocking chairs, and I thought better of the idea. I was feeling more nervous than ever, ten minutes away from meeting my new in-laws, and didn't feel like chatting with strangers.

So instead I veered toward a bulletin board at the edge of the parking lot; it was papered with flyers and labeled COMMUNITY ANNOUNCEMENTS. There were advertisements for yard sales and used cars and babysitting services, for cheap deals on ink cartridge refills and baby furniture and in-house massage therapy. And way at the bottom, a flyer for a missing woman named Dawn Taggart. Age twenty-three, five foot four, 105 pounds, brown hair, brown eyes. Last seen November 3. There was a hundred-dollar award for any information related to her disappearance. The bottom half of the flyer had torn loose and rippled in the breeze. I pressed it flat so I could get a better look at her photograph, a close-cropped image of Dawn's face. She looked proud, pretty, and defiant. The sort of girl who wouldn't be taken without a fight.

I heard footsteps approaching and turned around. The man from the porch was descending the stairs. He was my age, fifty or fifty-five, dressed in jeans and a black T-shirt emblazoned with the American flag. With his free hand, he carried an open Coors Light tall boy with an orange PAID sticker affixed to the side.

"You seen her?"

I shook my head. "I'm not from here."

"I could tell from your license plate. But you looked like you rec-ognized her."

"No, I've never seen her before." Which was the truth, technically, since I'd never actually seen Dawn Taggart in the flesh. "Did you know her?"

"She's my niece."

"I'm sorry. That's awful."

"It's a miscarriage of justice, is what it is." He seemed ready to elab-orate, then stopped and offered his hand. "Brody Taggart."

"Frank."

"What brings you to Hopps Ferry?"

I said I was traveling to a family get-together. I had the uneasy sense that telling him the full truth might not be a good idea.

"With your wife and son?"

"Actually, that's my sister. And her foster daughter."

Brody paused to reflect on this information, like it didn't quite add up. "I guess these days you see all kinds of females. But Dawn here, my niece? She wore her hair long. Classic all-American girly girl. Never missed a chance to dress up, even if it was just for Burger King."

Brody set down his tall boy and began rearranging the notices on the bulletin board. He ripped away outdated advertisements for church pic-nics and charity car washes, and then with trembling hands he moved

Dawn's flyer to the center of the board, where no one could possibly overlook it, and he tacked all four corners into place. He was clearly intoxicated and it wasn't quite twelve-thirty.

"Back when this country functioned properly," he continued, "you could handle this thing in an afternoon. You'd gather your friends and knock on some doors and get to the truth pretty fast. But these days you can't count on anyone. There's too much money changing hands. Lawyers and cops and soldiers of fortune. Everybody gets a piece of the action. Do you hear what I'm saying? These days, if you have enough money, you can get away with anything. You can take a beautiful, innocent girl and—" He snapped his fingers and then revealed his empty palm, like a magician vanishing a coin. "Poof! She's gone."

With a tiny jingle, the door to the restaurant opened and out came my sister and Abigail. They didn't notice me until they were down the stairs—and then Tammy veered in my direction, excitedly waving a newspaper. "Frankie, oh my gosh, you are never going to believe this! Look what I found inside. I told them who I was? And why we were here? And they let me have it for free!"

She showed me a small local tabloid, sixteen flimsy black-and-white pages. The *Hopps Ferry Messenger*. And right on the front page was an engagement photograph of Maggie with my future son-in-law. The headline read "Aidan Gardner to Wed Margaret Szatowski."

"Our little girl," Tammy said. "All written up like she's Meghan Markle. Can you believe it? And your name's here, too, Frankie, look!"

"I'll read it later, Tammy. We should go."

I tried directing her toward the Jeep but it was already too late. Brody stepped in front of me, moving so close I could see the dandruff in his hair and the squiggly red blood vessels in his bloodshot eyes. "Wait, hold up, you *know* the Gardners?"

"We've never met them."

"Please, Frankie, don't be modest!" Tammy said. "We're practically family!" She held up the newspaper so Brody could see for himself and directed his attention to a line in the third paragraph. "Listen to this: 'The bride is the daughter of Frank Szatowski, a United States Army veteran and a twenty-six-year employee of the United Parcel Service.'"

Brody turned to me in disbelief.

"You're letting your daughter marry Aidan Gardner? Are you out of your fucking mind?"

Abigail drew in her breath sharply. It couldn't have been her first time hearing the word; I think she was just frightened, because the man sounded unhinged. I put my hand on her shoulder, lightly gesturing for her to move behind me.

"Do you know *anything* about this family? Do you know how much evil shit they've gotten away with?"

Tammy was completely bewildered. "Would someone please tell me what the heck is going on? Who are you? And what gives you the right to say all these awful things?"

Brody yanked the missing persons flyer from the bulletin board and shoved it into her face. "This is my niece. She got pregnant with Aidan Gardner's baby and he killed her."

"Pregnant?" Tammy asked.

The door to the restaurant opened and a large bearded man in a greasy white apron stepped onto the porch. "Leave those people alone, Brody. Let them be on their way."

"It's a free country," Brody told him. "I can say whatever the hell I want."

The man descended the stairs and began untying his apron. "Not in my parking lot you can't. I want you off and I'm not going to ask you a second time, do you understand?"

Brody backed across the gravel while holding up both hands: *Hey, take it easy, calm down.* He was walking away but he refused to shut up. "You people have no idea what you're getting yourselves into. You all think Aidan's Mr. Wonderful. Everyone acts like he's Prince Charming. But you've got to believe me: he's the Prince of Fucking Darkness."

"Enough, Brody—"

"Look at the flyer," he told Tammy. "Look at my niece's face. She went to the camp asking Aidan for help, for a little financial support, and that's the last time any of us seen her. He killed her—"

"No—" Tammy said.

"—and buried her body at the camp. She's somewhere on that property, I guarantee it."

"Shut up, Brody. Stop talking."

"Trust your instincts," Brody said. "Deep down in your gut, you know something's off with this kid. Something's wrong. You can see the guilt in his eyes—"

A screech of brakes cut off the rest, and Brody turned in time to see the grille of a police cruiser bearing down on him. In his haste to walk away, he had inadvertently backed into the road. Amid clouds of gray smoke, the front bumper stopped within inches of Brody's knees. He laughed like a maniac, like some kind of freakish miracle had just occurred. "You see, Frank? You see how fast they came? Less than a minute? When have you ever seen the police get anywhere in less than a minute?"

A uniformed officer opened his door and stepped out of the car. "What's the problem here? Why are you walking into traffic?"

Brody kept backing up until he reached the far side of the highway and a long, wide grove of pine trees. "I'm warning you people. You have no idea what you're getting yourselves into."

The policeman advanced toward him and Brody finally turned his back on us, limping into the forest and then descending into a kind of valley until he vanished from sight. By this point, there were a handful of cars lined up behind the police cruiser, waiting to pass. The officer gave us a quick wave of apology before returning to his car and driving away.

Tammy was still staring into the woods, like she expected Brody to reemerge and continue his tirade. "What was that all about?"

"I'm sorry you had to hear all that," the man in the apron said. "Brody's kind of like our village idiot."

"Where's he going?"

"He lives down in the valley. With his sister. She's got a trailer on Alpine Creek."

Tammy was still holding the missing person flyer. I hadn't told her about the photograph I'd received in the mail or my conversation with Maggie.

"Who's Dawn Taggart?" she asked.

"Brody's niece. I knew her a little bit. Nice girl. Very sweet. Last November she went hiking and never came back. They found her car twenty miles south of here, in a state forest. Terrible thing for the family. Absolute tragedy. I feel bad for them, I really do. But blaming Aidan for their misfortune is just plain wrong. No rational person thinks he had anything to do with it."

"Well, of course he didn't!" Tammy said.

"I'll tell you the problem, ma'am. We got a couple bad apples in this town who like to blame the Gardners for everything. Too much traffic? Blame the Gardners. Too much rain? Not enough rain? Losing your hair? Raccoons in your trash cans? It's all the Gardners' fault. They have money, they must be responsible, right?" The man shook his head, as if human nature left him exhausted. "Meanwhile, they get zero credit for all the good things they've brought to our community. Like the new senior center. And the ice-skating rink. They built a new library at the elementary school. I could give you a whole list of places and people they've helped, myself included. If you ask me, Osprey Cove is the best thing that ever happened to this town."

"Well, we completely agree," Tammy said, and then she noticed Abigail leaning into her side and clutching her arm. Clearly the girl was shaken by everything she'd just witnessed. "Sweetie, listen to me. I want you to forget everything that bad man just said, okay?"

"Why?"

"Because he's crazy. He's not thinking straight. Aidan is a very, very sweet person and he would never hurt anyone."

Abigail seemed unconvinced. She looked to the flyer in Tammy's hand, to the photo of Dawn Taggart. "Then what happened to her? The girl who went missing?"

Tammy looked at the flyer in surprise, like she'd forgotten she was holding it. Then she crumpled it into a ball, suggesting that it wasn't worth thinking about.

"They don't know, sweetie. All we know for sure is that Aidan had nothing to do with it."

5.

We left the town in the rearview mirror and followed the highway for another mile or so. We were back in the woods, driving under a dense canopy of trees that blocked out the sun. Then the GPS ordered a sharp right turn onto a narrow single-lane road. It didn't have a name or a sign or anything to suggest we were traveling in the correct direction. But the computer insisted we were and told me to "follow UNKNOWN ROUTE for 0.7 miles."

I said, "This feels wrong," but Tammy encouraged me to keep going. We descended a long sloping hill, hurtling deeper and deeper into the wilderness. The asphalt was mottled with cracks and divots and sinkholes. All the bumps were doing a real number on my suspension and I pumped the brakes, slowing my speed to twenty miles an hour. There was a giant rock in the middle of the lane, about the size of a basketball, just waiting to destroy my front axle. I swerved to avoid it, and one of my tires nearly sank into a crater.

"We're going the wrong way," I said. "The Gardners would never live on a road like this."

"Let me tell you something about rich people," Tammy explained. "They're not all like Elvis Presley, buying mansions right in town so everyone can gape at them. Real rich people *hide* their money. They don't want you to know how much there is. And they *definitely* don't want you looking at it. So you have to work really hard to find their houses. Trust me, I watch a lot of HGTV."

The trip computer was counting down the distance to our destination—eight hundred feet, six hundred feet, four hundred feet—and still no houses or buildings in sight. Just dark, dank forest stretching as far as I could see. I slowed to a stop and the computer said, "You have arrived at your destination," which made me laugh, because we were very clearly lost.

"I told you so, Tammy. I knew we should have turned around. Now we're going to be late for lunch."

I cut the wheel to make a K-turn and Abigail tapped on her window. "Over there," she said. "Do you see?"

God, it was so easy to miss: a small break in the pines and a narrow strip of gravel, winding even deeper into the woods. It might have been the access road for a utility company—except for the bouquet of gold balloons, the only clue we were still on the right track.

"Bingo!" Tammy said. "Great eye, Abigail!"

The gravel driveway was even more rutted and ragged than the road we'd left behind. The trees and bushes were overgrown, and bright green leaves smeared against our windows as we drove along. But every so often there was another cluster of gold balloons, encouraging us to keep going. I wondered how anyone navigated this driveway in the winter, when it was likely buried under layers of snow and ice.

And then the road widened, the trees fell away, and we found ourselves crossing a large grassy meadow about the size of a soccer field. There were rows and rows of solar panels on both sides of the road, shiny black rectangles angled toward the sky. And at the far end of the meadow, we arrived at a small wooden hut with a lowered gate, like something you'd see at the entrance of a state park. A tall, large man with a bushy gray beard stepped out of the hut, holding a tablet computer and waving us forward. He was my age, more or less, and wore a blue mariner's cap and a cream cable-knit sweater, like he'd just returned from a voyage at sea.

"Welcome to Osprey Cove, Mr. Szatowski."

I had to laugh. It was like Aidan's apartment all over again. "How'd you know my name?"

"It's my job, sir. I am Hugo and I am the property manager." He had a curious singsong accent that rose and fell with every syllable. Swedish? Swiss? I had no idea. "Did everyone have a nice trip?"

"It was fine," I said.

"Oh, Hugo, it was wonderful!" Tammy exclaimed, leaning across my lap and shouting to make herself heard. "What a glorious morning!"

"I am happy to hear that, Ms. Szatowski." He wore a small radio in his right ear—a hearing aid, I supposed, or maybe some kind of communication device. Hugo reached inside the vehicle and stuck a small square of blue paper to the windshield. "This is your parking permit. If you could leave this up, you'll help us tremendously."

"We need a parking permit?"

"So we know you're a member of the family. We have a lot of guests coming, and a lot of cars to park."

There were two other men still inside the hut, trim muscular guys in black shirts and pants. One had a semper fi tattoo on his forearm, but even without it I would have flagged him as ex-military. There's a certain look you get when you come of age in the service, and for the guys who roll right into law enforcement or private security, that look never really goes away.

Meanwhile, Hugo was continuing his welcome-to-Osprey-Cove speech: "Now, has anyone told you about the time difference? You'll need to move your watches forward by fifteen minutes. We call it Gardner Standard Time. Because Errol Gardner likes to run fifteen minutes ahead of the competition."

I thought he was kidding, but he showed me his wristwatch, and sure enough the time was set to 12:53. "It's painless, I promise. You'll adjust right away, and the best part is: no jet lag!"

Tammy couldn't wait to get started. She asked how to override the clock on her iPhone, and Hugo was happy to walk around to her side of the car and give her a tutorial. Then he extended his hand, offering to fix my phone as well.

"I'll leave mine alone," I told him.

Hugo warned that I was making a mistake. "A lot of people try that approach? To add the minutes mentally? But sooner or later, everyone forgets. And you don't want to be late for Margaret's wedding!"

"I won't be late," I assured him. "I guarantee that's not going to happen."

Abigail leaned forward from the back seat, wriggling between me and Tammy. She wore a cheap Minnie Mouse wristwatch that looked like it came from a gumball machine. "Can someone fix mine?"

"You don't have to," I told her. "If you don't want to."

"I *do* want to," she said.

"Of course you want to," Tammy said. "You want to fit in this weekend and feel like part of the family." She adjusted the tiny dial on Abigail's watch, advancing the minute hand forward. "Mister Frank wants to stay stuck in the past."

"It's called Eastern Standard Time," I pointed out. "I'm pretty sure the president uses it."

"But we're not at the White House. We're at Maggie's wedding. And you need to quit being a party pooper."

Fair enough. I wore a digital Timex watch that Colleen gave me for our fifth wedding anniversary, and I futzed with its buttons until the clock read 12:53. "Is everyone happy now?"

"It's going to be a wonderful weekend," Hugo promised, and then he passed me a paper map illustrating the entire lakefront property with all its cottages and amenities. "Now, Margaret and Aidan are waiting for you at Osprey Lodge. Straight down this road, all the way at the end. But before you go, I still need to grab your privacy docs."

"Privacy what?"

"Just a simple waiver saying any privileged information you find on the property is treated confidentially. So you won't, you know, steal Mr. Gardner's secrets and start your own battery company." Hugo grinned at his own joke, then passed his iPad through my open window. "Just sign in the box with your finger."

"We're here for the wedding," I said.

"I understand, Mr. Szatowski. It is totally pro forma. Everybody signs a privacy doc."

I looked down at the iPad and a dense thicket of legal jargon, page one of fifty-six, like the user agreements for wireless phone carriers and health insurance policies. I scrolled through the text and found all of it incomprehensible: *The nondisclosure provisions of this Agreement shall survive the termination of this Agreement and Mr. Frank Szatowski's duty to hold Confidential Information in confidence shall remain in effect in perpetuity or until Fountainhead 7 LLC sends Mr. Frank Szatowski written notice releasing Mr. Frank Szatowski from this Agreement, whichever occurs first . . .*

"What's Fountainhead 7?" I asked.

"Oh, for crying out loud, give me the iPad," Tammy said, yanking the device from my hands and slashing at the screen with her finger. "Does Abigail need to sign, too? My foster daughter?"

"No, just adults," Hugo said.

"And can I sign my brother's name for him? Just to speed things along? We're late for lunch."

"I'm very sorry. He needs to do it himself."

"I'd just like to know what I'm signing," I told them. When I was a kid, my father told me I should never sign my name to a document that I didn't understand—but these days, it was impossible to live by that rule. You couldn't get cable TV or even a discount card at the supermarket without agreeing to thousands of terms and conditions. "I've never been to a wedding with a— What do you call this again?"

"Privacy document, sir," Hugo said.

"Why is it fifty-six pages?"

"I don't know, sir. To be honest, I don't think anyone's ever read it."

In the rearview mirror, I glimpsed a silver Tesla slowing to a stop behind me. I ignored the new arrival and concentrated on the screen: *The parties agree that any breach or threatened breach of this Agreement by Mr. Frank Szatowski entitles Fountainhead 7 LLC and/or members of the Gardner family to seek injunctive relief, in addition to any other legal or equitable remedies available to it, in any court of competent jurisdiction,* and what the hell did any of this actually mean? It was hard to concentrate with Tammy shrieking in my ear. She was already on the phone with Maggie, calling to complain.

"Yes, sweetie, we just got here. We're at the little tollbooth thingy? But the problem is your father. He's being an absolute *mule* about this privacy doc. No, *privacy* doc. On the iPad. Exactly! I know! I know! That's what *I* said. But you talk to him. He'll listen to you."

She smacked the phone against my ear.

"Dad, it's totally fine," Maggie said.

"I'm just skimming it. If your aunt would shut up for two minutes, maybe I could finish."

"Please don't make a big deal about this. It doesn't even apply to you."

"Then why do I have to sign it?"

"Everyone signs it. They won't let you past unless you sign it."

"Maggie, I'm your father. Are you telling me that Errol Gardner won't let me attend my own daughter's wedding if I don't sign this contract?"

"It's not a contract!"

"It's fifty-six pages written by lawyers. And no one can tell me what it means. I just want to ask someone."

"Seriously? Is this *really* how you want to start this weekend? By having a conversation with the Capaciti legal team? Can you please just do this the normal way, please?"

In my rearview mirror, I glimpsed a black Audi pulling up behind the Tesla. Hugo addressed both cars with a small apologetic wave, a quiet plea for a little more patience. I tried to read as quickly as I could—*This Agreement is binding on me, my heirs, executors, adminis-trators and assigns and inures to the benefit of the Company, its successors, and assignees*—but it was only page four of fifty-six and I realized I would never get through it all, so I just scribbled my signature and ticked a box marked I ACCEPT.

Tammy sighed with relief and told Maggie we were good. "It's fin-ished, sweetie. We'll see you in a minute."

Hugo took back the iPad, ensured that we'd done everything cor-rectly, and smiled. "Very good, sir. Now just proceed straight down this road. We call it Main Street. You'll pass a few smaller cottages but keep going to the big one."

"How will I know it's the big one?"

"I think you'll know. Enjoy the wedding."

The gate went up and I drove away without thanking him—which my sister interpreted as a slight. "You don't have to be rude, Frankie. He was just doing his job."

"We shouldn't have signed it. You have no idea what we just agreed to."

"Maggie says it doesn't apply to us."

"So why did we sign?"

She threw up her hands, the universal gesture for *I don't want to talk about this anymore.*

As we drove along, I glimpsed two more guards dressed in black. They were deep in the woods and walking along what appeared to be a ten-foot-high metal fence. It looked like something from *Jurassic Park*, designed to keep the dinosaurs from getting out. I could only glimpse a small section, but it seemed to wind through the woods in both directions.

Meanwhile, Tammy opened the map to take a closer look. It was the sort of cartoony drawing you'd get at an amusement park. All the buildings had numbers, and there was a legend at the bottom to help you identify them. Five cottages had lakefront views and another nine were farther inland—plus a game room, a spa/wellness center, a boat-house, and a few smaller buildings marked STAFF. Each structure was named after a different bird—from tiny one-bedroom bungalows like Hummingbird and Warbler to larger two-story buildings like Falcon, Bald Eagle, and Ibis.

Tammy read aloud from a history on the back side of the map: "'In 1953, the Lutheran Church purchased three hundred acres of land on Lake Wyndham to create Osprey Cove, a Christian overnight camp that operated for more than thirty years before falling on hard times and closing in 1988. The camp lay dormant for more than a decade until its purchase by Errol Gardner in 1999. Together with his wife, Catherine, and son, Aidan, he reimagined Osprey Cove as a sanctuary for the world's most innovative thinkers, leaders, artists, and entrepreneurs. We invite you to follow a good idea along our six miles of walking trails. Or relax and recharge in our spacious, well-appointed cottages. And paddle toward future inspiration on the shores of Lake Wyndham.' Oh, Abigail, doesn't this sound incredible?"

The kid had her hands and face pressed against the window, watching in fascination as the first few buildings came into view. The Gardners must have demolished the original cabins because all these log-and-timber cottages looked contemporary, with big picture windows and lots of expensive hand-finished construction details. Next to the front door of each residence was a wooden sign illustrating its namesake: Kingfisher, Loon, Woodpecker, Puffin.

"Which house is theirs?" Abigail asked.

"All of them," Tammy said. "They own everything you're looking at. And all these people work for them."

Everywhere we looked, employees were washing windows, shaking out rugs, pruning branches, painting fences, and sweeping dry leaves from porches. We passed a woman in a blue housekeeping dress pushing a wheeled basket piled high with white linen sheets. And then three sweat-soaked men kneeling at the side of the road, laying down mulch in a flower bed. They were all dressed in matching green polos and light khaki pants.

"Oh, for crying out loud," I said.

"What's wrong?"

"Look at them. And then look at me."

Tammy realized that I was dressed in a green polo and light khaki pants, too. "Well, I'm sure they could use a hand, Frankie. Maybe you want to pull over."

Abigail laughed so hard she sneezed, spraying a fine wet mist all over my window. But before I could complain about it, Main Street curved around a bend and Osprey Lodge came into view. Its design reminded me of the Old Faithful Inn at Yellowstone National Park; it was a three-story fortress of timber and glass and quarry stone, with wide balconies and long bannisters handcrafted from lengths of gnarled wood.

The road ended in a roundabout at the entrance to the lodge, and as we slowed to a stop I saw Aidan reaching for my daughter's hand. Maggie was dressed like a camp counselor in a pink T-shirt, khaki shorts, and tiny Converse sneakers, and she hugged me as soon as I got out of the Jeep. "I am so glad you're here," she said. "We're going to have so much fun this weekend!"

Aidan wore a long-sleeved sweatshirt and baggy pants spotted with little flecks of paint. I said it looked like he'd been hard at work, and he smiled but didn't elaborate. The wedding wasn't until Saturday, but already he seemed nervous, on edge.

"What a place!" Tammy exclaimed. "It's like the Garden of Eden." She breathed deeply, filling her lungs with the intoxicating scent of fresh pine. "We don't have air like this back home. It's all so clean!"

Abigail was still in the back of the Jeep, clearly not sure how she fit into the scheme of things, or if she should even come out to join us. Tammy waved at her through the glass, gesturing for her to open the door.

"This is Abigail," she explained. "She's staying with me for a couple days, and this is her first time attending a wedding!"

My sister must have briefed everyone ahead of time because Maggie greeted Abigail with a big hug, and I cringed when their heads touched. I wanted to warn my daughter not to get too close.

"Thank goodness you're here," Maggie said. "We have a really big problem, Abigail, and you're the only one who can help us."

The little girl blinked. "Me?"

"Aidan's cousin was supposed to be my flower girl, but she's got strep throat and she can't make it. But you're the same size and I bet you'd fit into her dress. If you're willing to step up, you'd be doing all of us a huge favor."

Abigail's mouth hung open, revealing the pointy tips of her little yellow fangs. "You want *me* to be in your bridal party?"

"I promise it's super easy," Maggie said. "All you have to do is—"

"'Precede the bride down the aisle and scatter flower petals on the runner!'" she said. "I already know! I have a whole book about it!"

"So that's a yes?"

Abigail glanced to Tammy for permission, and my sister flashed her a thumbs-up. "Yes! I'll do a great job. I'll go get the instructions!"

She dove into the Jeep to look for her book and I leaned closer to my daughter. "You don't have to do this, Maggie. I know you're trying to be nice, but it's your special day. You shouldn't have to compromise."

"I'm not compromising," Maggie said. "I want to do something nice for her."

Aidan didn't say anything. I couldn't tell if he was uncomfortable with the idea or simply uncomfortable with the presence of our family. "Abigail's in foster care," I told him, just to be completely clear. "I had no idea she was coming. Tammy just sprang her on me this morning."

"Maggie told me. It's fine."

But he didn't seem fine. He seemed annoyed, like we were some unwanted chore he'd been assigned to tackle. Abigail emerged from the Jeep with her etiquette book and thumbed the pages until she found the chapter for flower girls. Maggie was happy to review it with her while the rest of us stood around and watched. Then a tiny electric golf cart came whirring up a paved walkway, like a moon buggy from an old science-fiction movie.

There were two men in the front seat, and Aidan explained they had come for our things. I said, "Oh, that's not necessary," but it was too late. One man was already taking our bags out of the hatch while the other covered the driver's seat in a shroud of plastic wrap so he wouldn't soil the interior with his body. "Mr. Szatowski, could I trouble you for the keys?"

I didn't like the idea of turning them over, but everyone acted like it was a perfectly normal thing to do. And after the incident with the privacy doc, I didn't want to kick up another fuss. "How do I get my car back?"

The men laughed, like I had made a joke. I guessed someone would just tell me later.

After they drove off, I assumed we would go directly inside Osprey Lodge to meet Mr. and Mrs. Gardner. Instead, Aidan led us to a flag-stone walkway that wrapped around the side of the building. "We'll take the scenic route to your cottage. Lunch will be waiting when we get there."

I asked if his parents were joining us and Maggie said no. She explained that Errol was on a Zoom with Capaciti's board of directors because they were about to issue their second-quarter earnings report. But she didn't mention Catherine Gardner so I asked Aidan directly: "What about your mother? How's she feeling?"

"Not so great," he admitted.

"The stress is doing a real number on her," Maggie said, "and it's exacerbating all of her usual symptoms: the dizziness, neck pain, back pain—"

I didn't know much about migraines, but my sister nodded like these were all typical concerns. "I'll tell you something, Maggie: If I had three hundred people coming to *my* house for *my* child's wedding? The stress would cripple me. I'd be a useless puddle of goo!"

"She should be better by dinner," Aidan said. "She's really excited to meet you, Frank."

He bounded ahead and I stepped faster to match his pace and stay beside him. After our awkward first dinner and three months of failed meetups, I was ready for a fresh start. I didn't expect to become a second father to the kid, but I hoped he would consider me an ally, a dependable person standing in his corner and cheering him on.

"How are *you* feeling, Aidan?" I asked. "Are you nervous?"

"I'm fine," he said, with a tone that suggested he wasn't fine but didn't want to talk about it. "Thanks for asking."

Every window on the side of the lodge had its curtains drawn, concealing the activity within. We moved through a small copse of pine trees and I could hear the distant hum of an outboard motor; I smelled fresh-cut grass and the pleasant earthy musk of fresh water. And then the trail emerged from the trees and there was Lake Wyndham in all its glory, the sort of majestic view I'd only ever seen on postcards.

"Oh my goodness!" Tammy exclaimed. "Look at it!"

We'd arrived at the top of a wide and immaculately landscaped lawn. The soft grass descended a gently sloping hill before ending at a sandy beach, an L-shaped wooden dock, and a boathouse. And then the lake itself, ten square miles of royal-blue water, speckled with colorful kayaks and sailboats. Completing the view was a horizon with three green mountains and a sky full of cotton-puff clouds.

"This is where Aidan proposed," Maggie explained. "Back on Valentine's Day, so the lake was still frozen over. Snow everywhere you looked. Just this beautiful, majestic winter wonderland. I thought we were going snowshoeing, but next thing you know he was down on one knee with a ring."

"Sooooo romantic!" Tammy said. "I can't think of a more perfect spot for a proposal."

Aidan smiled through pursed lips, and I realized it was the same beach I'd seen in the photograph—the same beach where he'd posed for a snapshot with Dawn Taggart.

"And come Saturday, after the ceremony, this is where we'll have our reception," Maggie continued. "Our photographers love it, because the golden hour light is incredible."

There were large wooded areas on both sides of the lawn, dense New England forests crisscrossed with paved trails and smaller dirt paths, and Maggie warned that it was easy to get disoriented in the woods, especially at night. I showed her the map we'd received from Hugo and she seemed skeptical. "That's not going to help when it's after midnight and you can't see your hand in front of your face. My advice is to always carry your phone, so you'll always have a flashlight."

With my sister's permission, Abigail ran ahead to the beach and we all followed after her. The sand was soft and white and powdery. Aidan claimed it was imported from Waikiki, but I couldn't tell if he was joking, and I didn't push to clarify. At the moment, no one was swimming or sunbathing, but there were two dozen empty lounge chairs and umbrellas, suggesting that many more guests were expected.

Abigail stopped at a small fleet of kayaks, canoes, and sailboats. "Mister Frank, do you want to go canoeing?"

"We just got here," I reminded her.

"Maybe after lunch," Tammy suggested.

At the edge of the beach was another flagstone walkway, and this one followed the edge of the shore past the boathouse and around the lake. After a minute of walking we arrived at a two-story cottage made of steel and glass and stone, with a wide wraparound porch and big windows overlooking the lake.

"This is Blackbird," Maggie announced. "I think it's the cutest property at the camp and I wanted you guys to have it."

Aidan explained that every building on the property had keyless locks, so we would use Bluetooth technology to enter our cabin. Tammy and I surrendered our phones so Aidan could download and install the necessary app. The camp had lightning-fast Wi-Fi and the process took less than a minute. "I'm adding you to our family account," he explained, "so you can access all the main buildings. Now walk to your door and watch what happens."

As I climbed the steps to the front porch, the door clicked open and swung inward, as if released by a spring. I stepped inside a great room with hard pine floors, rough-hewn timber walls, and a stone fireplace that rose through a two-story atrium. The place was furnished with rustic decorations—elk antlers and vintage wooden oars and maps of the local terrain—plus enough chairs and sofas for a dozen visitors.

"How many people are staying here?"

"Just you three." Aidan pointed to the upstairs balcony and a pair of doors. "Your luggage should be waiting in the bedrooms. You're in the master suite, on the left, but Tammy's room is almost identical. I think you'll both be very pleased."

My sister and Abigail followed us inside, and Tammy clutched a hand over her heart. "Holy guacamole, look at this place! Abigail, have you ever seen anything like it?"

The kid spun around in a circle and pretended to faint on the floor. "Are you serious? This is our motel room?"

"Feel free to use anything in the house," Maggie said. "And if you need something you can't find, just pick up the phone and dial zero. Someone will run it right over."

I felt certain the cottage had everything we could possibly want. There were closets filled with extra blankets, pillows, towels, first aid kits, bug sprays, flashlights, and pullover water shoes. Plus an enormous flat-screen TV with dual soundbars, a big round table for playing cards, and a whole shelf full of board games: Mouse Trap, Snakes and Ladders, Trouble, and Taboo.

But my delight was short-lived because Aidan announced he was already leaving. "Glen's here," he told Maggie, and he showed her a text on his phone. "I better go lend a hand."

"Of course." She gave him a quick peck on the cheek. "Say hi for me, and we'll see you at dinner."

Aidan encouraged us to unpack and relax and enjoy ourselves, and then just like that he was gone. We'd been at the camp for a total of eighteen minutes.

"Where's he going?" I asked.

"College friend," Maggie said, as if this explained everything, as if I hadn't just driven three hundred and sixty miles to have lunch with my future son-in-law.

Tammy must have heard the irritation in my voice because she changed the subject. "Do I smell cinnamon rolls? Or is it just my imagination?"

"I'll show you," Maggie said.

She walked us through a dining area and into a thoroughly modern kitchen. Waiting on the countertop was an enormous spread of food: baskets of fresh-baked bread, platters of miniature sandwiches, a whole tray of fresh-cut fruit, and a mountain of pastries and cookies and brownie bites. There were enough provisions to last the three of us all weekend, but Maggie presented the vast buffet as simply "lunch."

"I figured you'd want something quick," she said. "Does this look okay?"

Tammy laughed. "Maggie, are you kidding? This is more than we have for Thanksgiving!"

Abigail asked for permission to start, then reached for a plate and started loading it up with chicken sliders, miniature BLTs, and three enormous scoops of potato salad. "Take it easy," I told her. "The food's not going anywhere."

"She's just hungry," Tammy said. "I'm hungry, too." Then she passed me a plate and grabbed one for herself.

"Go ahead and eat," Maggie said. "I'll give you some time to settle in, and then I'll swing back in a couple hours."

I couldn't believe it. "A couple hours?"

"Dad, I have wedding stuff."

"I thought we were having lunch together."

"No, I said there would be lunch *for you*. But I ate before you got here. Because I still have a million things to do."

I returned my plate to the counter. "Then let me help you, kiddo. Put me to work. What needs to be done?"

She shook her head, like I was failing to grasp the enormous magnitude of planning a wedding. "Dad, we have three hundred people coming this weekend. Sixty are vegetarian, twenty-six are vegan, eleven are gluten-free. There's a hundred guests staying at the camp and another two hundred staying in hotels, and I need three very nice charter buses to shuttle people back and forth." The pitch of her voice climbed higher and higher because she wasn't stopping to breathe. "However, the only charter bus company within a hundred miles just canceled on me for no reason at all. No apology, no explanation. Just 'Sorry, miss, we can't make it.' So unless you know three bus drivers, I don't think you can help me."

I actually *did* know three bus drivers—it's a popular second career for UPS drivers who get tired of hauling boxes—but none of them owned their own vehicles, and they certainly didn't drive the kind of luxury bus that the Gardners probably wanted.

"Oh, sweetie, that's terrible!" Tammy said. "Did you call the Better Business Bureau? It's their job to investigate these companies. Someone has to hold them accountable."

Maggie nodded patiently and waited for my sister to finish her suggestion. "That's a great idea, Aunt Tammy, but I already have a plan. I just need to go do it. If you all want to help me, you'll just stay here and unpack and relax."

I could see she was frazzled. I knew planning a wedding was a ton of work, and I didn't want to add to my daughter's growing list of burdens. So I tried to look agreeable, but she could still see the disappointment on my face.

"Listen, Dad, I'll try to be back by three o'clock. And then I'll give you a tour of the camp, okay? How does that sound?"

"That sounds great," Tammy said, hooking her elbow through mine and then leading me away from my daughter. "Go take care of business, Maggie. We'll be fine. Don't you worry!"

6.

Abigail ate too much and threw up. I saw it coming from a mile away. It must have been her first time eating from a buffet; she seemed to think she was required to try everything. I said, "Hey, Cookie Monster, take it easy!" and my sister got upset with me.

"Don't say that, Frankie."

"Why not? Look at her!"

Abigail had actual cookie crumbs all down the front of her shirt, and now she was eating fruit salad faster than she could swallow it. Her cheeks were stuffed with green grapes she hadn't gotten to yet, and still she kept pushing more in.

"She's had issues with food insecurity."

"You're going to choke, Abigail. Slow down."

"Don't regulate her. That's not what you do."

"She looks like a hamster. I don't want her eating like this in front of the Gardners."

"I'll take care of it. Just eat your lunch. Everything's going to be fine."

Then Abigail bolted for the bathroom and fell in front of the toilet, yakking her guts out. I reached for a handful of cherry tomatoes and popped one into my mouth. "What a shocker," I said. "Who could have seen that coming?"

Tammy frowned. "You promised you would be cool with this. And instead you're being a jerk. I don't know why you're so irritable, but it needs to stop."

She went to help Abigail and left me alone to finish my lunch. I knew she was correct: I *was* being a jerk. And I didn't know why I felt so irritable. Maybe it was my lack of sleep. Or maybe I just knew from the get-go that something about the camp was wrong.

So yeah, lunch was pretty much a bust, but our moods improved tremendously after we all went upstairs to unpack. Holy mother of God, you would not believe the size of my master suite. I could run laps around the place for exercise. There was a king-size bed. My own private bathroom. Another enormous flat-screen with Netflix, Hulu, Amazon, Apple, the works. And a little balcony just for me, so I could sit outside with a beer and watch the sun go down over Lake Wyndham.

Tammy was next door in a suite identical to mine, and Abigail was at the end of the hall in a tiny room for children with a nautical theme. There were colorful fish swimming all over the wallpaper and miniature bunk beds painted to look like sailboats. Abigail couldn't believe she had her choice of the upper bunk or the lower bunk; I think she'd been expecting to sleep on the floor.

Unpacking my suitcase only took a minute, and then I changed my clothes so I wouldn't look like a landscaper anymore. My suite had a small writing desk facing the window and someone had left me a calendar of events:

MARGARET AND AIDAN'S WEDDING WEEKEND

Thursday, July 21

12–5 pm: Unpack, unwind, relax, and explore!
5 pm: Welcome cocktails (main lawn)
6 pm: Dinner (main lawn)
8 pm: Campfire s'mores (beach)

Friday, July 22

11 am: Group hike to Cormorant Point

12 pm: Lunch at Cormorant Point

4 pm: Rehearsal (the Globe)

6 pm: Rehearsal dinner (main lawn)

8 pm: Karaoke contest (beach)

Saturday, July 23

11 am: Outdoor brunch (main lawn)

3 pm: Wedding (the Globe)

4 pm: Postnuptial cocktails (main lawn)

5 pm–???: Dinner, dancing, and more dancing! (main lawn)

The schedule was encouraging me to "unwind, relax, and explore" but I was far too anxious to nap or lounge in a rocking chair, and I didn't feel comfortable wandering the camp on my own. I was nervous about meeting Errol and Catherine Gardner in person, and I guess I wanted Maggie to be present when that first encounter actually happened.

So instead I sat down at the tiny writing desk and worked on my toast. I'd already cut it down to two pages, and then I'd spent the last few weeks rewriting them over and over. I'd try a line, cross it out, and then repeat the same sentiment with different words: ~~Maggie, I am so proud of the woman you've become.~~ And: ~~Maggie, you have always been such a kind and sweet and generous person.~~ And: ~~If Maggie's mother is watching us from heaven, I know she's pleased by what she sees.~~

I was trying to speak from the heart, but anytime I read my words out loud, they just felt cheesy and corny and false. And the more I revised, the worse everything got. I found myself wishing I knew some kind of professional writer who could give me advice, and that's what made me think of Vicky. She *wasn't* a professional writer, but her son was, and she read more books than anyone else I'd ever known.

I dialed the number of her salon and the receptionist got her on the line. "Frank?" she asked. "Are you okay?"

"Yeah, I'm sorry to bother you. I wanted to ask you for a favor." I explained my problem with the toast and asked if she'd be willing to read it over and give me some pointers. And of course I offered to pay her whatever she felt was fair.

"You don't have to pay me! It'd be my pleasure." She suggested that I text her the toast and promised to get back to me in the morning. "I'm sure it's better than you think. Everybody gets self-conscious about their writing."

I pleaded with her to be straight with me. I reminded her that in forty-eight hours I needed to stand in front of three hundred people and read the whole thing out loud. "If it sucks, I need you to be honest."

"If it sucks, I promise we'll make it better. Just send it over and I'll call you tomorrow." She sounded distracted; she explained that she had a toddler waiting in her chair and described the kid as a ticking time bomb. "If I don't finish her in five minutes, she's going to explode."

So I thanked her again and let her get back to work. Then I typed my whole toast into a single text and zapped it off to her. And after that I felt a whole lot better, because I knew I could count on Vicky to make it right. But there wasn't much time to feel satisfied because all of a sudden Abigail was screaming.

7.

Loud, terrified shrieks jolted me out of my chair. She sounded like she was being attacked. I opened my door and Tammy was already out of her bedroom. Together we ran down the hallway to find Abigail. Her door was closed but we could hear her on the other side, yelling like she'd stepped onto a bear trap. We went inside and found her backed into a corner, eyes wide with terror, gesturing furiously to an empty wall.

"Abby, what is it?" Tammy asked. "What's wrong?"

She was too hysterical to answer. She just kept pointing and shaking her finger at some invisible, unspeakable horror. Tammy approached her cautiously, both hands raised to show she meant no harm.

"It's okay, it's all right, you're safe here. No one's going to hurt you. Breathe, sweetie, breathe."

Abigail flipped face down on the rug like she was trying to bury her head in the floor. She was inconsolable. She hammered her fists and kicked her feet, and I started to think maybe she had much bigger problems than "food insecurity." Maybe she had a major behavioral disorder. Maybe she'd throw a temper tantrum at the wedding and fling all her flower petals into the horrified faces of Aidan's parents.

But as I looked around her bedroom in despair, I realized the blank wall wasn't entirely blank. There was a door to a closet, and it was still slightly ajar. I moved closer to investigate and Abigail shrieked like a teakettle at a full boil.

"Don't, Mister Frank! Don't!"

"Sweetheart, it's okay! We're here," Tammy said. By this point she was holding Abigail and smoothing her hair with the palm of her hand. "What's wrong? What did you see?"

She shook her head, refusing to answer, as if naming her discovery would somehow grow its power.

"Oh, for Pete's sake." I threw open the door to reveal an empty cedar closet. Nothing but a single high shelf, a wooden rod, and a couple of wire coat hangers. As I leaned inside, an overhead light flickered on, revealing a fuzzy clump of *something* on the shelf.

At first glance, I thought it was a wig. A long weave of curly dark brown hair. Then I looked more closely and realized it was quivering. Like it had a very faint pulse.

"What is it?" Tammy asked. "Frankie, what do you see?"

I grabbed a coat hanger and used one end to gently poke at the wig. A daddy longlegs climbed out of it, then another, and then suddenly dozens more. I realized it wasn't a wig; it was a nest, hundreds of daddy longlegs huddled together for safety and warmth in the darkness of the closet. Now they were fleeing from attack and scrambling across the walls. A big fat one dropped on my hand and I shrieked; I couldn't help it. I slapped myself silly trying to knock it off.

"Close the door!" Abigail screamed.

I slammed it shut, then looked down and saw a half-inch gap at the bottom. I yanked a blanket off the bed and used it to seal the opening. "It's spiders," I said. "Daddy longlegs."

"Daddy longlegs aren't spiders," Tammy said. "They're totally different animals."

I told her I didn't care: in my book, if a bug has eight legs and looks like a spider, then it's a spider. "They must have laid eggs."

At the mention of eggs, Abigail yowled, and I begged her to please, *please* stop screaming. "You've already got eggs in your hair, so let's not overreact."

She fell onto her side and hugged her knees, curling herself into a ball while my sister frowned. "That's not helpful."

"I'm sorry, but I can't think with her screaming. Can you please find some way to shut her up?"

Tammy rubbed her hand in gentle circles on Abigail's back, trying to soothe her. "Let's just call the Gardners and explain the problem. I'm sure we can switch cottages."

"No, I'm not doing that."

"Why not?"

"Because it sounds pathetic. What kind of man calls Errol Gardner and complains about spiders in his closet?"

"It's a serious infestation, Frankie. I think they need to call an exterminator."

"Those guys are a waste of money. They charge you three hundred dollars to spray a bunch of poison but all I need's a good shoe."

Tammy and Abigail waited outside on the front porch while I did all my dirty work with a Florsheim leather oxford—one half of the pair I'd brought to walk Maggie down the aisle. I didn't want the spiders to escape, so I sealed myself in the closet and started swatting. It was brutal, nasty work. There were hundreds of spiders and their mashed-up bodies excreted a foul odor, like something you'd squeeze from a boil. But I soldiered on, gagging on the awful stench until every last one was dead. Then I went downstairs for a bowl of warm water and a kitchen sponge and I proceeded to wipe down the cedar walls and ceiling, cleaning up all the broken legs and splattered remains. So much for "unpack, unwind, relax, and explore."

After I finished, I went outside to the front of the cottage and told Tammy the coast was clear. Then we spent a good ten minutes persuading Abigail that it was safe to return indoors. She was certain that I'd missed a few spiders and said she'd rather spend the weekend sleeping on the porch. I reminded her that most bugs lived outdoors, that the forest was alive with beetles, ticks, wasps, and centipedes—but this just set her off all over again.

"I won't go back in there," Abigail said. "I can't do it, Miss Tammy. Please don't make me do it. Please, please, please, please, please—"

So I figured fine, case closed, let the kid sleep on the porch. There were some really nice Adirondack chairs and we'd just bury her in blankets. Or dial zero on the house phone to request a sleeping bag. But my sister said she had a better idea, and she asked me to come inside the cottage. "I want to talk to you for a minute."

We went into the kitchen and Tammy used the little Nescafé machine to fix us both coffee. She made mine with milk and two sugars because she knows that's how I take it. Then she placed the tiny cup in front of me and lowered the boom: "I think you and Abigail should switch rooms."

"No way. Forget it."

"It's just a place to sleep. We're going to spend most of the weekend outside."

"Fine, *you* give her *your* room."

"*I* can't trade with her, Frankie. You know I'm scared of bugs."

"The bugs are gone." I was still holding the Florsheim shoe and I showed her the bottom. "I just killed a thousand of them. I was like John Wick in there."

"Right, but you couldn't have gotten all of them. There're more spiders in that room, I'm sure of it. And if we force Abigail to stay there, she'll be up half the night screaming. We won't get a wink of sleep."

I was struck by the maddening realization that Tammy was right: I had to choose between a sleepless night in my luxury suite or a solid eight hours in a child's bunk bed.

"This is why I didn't want to bring her! I *told* you there'd be trouble!" I pointed upstairs to the second floor. "That is nicer than any hotel room I've ever seen, and I shouldn't have to give it up."

"Don't blame this on me, Frankie. *I* wanted to call the Gardners and ask for a new cottage. But *you* said you'd take care of it yourself. And then all you did was chase those spiders back into their hidey-holes. How is this my fault?"

Out on the porch, Abigail was pacing back and forth in front of the window, furiously scratching her head with both hands.

"Please, Tammy. She *wants* to sleep outside."

"Frankie, that poor girl spent all of March and April sleeping outside. She and her mother were living behind a Taco Bell. There is no way I'm making her do that again. I want her in a proper bed with clean sheets and a pillow, just like me and you and the Gardners, do you understand?"

All I understood was that I'd already lost the argument—again—so I threw my goddamn cup in the goddamn sink and then went upstairs to move my stuff.

8.

My new bedroom had nowhere to sit, apart from a tiny "story corner" furnished with plump pillows and colorful picture books. I unpacked my things as quickly as possible, then went down to the kitchen and sat alone at the buffet. All the downtime was driving me crazy. I wanted to walk outdoors and see the entire camp. I wanted to go swimming and hiking and canoeing. And more than anything I wanted to meet my future in-laws.

I think that's the real reason I felt so irritable. I couldn't believe that Errol and Catherine still hadn't come over to welcome us. I was upset that Aidan had immediately bolted to spend time with his college buddy. And then Maggie rushed off into town and wouldn't even let me come with her. I tried to remind myself that she was very busy and sometimes the best way to help a person is to just get out of their way. But I already had the uneasy feeling that we were unwelcome, that we'd only been invited due to a sense of obligation.

At three o'clock I went outside to wait for my daughter. Abigail was sitting in a porch rocker and leaning over a checkerboard, playing a game against herself.

"Thanks for switching rooms, Mister Frank."

"It's fine."

She tapped the checkerboard. "Do you want to play?"

"I can't. Maggie's going to be here any minute."

"Where are you going?"

"She wants to show me the camp."

"Can I come?"

"Well, it's not going to be very interesting. We're just going to look at the buildings and, you know, talk about the history of the place."

She stood up anyway. "That's okay."

"Well, and the other thing is, Maggie wants to spend a little one-on-one time with me. Because we don't see much of each other." Abigail just stared at me, still not grasping the point, and I realized I had to spell it out for her. "It's better if you just stay here."

She sank back into her chair. "All right."

"What's Tammy doing?"

"She's taking a bubble bath. They didn't have bubbles in her bathroom? But she dialed zero on the house phone and a lady brought some right over. Three different scent options."

"Go tell her you're bored."

"I'm not bored. I just wanted to come with." Abigail returned her focus to the game and used a red checker to double-jump two blacks. I looked all around for Maggie, hoping she would materialize and rescue me from the awkwardness of the conversation, but there was still no trace of her. So I stood there and watched Abigail play an imaginary opponent until my phone started ringing. I checked the display—"Maggie ♥ ♥ ♥"—and then answered immediately.

"Hey, what's the holdup?"

"Sorry, I'm still here in town."

"What's wrong?"

"Everything," she said, before firing off a list of the latest disasters: the florist mixed up the table settings, the videographer tested positive for COVID, and she still needed a solution to the bus problem. All her problems seemed to be multiplying.

"What about your wedding planner? Isn't she supposed to handle this stuff?"

"It's a team effort, Dad. We're all doing the best we can. I should be back in time for dinner, okay?"

In time for dinner? "You mean six o'clock?"

"Dad, listen. You don't need me to see the camp. Take the map. Go exploring. Meet some people. There's horseshoes, a game room, a million different activities."

She spoke to me like I was a kid on summer vacation with no friends and nothing to do. She didn't seem to understand that I'd come to New Hampshire to spend time with family—not play horseshoes with a bunch of random strangers. But I could hear the aggravation in her voice and I didn't want to make things any worse. So I just said, "All right, see you soon," and ended the call.

Abigail was still hunched over the checkerboard and pretending that she hadn't been eavesdropping. But I'd been careful not to say anything that would reveal my change of plans.

"Heading out now," I told her.

"Where's Maggie?"

"I'm going to meet her at the lodge."

She flashed me a thumbs-up and I suddenly felt very silly for lying to a ten-year-old. But I guess I didn't want anyone to know I'd been ditched. Abigail said, "See you later, Mister Frank," and that was the end of it.

From our cottage, there were several different trails into the woods, but I just walked back the way we'd arrived, following the shore of Lake Wyndham for a minute or two until I was back on the beach. All the lounge chairs were still empty, and no one was swimming in the water. But up on the main lawn, closer to Osprey Lodge, men and women in white coats were rolling large tables across the grass and carrying out armfuls of folding chairs. They appeared to be setting up for the reception, even though it was only Thursday. I saw a carpenter in a Dartmouth sweatshirt firing a nail gun into a lumber frame. He was constructing a large platform, a kind of elevated stage, and I asked if he needed help. I suppose I was still looking for some way to contribute. He gave me a sideways look and asked, "You work here?"

I explained that I was Maggie's father, in town for the wedding, and he immediately straightened and set down his nail gun. "That's okay, Mr. Szatowski. You should just relax and enjoy the camp."

Why was *everyone* telling me to relax and enjoy the camp?

"I'm surprised you're setting up so early," I said. "What if it rains before Saturday?"

"This isn't for the wedding." He gestured to the big round tables, now draped with white linens and ringed by folding chairs. "All this is for tonight."

Up until that moment, I'd expected Thursday's dinner to be an intimate meal with just my family and the Gardners. But the caterers were setting out glasses and silverware for dozens of people. It might not have been the actual wedding, but it was already far more extravagant than any wedding I'd ever seen.

The carpenter returned to his work and fired a long line of nails into the platform. And as I stood there, deliberating my next move, Aidan emerged from the back of the lodge, accompanied by a woman with long red hair. I waved and called his name, but with the nail gun blasting, he didn't hear me. He and the woman set off on a narrow trail that disappeared into the trees. I hurried across the lawn, weaving around tables and caterers, trying to catch up. By the time I reached the start of the trail, they had already vanished into the woods.

But since everybody kept encouraging me to explore the camp, I decided to follow the path anyway. Inside the woods, it was cooler and darker and surprisingly quiet. The sounds of the camp fell away and soon I heard nothing but trilling cicadas and the occasional birdsong. From time to time I'd glance at the paper map and try to orient myself, but the trail wasn't marked. I was west of Osprey Lodge in a large cluster of trees labeled Imagination Grove, and the path was leading me to the outermost boundaries of the property. I began to understand that the map couldn't possibly be drawn to scale—that the wooded grove must have been much larger than shown, so all the areas would fit on a single page.

Or maybe I was just lost.

One of the most useful things I learned during my four years in the United States Army is a concept known as situational awareness. The idea is that you're always assessing your surroundings with a focus on threats, risks, and signs of recent disturbances. A very useful mindset for a scared nineteen-year-old kid patrolling Iraqi villages during the 1991 Gulf War, and I've found the habits hard to shake. To this day, I can't walk into a restaurant without taking note of the emergency exits. After several minutes of following the trail, I stopped and turned around, and I did not see a single living creature. There was no reason for me to feel nervous in an open wooded area with clear sight lines in every direction. But I had the uneasy feeling that an ambush was waiting just around the corner, that I was walking into some kind of trap.

The path brought me up a steep section of trail that was poorly maintained, and then I glimpsed a structure in the distance. Something resembling an old toolshed, and completely unlike all the modern buildings back at the camp. This one had worn-out wooden siding, dusty windows, and a gray shingled roof speckled with spongy green moss. I checked the map to orient myself but the building wasn't on it. I approached from the side, a flat and mostly featureless wall with two rusty vents and a single hung window. The curtains were drawn, but the screen was open and I could hear voices within.

One belonged to Aidan, but the other person—the woman—was doing most of the talking. I couldn't discern all of her words, just the general tenor of the conversation. She was angry and Aidan was placating her, or trying to.

"This isn't fair."

"I know."

"It's not fair *to me.*"

"I hear you. I understand."

"Don't say you understand, Aidan. Because if you *really* under-stood, if you actually agreed with me, you wouldn't be doing this."

He said something I couldn't make out, and I dared to move even closer, stepping softly across dry leaves until I was right beside the window.

Then he said, "What would you like me to do?"

"Tell the truth."

"Besides that."

"I'll help you. I still care about you. We can do it together—"

"No, no, no. *We* are not doing anything. There is no *we.*"

And then he said something I couldn't make out again. The woman was upset, but Aidan's tone was steady, stubborn, immutable. I glanced around, afraid that someone might catch me eavesdropping. But from what I could gather, the three of us were all alone in the forest. I side-stepped to the back of the cabin, to a larger window where their voices were easier to hear.

"... you're not seeing the big picture."

"Maybe I should talk to Margaret."

"*Do not* talk to Margaret."

"I just think—"

"Stay the fuck away from Margaret."

"Jesus, Aidan—"

"She cannot know about this conversation. If you say one word to her—"

The rest of the sentence was spoken under his breath.

"Are you threatening me?"

"No, I just—"

"Are you sure? Because that sounded like a threat."

"Relax, okay? Come here."

Hanging over the back window were faded yellow curtains that didn't quite reach the sill. I pressed my face to the screen and squinted through the open gap. I saw a cluttered room, dimly lit. Canvases leaned against the walls in stacks that were six or seven deep. There was a workbench full of paints and supplies and a large wooden easel. Aidan stood with his back to me, and the woman was embracing him. She was my daughter's age, tall with long red hair and a freckled complexion, and we immediately locked eyes. She straightened her shoulders and shook off Aidan's hands.

"Someone's here," she said.

The sun was at my back; I realized I had cast a shadow on the curtains. Aidan spun around and I leaped away from the window. He walked over and peered outside. "Frank? What are you doing here?"

I gave the first explanation that came to mind. "Just exploring the camp." Then I showed him the paper map, hoping it would add some credibility to my story. "It seems like I got myself lost."

"You're not lost. This is my studio. Come around to the front and I'll give you a tour."

Aidan was waiting in the doorway when I reached the entrance. "You've found my little secret. I've tried painting back at the lodge but it's impossible. Too many distractions. All the staff coming and going. But this place is perfect. It's the last surviving structure from the original summer camp. Super quiet and you won't find it on any of the maps. Most people don't even know it's here."

I followed him inside. The air was musty and smelled of chemicals—mineral spirits, turpentine, linseed oil. There were paintings everywhere—lots of haunted black-and-white faces like the ones in his penthouse apartment. But many more were incomplete or abandoned, and these canvases showed just *pieces* of faces: An open mouth. A long slender neck. A single ear half-concealed by lengths of hair. I found these face parts even more unsettling than the completed portraits.

The redhead was leaning against Aidan's workbench. She wore a cream-colored blouse, a long green skirt, and brown leather sandals. All her clothes and jewelry looked homemade and slightly primitive, like she'd come from a Renaissance fair.

"Frank, this is Gwendolyn," Aidan said, and I realized I'd misheard him earlier. He'd been running off to meet *Gwen*, not Glen. "We went to art school together. Now she's a teacher, like me."

She seemed amused by the comparison. "Aidan likes to make people sound important. I teach at a preschool on Tuesdays. Finger paints and Popsicle sticks. The rest of the week, I'm just driving for DoorDash."

"That's nothing to be ashamed of," I told her. "I've been at UPS for twenty-six years."

"Driving?"

"It's hard work but I guarantee we pay better than DoorDash." She seemed genuinely intrigued so I bragged a little about my union benefits—about the pension plan and the healthcare and the perks of being a Teamster. "Plus they're dying to hire more women right now. Because of MeToo and everything. Depending on your location, you could have a real good shot."

"You know, I might just look into it," she said. "How do you guys know each other?"

"Frank is Margaret's father," Aidan explained.

And it was like he'd flipped a switch. All at once, her entire demeanor soured.

"Wait, *you're* Margaret's father?"

"Yes, Frank Szatowski."

"Then I guess you'll be hanging up the brown uniform pretty soon, right? Have you delivered your last package?"

She wasn't the first person to make this kind of joke. A lot of my friends at work had made similar comments. Like they all expected Maggie to turn over some vast sum of money that would allow me to move to Key West and vacation in Hawaii and live a life of leisure with all my new Gardner relations. But I had no intention of taking a penny from my daughter. I've always felt that family fortunes should only travel in one direction—downhill, from parent to child, and not the other way around.

"I'm pretty happy with my life," I told her. "I'm not making any changes."

She didn't try to hide her skepticism—or her sudden inexplicable contempt for me. "And is Aidan going to call you Dad? Or do you think you'll keep things on a first-name basis?"

"We haven't talked about it." I turned to Aidan. "But since Gwen brought it up, I'm happy to answer to either one. Whatever makes you more comfortable."

"I know, Frank, and thank you. Gwen's just being provocative. It's kind of her brand."

She snorted at the assessment. "Sure, Aidan. Telling the truth is soooo edgy. I'm a real loose cannon." Then she leaned closer to me, squinting at my wristwatch. "Tell me something, Frank. What time do you have?"

"Three-thirty."

She shot a wry look at Aidan, as if this proved some kind of point. "All right, I'm going to go jump off a cliff. But it was great to meet you, Frank. I'm sure you'll have an amazing weekend. Give my best to Margaret."

Then she went out the door and bounded off into the woods, and maybe I was imagining it, but I thought she put some extra swing in her hips, like she knew we were watching.

"Sorry about that," Aidan said.

"Did I say something to offend her?"

"It's nothing you did. She's just weird about money."

He explained that Gwendolyn lost her parents at the age of seven, so she'd been raised by her grandmother, an Irish immigrant who worked as a housekeeper. Somehow Gwendolyn managed to attend NYU Steinhardt on a full scholarship, where she and Aidan struck up an unlikely friendship. They were close friends and confidantes for four years, then parted ways after graduation. Aidan moved to his penthouse apartment in Boston and Gwendolyn went back to Lawrence, Massachusetts, and her eighty-one-year-old grandmother. Because the world wasn't fair, Aidan said, and making a living as a visual artist was just about impossible.

"What does that have to do with me?"

"It's got nothing to do with you. She's just weird whenever she's here. Very critical of the camp. And she hates Capaciti. It was probably a mistake to invite her, but we used to be good friends."

I wanted to ask about the conversation I'd overheard, but there was no way to do it without admitting I'd been eavesdropping.

This isn't fair.

Tell the truth.

Maybe I should talk to Margaret.

I reminded myself that I hadn't heard the entire conversation, so they could have been talking about anything. But still:

Are you threatening me?

He was waiting for me to say something. Waiting to see if I'd make another move in this weird game we were playing. But I needed time to process everything I'd learned. I looked around the studio and noticed a metal spiral staircase in the far corner, descending through a hole in the floor. "Where does that go?"

"To the fallout shelter."

"Seriously?"

He nodded. "This camp was built in 1954, at the height of the Red Scare. Back when the government was subsidizing bomb shelters and everybody was building them." He was interrupted by a chirping from his pocket. Aidan reached for his phone and checked the screen. "It's my dad. I better take this."

He turned away from me, seeking some small measure of privacy, and I studied the spiral staircase. Narrow steps of grated metal wrapped around and around a black steel pole before vanishing into the darkness. It was like staring down into a well. "Yeah, I'm actually with him right now. . . . We're at my studio." Aidan listened for a moment before turning to me. "Dad wants to know if you're free for a drink."

"Of course."

Aidan said we'd be right over and then ended the call. As we exited the studio, he pulled the door shut and I noticed it was fitted with another Bluetooth lock. Aidan said his father was waiting for us in Osprey Lodge and I invited him to lead the way, but instead he turned in the direction of the lake. "Just one other thing, Frank. Margaret mentioned you received something in the mail? Some kind of photograph?"

"Right. It's in my suitcase."

He forced an awkward smile, apologizing for putting me out. "Do you think we could grab it on the way? My dad really wants to see it."

9.

Errol Gardner looked like the men you see in TV commercials for Viagra: tall and tan and broad-shouldered, with a full head of wavy salt-and-pepper hair. I knew from my research that he was fifty-seven years old; I'd read that he started every morning with an hour on the treadmill, fifty push-ups, a hundred crunches, and a sixteen-ounce wheatgrass smoothie. And I knew he wore variations of the same signature outfit nearly every day: a brown blazer, a white button-down shirt, and blue jeans. When asked by GQ about his personal style, Errol said it was "smart enough for Boston boardrooms, tough enough for factory floors, and good enough for drinks after work."

"Frank Szatowski!" He pronounced my last name like a kind of punch line, as if the sound of it was inherently amusing. "It's great to finally meet you. How was the drive?"

"Piece of cake."

"Good, good, good. That's what we like to hear. And your cottage? Is it comfortable?" He turned to his son. "Where did you put them?"

Aidan said, "Blackbird," and Errol nodded with approval.

"Great choice. Fabulous views. I can't believe you're finally here, Frank. I've waited months for this. Come inside, please!"

Osprey Lodge was enormous, and Aidan had hurried me upstairs to the second floor, so I didn't have much of a chance to look around. Errol Gardner's office was ringed with natural woodwork and tim-ber, as if the space had been carved from a giant tree. His desk was larger than your average dining room table, and the mahogany finish was inlaid with all kinds of decorative embellishments: birds, trees, flowers, and forest animals. Beside the desk was a matching pedestal displaying a narrow metal cylinder about the size of a small thermos. Errol called it an ultra-compact fuel cell: "The miracle in the Miracle Battery," he explained. "You're welcome to handle it, if you like."

I was already holding a bottle of Blanton's Single Barrel Bourbon, which I presented to Errol as a gift. "I read your profile in *New En-gland Living*. You said this was your favorite."

He accepted the bottle with a terrific smile. "Oh, Frank, I *hated* that interview! The writer got everything wrong—except the bourbon! It's the only honest thing she wrote about me!" He looked past me, over my shoulder. "Have you tried it, Gerry?"

I realized the three of us weren't alone. There was a fourth man near the window, perched on the edge of a sofa and dressed in a trim gray suit with a maroon bow tie. "I've not had the pleasure," he said.

"My best friend, Gerry Levinson," Errol said.

The man rose and crossed the room to welcome me. Gerry was a full generation older than Errol Gardner—old enough to pass as Aidan's grandfather. His face was lined with wrinkles and he walked with a slight limp, but his handshake was surprisingly firm. "It's won-derful to meet you, Frank. Margaret's told us so much about you."

Errol opened a cabinet in the wall that revealed a kind of hidden minibar. He uncorked the bottle of Blanton's and filled four glass tum-blers with bourbon. Then he proposed a toast to the bride and groom and we all clinked glasses. The whiskey was excellent. Just one sip and I felt the edge coming off. I'd been nervous about meeting the Gard-ners all day, ever since leaving my house at six o'clock in the morning. But now that introductions were underway, I already felt myself relax-ing. I took another sip and Errol laughed. "It's good, right?"

"Incredible," I said. "You weren't exaggerating."

The four of us gathered around a coffee table with our drinks, and Errol proceeded to sing Maggie's praises. He called her smart and ambitious and hardworking, a "rare kind of talent," and he said Aidan was lucky to have found her. "You and your wife did an amazing job of raising her. My only regret for this weekend is that Mrs. Szatowski can't be here to join us."

I was touched by this remark. I thought it was very kind of him to acknowledge her. "Colleen would have loved this camp. She was very outdoorsy. She loved nature. We used to go hiking when we were younger. Poconos, Catskills, Finger Lakes. But never any place as nice as this."

Once I get started on Colleen, it's hard for me to stop talking. I told them how we were classmates in elementary school and friendly in high school, but we didn't fall in love until after I joined the army. I spent six months in the Middle East around the time of Operation Desert Storm, and Colleen would write to me twice a week. She'd send long, detailed letters (this was right before email took off) chronicling everything happening back home. So when our local Blockbuster Video went out of business, or when the rector of our church was arrested for embezzling funds, or when any of our mutual friends got pregnant or arrested or whatever, Colleen would send me an update. I still have every single letter she sent me. If you've ever been deployed yourself, you know how important these messages from home can be. And over six months, her letters became more and more personal. She insisted that all the other guys in Stroudsburg were idiots, that I was the only one with half a brain, and she was mad at me for going away. She implored me to be very careful, to watch my back and get home safe. And by the time I got out of the army, I was already mad for her.

The whiskey must have really loosened me up because I hadn't meant to share all that. I apologized for talking too much. "Here I am, running off at the mouth, and I haven't even asked about *your* wife. How's Catherine feeling?"

Errol's perfect composure faltered, like I'd found a chink in his armor. "I'm sorry to say she won't be joining us tonight. She's been under attack since Tuesday, so we're hoping she'll be postdrome by tomorrow." He must have gleaned from my expression that I had no idea what this meant, so he proceeded to explain. He said that most of Catherine's migraine headaches were followed by a "postdrome phase," also known as a migraine hangover, that could last up to twenty-four hours. The hangover typically left her groggy and weak, but she was determined to power through it and join Errol in walking their son down the aisle.

"I'm so sorry," I said. "I didn't realize her condition was quite so bad." I reminded Errol that when we spoke back in May, he'd suggested that Catherine was making a nice recovery.

"I suppose that shows the depths of my ignorance, Frank. Migraine is a terrible disease—a brutal, debilitating scourge, and all the best doctors in Boston don't know a damned way to treat it. We've seen a dozen specialists and they've recommended a dozen different treatment plans. But as of two-thirty this afternoon, my wife is still in bed with her shades drawn, unable to move."

The topic seemed too painful for Aidan to discuss. Instead of participating in the conversation, he just clasped his hands around his glass and stared into his whiskey. Seated beside his father, he seemed smaller than I remembered, an inch or two shorter and several pounds lighter.

Gerry was the one who broke the silence. "There's a promising new medication with the FDA—"

"And it will be the sixth promising new medication she's tried," Errol said. "At this point, I've given up on the pharmaceutical companies. I'm ready to fund my own lab and research my own treatments. I figure I can't do any worse than the rest of the industry."

"There are ways to make that happen," Gerry promised. "But first we have a wedding to celebrate. Something to feel good about. Let's look for silver linings, shall we?"

Errol nodded good-naturedly and made a toast to silver linings, and we all clinked glasses again.

"Is Catherine here now?" I asked. "At the lodge?"

Aidan nodded. "Upstairs. Third floor."

"Would it be okay, do you think, if I said a quick hello? Just to introduce myself?"

Gerry's face clouded over, and Errol shook his head. "She'd be mortified, Frank. She's very ashamed of her appearance. The poor woman's simply exhausted. Planning this wedding took a lot out of her. And then you add the extra stress of this Dawn Taggart nonsense, all the verbal and emotional harassment, and she's been completely overwhelmed."

The name Dawn Taggart brought another abrupt halt to the conversation, and I was grateful for my glass of bourbon. After an awkward moment of silence, Gerry cleared his throat and continued in a soft, quiet voice: "Margaret told us you received something in the mail. We'd love to take a look, if that's okay with you."

I reached inside the pocket of my sports coat and found the plastic bag containing the envelope. I turned it over to Gerry and he inspected it carefully, studying the envelope through the plastic, as if searching for clues.

"Postmarked July seventeenth," he said. "Right here in Hopps Ferry."

"Nothing discreet about these people," Errol said. "Let's open it up. I want to see this thing."

Gerry reached inside his briefcase for a pair of latex gloves, then carefully stretched them over his long, spindly fingers. Then he removed the sheet of paper and unfolded it on the table where everyone could see it. Aidan took one glance at the photo and immediately shot out of his chair.

"That's a fake! I never brought her here."

"Of course it's a fake," Errol said.

Gerry nodded. "Dawn's mother must have found a picture of Aidan online, and then photoshopped her daughter into it."

Then the three of them looked at me, to see if I'd reached the same conclusion. "I don't know anything about Photoshop," I said, "but it looks pretty real to me."

"That's the idea," Gerry explained. "It's supposed to look real, Frank. In the right hands, this software can be very powerful. But once you've seen a lot of manipulated images, as I have, then you start to recognize the signs of digital tinkering. No court would ever admit this image as evidence." Using his finger, he directed my attention to the sandy beach at Dawn's feet. "Her shadow here, for example. Completely unnatural."

Errol agreed. "And look at the edges of Dawn's hair. Do you see how they look kind of jagged and pixelated? That's a bad cut-and-paste."

I leaned so close my nose practically touched the paper, but I couldn't see any jagged edges. I thought it looked like a perfectly normal photo.

Gerry took away the picture and resealed it in the plastic bag, as if the matter was settled. But Errol seemed to recognize that I wasn't satisfied. "Frank, I'm sure you have lots of questions, so let's just put everything on the table. How much has Margaret told you?"

"Not much. Just that Aidan wasn't involved."

Errol laughed. "Well, we can't take her word for it, right? She's a young woman in love! She has an unfair bias. You need to hear all the details so you can decide for yourself." Then he looked at Aidan, encouraging him to proceed.

"Right, okay," Aidan said, swallowing hard. He'd already finished his second bourbon and looked like he might appreciate a third, but Errol seemed to be holding the bottle at a distance. I could tell Aidan took no satisfaction in telling the story. He looked like a kid dragged in front of a classroom, unprepared to give an oral report. "The first thing you need to understand is that I never go into town anymore. Because everyone knows my dad, everyone knows who we are, and I'll have total strangers saying we should invest in their pizza shop. Or they'll pick a fight with me about electric cars. They want to argue about politics or tax subsidies, like I invented the Miracle Battery myself. So anytime I come to Osprey Cove, I always take back roads, to avoid driving through town."

Then one Friday morning—about a year earlier, in July of the previous year—Aidan was cruising along the back roads and punctured a tire. The spare in his trunk was also flat, and he'd found himself stranded in a forest without cellular coverage. There were no homes nearby, nothing but trees, and Aidan was contemplating a very long walk to town when a driver in a Toyota Corolla pulled up behind him. Dawn Taggart got out of her car and asked if he needed help. She had just finished her shift at Dollar General and was still wearing her sales vest and name tag. Aidan explained that he didn't have a spare tire and Dawn suggested they try hers, just to see if it fit. Aidan was then forced to admit that he didn't actually know how to change a tire—so Dawn got out her jack and lug wrench and knelt down in the gravel and showed him how to do it. "When she finished, I tried to give her some money. I had eighty bucks in my wallet but she wouldn't take it. She said I just needed to return the spare and buy her dinner. And after she'd been kind enough to stop and help me, I couldn't say no."

The next night, Aidan met Dawn at Millie's Bar and Grill, the only real restaurant in a county full of fast food and pizza shops. "Of course the whole place is full of busybodies. All the guys are staring daggers at me, like I've come to steal one of their women. I'm pretty sure they're going to follow me to the parking lot and beat the shit out of me. But the worst part of the dinner is Dawn Taggart. I mean, don't get me wrong: She's a very attractive woman. Very pretty. And I hope she's okay, wherever she is. But we didn't connect on anything. We had zero in common. All she could talk about was TikTok. Who she follows, who follows her, who she thinks I would like. She actually took out her phone during dinner and insisted on showing me her favorites. But she was nice enough to stop and change my tire, so I pretended to be interested. Then I paid the bill, drove her home, and I swear to you, Frank: That was the last time I ever saw her. Four months before she went missing."

All this sounded perfectly reasonable if I was willing to ignore the most obvious question: "If that's what really happened, why is her family blaming you?"

Aidan threw up his hands, suggesting that my guess was as good as anyone's. At which point Errol was happy to retake the floor. "Gerry has a couple ideas on that point," he said. "In addition to being my best friend, he's also our family attorney. One of the best litigators in New England. And he thinks he knows what they're after."

"Money, in a word," Gerry explained. "We think they'll threaten to file a civil suit. Do you remember the O. J. Simpson trials?"

I nodded, because everyone of my generation still remembered the O. J. Simpson trials. The criminal courts found him not guilty of murdering Nicole Brown and Ronald Goldman, so he never served any prison time. But the victims' families sued him in civil court, where the burden of proof was much lower, and they were eventually awarded $33 million.

"The Taggarts' lawyers will threaten to try the case locally," Gerry continued, "with jurors biased against wealthy out-of-town families. It's pretty easy to find twelve people in this county with a little class resentment. So the lawyer files the paperwork and hopes we come back with a settlement, to keep the story out of the media. Long story short, we pay them to go away. A hundred grand? Maybe two-fifty?"

"Not one fucking dime," Errol said. "Paying them is an admission of guilt, and my son didn't do anything. I'd rather go to trial."

"This is never going to trial," Gerry said softly. "They can't afford it, and their case is too weak."

"Not weak, Gerry. Nonexistent! The weekend Dawn disappeared, Aidan was in Boston! Two hundred miles away! With Margaret!"

I wasn't sure I'd heard this last part correctly. "Did you say Margaret?"

"We were at her apartment," Aidan explained. "The studio on Talmadge Street. Have you ever been there?"

Of course I'd been there. I helped her move in. It was the basement studio in the Victorian brownstone, the apartment with all the silver-fish. The place that Maggie couldn't stand. I remember worrying it wasn't a safe place for a young woman to live alone, because Maggie had to walk ten steps down a dark and narrow alley to reach the basement door. But my daughter said it was worth all the risk and inconvenience just to have a swanky address in Back Bay.

"Margaret invited me there for dinner on a Friday night. This would have been November second. The night before Dawn Taggart disappeared. She made us some food, and then we watched a movie, and then—" Aidan stumbled over the best way to describe what happened next. "It turned into a long weekend."

"Aidan, don't mince words," Errol said. "When you get evasive, you sound guilty."

Gerry agreed. "Frank needs to hear the truth. We're all grown-ups."

Aidan interlaced his fingers, flexed his hands, and tried again. "When we woke up Saturday morning, Margaret didn't have anyplace she needed to be. And neither did I, so we just, you know, hung out."

"In her apartment?"

"Yes."

"For how long?"

"Until Sunday."

"You stayed in her apartment all weekend?"

"Yes."

"It's three hundred square feet, Aidan. I wouldn't keep a dog in that space. What were you doing all weekend?"

I realized the answer as soon as the question left my mouth, and Aidan's flushed expression confirmed my suspicions.

"Young love," Errol said wistfully. "When you meet the right person, it's like the rest of the world just disappears."

Gerry nodded. "We've all been there."

And I wished they would stop talking, because I needed a moment to process what I was hearing: "So the day Dawn disappeared, you were inside Maggie's apartment?"

"Yes."

"The whole day? You never left?"

"Exactly."

"Did anyone see you there?"

"No, we didn't want any company," Aidan explained. "We were happy being alone together. Just the two of us. But that's why Margaret believes me. Because she was with me the whole time."

10.

We left Errol's office and went out to the lawn, where dinner was already underway. There were close to a hundred guests and every table was full, so the caterers were scrambling to carry out extra high-tops and chairs. A jazz trio was playing "It Had to Be You," and for the life of me I could not imagine how they had maneuvered a baby grand across the lawn without destroying the grass. The buffet table was a mile long, with a prime rib carving station, fresh New England crab cakes, huge ears of corn on the cob, and countless salads and side dishes. Plus three different cocktail stations so no one would have to wait for a drink. I drifted over to the closest one and was surprised to recognize the bartender.

"Mr. Szatowski," he said. "What are you having tonight?"

It was the man from the restaurant in town, the one who'd rescued us from Brody Taggart. He'd traded his dirty apron for a crisp white button-down shirt and a black vest and bow tie. I asked for a Coors Light and he offered me a Smuttynose lager. "Close enough," I said.

As he tipped the bottle into a pint glass, he encouraged me to pair it with the crab cakes, his wife's specialty. "She and my sister run a catering business. They're doing the whole wedding."

"Do you work here a lot?"

"In the summers, I'm here all the time. The Gardners have always done a lot of entertaining. But this wedding's taking things to a whole new level. We're cooking enough to feed an army."

I thanked him for the beer and then plunged into the crowd to search for my daughter. I needed to talk to Maggie right away. I needed to know if Aidan's story was true—and if it was, why hadn't she told me?

Maggie always compared her apartment on Talmadge Street to a dungeon prison cell. She called it dark and damp and claustrophobic, a place to sleep while she scraped together a living. When the company offered to let employees work remotely, Maggie refused. She even went into the office on weekends. Or she'd escape to Boston Common with her picnic blanket and laptop and work outside. Anyone who'd heard her complain about the apartment would have a hard time believing Aidan's story.

The crowd was younger than I'd been expecting—mostly people in their twenties and thirties—and I gathered most of them worked for Capaciti. Several wore zip-up fleeces with the Miracle Battery logo, and I spotted a woman in a tank top with a circuitry schematic tattooed across her bicep. There was no one on the lawn that I recognized, and certainly none of Maggie's friends from back home. But after several minutes of searching, I finally heard her calling me.

"Dad! Hey, Dad!"

I turned and saw Maggie hurrying toward me, running barefoot across the grass in a swishy yellow sundress and carrying her sandals.

"There you are! I've been looking all over for you!" She explained that she'd just returned from town, where she'd succeeded in finding a new bus company to handle the transportation. "So now I'm ready to celebrate. Do you want to come to the bar with me?"

"Could we talk about something first?"

"We'll talk in line. I really need a glass of wine."

"It's personal, Maggie. I don't think anyone else should hear this conversation."

She pointed me toward an empty high-top at the edge of the lawn.

It wasn't exactly private—we were still in full view of everyone at the party—but it would have to do. When we reached the table, Maggie stood with her back to the crowd, so no one would see her irked expression.

"What is it? What's the emergency?"

"I just had a drink with Errol and Aidan. And their attorney, Gerry Levinson? It was a really strange conversation."

"Why?"

"We talked about Dawn Taggart. The girl who went missing?"

"Yes, Dad. I know who she is."

"Right. Well, the weekend she disappeared, Aidan says he was in *your* apartment. The place on Talmadge Street. The dungeon."

Maggie waited for me to continue. "And?"

"You never told me that."

"Never told you what?"

"When we talked about Dawn Taggart, you said Aidan was two hundred miles away in Boston. You never said he was two hundred miles away in Boston *with you*."

Maggie shrugged, like I was getting hung up on a trivial and insignificant detail. "I'm sorry. I thought I mentioned it."

"You definitely did not mention it."

"So what? Why does it matter?"

I forced myself to keep a pleasant expression, because I could see the other guests stealing glances in our direction. Everybody look at the bride and her father, sharing a precious moment before the big wedding.

"Because you're his entire alibi!"

"Jesus, Dad. Is this *Law and Order*? Why are you talking like a special prosecutor?"

"Aidan says he spent the entire Saturday in your apartment. He says no one saw him there except you."

"Exactly."

"You hated that apartment, Maggie! You said it was dark and drab and you couldn't stand being there."

"Most weekends, that was true."

"So why was that weekend any different?"

She opened her mouth to answer and seemed to find herself at a loss for words. "Dad, that's a really personal question. I don't think you want to hear the answer. I mean, how graphic would you like me to get?"

"I just want a story that makes sense."

Look, I wasn't naive. I remembered what it was like to be twenty-five years old. I'd have no trouble believing that Maggie and Aidan spent the entire weekend in a nice hotel room, ordering room service and rolling around on a king-size bed. And I could easily believe they'd spent the weekend in Aidan's luxury penthouse, eating Lucia's cooking on the balcony and soaking in the LeBron James–size bathtub.

But nice hotels and luxury apartment buildings had security cameras and Maggie's shitty basement apartment did not. If any police officers from Hopps Ferry had traveled to Boston to see her place firsthand, I think they would have found her story very hard to swallow.

"I don't know why you're overthinking this," Maggie said. "Aidan didn't hurt Dawn Taggart. He has a beautiful soul. A gentle soul. I know him, and I trust him, and I have zero doubt."

But this just made me more confused.

"Are you saying you have zero doubt because he has a beautiful, gentle soul? Or because he was at your apartment when she disappeared?"

"Why does it matter?"

"Because there's a big difference!"

"Dad, please calm down. I don't know how many times I can answer the same question. I met Aidan on Halloween at a costume party. We went out the next night for dinner. And the night after that, I invited him to my apartment. He came over on Friday and left on Sunday, and we spent a wonderful weekend together. He is the sweetest, kindest, most compassionate man I've ever met, and I wish you could just be happy for me. Why can't you just be happy?"

"Because I'm worried, Maggie. I worry that maybe you love him so much, you're not seeing this situation clearly."

"Dad, believe me, I see the situation just fine."

My daughter could be very stubborn. Once she committed to a certain point of view, it was difficult to rattle her belief system. I'd always found it one of her most admirable qualities, but right now it was driving me bananas.

"Maggie, listen to me. Earlier this afternoon, we stopped at a restaurant in town—me and Tammy and Abigail—and we met Dawn's uncle. A man named Brody Taggart. And he's convinced that Aidan did something to her. He thinks her body's still here at the summer camp."

She laughed like I'd just told a joke. "Let me ask you something, Dad. When you spoke to Brody Taggart, was he intoxicated?"

"Yes, but—"

"So why would you trust a drunk over your own daughter?"

She had me there, but I wasn't finished. Next I told her about the conversation I'd overheard between Aidan and his art school friend Gwendolyn. "And I couldn't hear all of it, but he was threatening her, Maggie. He told her to stay the 'eff' away from you."

Again, she laughed. "That's because I don't like her. No one in the family likes her. Gwen's only here because Aidan feels sorry for her."

"They're keeping secrets, Maggie. There's something you don't know, and I think it's about Dawn Taggart."

"Oh my God, Dad. Enough with Dawn Taggart already. Are you going to talk about Dawn Taggart all weekend?"

"I think you should talk to Gwendolyn. Find out what she knows."

"That woman's a train wreck. She doesn't have any friends, so she just messes around in other people's business. And she's always giving

Aidan shit about his money. She hates Capaciti and she hates his dad and therefore she hates me, too."

"Why does she hate Capaciti?"

"She thinks we use too much cobalt. Or the wrong kind of cobalt? I have no idea. We get it from this tiny region of Africa where—it's true—the working conditions are not ideal. When your job involves digging tunnels into the earth, you don't always get central air and a good 401(k). But guess what? The exact same cobalt goes into Gwendolyn's cell phone, and her laptop computer, and her e-book reader, and her environmentally sustainable electric toothbrush, so why is she picking a fight with us?"

Once again, it seemed like I'd managed to work my daughter into a bit of a frenzy—and this last outburst must have traveled across the lawn, because heads were turning in our direction. But before I could respond, Errol Gardner came walking over with a smile and a glass of white wine. "This is for you, Margaret. I know you've had a long day. I figured you could probably use it."

"Oh my God, yes," she said, reaching for the glass with both hands and drinking like she was parched. "Thank you, Errol."

He clapped a friendly hand on my shoulder. "How are you, Frank? Have you tried the crab cakes?"

"Not yet."

"Phenomenal. Make sure you get some before they run out. And would you mind if we grabbed a quick photo? Just the dads?" I realized a woman with a large camera was trailing him at a respectful distance. "*Boston* mag is here."

The quick photo actually took several minutes, because the photographer coached us through a variety of poses and angles, and then she asked for my name and home city and occupation. I said that I worked for UPS and Maggie inserted herself into the conversation. "He *drives* for UPS," she said. "He's gone twenty-six years without an accident. More than one million miles without a scratch."

The photographer wrote everything down in her notepad. "They'll love those details. Thanks for letting me know."

Once our photo shoot was finished, Errol asked if he could borrow my daughter for a minute. "Patrick from GM is here, with his wife, Jenna. Can I make a quick intro?" He shot me a look of apology. "They're really good people for Margaret to know."

She didn't wait for me to grant permission. She just told me to go enjoy the buffet and said she'd catch up with me after she made her rounds.

"Sure," I told her. "Go make your rounds. I'll be fine."

"Good man," Errol said, and then he rested his hand on the small of Maggie's back and guided her through the crowd, leading her farther and farther away from me.

11.

"Mister Frank! Mister Frank!"

Abigail was squawking at the top of her lungs. I turned and found her waiting at the end of the buffet line, hopping up and down and waving her short arms without a trace of self-consciousness. For some reason she was dressed in a furry blue bodysuit, an elaborate costume that zippered up the middle. There was a hood with pointy blue ears and big googly eyes. She looked like a monster from *Sesame Street*. I hurried over and told her to please stop shouting.

"What are you wearing?"

"I'm Stitch!"

"What's Stitch?"

"From the movie."

Tammy came walking over with an enormous frozen piña colada. "*Lilo and Stitch*, Frankie. It's a cartoon."

Abigail pulled the hood over her head so I could witness the costume in all its glory. "Miss Tammy bought it for me. It's pajamas!"

"Then why are you wearing them now? Do you see anyone else wearing pajamas?"

"Oh, Frankie, she looks adorable. Now do the voice, Abby. Say something in his weird alien language."

Abigail screwed up her face and then sang nonsense lyrics in a squeaky high-pitched falsetto, like she'd just sucked in a lungful of helium. My sister exploded with laughter, spilling piña colada over the rim of her glass and drawing more stares. But since I'd made a promise to be cool about Abigail, I just smiled politely and then coaxed the child into the buffet line.

"Let's not repeat what happened at lunch, okay? You've got to take small servings. Pace yourself. You can always come back for seconds." She didn't hear a word of this. First she reached for the dinner rolls—three of them. Followed by an enormous scoop of mashed potatoes and two mini corn on the cobs. "Okay, see, you're doing it again. You're taking too much. You've already filled your whole plate."

I looked to Tammy for support, but she was chatting with the woman waiting behind us, talking about the secret to making a good mac and cheese ("panko breadcrumbs"). Abigail reached for a pair of tongs and started poking through a tray of chicken piccata, in search of the perfect cutlet. "Mister Frank, are there bones in these?"

"You don't have room. Come back for it later."

"What if they run out?"

"They won't run out."

"How do you know?"

I knew because no person in their right mind would choose a chicken cutlet over prime rib or a fresh New England crab cake, which is what I intended to eat. "Just keep moving."

Instead she pinched the tongs and dragged out an enormous cutlet that dripped lemon-caper sauce all over the table. She tried plopping it onto her mashed potatoes but it immediately tumbled off the side of her plate. I wasn't fast enough to catch it and the chicken landed on the grass between my shoes.

"You see! Didn't I just say—"

Tammy put a hand on my shoulder. "Easy, Frankie."

"I told her this would happen."

We'd brought the buffet line to a halt and I ordered Abigail to pick up the cutlet. She stared down at the grass and shook her head. In a very soft voice, she said, "I don't want it anymore."

"Doesn't matter. Pick it up."

Abigail shrank away from the chicken, like she was suddenly afraid of it. "I can't," she whispered. "I don't want to touch it."

Now everyone in line was staring at us so I had to reach down and pick it up myself. I put it on my plate because I couldn't let it go to waste, not with all the people watching. "Keep moving," I told Abigail. "Let's go find a table. This is ridiculous."

"Hang on," my sister called, and then she grabbed the last two crab cakes—one for herself and one for Abigail. "So she'll get some protein."

Tammy explained that she'd already saved seats for us and led us across the lawn. I assumed we'd be eating dinner with Maggie and Aidan and Aidan's parents. But the only people waiting at our table were Gerry Levinson and a woman in a sleeveless red dress. She was young—probably even younger than Maggie—and very attractive, with an impressive figure and a startling display of cleavage.

Gerry slowly rose to his feet and welcomed us to the table. "Hello again, Frank. This is my wife, Sierra."

I thought this was the start of a joke, but Sierra reached out to shake my hand and I spotted many large glittering diamonds on her ring finger. "So nice to meet you," she said, with a syrupy accent that was straight out of *Gone with the Wind*. "You must be so excited for Maggie."

I didn't know how to respond. What do you say to a beautiful woman in the prime of her youth who shackles herself to a shrunken elderly lawyer with skin like grilled cheese? As a couple, they looked unnatural, a freakish mutation of human biology. "Are you a lawyer, too?"

"Me?" She laughed. "No, I don't do anything."

"You're a writer," Gerry said. "Don't belittle yourself, Sierra. You're writing a children's book."

"I'm a writer," she said with a shrug. "I'm writing a children's book."

"You're looking at the next J. K. Rowling," Gerry explained. "We've tested the first five pages on my grandchildren and they love it. They can't wait for the next installment."

"Market research!" Tammy said. "That's very smart, Gerry. No wonder you're such a good lawyer."

Apparently my sister had already introduced herself to Gerry and Sierra and she'd accepted their relationship at face value, because she was happy to sit down and chatter away. She asked questions about Osprey Cove and Capaciti and everyone's role in the company while I forced myself to finish my dinner—to eat the chicken piccata that I hadn't even wanted. Under no circumstances was I going to throw a perfectly good chicken cutlet into the trash. There were little green specks all over the top, and I couldn't tell if they were chives or scallions or pieces of fresh-cut lawn. I just forked food into my mouth and tried not to think about it.

The jazz trio played one standard after another: "Moon River" and "Come Fly with Me" and "The Girl from Ipanema." Gerry told some hacky lawyer jokes, and Tammy and Sierra laughed at all of them. As the sun set over Lake Wyndham and dropped behind the mountains, I watched Maggie circulating through the party, moving from table to table to welcome her guests. She was a natural hostess and clearly admired by everyone.

But there was no sign of Aidan. And no sign of Gwendolyn, either. Maybe just a coincidence, but I didn't think so.

Eventually a waitress came around and lit the candles in the center of our table, revealing a daddy longlegs perched beside my water glass. I swatted it away before Abigail noticed. She'd brought her wedding etiquette book to dinner and now she was resting her face on the table and using one eye to reread her favorite pages.

"Always nice to see a child reading," Gerry observed, and Tammy assured him that Abigail was a huge bookworm, that she soaked up knowledge like a sponge. "Watch this," she said. "Hey, Abby, what are the five longest rivers in Europe?"

Abigail answered without raising her head. "Volga, Danube, Ural, Dnieper, and Don River."

Gerry used his phone to double-check the answer and held up the screen in astonishment. "Son of a gun!"

"Give her a harder one," Sierra said. "How about Asia?"

Abigail didn't miss a beat. "Yangtze, Yellow, Mekong, Lena, and Irtysh."

"She's faster than my Alexa speaker," Tammy said proudly. "I told her she needs to go on *Jeopardy!* and make some money. She knows every state capital, every US president, and every animated Disney movie since *Snow White*."

"That's extraordinary!" Gerry said. "Maybe you should come work for Errol Gardner, Abigail. What do you say? Would you like to join the Capaciti team after you graduate from college?"

She just turned the page of her book and shrugged. "I don't know. Maybe. We'll see."

And for the first time all day, I was grateful Abigail had joined us. I felt like leaning across the table and giving her buggy little head a kiss.

12.

We were all still sitting there when Hugo, the man from the front gate, came hurrying over to Gerry with a tablet computer. "I'm sorry, forgive the intrusion," he said. Gerry took a moment to read the screen and then tapped out a quick reply. "Thank you, Mr. Levinson," Hugo said. "Enjoy your evening, everyone."

He darted off into the night, and Tammy stared after him, utterly transfixed. "What a handsome man," she said. "And such a mesmerizing accent. Is it Transylvanian?"

"Dutch," Gerry explained. "But Hugo was actually raised in Congo-Kinshasa, after the country declared its independence from Belgium. He played a vital role in some of our business there. Now he's semiretired and stays at Osprey Cove year-round. Looking after the property but mostly just relaxing. It's incredibly peaceful here in the winters."

"Ab-so-lute-ly," Sierra said, stretching out all the syllables as if she was afraid of mispronouncing the word. She was slouched in her seat and absently twirling her long hair, well on her way to being drunk. I wondered how long she'd been married, if her father had attended her wedding, if any responsible adult male had played a role in her upbringing. The jazz trio went from "All of Me" to "The Way You Look

Tonight," and Gerry invited his wife to join some couples who were slow-dancing on the lawn.

Tammy stared fondly after them. "They're so sweet."

"You have to be kidding me. You're actually okay with them? As a couple? Don't you call yourself a feminist?"

Tammy sighed. "I used that word one time in high school and you've never let me hear the end of it." Then she reached for her water glass. It was empty except for ice so she tapped some of the cubes into her mouth and gnashed them with her teeth. "I say, the heart wants what it wants. They seem happy."

"You're out of your mind. She's barely finished high school and that guy's older than Count Dracula. It's disgusting. If I was her father, I'd be mortified."

Abigail was bored with the discussion. She slumped in her chair and pulled her furry blue hood over her head and down past her eyes and nose. She whispered, "Meep-meep-meep-meep-meep," for no discernible reason. I was glad Gerry and Sierra weren't there to hear it.

A waiter breezed past and offered me another beer but I asked for water instead. I'd already had enough alcohol and it wasn't doing anything to calm my nerves. Everything about the day had left me feeling unnerved. The conversation with Brody Taggart. The insane fifty-six-page privacy document. The swarm of spiders in my bedroom. My strange introduction to Gwendolyn. And then the conversation in Errol's office—all his assurances that the picture of Dawn and Aidan was obviously photoshopped. I wished I'd kept a copy for myself; I wished I still had it, so I could show it to an expert and get a second opinion.

Elsewhere, across the lawn, Maggie was still flitting from table to table and personally welcoming every guest. But there was still no sign of her fiancé. "Where's Aidan?"

"I don't know. I haven't seen him all night."

"Doesn't that seem weird?"

"You need to stop being so paranoid," Tammy said. "You're carrying on like he's Dr. Cell Phone, but look around you, little brother. Open your eyes. This is a totally different situation."

Abigail looked up from her book and grinned. "Who's Dr. Cell Phone?"

"Maggie's last boyfriend," said Tammy.

"No, no, no, don't call him a boyfriend."

"His real name was Oliver."

"But he wasn't a boyfriend."

Tammy shrugged. "I kinda think he was."

"For how long?" Abigail asked.

"For never! That guy was a creep and a pervert and an absolute fucking degenerate." I might have been shouting a little because Tammy clapped her palms over Abigail's ears, shielding her from my outburst.

"Frankie, calm down," she said.

"And you know what else bothers me? Where are Maggie's friends?"

Tammy gestured out to the lawn. "These *are* her friends."

"I mean her real friends. School friends. Girls from Stroudsburg." I tried to summon their names from memory, but it was hard because Maggie had brought so few of them around to meet me. She claimed that my shoddy housekeeping embarrassed her; she was always wishing we'd move to a nicer house on a better block. "What about the girl who lived on the corner? The Indian girl with the lisp."

"Priya Hattikudur," Tammy said. "I think they drifted apart after high school, Frankie. But that's normal. People develop different interests. Priya's doing real estate with her parents."

I understood that Maggie had chosen a different path for herself and now she lived in a different world—but I thought the point of a wedding was bringing everyone from your past together, so that people could celebrate your future.

"Instead of complaining about who's not here," Tammy suggested, "maybe you should go meet some people who are."

She pointed me to a table full of young men and women and explained that they were Aidan's groomsmen and Maggie's bridesmaids.

I went over to introduce myself and regretted the decision almost immediately. The chairs were full so there was no place to sit and I just had to stand there hovering while everyone introduced themselves. They all had exotic names like Bacchus and Mathilde and Tarquin, and I couldn't hear the rest because the music was too loud. There was talk of skinny-dipping later, and all the women wanted our waiter to join, because they claimed he looked just like Jeremy Allen White. Listening to their banter was like wandering into a movie thirty minutes late; they were referencing people I didn't know and things I'd never heard of: Slack, Chloé, Charli, Banksy, BeReal, Bad Bunny, NPCs, A24. I swear I'd never felt so old.

The woman closest to me was named Khalani. She was tan and pretty, with a starfish tattoo and long blond hair braided into ropes. She must have registered my discomfort because she encouraged me to move closer, then reached into her handbag for a tin of Altoids. She lifted the lid to reveal some two dozen gummy bears and encouraged me to choose one. "These are THC with a little extra wild card."

"What's wild card?"

Khalani whipped around her hair ropes and laughed. "Frank, you're so funny! If you knew, it wouldn't be wild. You just pick one and roll with it."

I told her no thanks, and she shrugged before choosing an orange bear for herself and passing the tin to her neighbor. I watched the box of gummy bears go around the table, and everyone regarded it matter-of-factly, like a basket of garlic bread at the Olive Garden. Some helped themselves; others just passed it along. I've never really felt comfortable around drugs, so I glanced up at Osprey Lodge, just to have a place to look. At a window on the third floor, I glimpsed the silhouette of a person standing between two curtains and looking down at the lawn. With all the light at their back, I couldn't discern their features—but the size and posture suggested a woman, tall and thin, with her hair pinned up.

Khalani saw me staring, then smiled up at the window and waved. "That's Catherine Gardner."

"How do you know?"

"It has to be. That's her bedroom."

"You've been inside?"

She nodded. "A couple years ago. She used to be a real mentor to a lot of us women. Such a shame she isn't feeling well." She continued waving, gesturing for Catherine to come downstairs and join the party, but the figure in the window didn't react. It was so rigid, it may as well have been a mannequin.

I explained that I still hadn't met her, and Khalani turned to me in astonishment. "But the wedding's in two days! You're kidding!" She placed a hand on my shoulder and gently pushed me in the direction of the lodge. "Go introduce yourself right now. Third floor, top of the stairs."

"Errol said she's napping."

"She's not napping now. Look at her! She's wide-awake and dying to talk with you."

I'd already seen enough of the lodge to know I could find my way to the third floor—but still I hesitated, afraid of doing something inappropriate. "I'll wait for Maggie to introduce us."

"She's too busy. Trust me, Frank. Catherine's a total sweetheart and she'll be thrilled to meet you. Don't be shy!"

I guess I didn't need that much of a push. I knew I wouldn't be able to relax until I met Catherine Gardner and properly introduced myself. So I stopped by the dessert table, arranged a small assortment of cookies on a plate, and walked up to Osprey Lodge. I retraced my route from earlier in the afternoon, through the massive front doors and into the house. The foyer was bustling with behind-the-scenes activity—lots of caterers wheeling boxes and trays to the refrigerated truck parked outside—so no one noticed me slipping inside and climbing the grand spiral staircase.

I paused on the landing where I'd met Errol Gardner and then continued to the third floor and a short darkened hallway. I waved my hand over the walls, feeling around for a switch, until motion sensors registered my presence and some lights in the ceiling flickered on.

I passed a bathroom and a kind of utility closet and a pair of darkened guest bedrooms before arriving at the final door. I gathered it was the master suite, so I screwed up my courage and knocked.

"Hello? Catherine?"

There was no answer. I knew there were probably multiple rooms in the suite and Catherine could be in any one of them; she probably hadn't heard me. So I tried the doorknob but it wouldn't budge. There was a Bluetooth sensor above the lock, and I remembered Aidan's promise to me—he'd said he put my phone on the family's network, so I could access all the main buildings. But even after I pressed my phone to the sensor, the door wouldn't open.

I knocked again, louder, and this time I was answered by sounds of movement. Soft, rustling footsteps.

"It's Frank Szatowski. Maggie's father? I was hoping to introduce myself. If you're up for having visitors."

More silence. I was beginning to think I was talking to myself. But just before I turned to leave, I heard the quiet squeak of a floorboard. As if someone was standing on the other side of the door and watching me through the peephole.

"She's not going to answer."

I spun around and saw a young woman in a long green skirt and brown leather sandals. Aidan's friend from art school, Gwendolyn.

"What are you doing here?" she asked.

I don't know why I felt guilty. I could have easily posed the same question to her. Instead, I told her the truth: "I came to see Aidan's mother. I wanted to introduce myself. See if she's feeling any better."

Something about my reply amused her. She smiled in a way that seemed gently mocking. "She's not feeling better. And she's definitely not going to open that door."

"How do you know?"

"Ask your son-in-law."

She turned and started down the hall, and I went after her.

"Wait, hold on, what are you talking about?"

"I'll be honest with you, Frank. When I met you earlier this afternoon, I thought you knew what you were getting yourself into. But apparently you don't. Because if you still haven't met Catherine Gardner, then you don't know anything."

"Tell me. What do I need to know?"

She didn't answer, just kept descending the stairs. I followed her past the second-floor landing and into a busy foyer full of catering staff.

"Gwendolyn, come on. Talk to me."

She shot me a stern expression that clearly meant "Not here." So I followed her outside into the night, past the large refrigerated truck and across the driveway. She walked into the darkness, heading toward a tall hedge of pine trees. Then she angled her body sideways and slipped through a gap, and I followed her into a small, private copse. She'd all but vanished into the night—but then a tiny orange flame illuminated her face as she lit up a cigarette.

"I followed you and Aidan this afternoon," I told her. "I was listening outside his studio, but I couldn't hear all the details. Why did he threaten you?"

"He doesn't want Margaret to know what I know."

"And what's that?"

She shook her head and smiled sadly, as if to say, *Nice try but not gonna happen.* "My advice to you is: Take your daughter and get the hell out of here. Convince her to call off the wedding before any more people get hurt. Because something awful is happening here. You can feel it, right? Don't you sense it?"

"Is this about Dawn Taggart?"

Gwendolyn took a long drag from her cigarette. "Dawn Taggart is the least of your worries. This is all so much worse than Dawn Taggart."

She was being so damn cryptic I wanted to shake her. "Just tell me the truth."

"You'd never believe me. I can see it in your face, Frank. You seem like a fundamentally nice person. You're not ready to hear it."

I yanked the cigarette from her lips, dropped it in the dirt, and stubbed it out with my shoe. "Listen to me, Gwendolyn. I'm not as nice as you think I am. I spent six months in the Middle East when I was barely out of high school. During this little thing no one remembers anymore called the Gulf War. And believe me: I saw things *you* cannot possibly imagine. So why don't you just tell me your big scary secret?"

Gwendolyn's face lit up with a harsh white glow—the narrow laser-like beam of a headlamp slashing through the night. Two guards dressed in black were off in the forest, trampling along a path on their nightly patrol. Gwendolyn stole an anxious glance in their direction and then lowered her voice.

"Tomorrow morning at eleven there's a group hike. People are walking up to Cormorant Point. Tell them you're not feeling well. I'll come find you and tell you everything. But until then you need to keep quiet. Don't mention this conversation to anyone."

The guards were walking in our direction, and Gwendolyn slipped away without another word. One of the men shined his flashlight directly into my eyes.

"Mr. Szatowski!" I recognized the voice as Hugo's. "You appear to have lost the trail. Is everything okay?"

With his cheerful demeanor and singsong accent, he could have been a kindergarten teacher addressing a classroom full of children.

"I'm fine. Just taking a walk."

Surely he had seen me talking to someone—but he didn't inquire who the person might be. He simply encouraged me to return to the dinner party so I wouldn't miss s'mores on the beach. "There's a beautiful bonfire going and all the young people are enjoying it. You should hurry and go now, before they run out of marshmallows."

13.

Back on the lawn, the jazz trio was gone, and somehow they'd taken their grand piano with them. Now there was electronic dance music blasting from someone's portable speaker. The device wasn't much larger than a softball, but it filled the night with a relentless, thumping bass that shook my entire body. Guests were shouting to be heard over the looping melodies. I returned to my dinner table but Tammy and Abigail were gone. In their place were a bunch of young people I hadn't met, drinking shots and slamming the empty glasses onto the table. I glanced up to the third floor of Osprey Lodge, but the silhouette in the window was gone.

It was hard to recognize anyone in the dark. My night vision isn't as good as it used to be. I circled the tables and studied all the different figures, scanning the crowd for Maggie's familiar silhouette. I passed two men making out on a chair; one straddled the other's waist, and they looked like they were trying to devour each other. The legs of the chair buckled beneath their weight, teetering on the verge of collapse. Elsewhere on the lawn, three women had started a game of horseshoes, even though it was too dark to see the pit; they were just hurling the rings into the black of night and listening for the clank of metal.

Then I felt a hand on my shoulder and turned to see my sister. She was carrying Abigail on her hip, and the little girl was drowsy with sleep. "There you are," Tammy said. "Where the heck have you been?"

"Looking for Maggie."

"You just missed her, Frankie. She came to our table while you were off wandering around. We had a nice long conversation but she got tired of waiting for you."

"What about Aidan? Have you seen him?"

"Not yet, but I need to get Abigail outta here. She's got a bellyache, and besides, this party's getting a little dystopian."

I agreed this was a good idea. Pennsylvania foster parents are expected to care for their children in safe environments free of drugs, alcohol, and promiscuity—so Tammy was currently failing her duties on multiple levels. If photographs of the party ever filtered back to DHS, she would never host another foster child again.

Abigail nuzzled her face into Tammy's shoulder, then opened her eyes and gave me a sleepy smile. "I'm sorry I dropped the chicken, Mister Frank."

I told her not to worry about it. The kid looked exhausted, and I knew it had been a long day for all of us. I said I'd be home soon, and I watched my sister carry Abigail into the night.

Then a steel horseshoe whizzed past my face, just inches from my nose, and a young woman ran bounding after it. "Sorry!"

I walked down to the lake and—as Hugo promised—there was an enormous bonfire blazing on the beach. Two shirtless guys were throwing more and more wood into the conflagration, coaxing the flames higher and higher. I thought they were being irresponsible. There was a gentle breeze coming off the lake and I knew there was a real risk of embers blowing into the woods; it would only take a single spark to ignite some dried leaves. I thought back to the news that morning, to the nine Americans dying every day in accidental fires.

And then a young woman in a white robe walked between me and the fire. She untied her belt, shook off the robe, and let it fall to the sand. Underneath, she was completely naked, with a slender back and long muscular legs. She marched confidently into the water, wading in until she was waist-deep. Then she dove forward and disappeared below the surface. Others were already in the lake and cheered at her arrival—a chorus of disembodied heads, all smiling and bobbing in the gently lapping waves.

And when I looked around the beach, I recognized another half dozen figures in various states of undress. Young people stripping down to their bras and boxers and thongs. I spotted Maggie standing among them, a white robe belted tight around her waist.

"Dad! Where have you been?"

"Looking for you. What are you doing here?"

"We're going swimming, as soon as you take off." She winked. "It'll be a little awkward if you stick around."

I told her this was a terrible idea. "Some of these people are taking drugs. THC with extra wild card."

She laughed. "They're just microdosing."

"What does that mean?"

"It's totally safe. Commercial-grade psilocybin and ketamine. They make it in labs, like vitamins."

"Does Aidan take them?"

"I *wish* Aidan took them. He could use them."

"Is he here? In the water?"

"No, definitely not."

"You're going skinny-dipping without him?"

"Trust me, Dad. This is not his kind of thing."

She took me by the hand and led me back to the lawn, and in my peripheral vision I saw boxer shorts dropping and robes springing open and long bare legs sprinting past us. "Where have you been all night? I've been waiting to talk to you."

"I know and I'm sorry, but I'll make you a deal. Go back to your cottage now. Get a good night's sleep. And I promise I will meet you first thing tomorrow at eight-thirty. We'll take an early morning canoe trip. Just like we always used to do, okay?"

She offered her hand, and I shook it.

"It's a deal," I told her. "But promise you'll be careful in the water, okay?"

"Good night, Dad. Get some rest. I love you."

"I love you, too, Maggie."

She left me on the lawn and bounded back to the beach, and I didn't turn to watch. I agreed that going back to the cottage was a good idea. I was exhausted from a long drive and a long day, and I was ready for a solid night of sleep in a child-size bunk bed. But as I walked up the lawn, I came to a pair of Adirondack chairs where Errol Gardner and Gerry Levinson sat facing the beach and drinking tumblers of bourbon. They recognized me and raised their glasses in a salute.

"There he is," Errol said.

"The father of the bride," Gerry said.

Sierra was standing behind her husband's chair and gently massaging his shoulders and neck. "How was your dinner, Frank?"

"Very nice."

Gerry winked at me. "You thinking of swimming tonight? Joining the youth contingent?"

"No, I was just saying good night to Maggie. I've scarcely seen her since I got here."

Errol drained the last of his bourbon, then set the empty tumbler in the grass. "You know, there's something I've been wondering, Frank. How long has it been since Colleen passed away?"

"Fifteen years, just about."

"I noticed you didn't bring a guest this weekend. Should we assume you're not seeing anyone?"

"Not right now."

"Think you'll ever remarry?"

Of course I'd thought about remarrying plenty of times. I knew I'd probably be happier if I did, and Colleen used to joke that I would never have any trouble finding a second wife, because I was always knocking on women's doors and delivering things they wanted.

And yeah, I guess I'd been keeping my eye on Vicky for the past year or so, but I wanted to patch things up with Maggie before making any moves. I wanted to make sure our father-daughter relationship was solid before introducing the notion of a stepmother.

I didn't feel comfortable sharing any of these things, so I just shrugged and said, "Getting married's a pretty big commitment."

"Oh, I'm not suggesting you get married," Errol said. "I just wondered if you'd enjoy some company this weekend."

"Weddings are a great place to meet women," Sierra said.

"It's true," Gerry agreed. "As soon as they hear Pachelbel's Canon, it's like they all lose their minds. Jump into the bed of whoever's standing closest." Sierra swatted his shoulder in protest, but her husband insisted that facts were facts.

"I'm just saying I would be happy to make some introductions," Errol said. "If you gave me a few basic parameters—hair color, body type, some kind of age range—I'm sure I could find someone. And then you could relax a little. Do you know what I mean?"

I thought I knew what he meant—but I couldn't believe he was actually suggesting it. "I appreciate that, Errol. But I want to be present for Maggie this weekend."

"She's fine, Frank! She's twenty-five years old. Your daughter is a fully grown, independent woman. I think you need to focus less on her and more on you."

And maybe on some level he was right, but I did not like the tone of these comments at all. I don't like anyone telling me how to be a father.

"You know, Errol, there's something I've been meaning to ask *you*. Where is *your* son tonight?"

"I don't know. He's around."

"No, he's not. I haven't seen Aidan since we left your study. Supposedly all these friends are here to celebrate his wedding. You have all these incredible crab cakes and cocktails and a bonfire but I don't see Aidan enjoying any of it. Where the hell is he?"

"Aidan's twenty-six years old. I don't babysit him."

"Maybe you should. Don't you think it's strange that you're here, and Maggie's here, and I'm here, and Aidan's been missing all night?"

"I don't know, Frank. What are you suggesting?"

I didn't know what I was suggesting. But I remembered all of Brody's warnings from earlier in the morning:

Trust your instincts.

You know something's wrong.

He's the Prince of Fucking Darkness.

Gerry cleared his throat and then spoke in his soft, quiet voice. "Frank, I think I can answer your question. Earlier this evening, I saw Aidan going into the lodge. He told me he was going upstairs, to sit with his mother. She isn't well enough to attend the dinner, but he didn't want her feeling left out. So he brought up some plates of food, and he's been keeping her company all night."

Sierra's mouth fell open, and she rested one hand on her breast. "Oh, now that is just about the sweetest thing I've ever heard. You raised a fine young man there, Errol Gardner."

"Aidan does look after his mother," Errol agreed. "He'd do just about anything for her."

I decided this all seemed plausible. Aidan could have been in Catherine's room when I knocked—maybe he was the person I'd heard shuffling on the other side of the door. And maybe Catherine had told him she didn't want visitors. Maybe she'd asked him to ignore me.

"I'm sorry, Errol," I said. "I wasn't trying to imply anything. I've been awake since three-thirty and I think I just need some sleep."

He stood up and shook my hand. "No hard feelings, Frank. It's a big weekend full of big emotions. Especially for us dads."

"Tomorrow's going to be a wonderful day," Gerry assured us. "The weather looks perfect for a hike, and then we'll all have fun on the lake."

I wished them all a good night, then crossed the lawn and walked toward the trees, following a trail that would lead me back to the cottage. Just before stepping into the woods, I took one last look back at Osprey Lodge—and I noticed the silhouette had returned to the third-floor window. And even though I could only see a general outline of her figure, I had the distinct sense she was watching me. I offered a small wave, as Khalani had done. And to my surprise, she raised her right hand, returning the greeting. Then she stepped back from the window and extinguished the light.

III.

THE REHEARSAL

1.

I woke to a gentle caress on my cheek. It felt like my wife's long brown hair tickling my face as she turned over in bed. I must have been dreaming of her again. Then the tickle crossed my nose on eight spindly legs and I sat up in the dark, blindly slapping at myself.

I reached for the nightstand and switched on the lamp. It was ten past four, Gardner Standard Time. I was sprawled across the tiny bottom bunk and there were three more spiders directly above me, suspended from the upper mattress. I grabbed a tissue from the box on the nightstand and squashed them. Then I looked around the room and discovered more spiders perched on the walls and ceiling and curtains. They must have come out while I was sleeping. I had to go around the room crushing them all before I felt comfortable turning off the light.

And by that point I knew falling back to sleep would be impossible. I had too many other worries on my mind: Dawn's uncle, in the parking lot of Mom and Dad's Restaurant, asking if I was out of my fucking mind. Maggie and Aidan's very unlikely story about the basement apartment on Talmadge Street. The fake photo of Dawn Taggart standing on the shore of Osprey Cove. And Gwendolyn's promise to come find me in the morning, to explain all the secrets. What was she going to tell me?

And when I'd exhausted all these new worries, I went back to re-
visit the classics, all my worst parenting failures. All the nights I forced
Maggie to stay at the dinner table and clear her plate; all the times I
grounded her for bad grades and blown curfews and chores left incomplete. I tossed and turned and wandered around this labyrinth of
regret, searching for memories of happier days that would allow me
to relax and fall asleep. I tried focusing on the good times—birthdays,
Christmas mornings, Waffle House brunches. But my mind kept dredg-
ing up all my biggest failures, like the time I threatened to call the police
on my own daughter.

Maggie must have been seventeen when it happened, because she'd
just started a part-time job at Dunkin' Donuts, serving up hot coffee
and Boston Kremes. She had saved quite a bit of money and she wanted
to purchase a $350 "vegan suede" jacket from one of those shady online
retailers that do all their sales on Instagram, so she needed to borrow
my credit card. I told her $350 was a ridiculous price for a coat with-
out any thermal lining, and I tried to explain that "vegan suede" was
just bullshit marketing speak for "fake leather." I warned that all these
glamorous social media influencers were peddling a fantasy lifestyle
that no normal person could afford. But my protests fell on deaf ears.
Maggie reminded me that she'd earned the money herself, and (per
our family agreement) she had the right to spend it however she liked.
Then she pushed a stack of wrinkled bills into my hand and dragged
me over to the family computer.

I used my credit card to order the coat—size medium, free standard shipping via UPS. A week later, Maggie received an email saying
that her jacket had been delivered—but when she went outside our
house to collect it, there was no trace of a package. Later that night,
after I got home from work, Maggie explained the problem to me and
wondered aloud if our driver had brought the jacket to the wrong
address. But I knew our driver personally; John "Speedy" Gonzalez
had been on the job fifteen years and we both worked at the same
package facility. He wasn't going to bring any box marked SZATOWSKI

to the wrong house. Speedy gave us VIP treatment and he always left our deliveries on the porch, where they'd be safe from rain and wind. The most likely explanation, I told Maggie, was that her package was stolen.

Porch pirates are a real problem in my line of work, and you'll find them trolling residential neighborhoods all over the country. They are vast networks of thieves and scammers who shadow package cars and then snatch boxes right after we deliver them. Several times a month, I'll suspect I'm being shadowed myself—at which point I will usually stop, pull over, and take a photo of the street behind me, making sure to capture the car and driver in the frame. That's usually enough to deter them. Unfortunately, the pirates are a lot like cockroaches. For every one you see, there's usually another three or four lurking around the corner, just out of sight.

Maggie was so upset by the news, she nearly started crying. But I assured her that she wasn't completely out of luck. I wrote an email to the retailer, identifying myself as an employee of United Parcel Service and explaining the situation. Their reply included a gift code for a replacement jacket, free of charge, and this time Maggie placed the order herself. Three days later, another vegan-suede jacket arrived at my house—and Maggie was waiting on the doorstep to receive it. I thought the coat looked cheaply constructed and wouldn't be much use in a snowstorm, but Maggie liked the style and wore it all the time.

Now, that should have been the end of it—except a few weeks later I stopped at the Sam's Club to pick up some grass seed and bumped into one of my daughter's friends, a girl from down the street named Priya Hattikudur. I liked Priya and thought she was a good influence on Maggie. Her parents were real estate agents and I saw their smiling faces on benches and bus shelters all over Monroe County. They seemed like smart, hardworking people with a lot of common sense.

So I was a bit surprised to see Priya wearing the same overpriced vegan-suede jacket that my daughter owned. And when I asked her about it, she said Maggie sold it to her.

"The company sent two by mistake," she explained. "She was going to list the extra on Depop, but she let me have it for eighty bucks."

I cannot tell you how awful I felt in this moment. If you've ever been disappointed by your children—deeply, seriously, *profoundly* disappointed—then maybe you have some inkling of what I mean. I was so shaken, I left the store without buying the grass seed. I had to go out to the parking lot and sit in my Jeep to steady my thoughts. And I pounded the empty passenger seat in frustration, striking it again and again until my fist was sore.

At dinner that night, I told Maggie about my conversation with Priya. She immediately confessed and apologized for lying. But she did it all with a sheepish grin, like she was Ferris Bueller caught playing hooky.

"You stole a jacket," I said. "You're a thief."

"Not a real thief," she said. "It's not like I carried the jacket out of a store."

"Yes! It's *exactly* like that!"

Maggie fired off every excuse in the book. The retailer was part of a massive international conglomerate, so they wouldn't feel the loss. The jacket was stupidly overpriced, so she *deserved* to have two for the price of one. And it was manufactured in Malaysia, probably by slave labor, so scamming the company was actually a kind of political statement. Maggie insisted that all her friends pulled the same kinds of tricks, that in the world of online shopping this was completely acceptable behavior.

"You used my credit card," I reminded her. "You made me complicit in your crime. We're talking mail fraud. Do you remember who I work for? How I put food on this table?"

My sister was joining us for dinner, so of course Tammy had to interrupt and give her two cents. She reminded me that no one else knew the truth of the situation, so there was no need to fly off the handle. And I guess that's when I *really* flew off the handle, because I threatened to report my daughter to the police. Maggie just laughed, because she knew I'd never actually do it.

"Let's be sensible," Tammy said, before proposing that Maggie simply return the jacket instead. But we couldn't figure out how to do it; there was no way to get a return label without triggering an automatic refund. So in the end I forced Maggie to donate the jacket to Goodwill. She was mad at me for a month, and out of spite she refused to wear any coat for the rest of the winter; she'd venture out in a blizzard dressed in a cotton hoodie, as if I'd left her with no other choice. And I didn't care, because back then I still had the courage of my convictions.

But these days, I'm not so sure. My three-year cold war with Maggie forced me to take a long hard look at all my parenting mistakes. I knew I'd pushed her away through a series of errors large and small—and now I needed to tread carefully if I wanted our relationship to survive. So I tried to relax and told myself everything would work out okay. Brody Taggart was clearly intoxicated. And Gwendolyn just seemed jealous of my daughter's good fortune. Neither one of them could be trusted.

I lay in bed for a long time and never returned to sleep.

2.

At seven-thirty I got up and made the bottom bunk, then showered and dressed and went downstairs to the kitchen. Waiting on the island was a warm platter of fresh-baked breakfast treats—muffins, bagels, scones, cinnamon rolls, and lots of odd-shaped pastries that I couldn't put a name to, plus bowls of oatmeal and yogurt and a massive urn of hot coffee. Clearly someone had entered our cottage to prepare the feast, but they'd completed their work in utter silence.

I fixed myself a coffee and filled a plate with carbs and then carried everything outside to the front porch. My sister was sitting in a rocking chair, dressed in a white Osprey Cove robe and slippers, watching mist rise from the lake with a mug of hot tea in her lap. "Good morning, little brother! How did you sleep?"

I didn't see the point in complaining, so I just slumped into the empty chair beside her. "Fine, you?"

"Best rest I've had in thirty years. I slept like Rip Van Winkle. It must be the fresh air. Or the sounds of the lake? The lapping of the waves on the shore. Soooo relaxing. I didn't even turn on my sound machine!"

She was in an exceptionally good mood. In all her life, Tammy said, she'd never awakened to a delicious breakfast prepared just for her.

As she savored every bite of her chocolate croissant, she told me all about her conversation with Errol Gardner, whom she'd met during dinner the previous evening. "I'll be honest with you, Frankie. I was a little intimidated about meeting him. Since he's so rich, I thought he might be uppity. But you know what? That man came to our table and he brought me a glass of white wine and a Shirley Temple for little Abby, and we must have talked for half an hour. Such a genuine and compassionate human being. Do you know he even promised to teach Abigail how to water-ski? There's three hundred Ivy Leaguers at this party and here's Errol Gardner making time to help a foster kid. That goes a long way in my book, do you know what I'm saying?"

I set my coffee on an end table and agreed that Errol was very generous. "Last night, he offered to find me some company."

"What kind of company?"

"Female company."

My sister was delighted. "I bet he knows some nice widows."

"Or prostitutes. One or the other."

She started choking on her chamomile tea. "Oh, Frankie, please! Did he actually use the word *prostitute*?"

"He said *companion*. But I could pick her age and hair color and body shape. Like I was ordering off a menu. It was really weird. And the whole time, Gerry's right next to us with his eighteen-year-old bride. God only knows how those two found each other."

"Errol just wants to know your type. I can talk to him on your behalf. I think I know what you're looking for."

"No, Tammy. Do not talk to Errol on my behalf. I don't want a companion for this weekend. I want to spend time with Maggie and Aidan and Aidan's family. That's it."

She let it drop, and I spent several moments simply appreciating the incredible view. The lake stretched out before us, placid and still in the quiet early morning. I spotted an osprey in flight, sweeping down to the water and skimming its talons along the surface; an instant later it was soaring skyward with a fish in its clutches. Then I turned my attention to my breakfast—a warm fresh-baked croissant, tiny round quiches with bacon and mushroom, a bowl of Maine blueberries in fresh sweet cream—and found my mood improving with every bite. Everything tasted fantastic and the coffee was sublime, and my sister shivered and sighed in blissful contentment, overwhelmed by the natural beauty.

Then the screen door creaked open and Abigail shuffled outside, dressed in her blue alien pajamas and clawing the side of her head.

Tammy said, "Good morning, potato bug!" and the little girl just groaned. "How did you sleep?"

Abigail scrunched up her face like she was constipated. "I'm all itchy, Miss Tammy."

"Really? Worse than yesterday?"

"Uh-huh."

"All right, honey, do me a favor. Go inside and get a towel. And bring the mayo from the fridge. And a rubber spatula. The kind you use to ice a cake. Do you know what I mean?"

Abigail nodded and disappeared inside the house and I glared at my sister. She waved off my concern. "It's probably just dry skin. Don't mind us. Go watch the birds or something."

There was a pair of binoculars on the front porch so that guests could sit in their rocking chairs and marvel over all the magnificent waterfowl. But Abigail's arrival ruined everything. She squirmed and fussed and groaned as Tammy worked the mayonnaise into her scalp, and all the birds flew off in search of peace and quiet. The smell was awful, like stinky, sweaty feet in polyester socks. I reached for the jar to check the expiration date.

"Tammy, this went bad in November."

She shrugged. "If these lice die from salmonella, it's all the same to me." Finished, she wrapped the bath towel around Abigail's neck so the condiment wouldn't drip on her pajamas. "These little buggers can hold their breath for an hour, so you need to leave this on until nine-thirty."

And with that, I realized I was late and stood up. "I have to go. I'm meeting Maggie for a canoe ride."

Abigail's eyes went wide. "Can I come with?"

Tammy shrugged. "Sure, why not?"

"No, no, no," I told her. "You should stay here and eat your breakfast."

"Frankie, she *really* wants to canoe," Tammy explained. "She was asking all day yesterday."

I promised Abigail that I would take her in the afternoon, if there was enough time. And she looked disappointed and so did my sister, but you understand my point of view, right? I was already sleeping in a baby bed and eating chicken cutlets that fell on the grass, and I refused to sacrifice the most important thing, which was quality time with my daughter. I didn't want Abigail coming between us and stinking up the whole boat.

"You could take her yourself," I reminded Tammy. "They've got a dozen canoes. Anyone can borrow them."

"I have no idea how to drive a canoe! I'd be scared to death."

"It doesn't matter," Abigail said. "I'll just stay here and read my book."

She shuffled back inside the cabin and my sister shot me a look of grave disappointment, but I refused to feel guilty about it. I set off down the path and followed the shore of the lake until I was back at the beach. The sand was littered with traces of the previous night's revelry: forgotten towels, empty glass tumblers, someone's bright yellow bikini bottoms, and lots of botched s'mores teeming with little black ants. The mess looked out of place in Osprey Cove, but there was already a trio of landscapers moving across the lawn and collecting the trash with long metal tongs.

I found Maggie standing near the shore, dressed in a 5K charity run T-shirt and khaki shorts. She held two insulated thermos cups full of coffee and passed one to me. "Milk and two sugars," she said, and I was so touched by this simple gesture, touched that she'd remembered my order and taken the time to think of me. Of course, I didn't know how I was supposed to canoe with hot coffee, but Maggie explained that modern canoes came with cupholders now, just like everything else in the world.

We grabbed a canoe and flipped it upright, only to discover it was full of daddy longlegs. I used a paddle to run them off and then together we pushed the nose of the boat into the lake. "I'll steer," Maggie offered. "I know where we're going."

I took my paddle and my coffee and settled into the front seat. My daughter pushed us off and then gracefully vaulted into the back seat without getting a drop of water on herself. She explained that our destination was Cormorant Point, a rocky ridge about a mile west of the cove. "We're going to hike up there for lunch, but I thought you'd enjoy seeing it from the water."

I still remembered Gwendolyn's instructions—how she'd told me to stay behind when everyone walked to the cliffs. "Are you and Aidan going?"

"Yes, everyone's going."

"Even Aidan's mother?"

I wish I could have seen Maggie's reaction, but I was facing the wrong way. "Well, no, Dad, obviously Catherine can't go. She's in no shape for a hike."

"How's she feeling this morning?"

"I don't know. I'm staying in Hummingbird. All the way on the other side of camp. I haven't been to the lodge since yesterday."

"So we're just going to leave her alone all day? That doesn't seem right. This is your mother-in-law."

We'd already traveled about a hundred yards from shore when Maggie angled her paddle, spinning us into a ninety-degree turn. Then we resumed our paddling so we were following the shoreline. "Catherine doesn't mind. There's a nurse in the house who looks after her. Keeps her company and makes sure she has everything she needs."

I was tempted to ask why her nurse didn't answer my knocking last night but decided against telling that story. I knew Maggie would just get upset.

"I'd be happy to stay home and have lunch with Catherine," I said. "If she's feeling better, and she's ready to have visitors. I can stay with her and keep her spirits up."

"Dad, that is really sweet of you, but I know how Catherine is and I know she will want you to do the hike. She'll feel bad if you're stuck in the house with her. She doesn't like to burden people."

I remembered Gwendolyn's words from the previous evening: *If you still haven't met Catherine Gardner, then you don't know anything.*

But how much did my daughter know?

And why was she being so evasive?

"I'm surprised you didn't bring Abigail," Maggie said. "She told me she wanted to go canoeing. She could have taken the middle seat."

"Her head lice came back. Tammy's putting mayonnaise on it."

"Seriously? That's just an old wives' tale. Mayonnaise isn't going to fix anything."

"Your aunt swears by it."

"That girl needs a doctor. When we get back to camp, I'll call the clinic in town. I'm sure they can send someone over."

"No, Maggie. You've already got a million things on your plate. I've barely seen you since I got here. You don't need any more responsibilities."

"Dad, why are you yelling?"

I didn't realize I was yelling. I lowered my voice and tried to explain myself in a calm, measured tone: "This weekend is about family, Maggie. After we drive home on Sunday, Abigail will go back to her mother—or some other foster parent—and we are never going to see her again. Thirty years from now, you'll be looking through your wedding photos and you won't even remember her name. You'll be like: Who the hell is this kid? What's she doing at my wedding?"

She laughed. "You're probably right, but I'm calling the clinic anyway. Someone will hurry right over."

You never hear about doctors making house calls anymore, but I guessed if you were in the Gardner family, you could pick up a phone and ask for anything you wanted. You could specify an age and hair color and body type and magically conjure up a female companion, like a genie summoned from a lamp.

We paddled along and Maggie enjoyed playing tour guide. She directed my attention to various landmarks around the lake, such as a small decommissioned lighthouse and a property that once belonged to Jimmy Stewart. I could tell she was proud of the camp and excited to show it off, that she already felt an ownership of the place.

Cormorant Point was a rocky gray cliff that jutted out from shore. Apart from being the tallest point on the water, there was nothing especially notable about it. A couple of early risers were already milling around the top, leaning against the safety railing while snapping selfies on their phones. Maggie explained that the top of the cliff was a fifty-minute walk from Osprey Lodge, just enough of a climb to work up an appetite. The caterers would have lunch and refreshments waiting when we arrived.

And then I realized that Maggie was already turning the boat around, as if our morning excursion was complete and now it was time to turn back. We'd been on the water for scarcely twenty minutes and there were still so many things I wanted to ask her about. We'd wasted all our time talking about Abigail and Jimmy Stewart's relatives.

"Maggie, listen to me. How are you feeling?"

"I feel great."

"I mean, about the wedding."

"I know what you meant."

"Are you nervous?"

"Not at all. I'm excited."

"How about Aidan? Is he nervous?"

"Aidan's fine."

"I didn't see him last night."

"Me, neither." I thought she might elaborate on this point, but she just kept paddling.

"Gerry said he was upstairs with his mother?"

"That sounds right."

"But you don't know? You haven't seen him?"

"He's staying in the lodge. I haven't seen him since dinner."

She said this all very matter-of-factly, but I couldn't wrap my head around it. "So you went skinny-dipping with all your friends and never saw him last night? Not even to say good night to each other?"

She laughed. "Dad, we're not like you and Mom. Aidan and I aren't joined at the hip. We're very independent people. We have different interests and friends. And Aidan's an introvert. He's an artist. He needs a lot of downtime. If you try to smother him, he'll resent you."

I could feel her paddling faster, putting more muscle into each stroke, like she was suddenly racing to get us back to dry land.

"I'm not trying to smother him, Maggie. I'd just like to talk to the kid. Understand what makes him tick."

"You talked for an hour yesterday! Errol said you guys were all drinking bourbon together. Doesn't that count?"

"We were with his father and the family attorney. Because I brought the photograph of Aidan and Dawn Taggart. They said it was photoshopped."

"It must have been," she said. "Aidan never brought her here."

Once again I wished I'd kept a copy. "It looked pretty real to me."

"Which is the point," Maggie explained. "It's supposed to look real. But these days you can't trust your own eyes anymore."

In the distance, I could see the side of the Gardners' boathouse slowly gliding into view. We were almost back at the camp, and I didn't want to end our outing on a sour note. We passed a few cottages on shore and I recognized the front of Blackbird. Tammy waved to us from her rocking chair on the porch and we both waved back. There was no sign of Abigail, though.

After another minute or so we found ourselves approaching the L-shaped dock. Osprey Lodge came into view and the main lawn was full of people; it seemed like all the guests had come outside to welcome our return. Or maybe they'd been roused from sleep by a fire alarm; many were still dressed in their pajamas and slippers and Osprey Cove bathrobes, like they'd hurried outside on short notice. I asked Maggie if there was some kind of group breakfast and she said, "No, no, this is weird. Something's not right."

Errol Gardner and Gerry Levinson were on the beach conferring with Hugo. Two of the security guards were standing knee-deep in the lake and wading toward us. Hugo spotted our canoe and then waved both arms toward the boathouse. "Stay out of the cove, please! Tie up on the dock!"

The sun had risen over Osprey Lodge, and I had to squint through my fingers just to orient myself; I couldn't tell what was happening. Maggie dug in with her paddle, spinning us around in a 180-degree turn, and then a cloud moved in front of the sun, allowing me a clearer look at the shore. The two men in the water were now waist-deep and advancing toward a large object floating just below the surface. I stared until it assumed a kind of form and its parts came into focus: slender bare legs, an open white robe, long red hair.

3.

Maggie hurried over to Errol and Gerry while I hastily tied up the canoe, and then I rushed over to join them. None of the guards objected to my arrival, perhaps because they were focused on a larger problem: the dead woman in the lake and how to bring her ashore.

Her robe had opened at the waist and expanded in the water, giving her figure the white-winged silhouette of an angel. The guards were using paddles to prod and push the body toward the beach. The guests on the lawn were keeping a respectful distance, but I noticed Khalani holding up her iPhone to record the events. Gerry noticed, too, and he sent a guard to speak with her. "Go remind that idiot she's signed an NDA. Then tell her to remind her friends they *all* signed NDAs. If I see any glimpse of this on TikTok, I am coming to her first."

Hugo knelt in the sand, pulled on a pair of thin gloves, and carefully turned the woman onto her back. I'd already recognized the long red hair, but I wasn't prepared for the shock of seeing Gwendolyn's face. Her eyes were still open and her lips were darkened and slightly parted; the overall expression was a look of surprise. Water trickled from her mouth and dribbled down the side of her face, like she was a vessel that had been overfilled.

"This doesn't make any sense," Maggie said. "My dad and I were just here at eight-thirty. The beach was empty."

"She was under the dock," Errol explained. "The landscapers came out to rake the beach and one of them spotted her."

Hugo pressed a finger to Gwendolyn's neck, feeling for a pulse. I thought it was a wholly unnecessary precaution. But maybe he did it because so many people on the lawn were watching. He turned to another of his men and said, "Bring us some blankets. Quick, quick, quick." Then he adjusted the folds of her robe, trying to preserve what remained of her modesty. "We need to talk to the other guests. See what we can determine before the police arrive. Find out if anyone saw her last night."

"I saw her last night," Maggie said. "It was around eleven o'clock—no, actually, eleven-thirty." Hugo encouraged her to continue. "A bunch of us were leaving the beach, heading back to our cabins, but Gwendolyn was walking toward the water. And she was alone. Dressed in the robe she's wearing now. I told her she was too late, everyone was finished swimming, but either she didn't hear me or she didn't care. She just kept walking."

"Did she appear to be under the influence?"

"I have no idea. She's never been especially friendly to me, so I didn't go out of my way to speak with her. But Aidan says she's done a lot of drugs, so it certainly wouldn't be . . ." Her voice trailed off, as if the right word had eluded her.

"It wouldn't be out of character?" Errol suggested.

"Exactly," Maggie said.

In fairness, I felt obligated to point out that lots of people were taking drugs the previous evening. I reminded Maggie about Khalani's gummy bears and the THC with extra wild card, but she responded like I was confused. "I don't mean microdosing, Dad. Gwendolyn was using street drugs. The real hard-core illegal stuff."

A guard came running up with a blanket and I worked with him to cover Gwendolyn's body. Just before lowering the blanket over her face, I noticed two red marks on the side of her neck. Each was about the size of a quarter. "What are these?"

Hugo held up one hand, signaling for everyone to halt. Then he knelt down and leaned over the body, moving so close to her face that I thought he intended to kiss her. Instead, he abruptly stood up and slapped his hands clean. "Those were caused by something in the lake. Like a rock or the tip of a branch." He pointed his index finger to demonstrate—poke, poke, poke—then motioned for us to finish covering the body. "We'll call the police, of course, and they'll bring the medical examiner." In the meantime, he asked his men to disperse the crowd, because he worried that onlookers might put the police on edge. "And of course someone should find Aidan and deliver the news."

"Me," Maggie said. "I'll do it. He'll be upset, and I want to be there for him."

I wanted to warn her to be careful. I had a hunch that Aidan already knew exactly what had happened to Gwendolyn.

"I'll come with you," I offered, but Maggie firmly shook her head, making it clear once again that my help was not required.

4.

"I think we can all agree she looked like trouble."

News of Gwendolyn's death must have traveled quickly because by the time I caught up with Tammy, she'd already formed strong opinions on the subject.

"I saw her last night in the buffet line and my first thought was, *This kid's an addict.* She had that glassy-eyed malnourished look they all get. Plus she barely took any food. Just green beans and corn and a little rice. What does that tell you?"

"She was vegetarian?"

"She was trouble, Frankie. With a capital *T* that rhymes with *D* and that stands for *drugs*."

I'd found Tammy and Abigail in the shade of Big Ben, the largest and oldest tree on the property, first planted (if you believed the plaque) by Union Army war hero Benjamin Butler in 1853. There were two wooden swings hanging from the lowest bough, but Abigail had ignored them and climbed up into the tree. Now she was high off the ground and reaching blindly into a knothole. I warned her that some animal living inside the tree was probably on the verge of biting her fingers, but she just ignored me and reached even deeper.

"I don't think Gwendolyn was an addict," I said. "I talked to her last night. She seemed perfectly sober."

"These people do a good job of hiding it, Frankie. Trust me. A lot of my birth parents are addicts and they're pretty good fakers. But if you know the warning signs, you can spot them." She sighed. "I just hope this doesn't impact the wedding. Do you think they'll postpone it?"

"They have to. The police are here. They're going to interview everyone at the camp. It'll cast a shadow over the entire weekend."

Something struck the back of my neck and I turned to see Abigail's sneaker swinging past my face. She had returned to the lowest limb and now she was stuck. "Mister Frank, I need help."

Even with both of my arms fully extended, I couldn't reach higher than her knees. "You have to jump."

She shook her head. "I can't."

"I'll catch you."

"No, no, no—"

"Just scooch your butt off the branch. Don't worry, Abigail. I promise I'll grab you. I will not let you fall."

Her lower lip was trembling, like she was going to cry. It was like her freak-out with the spiders all over again.

"I think we should ask for a ladder," Tammy said. "I can dial zero on the house phone."

I turned to look at her. "We don't need a ladder, Tammy. I can fix this. All she has to do is jump."

My sister's eyes widened in alarm and then seventy pounds of Abigail came crashing onto my shoulders. I fell to my knees, my palms slammed into the dirt, and something awful popped in my lower vertebrae. Like a muscle snapped in half.

"Abigail!" Tammy said.

I closed my eyes, gritted my teeth, and whispered a string of profanities. Abigail rolled off me and stood up and showed Tammy a thin red scratch on her wrist. "It burns," she whispered.

Tammy swept her up off the ground. "You're going to be okay, potato bug. I've got cortisone in my purse. Let's go back to the cottage and we'll get you fixed up." At last she noticed I wasn't moving. "Are you okay, Frankie?"

I said, "I'm fine," because I just wanted them to leave. Rolling onto my side made the pain slightly more bearable, but standing up was impossible.

In my line of work, there is nothing more dangerous than a back injury. You can lose an eye and still get behind the wheel, and I know drivers who have powered through arthritis, knee pain, and carpal tunnel syndrome. But there is no way you're hauling flat-screen TVs with a busted back. I was terrified that Abigail had left me unemployable, that I'd be forced to go out on disability, which was the worst thing I could imagine.

But after a short rest in the grass I managed to sit up, and then I slowly coaxed myself into a standing position. If it had been any other weekend, I would have gone straight to bed with two Tylenol and an ice pack. Instead I limped back to Osprey Lodge to find my daughter and see how her fiancé was coping with the news.

5.

Down on the beach, there were three EMTs and a half dozen police officers working side by side with members of Osprey Cove's security team. I watched from a distance, standing in the shade of the trees and observing their work. Apart from taking lots of photographs, no one seemed to be doing all that much. There was a stretcher in the sand, lying parallel to Gwendolyn's body, and the EMTs appeared to be deliberating the best way to get her on it.

Errol Gardner exited the back door of the lodge and walked over to me. He was holding an insulated mug of coffee and offered to bring me some but I declined.

"How's Aidan?" I asked.

"Oh, he's fine. He thinks this whole thing was basically inevitable. Said he always worried Gwendolyn was heading down this road."

"I don't think she overdosed," I said. "I talked to her last night. She was completely sober."

"I know, Frank. You mentioned that earlier. We'll just have to see what the medical examiner says. But it'll be well into next week before they issue a report."

I spotted Gerry and Hugo standing among the medics and the police officers. They were all engaged in easy, relaxed conversation; they could have been discussing the Red Sox.

"It's a shame about the wedding," I said. "Have you talked to the kids about rescheduling?"

"No one's rescheduling anything. The kids want to move ahead and so do I. And so should you. As soon as the medics clear out, we're going to proceed with the hike. Get everyone up to Cormorant Point." He seemed to register my tortured posture. "Though I'm not sure you're up for the walk, Frank. You look a little stiff."

I told him how I'd hurt my back and he winced in sympathy. Errol mentioned that the camp clinic had a heating pad and promised to have it sent over to my cottage. But first, he explained, he needed to talk to the police and encourage them to hurry things along.

I watched him march down to the beach and approach the police like he had every right to be there. I couldn't hear their conversation, but the officers seemed to be apologizing for taking so long.

Of course, Mr. Gardner.

We'll be finished in a few minutes, sir.

And then we promise we'll be out of your hair.

There were still plenty of guests hanging around the back of the lodge, but no one was bothering to interview them. The scene on the beach looked more like a coffee break than an actual police investigation. I was still watching it all in disbelief when my phone chirped with an incoming text. It was a message from Vicky, replying to my text from the previous afternoon:

> Frank, I've read your toast and I really think you nailed it. Your writing is warm and heartfelt and there's not a single word I would change. I guarantee people are going to love it. Especially Maggie. You got this!! ♥♥Vicky

She usually worked noon to closing and it was only ten-thirty, so I knew I had a good chance of catching her at home. I ducked into the trees for some privacy and dialed her cell.

"Hey, Frank! I just sent you a text!"

"I know. I just read it."

"Is everything okay?"

"No, not really. I'm sorry to keep bothering you—"

"What's the matter?"

I peered through the trees to the main lawn. The medics had lifted the stretcher off the ground, and now they were carrying Gwendolyn's body up the lawn to Osprey Lodge. "A woman died last night."

"Oh, no—"

"They're carrying away the body and then we're all going on a picnic. Except Aidan's mother, because she won't come out of her bedroom. So she missed all the skinny-dipping and microdosing last night. And did I mention all the clocks here are fifteen minutes fast?"

I could hear Vicky settling into a chair and popping the tab on a can of Diet Coke. "Frank, slow down. I think you should start from the beginning. Walk me back to yesterday afternoon. Tell me what's going on."

I walked her back even further—to Wednesday night, right after she cut my hair, when I came home to find the photo of Aidan Gardner and Dawn Taggart in my mailbox. I told Vicky about Hugo and the privacy docs and Catherine's mysterious illness, about Gerry Levinson and his absurdly young wife and Gwendolyn's promise to tell me everything, just hours before she turned up dead.

"I feel like I'm in the twilight zone. Everywhere I look, there's all kinds of crazy stuff, but people keep saying it's totally normal. I can't tell left from right anymore."

"What about Tammy? What's she think?"

"She's fallen down the rabbit hole. She's drank a whole big pitcher of crazy Kool-Aid and I can't talk to her."

"Then you need to trust your instincts. What's your gut telling you?"

I felt awful giving voice to my suspicions, but the words rang true as soon as they left my mouth. "I think Aidan did something to these girls: Dawn Taggart *and* Gwendolyn. I think my daughter is too lovesick to realize what's going on. And I think Errol Gardner is cleaning up his son's mess, because that's what rich parents do."

"Not just the rich ones," Vicky said.

"What's that mean?"

"I'm speaking from experience, Frank. When my daughter, Janet, started getting into trouble, I made a thousand excuses for her. 'Oh, she doesn't have a drug problem. She's just experimenting. She's just exploring her wild side.' I didn't want to see the truth. And by the time I admitted she had a problem, it was too late."

I felt awful for making her dredge up all these terrible memories. She'd told me more than once that losing Janet was the worst thing that ever happened to her. "I'm sorry, Vicky."

"It's fine, Frank. I'll tell you something I learned from hard experience: Every parent's an unreliable narrator. We think we know our kids better than anyone. But none of us can see them objectively. Not even a visionary like Errol Gardner. Your son-in-law sounds like Sam Bankman-Fried."

"Who?"

"The cryptocurrency kid? Don't you read the news?"

"I don't read about crypto. All that stuff's bullshit."

"Well, exactly, but Sam Bankman-Fried made a fortune off it. He stole billions from his customers. The judge gave him twenty-five years in prison, but the real kicker was his parents. They're both professors at Stanford Law. They know the rules of finance better than anyone. But they insisted their son was innocent. Claimed he never did anything wrong. Because they couldn't see him clearly. It's a willful kind of blindness, Frank, and I was the exact same way with Janet."

She offered to make a call to her son, the one who worked for the

Wall Street Journal, but I didn't want to do or say anything that might prompt an investigation. "They're trying to keep this quiet."

"You realize that sounds terrible, right?"

I could hear people behind me on the trail, approaching from the eastern cottages. "I gotta go, Vick."

"What are you going to do?"

"I've got an idea, but I'm not sure it'll work."

"Be careful, Frank. If you keep snooping around, you might get in over your head."

"I'm already in over my head," I reminded her. "Tomorrow at three o'clock, Maggie's supposed to marry this guy."

6.

I returned to Blackbird cottage and found Tammy and Abigail on the porch making last-minute preparations for the hike. My sister was never the outdoorsy type, but she was embracing the spirit of the event. She'd dressed in an old Dolly Parton concert tee and capri pants and gray Dansko sneakers—the official footwear of home healthcare aides everywhere. Abigail had changed out of her blue Stitch pajamas and was finally dressed like a normal kid. But she'd done a lousy job of applying her sunscreen, and there were gloopy streaks of zinc oxide all over her face. She welcomed me back with a big toothy grin. "Are you coming, Mister Frank? Maggie says that if we climb to the top, we can see all the way to Maine."

I told her that I hadn't slept well, that I was going to stay home and get some rest, but Tammy didn't seem to believe me. "Life is for the living, Frankie. I feel terrible about this accident, but Errol says we all need to forge ahead."

"You go forge ahead," I told her. "I need some downtime."

I went inside the cottage and watched through the window as Tammy and Abigail walked off to join the others. Then I moved to the kitchen and forced myself to eat an apple and a banana and a couple of slices of cheese. I knew I would be gone for a couple of hours, and I didn't want to be distracted by hunger. I also didn't want to be spotted by anyone in the hiking party, so I waited another ten minutes before leaving the cabin.

Instead of taking busy Main Street and passing Osprey Lodge, I followed the lake loop back to the beach and arrived to find the staff opening umbrellas and arranging the lounge chairs. All the police officers and EMTs were gone, and there was a large depression in the sand where Gwendolyn's body had been dragged ashore.

I crossed the beach and continued around the shore of the lake, passing more cottages and even a small spa, where guests were invited to register for hot stone massages and pre-wedding pedicures. Then I veered back into the woods, walking for another several minutes until I'd arrived at the entrance of the camp—the small wooden structure where we'd signed our privacy docs. Two security officers were drinking from sports bottles and having an animated conversation, but at the sound of my approach they stopped talking.

Then Hugo himself emerged from the shelter.

"Mr. Szatowski, you're going the wrong way! Cormorant Point is the other direction!"

"I need to go into town. How do I get my car?"

"Oh, I'll have Oscar drive you. Where would you like to go?"

"I can drive myself."

"Is there something you need?"

"Just odds and ends. Tylenol and what-not."

He smiled at me, revealing the whitest teeth I'd ever seen. "Our clinic has Tylenol. I'll send a bottle to your cabin and save you the trip."

"Well, there's still the whatnot."

Hugo encouraged me to elaborate. He explained that the camp received deliveries throughout the day and he could procure anything I wanted within an hour. "Batteries, computer chargers, extra clothing, personal items—"

"All I want is my Jeep," I told him. "How long would I have to wait for my Jeep?"

Nothing I said could dampen Hugo's cheerful enthusiasm. "Only a minute or two, sir." He ducked inside the hut and spoke into a radio, giving some whispered instructions I couldn't make out. Then he returned and announced the Jeep was on its way. "Would you like to wait inside my shelter? You might be more comfortable in the shade."

"No, I'm fine."

I asked Hugo if any police were still at the camp; he explained they'd worked quickly to minimize the disruption to the family. "Drugs are such a scourge in our rural communities. The police have seen enough overdoses to recognize the signs."

I looked around and saw that the other guards had walked off into the woods, following the border of the ten-foot fence. I pointed after them. "Does that go all the way around the property?"

Hugo nodded. "I know it's unattractive, but the camp is a serious target during the offseason. It's full of computers, kitchen gadgets, bedsheets, towels—there are thieves who will steal just about anything. And I'm just one man. I can't be everywhere at once."

"So you're still here in November?"

"All year round, Mr. Szatowski. Osprey Cove is my home. I have a little cottage called Nuthatch about a hundred meters into these woods."

"And it's just you? All winter long?"

"Oh, no, not by a long shot. Any given day I'm calling plumbers, painters, landscapers, gardeners, snowplows, you name it. With all these buildings, there's always something that needs fixing. But I keep everything tip-top so the place is ready when Mr. and Mrs. Gardner need it. They love visiting in the offseason. Especially when the leaves start turning."

"How about Aidan? Does he ever visit in the offseason?"

Hugo's smile faltered just a moment, like he was contemplating the question behind my question. "Almost never. Aidan's so busy with his artwork and his teaching in Boston. No time to relax and enjoy the finer things." Then the smile flickered back on. "But maybe that will change after his wedding. Your daughter seems very happy here."

I heard my Jeep before I saw it, heard the tires crunching gravel as it lumbered up the driveway. Hugo asked if I needed any directions but I told him I'd manage fine. I recognized the young man behind the wheel from the beach earlier that morning. He was the one who'd used the canoe paddle to poke and prod Gwendolyn's body back to shore. He shifted the transmission into park and left the vehicle running. "Have a good trip, sir."

As I pulled away from the entrance, I stole a glance at Hugo in my rearview mirror. He was reaching for his phone and pressing it to his ear.

I followed the winding gravel driveway back to the long, potholed access road, then turned onto a highway that brought me back to town. Once again, the parking lot of Mom and Dad's Restaurant was nearly full—a welcome sight, because I could leave my Jeep without drawing attention to myself. There was no trace of Brody Taggart (or anyone else) on the porch, but that was okay because I knew he lived nearby. In a trailer on the banks of Alpine Creek, or so I'd been told. I waited for a gap in the highway traffic and then hurried across the road and walked into the woods.

There was no obvious path to follow, so I just trampled along, stepping over ferns and fallen limbs, and sidestepping past sticker bushes. After a minute of walking, I heard the distant crack of a rifle shot. There were black-and-yellow NO HUNTING signs stapled to a few of the trees, but the signs were bleached by the sun and the staples were rusted, and I wasn't sure if the old rules still applied.

And then I found myself descending a steep and slippery hill— I fell from one tree to another, slamming into the trunks to steady myself, and repeatedly exacerbating the dull, throbbing pain in my lower back. For the umpteenth time, I silently cursed Abigail for leaping out of the tree and falling onto my shoulders. I knew I'd be scheduling a chiropractor visit as soon as I got home to Stroudsburg.

At the bottom of the valley, I stopped at the bank of a swiftly rushing brook, which I suspected was Alpine Creek. There was a narrow path alongside it, with footprints going in both directions, so I wasn't sure which way to go. But as I stood there, trying to make up my mind, I heard the bark of a dog from the west, and this settled the matter. The dog must belong to someone, and maybe that someone was Brody Taggart.

I walked about the length of a football field—just long enough to second-guess myself and wonder if I should have chosen the other direction. And then I spied the back of a small house. Based on everything Maggie had told me, I'd been expecting something like a FEMA trailer, one of those cramped metal boxes with all the furniture bolted in place. But this was a fairly large modular home, a double-wide-plus, with bright yellow aluminum siding and white trim around the windows. The whole structure was two feet off the ground on concrete supports, and someone had built a strong, sturdy porch on the front and filled it with houseplants and wind chimes and a United States flag. There were three vehicles parked in the gravel driveway—a Snowcat shrouded in a moldy black tarp, a silver Chevy Blazer, and a beat-up Toyota Corolla. And as soon as I saw the Corolla, I knew I'd come to the right place.

I climbed the steps of the porch and heard the dog barking again— inside the house now and going ballistic, snarling and snapping and flinging its body at the door. I thought I saw a flicker of movement in the big picture window, but it was covered by lace curtains and I couldn't be sure. The dog barked and barked, and I wondered if it had been a mistake to come. I was nervous about the encounter because I still remembered how my daughter described Dawn's mother: *She's drunk all the time; she spends the whole day in her nightgown. And she wears this horrible orange pancake makeup.*

I was reaching to knock again when I heard a soft little *click*. If you've spent any time in a combat zone, I guarantee you're familiar with the distinctive sound of a fire selector clicking from "safe" to "semi" or "burst." Moving very slowly, I raised both hands and turned toward the noise. Brody Taggart was holding an AR-15—the civilian equivalent of the M16 rifle that I carried all around Iraq. He'd equipped the slide with a special scope and laser sight, and now it was pointed right at my chest.

"I'm going to count to three," he said. "And then I'm going to fire at anyone standing on my porch."

I didn't make him count. I backed down the steps and past the cars and walked all the way to the end of his driveway. Only then did I stop and turn around. "We met at the restaurant yesterday," I reminded him. "You told me about Dawn, remember?"

"One," he said.

"I'm off your porch. Why are you still counting?"

"Changed my mind. Keep walking."

"A girl died last night. At Osprey Cove. They're saying she drowned in the lake. They're calling it a drug overdose, but I think they're lying."

"Not my problem," he said. "Two."

I raised my hands, imploring him to hear me out. "Is your sister here? Dawn's mother? Could I please talk to her?"

The front door swung inward, revealing a large woman dressed in a men's flannel shirt and blue jeans. She said something to her brother that I couldn't make out, and he lowered his weapon. A fluffy brown-and-white cocker spaniel charged outside and bounded over to me, circling my legs and leaping up at my knees. I reached down to let her sniff my hand and the dog immediately flipped onto her back, showing me her belly and pleading for affection.

"That's Bongo," the woman called out, "and I'm Linda Taggart. Dawn's mother."

"Frank Szatowski. My daughter's marrying Aidan Gardner."

"Oh, I know all about it, Frank. I'm the one who sent you the picture." She called me up to the porch and encouraged me to have a seat in one of the rocking chairs. To my relief, she seemed perfectly sober—and if she was wearing any makeup, it was so subtle I couldn't tell. Linda said she'd be right back, she was going to fix us something to drink. Then she looked sharply at her brother and told him to put the weapon away, because China wouldn't be invading anytime soon.

Brody flashed a look suggesting this fact was debatable, then grudgingly followed her indoors.

I moved to the porch and sat down, and Bongo settled happily at my feet. I gave her a good back rub and looked around at all the different houseplants. There were maybe some two dozen of them, wisterias and Boston ferns and a bunch I recognized but couldn't name. Linda must have had a real green thumb because everything was thriving.

She and her brother returned with three glasses of iced tea and a large glass bowl of animal crackers. "I teach second grade," she said with a shrug. "I wish I had more to offer you but I never imagined you'd actually visit us."

I sipped the iced tea—homemade, refreshing, and greatly appreciated after my short march through the woods. "I'm the one who should be apologizing," I said. "I'm sorry for barging in on you like this. I'm just scared and I don't know what to do."

"Tell us about the girl. What happened?"

I knew I was probably violating the terms of my nondisclosure agreement (or "privacy doc," as Hugo had so carefully described it), but I told her the whole story anyway, beginning with my introduction to Gwendolyn on Thursday afternoon and ending with the discovery of her body. Followed by the immediate assumption that she'd died of a drug overdose, despite the bruises I'd spotted on her neck.

"That's just how the Gardners work," Linda explained. "They think they can will any statement into fact, just by saying it out loud. Reality is whatever they say it is. If they want the time to be eight o'clock, they call it eight o'clock and expect *you* to adjust your watch. And the crazy thing is, people are happy to do it!"

"Gardner Standard Time," I said.

"Exactly. I'd call it a conspiracy but they don't even hide their actions. They just lie and expect you to go along with it."

"Aidan says your photo is a fake," I told her. "He says he never invited Dawn to Osprey Cove."

"Aidan's a goddamn liar," Brody said. "I'd like to rip off his head and shit down his neck."

He'd been leaning into the conversation, looking for a chance to contribute, and I suppose he couldn't hold back anymore. Linda shushed him and said he wasn't helping.

"It helps *me*, trying to imagine it," Brody explained. "I got a bunch of different visualizations. Like, say I shoot off his gonads and feed them to Bongo here."

At the mention of her name, the dog perked up, but Brody shook his head and urged her to be patient, saying that she'd need to wait a little longer.

"Tell me about Dawn," I said. "How did she meet Aidan in the first place?"

The first thing Linda Taggart explained to me was that every young woman in Hopps Ferry knew about Aidan Gardner. She said he was the closest thing the town had to a royal prince—young, educated, handsome, and wealthy beyond estimation. "We used to watch *The Bachelor* on Monday nights and Dawn used to joke that none of these TV bachelors held a candle to Aidan Gardner. And she'd never even met him! But if you grew up here, he was a kind of living legend."

Their chance encounter came in July of the previous year, Linda explained. Dawn was juggling two different part-time jobs—cleaning rooms at a Hampton Inn and stocking shelves at the Dollar General, both thirty minutes away toward Lake Winnipesaukee. One afternoon she was driving home from work when she found Aidan and his car on the side of the road with a flat. He didn't have a spare, so Dawn offered to loan him the one in her trunk. And when it became clear that Aidan didn't know how to operate the jack, Dawn knelt down in the road and quickly changed the tire herself. "And when she was finished, Aidan held out some money. Like a gratuity? But my daughter waved it off. Said he should buy her a glass of wine instead. A nice dry pinot grigio." Linda laughed at the recollection. "And I swear to you, up until that moment, my daughter never drank pinot grigio in her life. It was just something she heard about on TikTok."

Dawn came home feeling elated about the encounter, and soon she was seeing Aidan on a regular basis. He was a generous boyfriend and he showered Dawn with expensive gifts—a laptop computer and scanner, a Patagonia jacket, a Tiffany bracelet. Luxury items and appliances that a motel housekeeper could never afford.

"I suppose a lot of mothers would have been thrilled," Linda said. "But I didn't like it."

"Why not?"

"It never felt like a healthy relationship to me. They never did anything socially. With other people. None of her friends ever met him. And they never went out to restaurants or movies because Aidan didn't like 'the locals' all staring at him."

"Meaning us," Brody explained. "Like we're all so frigging impressed by his royal highness, we're just going to gape at him."

"I'll give you another example," Linda said. "Every year I do a cook-out for Dawn's birthday. Nothing fancy, just a small get-together in the yard, but Dawn wouldn't invite Aidan over. Said she was too embarrassed to show him our house. And I said to her, 'Honey, if this man loves you, he'll love where you're from, because your home is always part of you.' But then I came to realize the truth," she said, and here her voice broke a little bit. "And the truth is I think she was just ashamed of me."

I knew a little about this feeling myself. Even before Maggie left home for college, I could feel her pulling away, distancing herself from our family norms. She'd started criticizing the way I'd pronounced certain words, like *tortilla* and *supposably*. And she poked fun at my Timex wristwatch and Kirkland blue jeans, both purchased at discounts in the aisles of a warehouse store. I told myself it was healthy teenage behavior, that every generation needed something new to strive for. But her comments still stung.

"Aidan says there was just one date," I told her. "He swears they went out to dinner and that was the end of it."

Linda shook her head. "Then how does he explain the photo? I told my daughter, if you won't bring this young man to meet me, you can at least show me a picture. So she went to her computer and looked through her albums, and she printed out the one I sent you. It's plain as day they're on Lake Wyndham. Right on the Gardners' beach."

"Aidan says you photoshopped it."

Brody laughed. "There they go, bending reality again. Look where you're sitting, Frank. Do you think we know how to use a photoshop?"

"Dawn was seeing Aidan all summer," Linda insisted. "Then around mid-September it started to fizzle out. She said Aidan got too busy with his teaching. It was harder for him to get out to Osprey Cove. And I was like: good riddance. I thought she was done with him. But she saw him one last time on November 3. And that's the day she disappeared."

It was a Saturday morning, Linda continued, and Dawn was up early. She'd run out to the store because (she claimed) she needed shampoo. She was back within the hour but never took a shower, and Linda could hear her crying in her bedroom. She tried tapping on the door. Asking Dawn to open up and talk. But Dawn was on the phone. Linda could only hear one side of the conversation. "Aidan, I need to see you," Dawn said. "No, not next week, and not tomorrow. Get up here and talk to me right now. This is an emergency."

It was another two hours before Dawn finally left her bedroom. Linda tried to coax the truth out of her, but she wasn't interested in talking. She said she was going shopping for new winter boots.

"And I knew my daughter, Frank. I knew she was lying, just like every parent knows when their kid is lying. And I wish I'd stopped her from leaving. I wish I'd forced her to tell me the truth. If only I'd stopped her—"

Brody put a hand on her knee. "Don't go down that road," he said. "Just tell him what happened next. What you seen on your phone."

Linda took a deep breath. "Right, I guess I need to explain that part. The thing is, I've always paid Dawn's cell phone bill. Ever since she was in high school. I just got in the habit and I didn't mind. I tried to make her life a little easier. One less bill to worry about and all that. Plus I liked knowing her whereabouts. Anytime she'd stay out late, I could open my phone and look at the map and there she'd be, this blinking blue dot."

I knew exactly what she was talking about. Maggie and I used to share a cell phone plan, and I tracked my daughter's location all through high school, always making sure she was getting to class on time and staying out of trouble.

"So when Dawn left the house, I had a pretty good idea where she was going. But I opened the map just to be sure. I watch the blinking blue dot, and I see it go right up the highway to Osprey Cove. I see Aidan's agreed to come meet with her. And then I felt guilty for spying on her. I knew I ought to mind my own business. So I put away my phone and started doing my chores. I went around my house and emptied all the trash cans. And while I was in Dawn's bedroom, emptying her wastebasket, I found something."

She slowly pushed herself out of her chair, stood up, and encouraged me to follow her inside the house. The three of us walked down a short hallway and then squeezed inside a very tiny bedroom; the door only opened halfway before colliding with a bed. It looked like a space in transition, with ivory-white walls and white curtains. But when I peered closely into the corners, I could see glimpses of the previous color, little spots of hot pink that were mostly painted over. Here and there were other remnants of a younger teenage girl: Polaroid photos of teenage friends. A medal from a high school volleyball tournament. A postcard of a goofy grinning polar bear.

Linda brought my attention to a wastebasket next to the bed. "I looked in here and I found this." It was the package for a Walgreens one-step pregnancy test, promising early detection with 99 percent accuracy. "Just the box but not the actual test, so I assumed Dawn brought that with her. To show to Aidan. Now, my first impulse was to text her and tell her to come home. I wanted her to know that she didn't have to beg Aidan for help. We could give her all the support she needed. But the blue dot said she was already in Osprey Cove, so I figured I was too late. I'd just have to wait and see what happened."

Simply being in her daughter's old bedroom seemed to overwhelm her, and I suppose I could relate to those feelings a little bit. She sat at the edge of Dawn's bed and gestured for me to sit beside her. Brody remained standing in the doorway, like a sentry, and Bongo turned around in a circle before settling onto the rug. Linda quickly summarized the next part of the story: Dawn never came home on Saturday night—and when Linda checked the map to determine her daughter's whereabouts, the blue dot had disappeared. LOCATION UNKNOWN. Linda didn't panic right away. She said it wasn't the first time Dawn had stayed out all night, and it wasn't the first time her phone ran out of battery. She imagined there might even be good news—maybe the kids were talking to each other and possibly working things out. Linda went to sleep hoping for the best and then woke the next morning to an irritable phone call from the manager of the Hampton Inn, complaining that Dawn was late for work and did anybody know where she might be?

Linda called all Dawn's friends, but none of them had seen her all weekend. And no one had Aidan's phone number. But one of them knew Osprey Cove had a landline, a general number for deliveries and such. Linda tried calling, and a man with a Dutch accent answered the phone. He said he'd been working the entire weekend and the camp was empty. He said the Gardners were all in Boston and there hadn't been any visitors. Instead of expressing sympathy or concern, he simply advised Linda to dial 911.

The police found Dawn's Toyota Corolla in a state forest twenty miles south of Osprey Cove, in a parking lot with a popular trailhead. They took a pair of dogs up and down the mountain. They never found Dawn, but they did find her sweatshirt, a little gray hoodie— she'd been wearing it when she left the house. So when Linda insisted that her daughter vanished at Osprey Cove, no one took her seriously.

"The chief of police came here to talk with me, and I told him everything I just told you. I showed him the pregnancy test box, and I told him about the little blue dot. And then I did the dumbest thing I could have done."

"What's that?" I asked.

"I gave him my phone. For evidence. He said maybe my phone could prove that Dawn had visited Osprey Cove. He said maybe her trail was still in the memory chips and they could fish it out. And I desperately wanted to believe him, so I turned it over." Linda shook her head. "A week later, he brought it back. Said no one could find anything. But I think they *did* find something, and they erased it."

"You have to remember," Brody said, "a lot of these cops work part-time for the Gardners. Off duty, they're private security guards. Sixty bucks an hour. That's a lot of reasons to look the other way."

"But they must have talked to Aidan," I said. "Didn't the police interview him?"

"Sure, they interviewed him. He claimed he hadn't seen Dawn all summer, and no one could prove otherwise. The day she disappeared, he says he was in Boston with your daughter. And now nine months later they're getting married. Doesn't that timing seem unusual?"

I agreed it was a little disconcerting, and Linda warned me that Maggie was in real danger. "If anything happens to her, no one in this town is going to help you."

"What about the security cameras? I've seen them all over the camp. Did the police ask to see the footage?"

"Oh, sure, the Gardners were very cooperative. They turned over a whole weekend of video. All time-stamped and dated. But I think anyone who invented a Miracle Battery could probably forge a time stamp, don't you?"

I agreed that these days it seemed possible to fake just about anything. I've seen a video going around YouTube where Joe Biden's talking and Donald Trump's voice is coming out of his mouth. You used to be able to trust your own eyes and ears, but these days it's getting harder and harder to believe in anything.

Linda must have seen the uncertainty in my eyes because she doubled down on her statements. "I know my daughter went to that camp. They moved her car, and they moved her sweatshirt. But I'm convinced she's still there."

7.

When I left the trailer, Brody noticed I was limping—my lower back was still aching and messing up my entire gait—and he suggested I follow their access road out to the highway. "No offense," he said, "but you don't look like you're in any shape to climb out the gorge."

I took his suggestion. The route was long and quite a bit out of my way, and I didn't make it back to Mom and Dad's Restaurant until nearly two o'clock. I was backing out of my parking space when the door to the restaurant opened and my friend the bartender stepped outside. He recognized my Jeep, then squinted at me through the windshield and gave me a puzzled wave. I waved back, grateful to be in motion, so I wouldn't have to stop and explain why I'd parked there.

Back at Osprey Cove, there were a half dozen cars waiting to enter the camp—a long line of new guests arriving for the wedding. The security team was stopping every vehicle to check IDs and collect signatures, so I settled in for a long wait. But then Hugo recognized me and came trotting over, insisting that I get out of my Jeep. "Margaret's been asking for you. It's her big weekend and you should be with your daughter. Not waiting for my team to do their job."

He was already opening my door, so I couldn't refuse him. "Thank you, Hugo. I appreciate it."

"No problem, Mr. Szatowski. Did you find what you needed in town?"

I realized I was empty-handed, that I hadn't brought back any kind of bag. And from the way Hugo smiled, I think he knew he'd caught me in a lie.

"I found more than I expected," I told him. "Has there been any news on the girl?"

"What girl?"

I couldn't believe he had to ask.

"The dead one. Gwendolyn."

"Oh, no, sir, I don't think we'll hear anything until next week." Then he lowered his voice. "But since you are family, I will share some confidential information. The police found xylazine in her suitcase. You're probably not familiar with the name but it's a deplorable drug. Much more dangerous than heroin or even fentanyl. Some kind of animal tranquilizer used by farmers. But for the girl's sake, Mr. Gardner wants to keep that information private."

I turned over my keys and followed Main Street back inside the camp. Now that the guests were arriving in force, Osprey Cove had taken on a whole new level of energy. The landscapers and housekeepers had moved out of sight, and all that remained were the fruits of their labors—trees and flower beds popping with color, well-swept walkways, and immaculately clean cottages. Guests were everywhere—unpacking their cars, swinging in hammocks, whipping Frisbees, and greeting friends with hugs and high fives. It seemed like cocktail hour was already underway because everyone was holding a wineglass or plastic cup. No one seemed to be acknowledging that a woman had died here, that a body was found with two curious bruises and an investigation was still pending.

I was passing a cottage nicknamed Woodpecker when a young woman came bounding down the steps, waving to me. "Mr. Szatowski! It's Minh! From Babson College!" She threw her arms open wide, revealing a Babson College sweatshirt. "Do you remember me?"

Of course I remembered her. Minh and Maggie were roommates all four years of college. They'd been randomly matched by a computer but grew into close friends and joined the same sorority. She'd always struck me as a sweet girl and a loyal friend, and I was thrilled to finally reconnect with a person from Maggie's past. She greeted me with a hug, and I thanked her for coming.

"Well, if you think I'd miss this wedding, you don't remember me very well. I can't believe the size of this place!"

She explained that she was recently married herself and waved over her new husband, Brian. If you told me he was still in high school, I would have believed you. He had bright eyes and an impish smile, and he seemed completely enamored of his new wife; I noticed that he reached for her hand in a gesture that seemed reflexive. They'd been married a little over a year but still looked and sounded like giddy lovebirds on their honeymoon.

"It's a funny thing, Mr. Szatowski. I was just telling Brian about Babson College and all those lousy admins ready to throw Maggie under the bus. They were all so mean to her, do you remember? But I'm making a prediction. After this weekend, I bet all those same deans and provosts will be knocking on her door and asking for donations. And I hope Maggie tells them to go to hell!"

She laughed at her own joke, but I had trouble seeing the humor in the subject. I told her I didn't really like to think about it.

"Well, I promise Babson has already forgotten. Their Annual Giving office has a very short memory. She'll make the cover of their alumni magazine before she turns thirty, I guarantee it."

One of the biggest regrets of my life was sending Maggie out of state for college. You have to remember that I joined the US Army right out of high school, so when it came time to file Maggie's applications, we were both flying blind. I wanted my daughter to go to Penn State, so she'd be close by in the event of an emergency. But Maggie argued that Nittany Lions were a dime a dozen. She said she needed to attend a more prestigious school to have a competitive advantage, and she quickly identified Babson as a "feeder school" to Amazon, Google, Microsoft, Bank of America, and other Fortune 500 companies. The tuition was ridiculous but I could afford it, and I wanted her to have every advantage that money could buy.

Her grades were fantastic, all straight As, and she rushed the college's most popular sorority for business majors, which exposed her to a vast network of professional contacts. The problems started halfway through Maggie's senior year, when a sister named Jessica Sweeney got in trouble for selling test answers. She was dragged in front of the Board of Academic Integrity, and instead of taking responsibility like a mature adult, she tried to pin all the blame on Maggie. Claiming that Maggie was the *real* mastermind of the operation and Jessica was merely an assistant. Most of the sisters united behind Maggie but two insisted that Jessica was telling the truth, and the rest of the semester was an all-out civil war, with accusations and threats flying back and forth. Maggie called me crying every night. I'd never heard her sound so frightened and hopeless and terrified—and I was three states away, unable to help. I begged her to talk to a therapist, and I hired her a lawyer to help sort everything out. In the end, my daughter was completely exonerated, and Jessica Sweeney left the school in disgrace. But the experience ruined college for Maggie, and she refused to walk at her own graduation ceremony.

"I'm sorry she had to go through all that," Minh said, "but do you know something? I think the experience made her stronger. I bet no one messes with her anymore."

I wasn't so sure about this last part. In fact, after hearing Linda Taggart's story, I was more certain than ever that Maggie was being played, and she was going to need my help to make things right. I told Minh and Brian that I would see them at dinner, and then I walked down to Osprey Lodge in search of my daughter.

The catering team was already hard at work on the main lawn, assembling twice as many tables and chairs as they'd brought the night before. And now the beach was full of sunbathers—beautiful young people with bronzed skin sprawled out on lounge chairs, scrolling through their phones and sipping on piña coladas. There were more of them out in the water, swimming and paddleboarding and kayaking in the cove. I moved just close enough to make sure none of them was Maggie, then followed the path around the lake until I was back at my cottage.

"There you are!" Tammy exclaimed. "Where the heck have you been?" She and Abigail were sipping iced tea on the porch. Their faces were slightly pink with sunburn, as if they'd spent the whole afternoon outdoors.

"I had to run to the drugstore."

"Why?" Tammy asked.

"It doesn't matter. What did I miss?"

According to my sister, they had been enjoying the most wonderful afternoon. First they all hiked to the top of Cormorant Point, where the views were "glorious" and the lunch was "exquisite" ("Best potato salad I've ever tasted," Tammy said, before miming a chef's kiss). Then Errol Gardner himself took them out on the lake in his speedboat so that Abigail could learn how to water-ski. "Maggie came, too, and we had a wonderful time."

Abigail seemed a little less enthused. "I *wanted* to canoe," she explained. "But Errol said water-skiing was funner, so that's what we did."

"And I haven't even told you the best part," Tammy continued. "After we came off the lake, Errol said he had something for me." She lowered her voice. "Like a kind of wedding gift. Because I played such a big role in bringing up Maggie." And only then did I realize my sister was holding a thick sheaf of papers in her lap. They were bound in a navy blue folder embossed with gold foil letters, like something you'd receive from a bank. "This is one thousand shares of Capaciti stock. In my own private brokerage account that Gerry set up for me. He's going to wire the transfer on Monday, after we're back in Stroudsburg. Isn't that the most generous thing you've ever heard of?"

Last time I checked, Capaciti stock was trading for $262 per share. The gift was more money than my sister earned in the last five years combined.

"And don't hold me to this," Tammy continued in a low whisper, "but I'm pretty sure you're getting some, too."

There was no time to elaborate because Maggie was emerging from our cottage with a glass of lemonade. "Dad! Where have you been?"

"I'm glad you're here. Can I talk to you?"

"What is it this time?"

"In private," I said. "I'm sorry, Maggie. I hate to ask you again but it's really important."

She seemed exasperated by the request but followed me down a path to the lake, anyway. I wanted to walk even farther, just to make sure Tammy and Abigail couldn't hear us, but Maggie insisted we'd gone far enough. "We're already miles from civilization," she said. "What is this very urgent super-private thing we need to discuss?"

"You're not going to like what I have to say. But I need you to promise to listen and really hear me, okay?"

She exhaled and then smiled, to show she was still keeping an open mind. "Yes, Dad. You have my complete attention. What is it?"

"I drove into town this afternoon. I met Dawn's family."

She opened her mouth to reply and nothing came out. The news had left her speechless.

"I wanted to hear their side of the story. You told me they were crazy, but I don't think they are. I think they're telling the truth."

She stepped closer to the lake, putting some extra distance between us. She seemed ready to jump in the water and start swimming. "Please tell me you're joking, Dad. Please don't say you went to meet them *the day before my wedding?*"

"I think you should hear Linda's story. She wasn't drunk and she's not crazy. Something bad happened here."

All my language seemed to wound her. She was gesturing wildly with her hands, like she was trying to shield herself from my nonsense. "Dad, if I knew you were going to do this, I never would have invited you here. You're making me wish I never called you. Why can't we just have a nice weekend?"

I told Maggie the basics of what Linda Taggart had told me: how she'd traced her daughter's journey to Osprey Cove using the GPS app on her smartphone—monitoring her activity at the camp until the blue dot disappeared. "How do you explain that, Maggie?"

"The explanation is: She's lying! She's making it up!"

"No, Maggie, I think *you're* lying." She gaped at me like she'd been slapped, but there was no turning back now. "I think you love Aidan very much, and you want to protect him, so you lied to the police and told them that he spent the weekend in your apartment. And maybe everyone here believes you, but I'm your father and I know how to read your cues. I have *never* believed this story. You're hiding something."

"That's a great thing to hear, Dad. Thanks for sharing that with me. But now let me ask you: What secret do you think I'm hiding? Is Aidan a serial killer? Is he murdering women at Osprey Cove? Oh my God: Did he murder Gwendolyn, too? Is that what you think? Have I fallen in love with Jeffrey Dahmer?"

"I don't know, Maggie. I don't know what to believe."

She screamed at me: "That was sarcasm! He's not Jeffrey Dahmer! What the hell is wrong with you?"

I struggled to keep my voice from rising because I didn't want to match her volume; I didn't want to yell. "Maggie, you have to agree there is something very weird about this place. Just last night a woman died and now your coworkers are building sandcastles where her body washed up."

"The police found drugs in her suitcase. Something called xylazine."

"Yes, I heard that. But tell me something else: Have you seen Catherine Gardner yet? Has she come out of her locked room?"

"She's sick! How many times do I have to say it?"

"And what about Aidan? Where is he? I haven't seen him in twenty-four hours!"

"Here we go again—"

"I think you should take a pause, Maggie. Make sure you want to be on this train."

"There are two hundred people at the camp right now. And another hundred coming tomorrow. The train's already left the station."

"No, it hasn't. The train doesn't leave until tomorrow. You still have time. Just look at all the question marks: Gwendolyn, his mother, the photo of Dawn Taggart—"

And then all of a sudden Maggie seemed to remember something, and all the tension drained from her body. She relaxed and started to laugh. And I was foolish enough to believe that maybe, *maybe* I had finally reached her.

"What's so funny?"

"I just realized something," Maggie said. "You were gone all afternoon, so you don't know about the photo. The one you received in the mail. I wish I had it with me."

As it turns out, I had a copy in my pocket. I'd asked Linda Taggart to print it before I left her house, and she'd run it off using the equipment in Dawn's bedroom. I removed the sheet of paper from my back pocket and unfolded it.

"Gerry sent a scan to his office so his interns could analyze it. They have special software they can use to calculate the shadow length and whatnot. But turns out they didn't need it. One of the interns spotted the flub right away."

Maggie pointed to the photo of Aidan, looking fifteen pounds heavier and smiling with a lightness of spirit I'd never seen in person. I didn't understand what I was supposed to be noticing.

"His hands," Maggie said. "Look at his hands."

His left arm seemed fine. It hung at his side and his left hand looked normal. His right arm was wrapped around Dawn's waist, and he was resting his right hand on her hip. And I still didn't see the problem so Maggie had to point me to it. "Look at his thumb," she said. "Don't you see it?"

And at last I realized what she meant.

His right thumb was on the wrong side.

In the photograph that Linda Taggart shared with me, Aidan Gardner was a man with two left hands.

8.

We rehearsed the ceremony in the Globe, an old outdoor theater constructed by the original summer camp. It was deep in the woods and hidden by tall trees, a deep crater ringed by wooden benches with a stage in the center. It had the feeling of a sacred space, a kind of secret sanctuary deep in the forest, and it might have been quiet and peaceful if there weren't so many people hanging around. I'd assumed the rehearsal would be a private affair for the bride and groom and family, but several dozen guests had come to watch, many with glasses of wine or small plates of food, like this was just the next stage of the weekend entertainment. I was disappointed that no one chased them off.

At the base of the stage were four women in black dresses with violins and violas; they were tuning their instruments and arranging their sheet music with quiet, well-practiced efficiency. I was watching them set up when a young man with wild curly hair approached and pulled me into a hug. "Hey, Dad, it's great to meet you! Are you ready for this? I'm RJ, and I'll be hosting the ceremony."

He was dressed in chinos and sneakers and a yellow T-shirt advertising Kodak film. "You're hosting? Are you a pastor?"

"Sometimes it feels that way! But no, I work in human resources. With Errol and Margaret." He explained that he also dabbled in stand-up comedy and taught improv on Saturday afternoons, so he was accustomed to working a room. He'd paid a sixty-five-dollar fee to a website to become an ordained minister, strictly for the purposes of officiating Margaret and Aidan's ceremony.

"Now do me a favor," he said. "Can you point me to the groom? Because I want to say hello before we start."

Aidan was sitting on a bench with three other young men (his groomsmen, I would later learn, all colleagues from MassArt), and he looked a little sickly—almost feverish. His face was pale and clammy and some kind of rash had broken out on his forehead, a sprinkling of little red dots. RJ greeted him with a double fist bump. "My man!" he exclaimed. "How are you, my brother?"

Errol Gardner arrived with Gerry and Sierra and copious apologies for his wife's absence. He told everyone that Catherine was still feeling poorly but expressed confidence she would be "ready to rock" for the big ceremony Saturday afternoon. Meanwhile, Tammy showed up with Abigail to practice her flower girl duties. But instead of sitting with us and waiting patiently for the rehearsal to start, Abigail was following Maggie all around the Globe like her little shadow and introducing herself as "the cousin of the bride."

"That's not even true," I told Tammy. "I wish she would stop saying that."

"It's adorable, Frankie. People love her."

"She's bouncing around like a pinball. How much iced tea did you let her drink?"

Tammy frowned at me. "You need to understand something about Abigail. She is the product of a broken home. Everyone she knows is from a broken home. Outside Disney cartoons, I don't think she's ever seen a good marriage. But this weekend, she's finally meeting two people who really love each other. She's going to watch them make the ultimate commitment, the biggest promise you can make to another person. 'To have and to hold, till death do us part.' You're so old and jaded and cynical, you've lost sight of what those words actually mean.

But Abigail's seeing everything for the first time, so of course she's excited. And if you took your head out of your ass for one minute and looked around this beautiful space, you'd be excited, too."

I waited for her to finish her little rant and then I said, "Well, I don't think Aidan looks too excited. I think he looks like his friend just died and everyone's pretending nothing bad happened."

"It's just nerves. I still remember *your* rehearsal dinner, and you were a pretty anxious groom yourself."

And then she turned and introduced herself to the woman on her other side, because once again she was sick of talking to me.

I told myself to calm down and chill out. The fake photo proved that Linda Taggart's story was bullshit. Dawn had never been to Osprey Cove. And maybe Gwendolyn really did overdose. There were certainly plenty of drugs going around the party. Maybe Aidan was genuinely grieving the unexpected death of his friend—but loved my daughter too much to postpone the wedding. All these ideas seemed entirely rational and plausible. So I made a conscious decision to stop worrying and start having a good time.

At a quarter past four, the rehearsal got underway. RJ stood center stage, holding a large hardcover book that appeared to be a Bible, and he coached us through the procession. Abigail went first, pretending to scatter flower petals as she walked. Next were three pairs of bridesmaids and groomsmen, followed by Aidan and Errol Gardner. And then it was my turn to practice escorting Maggie.

She'd been cold to me since we'd left the lake, since she'd proved without a doubt the photo was a hoax. She'd asked me "what kind of father" would side with a complete stranger over his own daughter, and I had to admit I felt bad for not trusting her instincts. I suggested we link arms, like I'd seen fathers and daughters do at other weddings, but Maggie said we could save the physical contact for tomorrow. Then she walked very purposefully down the aisle, a half step ahead of me, and I could hear spectators chuckling as I struggled to keep up with her.

Up on the stage, I realized RJ's Bible was just a prop, a Harry Pot-
ter book with the jacket removed. "Now I'll ask, 'Who presents this
woman to be married?' And that's your cue, Frank. You say, 'She presents herself, with her father's blessing.' Then you hug your beautiful
daughter, you shake hands with the groom, and your work is finished.
Sit down, relax, and enjoy the rest of the show."

I joined Tammy and Abigail in the front row and my sister patted my knee, congratulating me on a job well done. "Just remember to
smile tomorrow," she suggested. "You looked pretty spooked up there."

RJ sped through the rest of the rehearsal. He assured Maggie and
Aidan that he'd go easy on "the God stuff" and then wondered aloud
if, given the setting, a little Capaciti humor might be warranted. Everyone looked to Errol for a judgment and he shrugged. "Just don't go
overboard," he said. "It's their wedding, not a shareholders meeting."

Most of the participants seemed too nervous and self-conscious to
practice their parts in earnest. The sole exception was my sister, who'd
been tasked with a short Bible reading. She asked for permission to
rehearse it onstage, to make sure she was loud enough.

"Of course," RJ said, inviting her forward with a dramatic sweep of
his arm. "The stage is yours, madame."

Tammy had printed her lines on paper in a giant font so she could
see them without her glasses. "This reading is from Paul's first letter to
the Corinthians," she said. "Can everyone hear me okay? Am I being
loud enough?"

I gave her a thumbs-up, and she proceeded to recite the passage in
its entirety:

> Love is patient. Love is kind. It does not envy. It does not boast. It is
> not proud. It does not dishonor others, it is not self-seeking, it is not
> easily angered, it keeps no record of wrongs. Love does not delight in
> evil but rejoices with the truth. Love always protects, always trusts,
> always hopes, always perseveres. Love never fails.

Tammy finished with a smile and a small sigh of relief, and for a moment there was absolute silence in the Globe, as if the power of her words made all other speech seem frivolous.

Then RJ looked to Maggie and saw something in her face that he didn't like. "Is it too cringe? Should we try something, I don't know, more contemporary?"

And for a moment I worried Maggie might agree with him. But then she shook off whatever was bothering her, took both Aidan's hands, and stared meaningfully into his eyes. "No, no, it wasn't cringe at all. That was perfect."

9.

The theme of the rehearsal dinner was Lobster Night and each place setting included hand wipes, a checkered red-and-white napkin, a souvenir lobster cracker, and a custom-printed dinner bib (MARGA-RET AND AIDAN'S WEDDING: A CLAWS FOR CELEBRATION!).

The seats were assigned, and I was grateful to find myself at a table with Tammy, Maggie, Aidan, Errol, and Abigail. There was an extra chair reserved for Catherine Gardner, in the event that she was well enough to join us, but by this point I had stopped expecting to ever meet her.

Aidan took a seat between Maggie and Abigail, and I called across the table, "I'm sorry about Gwendolyn."

"Thank you, Frank."

"Has anyone spoken to her family?"

"Gerry's office is doing some research. Gwen was raised by a grand-mother who's not with us anymore, so they're not sure who to call."

Maggie leaned forward in her chair. "Dad, it's the rehearsal dinner, remember? Can we stay focused? Is everyone having lobster?"

Tammy raised her hand. "Yes, please!"

Abigail was more reticent. "They look scary."

Aidan encouraged her to try one, anyway. "New England has the best lobster in the world. You'll never get a better chance."

And when the waiters brought over our meals—one whole lobster per person, jumbo-size crustaceans with massive foreclaws dangling off the sides of the plates—Aidan patiently taught Abigail how to break apart the shell and pry out the tender meat within. He spoke to her with a gentle tone that was wholly unfamiliar. I heard him asking patient questions about her interest in world geography—about her favorite mountains, rivers, and volcanoes. It was the most I'd heard Aidan speak to anyone all weekend—except for Gwendolyn, I suppose. He seemed happy to focus all his attention on the little kid and ignore the rest of the table—and the rest of the reception.

The vibe of the dinner was country-casual. There was a jug band with banjos and washboards, and they performed silly songs about bullfrogs and sunbeams and falling in love under the harvest moon. Waiters walked around with pitchers of beer, but no one was getting too sloppy; it seemed like people had learned a lesson from the previous night's tragedy. Every so often some joker would start clinking his fork against a wineglass and others would join in and the sound would crescendo until Maggie and Aidan kissed. Abigail stood up and applauded every single time. She couldn't believe it was a real tradition; she said her wedding book never mentioned it.

There was a microphone and a stage for people who wanted to deliver a toast to the bride and groom, and Errol asked me if I planned to say anything. I told him I was saving my remarks for tomorrow's wedding, and he kept his own speech very brief. He thanked everyone for attending. He acknowledged the absence of his wife and her continuing health problems but promised we would see her in the morning. And then he raised his glass to the bride and groom. "Margaret is a smart, hardworking, and beautiful woman, and I am so grateful that she and Aidan found each other. I love you both so much." He finished to a standing ovation and thunderous applause, like he'd just recited

the "I Have a Dream" speech. My sister grabbed a red-and-white napkin to dab the tears from her eyes. "I always cry at weddings," she told
everyone.

Aidan clapped politely, then removed his phone from his pocket
to view an incoming text. He frowned at the screen before setting the
device face down next to his plate. Then he leaned over to Abigail and
asked if she'd ever been to the Grand Canyon, if she knew it was deep
enough to hold four Empire State Buildings stacked on top of each
other.

There were a lot more toasts. In the wake of Errol's speech, it seemed
like every Capaciti employee wanted to get onstage and share a story of
how Maggie had touched their lives. And then RJ got up and did ten
minutes of crowd work, gently poking fun at all the married couples
in the audience ("What is the deal with mothers-in-law, amiright?"). I
had a hard time focusing on any of it. My thoughts kept drifting back
to the mystery photograph of Aidan with Dawn Taggart. I understood
that Maggie was correct—the photo was clearly manipulated, an obvious fake. But after meeting Linda and Brody, I couldn't believe they
were capable of doing the work.

Which left Dawn Taggart. She had an expensive-looking computer in her bedroom. It was possible that she photoshopped the image herself—but why?

Why invent a relationship with Aidan?

Up on the stage, Gerry and Sierra were delivering a joint toast to the
bride and groom and sharing secrets from their own successful marriage. And then I glanced at my future son-in-law, sitting silently and
wringing his hands in his lap. I could tell his thoughts were elsewhere,
that he wasn't hearing a word of their speech.

And resting beside him was a key that would unlock the answers
to all my questions.

10.

After the sun went down, a waitress came around and lit the candles in the center of our table. We'd all shuffled to new seats to change conversation partners. Now Errol was seated beside Abigail and explaining how the Miracle Battery functioned while Tammy spoke with Maggie and Aidan about their upcoming honeymoon in Spain; they were planning to spend two weeks in the north country, to avoid the sweltering summer temperatures. Aidan had left his cell phone resting face down on the table, and I'd moved close enough to toss my red-and-white napkin on top of it. Then I looked around to make sure no one was watching, and I deftly slid his phone off the table and into my lap.

I excused myself to use the restroom, then walked around Osprey Lodge to the main entrance. Inside the foyer was a long line of women waiting to use the powder room. A few of them smiled at my arrival, and I smiled back before starting up the stairs. I imagine they thought I had every right to be there, as a houseguest of my future in-laws. I climbed to the third floor and returned to the hallway where Gwendolyn had found me. *If you still haven't met Catherine Gardner*, she had warned me, *then you don't know anything.*

I walked to the door of the master suite and knocked.

"Mrs. Gardner? Hello?"

There was no answer. I pressed Aidan's phone to the black sensor panel, and with a gentle click the door unlocked. I pushed it open, revealing a short, dark hallway. At the far end were flickers of blue and white light, and faint sounds of a studio audience cheering and applauding. Behind me, the door swung shut, and I heard the churn of the electronic dead bolt cranking back into place.

I took a step forward and my foot sank into something soft. It was fabric, some kind of blouse. There were clothes all over the floor—dresses and sweaters, skirts and slacks, enough pieces to outfit a dozen women. I stepped lightly through the clutter. "Hello? Is anybody here?"

As I followed the passage, I became aware of an odor—a sour, pungent bouquet that smelled like the back of a garbage truck. The hallway ended and I found myself in an empty bedroom. It was too dark to see very much. All the curtains were drawn and the only light came from a large flat-screen television playing *Family Feud*. "We asked one hundred Americans: name a food that reminds you of the human body." A contestant buzzed in with "Banana!" and the audience went wild, cheering and applauding and stamping their feet while the host pretended to keel over in shock, like he never saw it coming.

Women's clothing was everywhere, strewn across the floor and most of the furniture. All the items looked new and never worn; most still had their tags attached, and a few were still sealed in plastic bags. There were so many outfits piled on the sofa, I nearly overlooked the person seated among them. She wore the same white bathrobe that all the guests had in their cottages—but hers was mottled with brown and yellow stains, and she'd neglected to close it all the way.

I'd seen photographs of Catherine Gardner online. She was an elegant, smartly dressed woman who sat on the board of Boston's Museum of Fine Arts—and this person scarcely resembled her. She was alarmingly thin, almost skeletal, and her makeup looked like it had been applied by a child. Her cheeks were plastered with a fleshy paste that didn't match the color of her ears or neck. And her eyes were ringed with pink shadow that looked like a bacterial infection. She watched the television with a blank expression, not seeming to comprehend a word of it.

The game show host was cheerfully greeting family members and then repeated the survey question to an elderly grandmother: "Name a food that reminds you of the human body."

"Eggplant!" she shrieked, to the cheers of the crowd, while the host reeled in astonishment, staggering around the set like he'd been punched in the face. And still Catherine Gardner showed no reaction. I had to move between her and the screen before she finally registered my presence. In a quiet voice she asked, "Where's Aidan?"

I could scarcely hear her over the cheers of the studio audience. "He's downstairs, Mrs. Gardner."

"Who are you? What are you doing here?"

"My name is Frank Szatowksi."

"You're not supposed to be here. I'm calling my son."

Then she reached into the piles of clothing, burrowing under the garments in search of a phone.

"My daughter is marrying Aidan tomorrow," I told her. "I'm Margaret's father."

She stopped searching for her phone and reached for a table lamp, switching it on to get a better look at me. "Of course you are. I see the resemblance now. But where are my manners?"

Suddenly she was pushing herself off the sofa, making a wobbly attempt to stand up. The folds of her robe fell open, leaving her naked and frail body completely exposed. With a sweep of her arms, she pushed all the clothes off the sofa, clearing a space for me.

"Would you like to sit down?"

I forced myself to hold eye contact. "Do you need some help with your robe?"

Catherine looked down and then laughed at the oversight, like I'd just pointed out that her shoelace was untied. She pulled her robe tight and clumsily knotted the belt. "You must think I'm a terrible hostess.

Let me turn down the television." She reached for the remote to lower the volume but didn't seem to understand she was holding it the wrong way. I offered to do it for her and turned the volume all the way down. "Oh, that's kind of you, Frank. Now please sit down so I can serve you something. I won't feel right until you let me."

I perched on the edge of the sofa, and she brought over two tumblers and a bottle of Tanqueray. With trembling hands, she poured the glasses full of gin. No ice, no lime, just pure colorless alcohol all the way to the rim. Then she sat beside me and lifted her glass, spilling much of the alcohol down the side and over her hand and wrist. "To Margaret," she said. "A wonderful young woman."

Her toast was interrupted by a high-pitched pinging. I realized the sound was coming from Aidan's phone—it was emitting some kind of siren to help the owner recover it. No doubt he'd discovered it was missing, and now he was trying to find it. I pressed every button on the surface of the device until it finally went silent.

"I hope you'll forgive the clutter," Catherine continued, and she gestured to the piles of tangled clothing at our feet. "It's impossible to do any shopping here in the wilderness, so I buy all my clothes online. But that makes sizing tricky. There's endless trial and error. I just want to look nice for the big day."

In the span of just a minute or so, she'd shaken off her stupor to become a lively, animated hostess. She sat across the coffee table from me and took both my hands, like she was afraid I might try to leave. "I'm sorry for hiding away all weekend. The doctors say I need to ration my strength. But now that you're here, is there anything I can do for you?"

"I'd love to ask you about my son-in-law, if that's okay. The wedding's tomorrow, and I still don't know him very well."

At the mention of her son, Catherine brightened.

"He's my favorite subject. You can ask me anything you like. I'm an open book."

"I want to know about the rumors. And Dawn Taggart."

She released her grip on my hands and sank back into her chair. "Well, that's totally understandable. I know what her family's saying about him. But I assure you, he never laid a finger on that girl. He's very gentle. Very sensitive. And he'll be a loyal and faithful husband. You've got nothing to worry about."

"I met with Linda Taggart this afternoon."

"That woman's a fool."

"You may be right about Aidan, but I don't think Linda Taggart is a fool. I think she's just confused."

"How so?"

"Linda Taggart made a habit of snooping on her daughter. She'd track the location of her phone. So she knew Dawn was coming here to Osprey Cove. That's a fact. Dawn Taggart was visiting someone here at the camp. And bringing home all kinds of jewelry and expensive gifts, so she had to explain where everything was coming from. So she told her mother she was seeing Aidan Gardner. She even photoshopped a picture of the two of them together. Dawn invented a relationship because she was too embarrassed to tell her mother the truth."

"Which is?"

"Dawn was having an affair with a married man."

Catherine smiled and nodded, the way a tutor might encourage a student who is making progress in the right direction. "That's very good, Frank," she said. "You must be a very perceptive person."

"I need to know the truth. Did Errol do something to Dawn Taggart?"

"My husband? Oh, no, Errol would never hurt anyone. Not with his own hands, at least. But now, if you don't mind, I'm going to have a second cocktail."

I hadn't realized that she'd finished the first. With shaking hands she lifted the bottle and refilled her glass before continuing: "My husband has some very old-fashioned ideas about men and women. He keeps them to himself, because these days you have to be so careful. With the internet and everything. But if you get a few drinks in him, he'll tell you his theories. Errol believes that men are incapable of monogamy. He believes that men—especially wealthy and powerful men—have an evolutionary imperative to mate with as many women as possible. He insists they all do it, all the titans of industry. Jeff Bezos, Bill Gates, all your movie stars, all your NFL quarterbacks, and of course all your politicians." Catherine shrugged. "I wonder, Frank, if you think he's right?"

I told her I did not. I felt certain there had to be plenty of wealthy and powerful men who didn't cheat on their spouses—but when she pressed me for an example, I couldn't think of a single one. Tom Hanks, probably? Jimmy Carter? Mister Rogers?

"Well, if my husband had any sense at all, he would use an escort service. That's what all his friends do. That's how our lawyer Gerry met his twenty-one-year-old bride. These services will deliver beautiful young women anywhere in the world—even here to Hopps Ferry. But my husband hates paying for it. He likes the thrill of the chase. He needs it to feel like a conquest—the more illicit and forbidden, the better. There have been dozens of women, Frank. Maybe even hundreds. I've no idea. I lost track of how many times I've been tested for venereal diseases—about the most humiliating procedure you can imagine." She reached toward the end table for a half-empty bowl of cereal, a mass of soggy brown flakes in an inch of tepid milk. "Forgive me for eating, but you caught me in the middle of supper. What was I saying?"

"How did your husband meet Dawn Taggart?"

"Well, now, that's an interesting story. One evening last summer, Dawn came to Osprey Cove looking for Aidan. My son had already taken her out to dinner, because she'd helped him change his tire. But one date was enough for Aidan. He didn't want any more to do with the birdbrain. Now, my husband, on the other hand, he was happy to welcome a pretty young thing into the camp and give her a tour. Aidan and I were back in Boston at the time; we had no idea what was happening." She slurped another spoonful of cereal, and I looked down at my lap so I wouldn't have to watch her eat. "And I suppose he liked having her around, because she'd come visit anytime he had the camp to himself. Just your classic sugar daddy–gold digger scenario. She'd show up with frilly lingerie and he'd send her home with laptops and Tiffany bracelets."

Catherine held up one finger, gesturing for me to hold that thought, and a stream of thin brown liquid spewed from her lips, spilling over her chin and spattering into the bowl of milk. It was all over in a moment and then she studied my expression, trying to see if I'd noticed. If I hadn't reacted, I think she might have just proceeded with her story. But the smell of vomit rocked me back in the sofa and she apologized.

"Are you okay?" I asked. "Can I get you something?"

"I'm fine. This just happens sometimes." Then more brown sludge gurgled out of her mouth and she held the bowl under her chin to collect it all. She motioned with her finger that she was okay, that she just needed another moment. After she'd finished gagging and she'd cleared her throat, she pushed the bowl of milky vomit to the far end of the table, so we wouldn't have it resting between us.

"Are you sure you're all right?"

"Don't patronize me, Frank. I said I was fine. Now, the problem with Dawn Taggart is that eventually my husband got tired of her. He found some new flavor of the month and decided to say bye-bye to Birdbrain. And that's when she springs her big surprise: Guess who's having a baby? And guess who wants child support? She must have felt like she hit the Powerball. She called Aidan and told him first. Said she wanted to talk to me instead of my husband. She claimed that only another mother could see the situation clearly and make things right."

Errol was away on business in Singapore, so Aidan and Catherine were unable to confer with him. They drove from Boston to Osprey Cove on the morning of November 3 and arrived at the camp just before noon. It was a Saturday deep in the offseason, so Hugo was the only person working on the property, and they knew they could count on his discretion.

"I hated the idea of welcoming this girl into my home, but I brought her into Errol's office and she showed me her pregnancy test. And then she shared her list of demands, like Christmas was coming and she could name everything she wanted. Money for rent because the baby needed a place to live. Money for utilities, for clothes, for groceries. Gas for her car. A college savings fund. And then she tallied up all the numbers and hit me with the total: forty-five grand a year. I just about died! This girl had no concept of money, no idea what Errol and I were actually worth. Last year, I gave one-point-four million to an aquarium! For a jellyfish exhibit! I've got forty-five grand in pennies at the bottom of my purse. But this girl was so entitled, so disrespectful, I turned her down on principle. I said I didn't give charity to whores." Her voice was shaking, and each new detail seemed to wound her, like she was cutting out pieces of her heart. "I suppose that's when things got a little out of hand."

Now Aidan's phone was ringing—I could feel it buzzing in my pocket—but I just urged Catherine to continue. "Dawn started listing all the things my husband liked to do to her. Really vile and unpleasant things, with my grown son seated right beside me. It was horribly inappropriate and I asked her to stop but she just kept going. She was determined to hurt me and hurt me and hurt me until I agreed to pay. And finally I couldn't take any more. I grabbed the closest thing I could find—this little fuel cell Errol keeps near his desk, it looks like a water bottle—and I bopped her on the head."

"You bopped her on the head?"

Catherine nodded. "Just a couple taps to remind her who she was talking to." She pantomimed like she was hammering a nail. "Bop-bop-bop. 'Shut up, you stupid whore.'"

There was a loud knock at the bedroom door. Someone in the hallway was calling Catherine's name, but I urged her to finish the story.

"Well, that's pretty much the end of it. Aidan grabbed the fuel cell away from me and of course Birdbrain didn't know what hit her. There was blood in her hair, running down the front of her face, so of course she got upset. Aidan went after her, tried to calm her down, but now *he's* holding the fuel cell, so she panicked. She ran out to the stairs and then it was whoopsy-daisy and bang-bang-bang all the way down." Catherine shrugged, as if to suggest these sorts of things happened all the time. "At the end of the day, she was a victim of her own clumsiness. I certainly don't take the blame for what happened."

I wasn't sure a jury would agree with her, but I could hear the dead bolt turning as someone unlocked the door, and I realized there was only time for one more question: "Does my daughter know *any* of this?"

Catherine laughed. "Oh, Frank! You missed the whole point of the story! Or maybe I told it wrong? Did I leave out the part with Margaret?"

"Yes! What do you mean?"

I never found out. Hugo rushed into the bedroom, followed by Aidan and a middle-aged woman in nursing scrubs. "Mr. Szatowski, you really shouldn't be here," he said. "We told you Mrs. Gardner isn't feeling well."

I ignored him and kept my eyes trained on Catherine. "Please just answer me. What's the part with Margaret?"

"Your daughter is a blessing." The nurse was already rolling up Catherine's sleeve and giving her an injection and within seconds her eyelids were fluttering. She said, "We'd be lost without her," and then she was gone. The nurse proceeded to tend to her with a well-practiced efficiency while Hugo ushered me out into the hallway and Aidan followed behind us.

"Mrs. Gardner is very ill," Hugo said.

"Yes, I can see the migraines have taken a real toll on her. Or maybe she's had a complete and total mental breakdown."

"All good reasons to ignore what you just heard," Hugo said. "She's in a very fragile place. Her memories are not reliable."

"She remembers Dawn Taggart falling down the stairs and cracking her skull. Was that reliable?"

Aidan started to answer but Hugo interrupted him: "We have no idea what happened to Dawn Taggart. We've already shared our sur-veillance video with the police, and there's no indication that she ever visited Osprey Cove. Her disappearance is a terrible tragedy, and we extend our thoughts and prayers to her family and the entire commu-nity. Now, I need to know if you're comfortable with that explanation, Mr. Szatowski. And when you answer that question, I need you to be very convincing."

"My answer depends on Maggie." I turned to look at her fiancé. "She's obviously lying to protect you. But does she know the truth? Did you tell her what really happened?"

Aidan nodded. "Margaret knows everything. We should have been more honest with you, but she worried you wouldn't understand."

And I didn't understand, because this new information made their entire relationship look like a sham. "She said she met you on Hallow-een. At a costume party. And then three days later, she agreed to lie to the police on your behalf? How does that happen?"

"No more questions," Hugo said. "Let's go find Mr. Gardner, and then we'll have this conversation together."

"*You* find Mr. Gardner," Aidan told him. "I'll make things right with Frank. We could have saved ourselves a lot of trouble if we'd just been honest with him from the beginning."

11.

Aidan didn't say another word until we were outside Osprey Lodge. He led me across the driveway and into the dark copse of pine trees where I'd met Gwendolyn the night before, and only then did he finally speak: "You stole my phone?"

I returned it to him. "I'm sorry, Aidan. I needed to know the truth. But I feel like I only got part of it."

"You're safer not knowing the rest. I was honest with Gwendolyn— I trusted her with everything—and look what they did to her."

"Who is they?"

"Please stop asking questions. There are lots of different ways to have an accident at Osprey Cove, and you're already on Hugo's radar."

"I'm not afraid of him."

"You should be." Aidan glanced around anxiously, making sure no one was lurking nearby. "He used to run the cobalt mines down in Congo-Kinshasa until the people at Amnesty International caught up with him. My father got him out of the country on a Capaciti jet. He was facing all kinds of criminal charges: human trafficking, exploitation of children, workplace 'accidents,' I'm talking real crimes against humanity. He's been hiding here for two years and I still don't even know his real name. I just know he is very dangerous and very loyal to my father. And now he's watching you closely. My advice is: forget what you heard, go back to the party, and just act normal."

"Your mother needs help, Aidan. If you don't get her into treatment—and I mean real treatment, in a real clinic—she's going to drink herself to death."

"It's too late, Frank. She's always been a drinker. She had to be, with all the sleeping around my father did. But the visit from Dawn Taggart sent her spiraling. Just a complete and total mental breakdown. Not the sort of thing she can unpack with a therapist. Not unless she wants to go to prison."

"She said Maggie's involved."

"Here's what I can promise you, Frank: your daughter is completely safe, and she's getting exactly what she wants. But she is never going to tell you the truth about this wedding, because she doesn't think you can handle it."

"What does that mean? What could be worse than Dawn and Gwendolyn being murdered?"

And he looked like he really wanted to tell me—but instead he pushed through the trees and stepped back onto the driveway, returning to full view of all the wedding guests outside Osprey Lodge. A trio of young women recognized him and came hurrying over. "Karaoke time!" they exclaimed in unison, swarming around the groom and insisting that he join everyone back at the party.

"Come on, Frank," he called to me. "It's karaoke time. Let's get back to the party."

I didn't follow, and his female admirers showed no interest in persuading me. Aidan followed them around the side of the lodge with the resigned expression of a man being led to a firing squad. I knew my only path forward was to confront Maggie with all my new information and demand the truth. But that conversation was never going to happen on the main lawn, not in full view of Errol and Gerry and everyone else.

Fortunately, I still had the map of Osprey Cove folded away in my pocket, and I remembered that my daughter was staying in Hummingbird—"all the way on the other side of the camp" and far from all the excitement of Osprey Lodge and the main lawn. I decided to go there and wait for her to come home, and I wouldn't leave until she came clean about everything.

I followed a trail into the woods and immediately tripped over a root. This late at night, there was scarcely any moonlight in the forest. I took out my phone, swiped on the flashlight, and used it to help guide my way. The trail descended into a valley, and I passed a pair of cottages named Grackle and Crane. Both buildings were dark, presumably because their occupants were still at the party.

And then I walked for a long time without seeing anything. Further proof that the map of Osprey Cove was not drawn to scale, because the cottage marked HUMMINGBIRD was nowhere in sight. The silence and near total darkness had a way of narrowing my concentration. There was nothing to think about except the next step in front of me, and I felt hyperaware of my surroundings. Once again, all my old situational awareness habits kicked in. Once again, I had the uneasy feeling that I was walking into a trap, that something awful was waiting just around the bend.

Or perhaps something awful was creeping up behind me. A branch cracked and I spun around in a circle, aiming my feeble phone flashlight into the darkness. I didn't see anyone, but I did see countless places where a person might hide.

"Aidan?" I called out. "Did you follow me?"

There was no answer. I turned around and resumed walking. Eventually I spied three glowing squares on the horizon—they were the small windows of a cottage, softly illuminated from within. I had finally made it to Hummingbird. I climbed the steps of the porch and tried the door. It was locked—but when I pressed my phone to the sensor, the bolt turned and the door swung inward.

I entered a cottage that was much smaller than mine. There was scarcely enough space for a sofa, a small dining table, and a tiny kitchenette. Almost immediately, I sensed that I wasn't alone. The door to the back room was slightly ajar and I heard movement on the other side. I reached into the kitchen sink for an empty wine bottle; I grabbed it by the neck, holding it like a club, and then pushed the door open.

Maggie lay on a bed, stretched out on flannel sheets with her back slightly arched, her dress hitched up to her waist. She faced the ceiling with her eyes closed, biting her lower lip and breathing fast and gripping the edge of the mattress. And crouched before her was a pale fleshy monster with its face between her thighs. I didn't realize I'd dropped the bottle until it hit the floor and shattered. Errol Gardner turned to me with wide eyes and wet lips, and I charged forward, knocking him off the bed and onto the floor. I straddled his hairy naked torso before he could wriggle away from me. Maggie screamed and Errol bucked his flabby, sweaty belly, trying to throw me off, but I had all the leverage. I had him pinned. I smashed the flat of my palm into his face, then squeezed my hands around his neck, pushing my thumbs deep into his throat.

Maggie kept screaming, but it was just noise. She reached for my shoulder and pulled, and I felt a sharp stabbing twist in my lower back. Just enough of a distraction for Errol to swing out—a sloppy thunderclap to the side of my head that deafened my left ear. I felt concussed, like I might throw up. My arms went limp. I looked up at the bedroom window and saw a reflection of the open doorway. I saw Hugo rushing into the room with a black baton raised high over his head.

And right before everything went dark, I realized my daughter had stopped screaming. She was facing the door—she had seen Hugo rushing in—and she hadn't even tried to warn me.

IV.

THE WEDDING

1.

Morning light filled my window. I squinted and turned away from the sun, pulling the blankets over my shoulders. A daddy longlegs crouched on my pillow, just inches from my face, and I brushed it away. Another spider watched me from my bedpost, but I left that one alone; I would deal with it later. I just wanted to sleep.

But then I remembered.

I sat up and swung my legs out of bed, and a sudden stabbing pain fired through the base of my skull. Holy mother of God. My brain felt skewered. I closed my eyes and gritted my teeth and tried to gather my bearings. I was back in my cottage. Back in the kiddie room with its storybook corner and brightly colored fish wallpaper. Back in the bottom bunk, though I had no recollection of coming here.

The last thing I remembered was wrestling a naked, sweaty Errol Gardner to the floor. I remembered mashing the flat front of my palm into his face.

A dream, I told myself.

A horrible, anxiety-fueled nightmare.

Except my knuckles were split. My lower back was sore. And I was dressed in all my same clothes from the night before.

I reached for my scalp and felt a tender, throbbing lump. My hair was caked with dried blood. And before I even understood what was happening, I was throwing up. I made it to the bathroom but not the toilet and vomited all over the sink.

I gripped the towel rack to steady myself and tried to collect my thoughts. *Love is patient. Love is kind. He's the Prince of Fucking Darkness. There they go, bending reality again. Dawn Taggart is the least of your worries. Your daughter is getting exactly what she wants.* The hurt inside my head was excruciating. It felt like a piece of my brain had been cut out and now the raw, tender wound was exposed.

I switched on the light and cleared the spiders off the mirror so I could see my reflection. My shirt was streaked with dirt and blood. Two of its buttons were missing. I looked like an extra in a zombie movie, one of these businessmen commuting to the office who gets infected by the virus. I turned on the tap, splashed cold water on my face, and rinsed out my mouth. I had a couple of toiletries on the counter—a toothbrush, deodorant, a bottle of cologne—but I did not bother to collect them. I only cared about two things: getting Maggie, and getting far away from Osprey Cove.

The display on my Timex said 11:53, but of course this was still Gardner Standard Time. I fumbled with the little buttons and turned back the clock to 11:38, Eastern Standard Time. No more bullshit. Then I went into the closet to grab my suitcase. As soon as the motion light flickered on, dozens more spiders scattered across the walls, panicked by my sudden arrival. I just grabbed my bag and closed the door because they didn't matter anymore. In another five minutes I would be gone.

I found my cell phone in my pocket and discovered the battery was down to its last 8 percent. And there was one new notification—a voice mail from Vicky, left at 10:52 a.m. I pressed play and listened:

"I didn't hear back from you last night so I hope everything's okay? I wanted to let you know, I did reach out to my son, Todd. The one at the newspaper? Now, don't worry, Frank. I didn't say anything. I just asked if he'd heard anything squirrelly about the Gardners. Because a lot of

THE LAST ONE AT THE WEDDING   229

times, these writers have hints of a story, but not enough sources to put the whole thing into print? And I get the feeling this might be one of those situations. Because Todd got pretty quiet and said he couldn't tell me anything. Which is his way of saying there *is* something. And you should be careful. So give me a call when you get this. I'll explain it better over the phone."

But I didn't need her to explain it any better. I didn't need advice from Vicky or anyone else. I put my suitcase on the bottom bunk and unzipped the lid, just as Tammy appeared at my bedroom door. She gave a quick perfunctory knock before opening it.

"Listen, Frankie, I just wanted to check on you, make sure you're— Oh my goodness, look at your face! And your shirt!"

"Pack your stuff. We're leaving."

She smiled uneasily, like she was expecting me to follow my announcement with a punch line. "What are you talking about? What's going on?"

"I don't know, Tammy. I have no idea what's happening. But I know this wedding's a joke. Maggie's made a terrible mistake, and we need to get her out of here."

"Frankie, Frankie, calm down." Tammy moved closer and rested a gentle hand on my arm. "Maggie is fine, okay? I just saw her. We just had breakfast together. Me and Maggie and Abigail, we had strawberry pancakes and Maggie is one hundred percent all right. Today is her wedding day, remember? She's marrying Aidan Gardner."

"I know what day it is. Why are you talking to me like I'm a toddler?"

"Because you sound confused. I was here last night when they brought you home. Maggie said you had too much to drink. She said you fell and hurt your head."

"And you believed her?"

"Of course!"

"You think I got drunk? And blacked out? At my own daughter's rehearsal dinner? Does that sound like *anything* I've ever done?"

"Well, no, Frankie, but if I'm being honest, you haven't been your-self these past few days. I think you're under an enormous amount of stress. What do *you* think happened last night?"

I didn't want to tell her. A part of me hoped that if I kept my dis-coveries to myself, they wouldn't be true. But I knew I wouldn't get far without my sister's help. I sat down on the lower bunk and invited her to sit beside me, because I knew the story would take a while. "Last night during dinner, I went inside Osprey Lodge and I met Catherine Gardner. She's not sick, Tammy. She doesn't have migraines. She's had some kind of mental breakdown. She's completely intoxicated around the clock, and that's why she hasn't joined us. And *she's* the one who killed Dawn Taggart."

Tammy leaned away from me, like she suddenly feared I was con-tagious. "Okay, stop."

"She crushed her skull with a car battery. And Aidan was here when it happened. He saw the whole thing."

"Stop-stop-stop. I don't need to know."

"Tammy, you're not hearing me clearly. I am telling you that Cath-erine Gardner murdered a pregnant woman. Right here in the camp. And Aidan helped her cover it up."

"I *am* hearing you clearly. And I'm telling you: it's not our dirty laundry. Every family has secrets. Let's mind our own business."

I stared at my sister in disbelief. This was a woman who had devoted her entire life to helping others—dozens of foster children and count-less senior citizens. She'd always been quick to rail against injustice, but now I felt like I was speaking to a different person. And I still hadn't told her the worst part: "After I talked to Catherine, I went to Maggie's cottage. Way off deep in the woods. And I found her in bed with Errol Gardner." I searched my sister's face, looking for any kind of reaction, but her expression didn't change. "Do you understand what I just told you? She was having sex with her future father-in-law. The night before her wedding. I threw him on the floor and started hitting him, then Hugo clubbed me over the head and that's the last thing I remember."

For a long moment, my sister didn't say anything. I assumed she was overwhelmed by the story and struggling to make sense of it. But when she finally spoke, she surprised me.

"I hear that you're upset."

I blinked. "You *hear* that I'm upset?"

"I believe everything you're saying is true. And I understand why it bothers you. It bothers me, too. I wish Maggie had made different choices. But this *is* Maggie we're talking about. You can't say you're surprised."

"Yes, I can. I am."

"Frankie, come on. I helped you bring her up. And I love that girl as much as you do. But be honest with yourself. She has a history."

"What kind of history?"

"Of manipulating people. Using them to get what she wants. All that business with her sorority sisters. And Dr. Cell Phone. Think about the whole reason Maggie stopped talking to you."

"She stopped talking to me because I let her down. She asked for my help and I turned my back on her."

"No, Frankie, that is not what happened. She's manipulated you into seeing things that way. Because—again—she is very good at manipulating people. Especially you. As I recall, you were just trying to do the right thing."

I couldn't process what she was saying. Things were moving too quickly and I just wanted everything to stop. "We need to help her."

"She doesn't need help. This isn't *Taken* and you're not Liam Neeson. You don't need to rescue Maggie. She knows exactly what she's doing. I don't understand the choice she's made, but it is clearly her choice. She *wants* this. I think we'll be a lot happier if we just accept it."

"Dawn Taggart was *murdered*. And then Gwendolyn found out and she was murdered, too. Hugo drugged her and drowned her and dumped her body like it was garbage."

"But Maggie didn't hurt either one of them. And you know the

Gardners are going to get away with it. These kinds of people always get away with it. They hire their lawyers and work the system."

"So you're just going to pretend nothing happened? You think you can actually do that?"

"Frankie, I know I can. Because I'm tired, okay?" She could tell I was bewildered, so she tried to frame her answer differently: "We have very different circumstances, little brother. In three more years, you're going to retire with a pension and healthcare and the freedom to do anything you want. But me? There's no pension for me. If this wedding falls apart, if Errol takes back his thousand shares, I've got forty grand in an IRA plus whatever I shake out of social security. At that rate, I will never stop working. I'll be lubing catheters and treating bedsores until I'm ninety years old. And I don't want that life for myself anymore." She gestured out the window to the rest of the camp. "Especially after seeing all this. Everything's so beautiful here."

"I would take care of you, Tammy. I'm not going to let you end up in the poorhouse."

"I don't want to leech off you. I don't want to ask for a handout every time my car needs new tires. I want to keep my thousand shares and have a nice quiet retirement."

I felt another wave of pain coming on and gritted my teeth and squeezed the edge of the mattress, bracing myself for the worst. My big sister had always looked after me, always supported me, always stood by my side, but now she was a Capaciti shareholder and I didn't recognize her anymore. She swiveled her fanny pack around her waist and unzipped the tiny pocket and removed a small bottle of Advil. She shook out two of the little brown tablets and gently placed them in my hand.

"Tell you what I'm going to do. I'm gonna find Maggie and have her come over so you can talk. But before she gets here, you need to shower. You look awful and you smell absolutely foul. Go clean yourself up. And while you're in there, I want you to remember why you and Maggie stopped speaking. Be honest with yourself. Because this whole situation feels very familiar, Frankie. It feels very three years ago. And I don't want to see you make the same mistakes. You can trust that Maggie is ready to make adult choices with adult consequences, and you can have a real relationship with her. Or you can keep fighting her and undermining her decisions and destroy any chance of a future together. And as someone who cares about you, I am going to suggest you choose the former." She patted my knee and then looked at her watch and discovered it was almost noon. "And you better get going, because you've only got three hours."

2.

I took a long, hot shower and washed the blood from my hair as I reflected on my sister's advice. I tried to understand how I'd screwed up so badly, how I'd raised someone capable of making such disastrous choices. I didn't like dwelling on the recent past, but Tammy seemed to think I could learn a lesson or two from it, and maybe she was right.

After Maggie finished college, I hoped she would move back home and take a job in Allentown or Reading. But she insisted that all the best career opportunities were in Boston. She needed a place to live, so I cosigned the lease on the basement studio apartment and I agreed to pay her rent for the first year until she got on her feet. I knew it was only a matter of time until someone recognized her value and paid her a real salary.

In the meantime, she worked thirty hours a week at Dr. Cell Phone, one of these rinky-dink places that repairs the cracked glass screens of electronic devices. I only visited the "store" once, and my first impressions were not positive. It was a cluttered and stale room with bad artificial lighting. The carpet was worn. The windows were smudgy. In many ways, you could say the business was a reflection of its owner. Oliver Dingham was forty-six years old with pale, blotchy skin and a bad comb-over. Most days he dressed in nylon tracksuits, though it was hard to imagine him running on a track or any other surface. He'd inherited the business from his father, and he showed zero interest in growing it. Outside work, he was a self-described AFOL—an adult fan of LEGO—and he'd filled his two-bedroom condo with intricate three-thousand-brick re-creations of Hogwarts Castle and the *Millennium Falcon*. And if I sound like I'm being overly critical of the man, it's only because he was clearly infatuated with his new twenty-one-year-old employee.

"Not true," Maggie insisted, after I confronted her with my fears. I told her she was blind to the basic calculus of the situation. Oliver was a balding middle-aged incel who hadn't been on a date in years. Maggie was a bright and beautiful young woman. And together they spent thirty hours a week in a tiny room that saw little foot traffic. They might as well have been marooned on a deserted island. I pleaded with her to quit and find another job—at a restaurant, or a bowling alley, or anyplace she'd be around other young people. "You shouldn't be cooped up all week with that guy. You're wasting the best years of your life."

But my concerns fell on deaf ears. Maggie claimed that *any* job in technology would look good on her résumé. And she pointed out that Oliver was paying her twenty-two dollars an hour, well above minimum wage—which to me was just another red flag. She insisted that Oliver never made a pass, but I knew it was only a matter of time. I started searching the help wanted ads on my daughter's behalf, looking for any kind of job that would get her away from Dr. Cell Phone. I sent her all kinds of leads but she never followed up on them, and I suppose this is when our relationship started to deteriorate. She called me meddling and hypercritical. I called her lazy and unfocused. Is it any wonder she stopped calling home? Or that our conversations became less and less frequent? When she announced she was staying in Massachusetts for Thanksgiving and Christmas, to celebrate with friends, I was gutted.

Then one Saturday morning in February I woke to the sound of a car pulling into my driveway. It was early and still dark, just a little past five-thirty. The vehicle pulled all the way up my driveway and around the back of my house, and then I heard a car door quietly open and close. As if the driver was taking pains not to disturb anyone. I hopped out of bed and went downstairs to my kitchen, arriving just in time to see my daughter unlocking the back door.

"Surprise," she said. "I hope I didn't wake you."

She was dressed in ripped jeans, a dirty green sweatshirt, and beat-up Nikes, and she looked exhausted. I welcomed her with a hug and I thought I smelled cigarette smoke in her hair, but I decided to let it slide. She explained that she'd been struck by a bout of homesickness, so she'd driven through the night to visit me—and now she was desperate for a shower and a nap. I made her scrambled eggs while she cleaned herself up and changed into fresh clothes. And while she slept, I did a little work on her car, topping off the fluids and checking the tire pressure and vacuuming the crumbs out of her floor mats.

Later that morning it started to snow, so we stayed around the house all day. Tammy came over with two of her foster kids and the five of us made an enormous vat of chicken soup and loaves of fresh-baked bread. Once the yard was blanketed in white, Maggie took the kids outside to make snow angels and build an igloo while Tammy and I watched through frosted windows with mugs of hot chocolate. After dinner we put on some Billy Joel CDs and taught the foster kids how to play Euchre and Aw Shucks, and it was pretty much a perfect day from start to finish.

Sunday morning, Maggie seemed different. She'd emerged from her bedroom looking shaken. I'd heard her on the phone having a strained conversation, but I'd resisted the urge to eavesdrop. I asked her if everything was okay, and she said she was fine. We drove over to the Waffle House for brunch and the waitresses welcomed her back like a homecoming queen. I ordered my usual farmer's omelet and Maggie got the strawberry pancakes, but she barely touched her food. She seemed anxious to get back to Boston. I tried to make small talk and I asked about her job search, but I didn't push too hard. She seemed frustrated by her lack of progress and I didn't want to make her feel any worse.

We were back at the house by eleven that morning, and she gathered her things to leave. I remember walking her out to her car, which had remained parked in my backyard all weekend. "Oh, listen," she said as she unlocked the driver's door. "Could I ask you for a favor?"

"Of course, kiddo. Shoot."

"If anyone asks what time I got here, could you say you're not sure?"

Maggie slipped inside her little Honda and rolled down the window to hear my answer. Like she'd just asked me to water her plants or borrow twenty dollars.

"You got here Saturday morning."

"Right, and I'm asking if you could be a little less specific. Like say you went to bed Friday night and never heard me come in. Because I have my own key. And when you woke up Saturday morning, I was asleep in my bed."

"But you weren't asleep in your bed. You were awake in my driveway."

She replied with a long, exasperated sigh, as if I was missing the point. "You don't have to lie. You just have to pretend you didn't see me pulling in."

"That *is* lying. That's not what happened."

"It's what *almost* happened. If you didn't wake up so fucking early, you would think it's the truth. Because you would have found me in my bed, and I would have told you I was there all night."

My pulse started to quicken. This was bad; I knew it was bad. "Maggie, get out of the car, please. Let's go inside and talk about this."

Instead she started the engine. "I have to leave."

"I'll help you, but you need to answer some questions."

"Since when? What happened to Mr. No Questions Asked?"

This was always my rule back in high school, when Maggie started going to parties and staying out late. I told her that if she ever needed a ride home or any other kind of assistance she could call me at any hour and I would rush to get her—no questions asked.

"That's who I need right now," she said. "I need Mr. No Questions Asked. Please don't overcomplicate this, okay?"

She was already backing out of the driveway as she made her final plea. She was going a little too fast and clipped my trash bin before rolling off the curb and veering out into the street. Then she shifted into drive and sped out of sight.

I walked back inside the house and started to rehearse my story. I didn't understand what was happening, but I knew a call was coming and I wanted to be ready. *I'd gone to bed early Friday night, and I didn't hear Maggie come in. When I woke up Saturday morning, I found her asleep in her bed.*

That night I had leftover chicken soup for dinner. It was usually better the second day, but not this time. After I finished washing the dishes, I emptied my kitchen trash and carried the bag out to my driveway. When I lifted the lid on the bin, I noticed there was another bag already inside. It was a ten-gallon bag but mostly empty, and I knew I hadn't put it there. I pulled it out and carried it to the privacy of my backyard and then patiently worked out the knot. Inside were Maggie's ripped jeans and dirty green sweatshirt. And her socks, sneakers, bra, and underwear. Plus a pair of cheap yard gloves and a plain navy ballcap. I put it all back in the bag, then put the bag back in the bin, and then I dragged the bin out to the curb so it would get picked up the following morning. It was a long and mostly sleepless wait until sunrise, when I heard the low groan of the garbage trucks turning onto my street. They carried away all the evidence but none of my worries.

The days passed, then weeks, and then a full month, and I almost allowed myself to relax. It seemed like Maggie was correct: everything was fine. No one called me with any questions, and I'd been seeing problems where problems didn't exist. I sent a few casual texts to my daughter and asked how she was doing; her replies were brief but friendly. She told me that she'd stopped working for Dr. Cell Phone and found a new job as a barista. Meanwhile, she was emailing lots of résumés and hoping to find a better gig. All positive signs for a brighter future.

And then Maggie got the offer from Capaciti. She called me to share the good news and we celebrated for close to an hour. It was her first professional job in a brand-new office in downtown Cambridge, with a modest entry-level salary plus performance bonuses, Blue Cross health insurance, and a slew of corporate benefits. Capaciti employees had free access to the Museum of Fine Arts and the New England Aquarium. They received 10 percent off all purchases from Hertz, Avis, Southwest Airlines, and a hundred other businesses; she read from a list that went on and on. And I remember feeling so proud of her. I knew it was hard to get your foot in the door when you didn't have any personal connections, and Maggie had risen to the challenge. The road to this point had been a little bumpy, but she'd finally made it. Now her future was wide open, and I sent her a large bouquet of flowers with a card: *Congratulations! You did it!*

About three weeks later I came home from work to find a white Chevy Impala parked in front of my house. At my arrival, the driver opened his door and waved to me. He was a Black man dressed in a shirt and tie, and there was something in his demeanor that reminded me of my father. Not so much his age (he was only a half generation older than me) but his overall attitude. He had the kind of leisurely gait that I see on a lot of older guys who choose to work well past their retirement age. The pensions are locked up, so all the pressure's off, but they're enjoying themselves too much to quit.

"Mr. Szatowski?" He was walking up my driveway. "I'm Leonard Summers. I work with the state fire marshal of Massachusetts. Could I ask you a couple questions?"

"Was there a fire?"

"Yes, sir. Pretty big one. Margaret didn't mention it?"

"Is she all right?"

He nodded and said my daughter was safe, and then he repeated his question: "She didn't mention any fire?"

"I haven't spoken to her in a while. She just started a new job."

"Right, I heard about that." He reached into his pocket for a tiny notebook and opened it. "Something called Capaciti, right? Spelled with two *i*'s?"

Up until this moment, I'd hoped that Leonard Summers was mistaken, that he'd come to the wrong house for the wrong Margaret Szatowski. But evidently not.

"That's correct," I told him. "C-I-T-I."

"Gosh, my mother would have hated that," he said with a smile. "She taught second grade in Roxbury, and she was a stickler for spelling. Always railing against Froot Loops and Kool-Aid for making her kids illiterate. And nowadays it's so much worse. Lyft, Chick-fil-A, Capaciti with two *i*'s. It's good she's not around to see it, you know?"

He spoke like we had all the time in the world, and I just smiled politely and endured the anecdote and wondered why this man had come to see me.

My next-door neighbor opened her front door and stepped outside, making a pretense of reaching into her mailbox but clearly just eavesdropping. Leonard Summers offered her a friendly wave and called out, "Good afternoon!" and then suggested we speak indoors.

We went into my kitchen and I offered to make coffee. He said he never drank coffee after lunch because the caffeine kept him awake, but a glass of water would be nice. So I poured two glasses of water and joined him at the kitchen table.

"I want to ask you about Margaret's previous job," he explained. "Last week, I arrested a man named Oliver Dingham. Have you ever met him?"

"Once."

"When was that?"

"A couple months ago. I went to Boston to visit my daughter and she showed me where she worked."

"So you've been to the store? Dr. Cell Phone?"

"Briefly but yes, I've been there."

"Good, good, good. That saves me some time. About two months ago, on the night of February 7, Oliver Dingham started a fire that destroyed the entire building." He removed a laptop from his satchel, then opened the screen to show me photos of the wreckage. The building had been reduced to a smoldering pile of rubble and twisted steel. "Now, I have been doing my job for a long time and I have met some very bad arsonists, but Mr. Dingham is easily the worst. The poor fool made just about every mistake in the book. For example, most accidental fires can be traced back to a single point of origin—a space heater, say, or a dropped cigarette. But the fire at Dr. Cell Phone had three separate and distinct points of origin. Three giant red flags screaming 'Not an accident,' do you follow? And on top of that, we found traces of acetone all over the interior, which simply makes no sense. If it was a nail salon, sure, you'd expect to find acetone, toluene, formaldehyde, lots of highly flammable chemicals. But not in a phone repair shop. There's no reason for him to have so much liquid accelerant on-site. Just another huge red flag."

He paused to take a sip of his water, and perhaps to give me a chance to speak, but I just rubbed my sweaty palms on my pants and waited for him to continue.

"So I visited Mr. Dingham at home to ask why he kept so much acetone in his store, and it was the shortest interview in the history of my career. Within five minutes the man just cracked like an egg. Crying and apologizing and fessing up. So we arrested him on charges of first-degree felony arson and felony homicide."

"Homicide?"

"That's the worst part of the story. One of the first responders was a firefighter named DeShawn Wilson. Twenty-nine years old. The floor gave way and DeShawn fell into the basement. Half the building came down on top of him." He paused to show me a photograph of the deceased hero: DeShawn posed in his firefighter's cap and uniform with a young woman and a baby boy. "That's his widow, Kim, and their son, DeShawn Junior. Are you sure your daughter hasn't mentioned *any* of this?"

"She's been really busy. With her new job. There hasn't been a lot of time for phone calls."

He nodded and then made a small notation on his pad. "Well, I'm sure you're busy, too, so let me cut to the chase. Mr. Dingham is getting sentenced on Friday and I've been helping out the prosecutors. We want the judge to have all the relevant information. And the more I get to know Mr. Dingham, the less I understand his motivation. Why burn down the business? He says he did it for the money. But when I asked why he *wanted* the money, how he planned to *use* the money, he couldn't answer me. He had no idea. Isn't that strange?"

I lifted my glass to my lips and swallowed some water and tried to look like I was thinking. "Maybe he had financial problems."

"I thought the same thing! So I looked into it, Mr. Szatowski. And you know what? Turns out his grubby little business did all right! When you charge people sixty bucks for a little piece of glass, you make a real nice profit margin. Plus the man has zero debt. No sick relatives, not much family at all. And no real ambitions, which was the biggest surprise. Arson is a lot of hard work. A massive endeavor. And I got the sense Mr. Dingham never really worked hard at anything. He seemed happy to coast along at his store, build his crazy LEGO models, and watch a staggering amount of internet pornography. All of which led me to wonder if *mayyyyybe* Mr. Dingham had a partner." He paused for another drink of water, then asked, "Did you know he was paying Margaret twenty-two dollars an hour?"

"I think he really valued her."

"Oh, I agree. I think he valued Margaret a real lot. I've read a couple hundred of their text messages, and it's clear they were very close."

I didn't like what he was insinuating. "The man was forty-six years old. If he had feelings for my daughter, I'm sure they weren't recip-rocated."

"I have some images suggesting otherwise. Found them on his phone. 'Boudoir photos' is what I think they're called. Not the sort of pictures you'd normally share with your supervisor." He tried swivel-ing his computer to show me but I held up my hand, indicating that I did not wish to see them. "Anyway, I visited your daughter earlier this week. I asked her about the fire and she said she was home that weekend. Visiting you and—" He checked his notes. "You and Aunt Tammy. Does any of this sound familiar?"

"Very familiar. There was snow on Saturday and Tammy came over with her foster kids. Maggie played with them in the backyard."

He smiled at my use of the name Maggie and scribbled something on his notepad. Then he placed a little paper calendar on the table between us. It showed all the weeks and months of the year, and he pointed to the first weekend in February. "Is this the Saturday you're describing? February seventh?"

"Yes, I think so."

"It's better for me if you're sure. Can you say with absolute certainty that Maggie was here in this house on Saturday, February seventh?"

"Yes, I am absolutely certain."

"And what time did she arrive?"

I repeated the question word for word: "And what time did she *arrive?*"

Leonard Summers allowed himself a small smile. I suppose in that moment he knew he had me. "Correct, Mr. Szatowski. You said there was snow on Saturday afternoon, and your sister Tammy came over with her foster kids. So I'm just asking you to think back a tiny bit further. What time did Maggie get to your house?"

"I don't remember."

"Well, it's really important that you do. It's the reason I drove all this way to speak with you." He sat back in his chair and drank his water and then let his eyes wander around my kitchen. "Just take your time and think back."

"I'm sorry," I told him. "I'm drawing a complete blank. I have no idea."

He nodded, like this was precisely the answer he expected. "I know I'm putting you in the hot seat. This is your daughter we're talking about. Your only child, am I right? So here's what I'm going to do. Before I repeat the question, as a show of good faith from one father to another, I'm going to lay all my cards on the table. I think this fire was Maggie's idea. I think she read somewhere that eighty percent of arsons are never solved and she decided those odds were pretty good. So she convinced Oliver to start the fire and split the insurance money."

"Is that what he says?"

He shook his head. "No, sir."

"Then what proof do you have?"

"Not a whole lot, since I'm being honest. But we did find two sets of footprints in the lot behind the building. A men's size eleven and a woman's size seven. Both with traces of acetone. Do you know your daughter's shoe size, Mr. Szatowski?"

"I haven't bought her shoes in a long time."

"She's a size seven."

"So are lots of women."

"True, but Oliver Dingham doesn't know lots of women. He doesn't know *any* women. I've been through his phone; I've been through all his contacts and photos. He had a pretty solitary existence before your daughter came along. He certainly didn't have anyone sending him boudoir photos."

Some part of me knew he was telling the truth, but I couldn't bring myself to admit it. "I don't know anything about the photos. But she's not a criminal."

"Oh, I think we're all criminals to some degree. There's a whole wide spectrum of illegal and immoral behavior." He drew an arc in the air to help illustrate his metaphor. "At the one end, you've got your Jeffrey Dahmers and your Ted Bundys. And on the other end, you've got millions of morally upright citizens who cheerfully drive ten miles over the speed limit because they know they'll never get ticketed. And we're all at different places on this spectrum, don't you agree? I bet your Maggie's somewhere right in the middle."

"She's never been in trouble!"

"Well, that's hardly true. Wasn't she caught shoplifting? As a kid?"

"All kids shoplift."

"But she got in fights, too. That's rare for girls."

I shook my head. "No. She never got in fights."

"I guess you didn't hear about them. But there's video online, if you look back far enough. Kids love sharing this stuff. They post a fight on YouTube and ten years later they forget all about it, but the internet *never* forgets. Maggie had a pretty explosive temper back in high school, wouldn't you say?"

"She lost her mother. Those were tough years."

"Of course they were, Mr. Szatowski. And I'm sorry for your loss. But college was tough for Maggie, too, right? That whole sorority business? Selling answers to tests?"

"She had nothing to do with that."

"Right, right, all the blame went to that other girl. The one who dropped out of school, Jessica Sweeney. You know I called her the other day, to get her side of the story? She lives in Arizona now. Back home with her parents. Trying to put her life together. She told me your daughter was 'a narcissistic sociopath.' I wasn't familiar with that term, so I had to go home and look it up. It's a kind of person who doesn't feel any empathy or guilt. No close friends, just lots of superficial acquaintances. People she can manipulate to get what she wants."

I reminded him that Maggie was completely exonerated, so what was the point of listening to a nutcase like Jessica Sweeney?

"Because her story fits my pattern, Mr. Szatowski. And I see this pattern continuing, escalating, accelerating. If we don't stop it now, if we don't get Maggie the help she needs, where does it go from here?"

I reminded him that she had a new job, that she had a whole bright future ahead of her.

"Maybe so," Leonard Summers said. "Or maybe she just keeps on making bad choices. I think there's a real risk of that happening. I once heard a doctor say that the human brain isn't fully developed until the age of twenty-five. Which means there's still time, if we get her the help she needs. Or else she keeps going down this same path, and I don't know where it ends."

"She's on a good path now," I told him. "She'll have a bright future."

He sighed, as if he'd reached the conclusion that he was never going to convince me. "I didn't come here to argue about Maggie's future," he said, and again he tapped the paper calendar on my kitchen table. "I'm just asking what time she arrived at your house on Saturday, February seventh. And I encourage you to answer the question very, very carefully."

After he drove away, I poured myself a drink to make my hands stop shaking. Then I went over to my computer and searched for information on DeShawn Wilson. YouTube had a television clip from WCVB, one of the local Boston news affiliates, titled "Watertown Firefighter and Father Dies After Battling Blaze: 'Tragic Loss.'" His wife, Kim, had rushed to the scene of the accident, and the news anchor was interviewing her in front of the smoldering wreckage. She was wrapped in a gray emergency blanket and cradling her infant son and openly weeping. She said, "This is a terrible, terrible day," and I had to turn it off; I couldn't bring myself to watch.

Then I called my daughter and told her about my visitor. "It's over, Maggie. He knows everything."

"What are you talking about?"

"The fire. Dr. Cell Phone."

"Dad, I had nothing to do with that fire. I was at your house that weekend, remember?"

She spoke like there was an unknown third person sharing the line and listening to our conversation—and who knows, maybe there was.

"You need to tell the truth, Maggie."

"It *is* the truth."

"I'm going to help you. I'll hire another lawyer."

"I don't need a lawyer. I didn't do anything."

"Maggie, listen to me. He asked about February seventh. He asked what time you came to my house."

"And?"

I took a deep breath, like I was getting ready to dive underwater. "I said you got here Saturday morning. Just before sunrise. About five-thirty."

"You lied?"

"I didn't lie."

"I got there *Friday*, Dad. Almost midnight."

"No, Maggie."

"You were already asleep. So I came through the back door and went to bed."

"Enough, Maggie. It's time to come home."

"Fuck you."

"Maggie!"

"Why would I come home? Why?"

"So I can help you."

"This isn't helping! I asked you for *one* thing. One thing!"

"We'll make things right—"

"No. Never. I don't want to see you anymore."

"Maggie, come on—"

"Stay out of my life, do you understand?"

After she hung up, I went to Tammy's condo and told her what happened, and she tried reaching out to Maggie on my behalf, all to no avail. We resigned ourselves to the fact that she would be arrested and arraigned on charges of arson and homicide. Instead, she flew with her corporate coworkers to a weeklong sales conference in Cabo San Lucas and five nights of luxury at a Four Seasons resort. I never received any official explanation, but my understanding (based on the trial transcripts) is that Oliver Dingham refused to name Maggie as an accomplice or conspirator. He insisted that he acted alone and refused to place her at the crime scene, so all the prosecution's evidence was strictly circumstantial. And since Oliver was the sole beneficiary on the insurance claim, the state was happy to prosecute him and put the whole matter to rest. He was sentenced to ten years in a medium-security prison but only lasted six months before dying in an "inmate-related dispute."

And in the years that followed, I've come to see the situation from Maggie's point of view. As parents, we always say we'd do anything for our children—but would we really? CNN just ran a story about a forty-year-old mother who leaped from the deck of a cruise ship to save her daughter from drowning. All I had to do was tell a simple white lie—and instead I'd nearly sent her to prison.

As Maggie pulled the rest of her life together—as she demonstrated she was capable of making an honest and successful living with a real job at a real company—I felt worse and worse about my decision. I wished I could go back in time and give Leonard Summers a different answer. It would have been so easy to play dumb, to say I'd gone to bed early and never heard Maggie come home.

And now I was facing the same choice all over again.

Could I really stand by my daughter's side as she prepared to make the biggest mistake of her life?

Or would I choose to walk away, with the knowledge that I would never see her again?

3.

After my shower, I put on some clean clothes and went downstairs to
the living room. Abigail was standing on a chair in an ivory lace dress,
arms stretched high above her head, while Tammy and Maggie made
careful adjustments to her hem and sleeves.

"Can I put them down yet?" she asked.

"Five more seconds," Tammy said. "Almost."

"I'm tired!"

"I know, honey, hang on—"

"Done!" Maggie said. "You can relax."

Abigail dropped her arms and exhaled with relief as I reached the
bottom of the stairs.

"You're just in time," Tammy said. "What do you think of our little
flower girl? Doesn't she look wonderful?"

And I had to admit, the sight of Abigail brought me up short. I almost didn't recognize her. She wore a crown of white summer daisies
that concealed the sharp contours of her buzz cut, and her dress had
little sparkles that twinkled when she moved. "It's beautiful," I told her.
"You look like a princess."

Her face turned red. "Aw, Mister Frank, stop!"

Maggie set down her sewing basket and rushed to my side. "How are you feeling, Dad? Is your head okay?" I just stared back at her. I supposed she was just going to pretend that nothing out of the ordinary happened last night. Reality was whatever she wanted it to be. "Can I get you some coffee? There's still plenty of breakfast left in the kitchen. Croissants, fruit salad, some quiche—"

"Maggie, I just want to talk for a bit. Would that be all right?"

"More than all right," Tammy said. "This is a big day for you two! A big day with big emotions." She swept both of us across the room and out the front door. "Go have your conversation outside while I finish here with Abby. And then *she's* going to help *me* fit into my dress. Because, let's be honest, I'm going to need a lot more time!"

I followed my daughter out of the cottage and into the woods. We walked on a trail for a long time without saying anything. It was like that first out-of-the-blue phone call back in May, when she'd reached out with her big news. Clearly we needed to talk, but neither one of us knew where to start.

"I'll answer your questions," she finally said. "And I promise I'll tell you the truth. But *you* have to promise to listen. You need to hear me out."

"Is he blackmailing you?"

"Who? Errol? No! Of course not. Everything you saw last night was consensual."

This seemed impossible. Maybe consensual didn't mean what I thought it meant?

"We've been together awhile now."

"How long?"

"Almost a year."

"I don't understand. How are you 'together' with a fifty-seven-year-old married man? What does that even mean? How in the world—"

"Dad, I will explain everything, but I need you to listen. Don't judge, don't criticize, don't moralize. Just hear me out. Can you do that?"

I gritted my teeth and nodded, and she began to tell me her story. She said that during her first year at Capaciti, Errol Gardner barely spoke a word to her. He was the sort of CEO who rarely acknowledged or even noticed all the young assistants working long hours on his behalf—or so she thought.

Then one day she received an invitation to lunch. Errol described it as a new company initiative—an attempt to foster mentorship between senior executives and junior employees. Maggie said it was the least convincing pickup line she'd ever heard, but she was flattered that he'd taken an interest. She said there were a dozen other women he could have asked, and they would have all agreed to the lunch in a heartbeat.

What followed, according to my daughter, was an increasingly intimate series of encounters, all under the guise of career development. Brainstorming sessions, dinner after work, late-night drinks at sales conferences. A week in Chicago at the Auto Show. Trips to Munich and Singapore and Sydney on Capaciti's private jet. "Discretion was very important," Maggie explained. "We were never together in Boston or Cambridge. Only out of state and ideally out of the country. And I know these stories always sound cheap and tawdry, but I promise you, this is not a Harvey Weinstein situation. It's a real relationship built on respect. We go to museums, we read the same books, we like the same TED Talks—"

I had to stop her right there. "You know you're not the only one, right? Catherine says he's been cheating on her for years. Dozens of women. You're just his latest flavor of the month. You're the new Dawn Taggart!"

"I'm getting to her," she said. "You promised you would listen, remember?"

We had reached the clearing with Big Ben, the tall tree with the two wooden swings. No one else was around, so my daughter took one and I took the other, and then Maggie continued her story: "After we were together a couple months, Errol invited me to visit Osprey Cove. This place is so important to him. He's had all of his best ideas here. All his biggest innovations were born on this lake. It was the first weekend in November and he promised the foliage would be beautiful. We left Boston on a Saturday morning, and when we arrived in New Hampshire, he showed me the back roads that he liked to use. So he could bypass Hopps Ferry and not draw attention to himself."

But upon arriving at the camp, Errol realized that something was amiss. The first sign was the empty guard station. Hugo, the property manager, was absent from his post. Errol proceeded into the camp, and when he arrived at Osprey Lodge, there were two other cars parked in the driveway. A black BMW belonging to his wife and a silver Toyota Corolla that belonged to Dawn Taggart.

"As soon as I saw the cars, I knew something was wrong. Errol turned white as a sheet. He drove all the way around the rotary and started making excuses, saying we'd have to visit some other time. But it was too late. Catherine heard his car and opened the front door. She was standing there with Aidan and they both looked awful. I assumed it was because of me. I thought we'd been caught red-handed. But then I looked past them and saw a third person in the doorway. Sprawled at the bottom of the staircase with a broken neck. If we'd arrived ten minutes earlier, we could have stopped the whole thing from happening."

Hugo was already at work inside the lodge, assessing the situation and plotting the best course of action. Maggie explained that he had experience with these kinds of situations, from his work in Congo-Kinshasa. He assured the Gardners that everything would be okay, that he could make the girl and her car disappear. But Errol knew that Linda Taggart would report her daughter missing, and she would point the police to Aidan as the most likely suspect. His son needed an alibi from a third party. Someone outside the family willing to testify he wasn't anywhere near Osprey Cove. So Maggie raised her hand and volunteered.

"We were back in my apartment by four o'clock that afternoon, and we stayed up half the night talking. Aidan felt terrible about what happened. He thought we were all going to jail. But Hugo promised the local police wouldn't look too hard, and he was right. The town has too much to lose if Osprey Cove goes dark. I bet Errol Gardner could walk into Hopps Ferry and shoot a person in broad daylight and everyone would just look the other way."

While Maggie and Aidan were hunkered down in the basement apartment, Errol and Catherine were at Boston's Museum of Fine Arts; they had several friends on the board who recalled spending the entire afternoon with them. And all the while, Hugo was cleaning up the camp and relocating the body to some unknown location. "He waited until dark and then drove Dawn's Toyota to the state forest. Then he put some of her clothes on the trail, just to confuse the police." Maggie laughed. "It's very easy to conceal this sort of thing, if you've got enough resources. That's why the jails are full of poor people."

I couldn't believe the levity in her voice. She almost sounded boastful—proud of her role in the cover-up. "There was quite a bit of acting involved, but I'm getting pretty good at it." Then she transformed her expression, widening her eyes and clutching her hands to her chest, like she was Cinderella meeting her fairy godmother. And in a singsong voice she quoted an old conversation back to me: "'Sometimes we're talking and I feel like Aidan can read my mind. Like we have a telepathic connection. Did you and Mom ever feel that way?'"

I stared back like I'd been slapped, and she laughed at my reaction. "Oh, Dad, come on! Have I ever talked that way about anyone?"

"I thought you'd fallen in love. I was happy for you."

"I never said I loved him. You *assumed* I loved him, because I *am* excited for this wedding. But the marriage is strictly business. We'll make public appearances as husband and wife, but in private there's no commitment. Aidan can sleep with whoever he wants. Not Gwendolyn, unfortunately, and that's a shame. I think he always had a little crush on her. But he's rich and good-looking. He'll find someone new."

She seemed oblivious to the cruelty and callousness of her words. "Gwendolyn was *murdered*," I reminded her. "And now you're an accomplice to her murder."

Maggie shook her head. "No more than you or Tammy. Or anyone else at the camp. I don't know what they did to her. I never saw anyone lay a hand on her."

"What if Aidan changes his mind?" I asked. "He's looked miserable all weekend. What if he goes to the police and confesses?"

"Never gonna happen. He loves his mother too much. He doesn't want to see her go to jail. This is his only viable option."

"And you? What are you getting out of this?"

"Well, I'm not Dawn Taggart, I'll tell you that much. Forty-five grand isn't going to cut it. I insisted on an ironclad prenuptial agreement. Following a period of at least six months and no more than twelve, Aidan and I will announce our separation and file for divorce. We'll split all our combined assets fifty-fifty, including his penthouse apartment and his eighty thousand shares of Capaciti stock. At which point I promise you will never have to work another day in your life. You can wave a giant middle finger at UPS and tell them all to go to hell."

"I like UPS, Maggie. UPS has put food on our table for twenty-six years."

"Fine, Dad, whatever. Run your body into the ground if it makes you happy. I'm just saying you'll have a choice."

"And in the meantime you'll keep sleeping with Errol Gardner? While you're married to his son?"

"I'm not asking for your approval," she reminded me. "I'm asking you to respect my decisions."

From our perch on the swings we had a partial view of Lake Wyndham and we could see dozens of brightly colored sailboats moving across the water. All these happy families spending time together— parents, grandparents, aunts and uncles. I found it hard to square the beauty of my surroundings with all these ugly confessions.

"Maggie, we have to leave."

"I'm not going anywhere."

"You can't go through with this. It's a perversion of marriage. The opposite of everything your mother and I believed in. We *forbid* this marriage."

She laughed an ugly laugh—a short, harsh bark. "Oh, you forbid it? What is this, a Jane Austen novel?"

"Let's get out of here. Quit your job at Capaciti and come home. Stay with me until you get back on your feet and I promise I will never breathe a word to anyone. But if you don't, if you go through with this wedding and marry Aidan Gardner, I am going straight to the police—to real police, not the local Keystone Kops—and I will tell them everything."

Maggie glanced around, checking to make sure no one was walking nearby, and then she lowered her voice. "Dad, please don't make threats like that. I know you're not serious. But the wrong people could overhear you and jump to false conclusions."

"I *am* serious. I can't stay here and watch you do this."

"You don't have a choice. They have your Jeep. They have your keys. And Hugo knows what happened last night. You're not leaving this camp without his permission. And even if you did, where would you go? You have no proof and no evidence. Errol and Catherine have donated millions of dollars to hundreds of charities and you're just the UPS guy. No one is going to believe you."

I pointed out that Linda and Brody Taggart would help support my story.

"Sure, a second-grade teacher and a drunk janitor. And meanwhile Gerry and his team will get to work and they will absolutely destroy you. They will take you apart brick by brick. You'll lose your job, your house, your reputation. I've seen them do it to other people, Dad, and it's brutal."

"It's a risk we have to take. You can't trust these people. What if they're playing you? What if they turn around and try to pin this whole thing on you?"

Maggie was confident this could never happen. "We spent a long time planning this wedding and I've got hours of conversations on tape. Me, Errol, Catherine, Aidan, even Gerry. If they ever tried something, I'd bring them all down with me."

This was a revelation. "Maggie, if you've got those conversations on tape, you've got all the power in the world. You can turn them over to the FBI. You could be their star witness."

She stared back at me like I was missing the point. "If I go to the FBI, I get nothing. I've invested a whole year with this family. I'm two hours away from lifelong financial independence. And you're suggesting that I quit?"

"I'm *begging* you to quit."

"Dad, I'm going to say something, and it's going to hurt, but you need to hear it: I am never coming home to Stroudsburg. It's too small. It's too cheap. And all the people are too sad. You all have no idea what you're missing. This world we live in—it's so much bigger and more amazing than any of you realize. It's like—how can I put this? You don't even know *what you don't know*." She shook her head. "I'll never go back. I'd rather put a bullet in my brain."

I heard footsteps, and we turned to see Sierra Levinson sauntering up the trail, dressed in a wide-brimmed straw hat and a slim-fitting floral dress. "Sorry to interrupt y'all's daddy-daughter time, but I wanted Margaret to know the stylists are here. To do everyone's hair. They can start with other people, but we thought you might want to go first."

"Thank you, Sierra," Maggie said. "I'll be there in five minutes. Have her wait for me, okay?"

"Of course, no rush," she said, and then she swatted a playful hand across my shoulder. "Don't look so nervous, Frank! You're going to do great today!"

Maggie waited until Sierra was down the trail before speaking again. "I know you're unhappy. But if you love me as much as you say you do, you'll respect my decision. Put on your tuxedo, walk me down the aisle, and say something sweet during the reception. That's all I'm asking. You've spent the last three years saying you would do anything for me. Well, this is what I need. Today. Right now. Are you going to support me or not?"

And when she framed the question like that, I didn't have much of a choice.

4.

I returned to my bedroom and found my suitcase had been moved. It looked like a housekeeper had come through and cleaned up my mess. All the vomit in the bathroom was gone and my sailboat bunk bed had been remade with fresh linens and blankets. All my clothes were folded and put away in the dresser. And somebody must have gone around and chased away all the daddy longlegs because I didn't see any more. Even the cedar closet was finally free of them.

I unzipped my garment bag and carefully unpacked the components of my tuxedo. It was a beautiful suit, hand-tailored in Italy—a pearl-gray jacket with matching vest and flat-front pants. The white twill shirt was immaculately pressed and cool to the touch; I carefully pushed the black onyx studs through the buttonholes. The accessory package included a clip-on bow tie, but in the weeks leading up to the wedding I'd spent many hours in front of my bathroom mirror, practicing and mastering the real deal. Now I could knot a real bow tie in ninety seconds flat. I wasn't sure if anyone at the wedding would notice the difference, but I felt better knowing it was done right.

I was fastening my cuff links into my shirt sleeves when my cell phone buzzed with an incoming call: SUPERCUTS.

"Hey, Vicky."

"Frank, is everything okay?"

"Yeah, yeah, sorry. Everything's fine."

"I've been so worried about you. I thought you were going to call me last night. What happened to the girl?"

"They found drugs in her cottage. Something called xylazine." The words stuck in my throat like glue, but I managed to force them out. "She seemed like a very troubled person."

"And Dawn Taggart? What about her?"

"It was just a big misunderstanding, Vicky." I hated myself for lying but I sure couldn't admit the truth. "I think what happened is, I'm just not used to these kinds of people. Because Stroudsburg is such a small town? I've been misinterpreting a lot of things. But everything's better now. It's all straightened out."

She must have heard something in my voice that she didn't like. "Are you sure? My son seemed pretty worried about you, Frank. He wouldn't go into detail. Citing his journalistic code of ethics or what have you. But he seemed very uncomfortable with the whole situation."

I assured Vicky that Todd was wrong, that everything was fine, and then added that the ceremony was starting in an hour. "So I need to finish getting dressed."

"Okay, I'll let you go," she said, but then instead of hanging up she stayed on the line. "Are you *sure* everything's okay?"

"I'm fine. I'll call you when I get home."

"All right. Good luck with your toast!"

Right, the toast. After I ended the call, I opened my desk drawer and took out the single sheet of yellow lined paper with my final draft. *I know her mother's watching us from heaven, and I know she's pleased by what she sees.* And at last I realized why I'd struggled so much with the toast, why my speech had always felt so false and phony. I suppose deep down inside I had never believed a word of it.

5.

At two o'clock, the wedding party assembled on the beach of Lake Wyndham for a photo session. I assumed it would be a small and private affair, but as with the rehearsal, there were dozens of guests milling around and enjoying the preshow spectacle. There was even a bartender mixing cocktails up near Osprey Lodge. It was the man from Mom and Dad's Restaurant, the same man who claimed the Gardners deserved more credit for all the good things they'd brought to the community. He already had a long line of guests waiting for a drink.

Meanwhile, Maggie and her bridesmaids were out on the dock, posing in front of the lake while a team of photographers snapped camera shutters and a videographer captured wide panoramic shots. A woman with cat's-eye glasses and a clipboard was shouting instructions—"Show me shy! Show me demure! Okay, now show me flirty! Show me sexy! Come on, ladies, vamp it up! Show me those bedroom eyes!"

They say there's nothing quite like seeing your daughter in her wedding dress on her big day. It's the last major milestone of fatherhood, a huge emotional moment for every dad. But when I looked at Maggie, I just felt numb. Her lace tiered ball gown reportedly cost $15,000 and came from a famous designer based in Paris, but I thought it looked flimsy and insubstantial, like the costumes for sale at a Halloween store.

I dragged an Adirondack chair into the shade of the trees and sat down to watch the photo shoot. More and more guests were wandering out to the lawn. The men wore summer suits in neutral shades of blue or light gray, while the women were a bit more showy in brightly colored gowns. I wondered if any of the Capaciti employees knew my daughter's secret. Surely there had to be rumors. Anytime a young woman straight out of college starts joining the boss on international work trips, there's bound to be gossip and speculation. Yet everyone I'd met seemed convinced Maggie was a rare and extraordinary talent who'd earned her place in senior management. I suppose it's easy to make a person believe something when their paycheck depends on their believing it.

A trio emerged from the crowd to approach me. Errol Gardner pushed a wheelchair occupied by his wife, and they were accompanied by a man who looked strangely familiar.

Errol wore a black tuxedo and dark sunglasses that helped to conceal the bruise I'd left on his face, and Catherine scarcely resembled the woman I'd met the night before. Her makeup was subtle and very precise; her hair was clean and artfully styled. She wore an elegant sequined gown with pearl earrings and a glittering diamond necklace. Above all, she was medicated within an inch of her life. Her hands were folded in her lap, and she cast her blank stare all over the lawn, seemingly overwhelmed by so much movement and activity.

Errol proceeded like this was our first introduction. "Catherine, this is Frank. Margaret's father. He's very excited to meet you."

I thought I saw a flicker of recognition in her eyes—a small sign she remembered our conversation from the previous evening. But she simply apologized for not coming downstairs sooner. "My medicines aren't working so well," she said in a voice scarcely louder than a whisper. "I'm afraid they've left me very fatigued."

"The doctors ordered her to stay in bed," Errol explained. "But she refused to listen. She said there was no way she'd miss this ceremony."

I was ready to suggest that we all just cut the bullshit when the third person spoke up, and his voice was instantly familiar. "I'm glad you made that decision, Catherine. No mother should ever have to miss her son's wedding."

The man was my age, bald, with a face I knew I'd recognized. But I was seeing him out of context and simply couldn't place him.

"Frank, I'd like to introduce you to a good friend of mine," Errol said. "This is Armando Castado. I believe you two work together."

Holy mother of God. I suddenly found myself shaking hands with the chief executive officer of the United Parcel Service. "It's a real pleasure to meet you, Frank. Congratulations."

"Thank you, Mr. Castado."

"Armando, please."

"Okay. All right. Armando." I was so blindsided, I managed to forget the events of the last seventy-two hours and focus on the immediate present. "What are you doing here?"

"The Gardners invited me. And Margaret, of course. We've all been working together these past few months, so I was pretty excited to receive their invitation. And when I learned the father of the bride was a fellow UPSer, that just sealed the deal. Circle of Honor, right?"

"Yes! Twenty-six years."

Armando took a moment to explain the Circle of Honor to Errol and Catherine. He said that only a small fraction of UPS drivers ever managed to join its ranks because going twenty-five years without a scratch was nearly impossible. "It takes extraordinary skill, discipline, and intelligence, day after day and mile after mile. Most people simply cannot do it."

"I know I couldn't do it," Errol said. "Just last week, I dinged my bumper at the airport."

Catherine smiled uneasily and stared down at her hands. I didn't think she could follow the conversation at all. A waiter came by with a tray of champagne glasses and asked if we were interested in a little pre-wedding celebration. Armando took flutes for everyone and passed them around. "Let's raise a glass to the father of the bride," he said. "Remember, Frank: You're not losing a daughter. You're gaining a son. Congratulations."

"Hear, hear," Errol said.

Then he held a glass to his wife's lips. Champagne dribbled down her chest and into her lap, but we all pretended not to notice. I suppose I had fully resigned myself to the situation. I realized that if I ignored everything I'd learned in the last twenty-four hours, the wedding was everything I dreamed it would be. The sky was clear, the sun was shining, my daughter and her bridesmaids looked beautiful. My new in-laws had graciously welcomed me and Tammy into their extended family, and now the CEO of my company was showering me with praise. All I had to do was relax, drink the delicious champagne, and repeat all the old familiar clichés: We couldn't have asked for a better day. Marriage was hard but well worth it. Grow old with me, the best is yet to be.

A photographer hurried over and interrupted our conversation: "We need all the family members on the dock, please. Mom and both dads. Everybody get their smiles ready!"

"We'll talk more at dinner," Armando promised. "Good luck at the ceremony, Frank. It's going to be wonderful."

I followed my in-laws down to the beach, where all the groomsmen and bridesmaids and Maggie were waiting. Aidan was running late, so the photographers were ticking off the shots that didn't require him: me and Maggie, me and Maggie and Tammy, and of course me and Errol Gardner, with Maggie standing between us. "Big smiles, Frank!" the photographer called, clicking the shutter again and again. "Look happy! Oh, that's perfect! That's wonderful!" As soon as we finished, I called to the waiter for a second glass of champagne. I realized that if I was going to make it through the ceremony, I would need to give Catherine Gardner a run for her money.

By two-thirty Errol was confronting the groomsmen and asking what the hell was taking Aidan so damned long. No one had a satisfactory answer. No one had seen him in more than an hour. They'd all tried texting Aidan on their phones, and he'd replied with numerous assurances that he was on his way.

The clipboard lady promised everything would be fine; she said it would be easy to take the remaining photographs *after* the ceremony. "It's normal for grooms to get confused," she assured us. "I bet Aidan went straight to the Globe, and now *he's* wondering where *we* are."

I thought this seemed unlikely, but the clock was ticking and there was a consensus that we all needed to move to the ceremony. I followed the crowd up the lawn and watched Abigail "processing" in front of the bride, clearing a path for my daughter to follow. Tammy sidled up alongside me. "You look very handsome, little brother. I'm glad you're finally getting into the spirit of things."

"I don't think the groom is coming."

"Of course he is. Don't jinx us."

"He's gone, Tammy." My heart felt light as I voiced the idea, as if a crushing burden had been lifted. "I think he came to his senses and got the hell out of here."

"Oh, you think he just drove out the front gate? With Hugo and his whole SWAT team on standby? Don't bet on it, Frankie." One of the photographers walked alongside us, snapping candids, and my sister's cheerful smile didn't falter. "He'll be waiting at the Globe."

But she was wrong. When we arrived at the outdoor theater, there was still no sign of Aidan, and the ceremony was due to start in twenty minutes. Now everyone was texting the groom but no one was getting a reply. Errol sent Gerry to check Osprey Lodge and Hugo radioed his team and ordered a full sweep of the property. I was surprised that no one proposed a visit to Aidan's studio—the place he always used to escape the chaos of Osprey Cove. "You discovered my little secret," he had said to me. "Most people don't even know it's here."

Without a word to the others, I ducked into the woods to check the studio myself. I still remembered the route from two days earlier, when I followed Aidan and Gwendolyn to the outer boundaries of the property. After several minutes of walking, I checked the time and then quickened my pace. It was just about quarter to three, and I realized that if my hunch was wrong—if Aidan *wasn't* at the studio—I'd never make it back to the Globe in time. I'd miss the chance to walk my daughter down the aisle.

But when I finally arrived at the cottage, the door was unlocked. I stepped inside. There was no sign of Aidan, but I didn't feel alone. The black-and-white faces watched me with their strange, haunted expressions. I stopped at the spiral staircase and peered down through the hole in the floor. At the bottom was a faint glimmer of light.

"Aidan? Is that you?"

"Don't come down here, Frank."

"Everyone's looking for you. Gerry, Hugo, the photographers—"

"Fuck them."

I didn't know how to answer that. I turned around in a circle, casting a glance around the studio and surveying all the paintings in progress. I recognized one of the subjects as Gwendolyn. Her eyes slightly lowered, looking out at the viewer with a shy and slightly flirtatious smile.

"I'm coming downstairs, Aidan."

"Please don't." His voice was shaking. Like he was engaged in some kind of physical exertion. "Just leave. And don't tell anyone I'm here."

"Aidan, I just want to make an observation, okay? You don't need to go through with this wedding. I know you lied to the police. To protect your mother. That's an honorable thing. Anyone would understand why you did it. But Maggie lied, too. You're both guilty of the same thing. So if you call off this wedding, she can't hurt you. She's powerless."

"If you think she's powerless, you don't know her very well."

"Believe me, I know her better than anyone. I've just spent a lot of time unwilling to see the truth."

One pretty obvious tenet of situational awareness is that you never want to voluntarily enter a dark basement with just one exit. But I knew I would never convince Aidan of anything until we talked face-to-face, so I ignored my better instincts and descended the staircase. The steps were short and narrow, and I had to grip the steel pole and twist my body into unnatural positions just to reach the bottom. I found myself in a kind of small, cramped vestibule with a round metal door, like the entrance to a bank vault.

Just beyond was a tunnel lined with tall metal shelves, still well stocked with provisions after all these years. There were large rusted cans of stewed tomatoes, creamed corn, pork and beans, tuna fish, and Del Monte fruit cocktail. There were moldering cardboard boxes labeled BISCUITS—SURVIVAL—ALL-PURPOSE and enormous barrels marked DRINKING WATER and lots of vintage 1950s household products: Charmin toilet paper, Ajax detergent, Ivory soap, and Eveready batteries. Plus a small library of paperback novels, how-to manuals, and sets of encyclopedias. The entire shelter had the musty, pleasant smell of a used bookstore.

At the far end of the tunnel, the passage widened into a kind of living area with a sofa, a dining table with chairs, and four pairs of army-style bunk beds. Aidan sat at the head of the table, dressed in his black tuxedo, as if welcoming me to a formal dinner. On the table before him was an open metal case containing a black Colt revolver. Because a bomb shelter would need to be defended from external threats, after all, and the builders had prepared for every worst-case scenario.

"Don't come any closer, Frank. You should have stayed upstairs."

"Talk to me, Aidan. What are you thinking right now?"

He wouldn't look at me. I glanced at the gun, but I couldn't tell if it was loaded. After sixty years in a musty, humid basement, I didn't know if the weapon would still fire properly, or if the bullets were still functional. And I didn't want to know.

"You're the only person in this camp that I trust," I told him. "If anything happens to you, I don't think I'll be safe here."

"You'll be fine, Frank. I went by your cottage a little while ago. I left a gift in your suitcase."

"What kind of gift?"

"You'll see. It's enough to protect you. Don't worry."

There was a kind of resigned sadness in his voice, like he had no intention of ever leaving the basement.

"Aidan, listen to me: I have a friend of a friend who works for the *Wall Street Journal*. It sounds like they're already investigating your family. I bet they know people who would help you."

"Frank, if I talk to the *Wall Street Journal*, your daughter is going to be in an awful lot of trouble."

"I'm not worried about her. Right now, I'm just worried about you and the gun on the table. Could you close that case for me, please?"

He shook his head, still refusing to make eye contact. His face was flushed. Clearly he had been crying.

"I have an idea, Aidan. Right now, everyone's waiting for you back at the Globe. Let's use this moment to get out of here."

"How do you mean?"

"I mean leave Osprey Cove. Never come back."

He chuckled. "As if it's that easy. I'm sure they've got Hugo on high alert. We'd never make it past him."

"How about the fence? Is there a section that's broken? Someplace we could get through?"

"Not that I've ever seen. We could go look, but there's always security walking the perimeter."

"What about the lake?"

"You want to swim?"

"We can take your father's boat. They can't stop us once we're on the water. There are too many witnesses. All those sailboats. We'll cross the lake and find some town and I'll call the Taggarts."

"Those people hate me. They won't help us."

"They will, if you start telling the truth. Your parents ruined their lives. They deserve to know what really happened."

I could tell that he agreed with me, but I could also see he was terrified.

"Look, Aidan, if you won't do this for yourself, and you won't do it for the Taggarts, how about you do it for Gwendolyn? She liked you. She cared about you. She wanted you to stand up for yourself. And look what they did to her. I know you must feel awful about it."

He still wouldn't look at me, but he nodded his head, and I knew I was reaching him.

"If she was still alive, she'd want you to put away the gun and come upstairs with me."

"You're right. She would."

"But we need to go now. Before people start leaving the Globe." It was already ten past three; we'd have to run if we were going to make it. We'd be very conspicuous in our tuxedoes and black oxford shoes, but maybe with enough of a head start we could do it. "Are you ready?"

Aidan thought for a moment before answering. "I told Gwen the marriage was just for show. I said it was only going to last a year. And in the meantime I was free to see other people. But she refused to play along. She was too principled. She said she wanted nothing to do with me. Not unless I turned my back on all the money and told the truth."

Then Aidan stood up and straightened his jacket, like he had finally resolved to do just that. He closed the lid on the gun, locked the case, and returned it to a high shelf.

"I know a shortcut we can take," he said. "There's a path through the woods that'll get us to the boathouse."

"Let's hurry," I told him.

I followed Aidan up the spiral staircase and across the studio, but as we approached the door I heard footsteps on the porch outside and realized my miscalculation.

It was indeed ten past three, but in the world of the Gardners it was already three twenty-five—they'd already had plenty of time to start looking for us. Aidan opened the door to discover not just his father and Gerry Levinson but Hugo, too.

"Aidan! What are you doing here?" His father was furious. "We've got three hundred people waiting!"

His son turned on his heel and ran back to the stairs. I lunged to stop him but wasn't quick enough. I called his name but he just spiraled down into the hole.

Errol turned his rage on me. "And what are *you* doing? Why aren't you at the Globe?"

I ignored him. I ran to the top of the stairs and called down to the cellar. "Aidan, wait, please—"

And then we all heard it—a single loud pop, amplified and echoing off the basement's hard concrete walls—and I knew the wedding was off.

6.

Within an hour, the catering staff was stacking chairs and clearing all the tables. They shook out all three hundred artfully folded linen napkins; they collected all the silverware and sorted the utensils into plastic trays. Dinner plates, salad plates, and bread plates were stacked onto dish dollies; tablecloths were swept into bins to be laundered and pressed. Guests were encouraged to take home a centerpiece so the flowers wouldn't go to waste, and the subtext of the invitation was clear: please depart as quickly as possible, so our family can grieve in private.

"A terrible accident" was the term used by guests who approached me to express their condolences. I suppose it was the most polite thing to say: let's all pretend Aidan entered a bomb shelter to clean a vintage handgun at the precise moment he was supposed to be speaking his vows. But as soon as these guests turned their backs to me, I could see them congregating and comparing notes. It was an open secret that Aidan had been in therapy for years, that he'd always been aloof and a bit of a loner. He had an "artist's temperament." The subjects of his paintings always looked so troubled. And of course he'd just lost a dear friend to a drug overdose. Clearly he'd been suffering and internalizing a great deal of pain. And it was so easy to overlook all the warning signs. . . .

Luxury buses shuttled the hotel guests back into town, and by four-thirty the cottages were emptying out. Still dressed in my tuxedo, I grabbed a bench on Main Street and watched the guests dragging their rolling bags out to their vehicles. Whenever possible, they avoided making eye contact. No one really knew what to say. It was one of those awful situations where words were simply inadequate.

One of the few people who did try to speak with me was Armando Castado. He sat beside me on the bench and gave me a business card with his personal phone number, and he encouraged me to use it. "Anytime you need someone to listen, I hope you'll reach out to me. I'll be waiting for your call, Frank."

I had no intention of ever discussing this incident with anyone—especially not Armando Castado—but I appreciated the gesture. "Thank you."

"Margaret will get through this," he promised. "With your love and support, your daughter is going to be fine."

I wasn't so sure of that. I hadn't seen Maggie since I'd left everyone at the Globe, but I'd heard she was somewhere inside the lodge, grieving in private with Aidan's parents, and I couldn't bring myself to join them.

Immediately after the gunshot, Hugo cautioned all of us to stay upstairs while he went down the spiral stairs to investigate. He said it was safer if he went alone. Errol and Gerry were happy to oblige, but I followed Hugo, anyway. To this day, I wish I hadn't; I'll never unsee what we found in the basement. Aidan lay sprawled on the floor and most of his head was dripping down the wall. And yet somehow the rest of his body was still alive. He was still *moving*. I reached for my phone to call 911, but Hugo smacked the device out of my hand. "Don't be stupid."

I went to retrieve it and he shoved me against the wall, then chopped my lower back with the sharp edge of his hand. I felt like I'd been tasered. I would have collapsed if Hugo wasn't right behind me, twisting my arm and pinning me to the wall and forcing me to endure the horrible wheezing gasps of Aidan's last breaths. Hugo calmly whispered it would only be another minute, and it felt like the longest minute of my life. To this day, I'll sometimes hear a random stranger clearing their throat in a bar or restaurant, and suddenly I'll be back in the basement, my face pressed to the cool cinder-block wall, immobilized and unable to help.

When at last the breathing finally stopped, Hugo released me and I fell to the floor. He announced that it was safe for Errol and Gerry to come downstairs, but neither man moved in a hurry. I suppose they already knew what they were going to see, and they only came halfway into the shelter, sparing themselves the worst of it. Errol didn't show any kind of remorse. He looked like a man encountering a nuisance, like he'd arrived to discover his basement was flooded. He simply turned to his attorney and asked, "Now what?"

Gerry thought for a moment, then proceeded to outline a plan: "Hugo will have to dial 911 so there's an official record of the call. And after yesterday's episode, I think the police will be surprised to hear from us so soon. But this time, fortunately, we have a much simpler story: Aidan was late for the wedding, the four of us came looking for him, and we found him like this. We have no idea why. We're all still in shock." Gerry looked from Errol to Hugo to me. "Can we agree that's what happened?"

Errol nodded and Hugo said, "Of course," and I asked, "What's the alternative?"

"I don't follow, Frank."

"I'm asking what happens if I don't agree. Will the police show up and find my body next to Aidan's? Or do I just go missing like Dawn Taggart? When does this end?"

Gerry ignored my questions. He seemed to dismiss them as pointless. "Right now, there are three hundred people waiting for us at the Globe. I'll go there now and explain there's been a terrible accident. I'll break the news to Margaret and to Catherine, if she's lucid enough to hear it. After Hugo calls the police, we'll start encouraging guests to be on their way. Meanwhile, you two men need to reach an understanding. You've got ten minutes to get your shit together."

We followed them upstairs out of the cellar. Hugo and Gerry were already leaving the studio, but I paused to linger over Aidan's paintings and Errol stayed with me. In the moment, I could think of no better way to honor Aidan's life than to stop and appreciate his artwork. All the black-and-white faces of regular people, all the nurses and teachers and line cooks and bus drivers. With their wrinkles and blemishes and imperfections, they didn't look anything like the wedding guests at Osprey Cove, and I wondered if maybe that was the point.

"I don't know how you can live with yourself," I told Errol. "Your son was a good man. And incredibly talented. And now he's dead. Because of you."

He shrugged, casual, making it clear that none of my words had landed. "The truth's a little more complicated, Frank. Would you like to know it, or do you just want to judge me without having all the facts?"

I couldn't believe he was going to try to defend his actions, and yet that's exactly what he proceeded to do: "About fifteen years ago, I had a chance to invest in a little start-up called Atavus Genetics. The company didn't survive; it was crushed by 23andMe because it was basically the same idea: you spit in a cup and mailed it to their lab, and they sent back all the secrets of your DNA. The CEO gave me a bunch of sample kits to share with my friends, and on a whim I decided to test my son. Back then he was maybe ten years old, and I was curious to see what he'd inherited from me. And it turns out the answer was zero. Which might have surprised a lot of other people, but not me. The truth was, I always suspected it. The boy didn't look anything like me. And our personalities were totally different. He was always so timid, so cautious, so afraid. It was a genuine relief to know he wasn't mine. I decided to just leave him to Catherine and focus on my work."

"Did anyone tell Aidan the truth?"

"I don't know. I certainly didn't."

"So you just rejected him but never explained why? Does that seem fair to Aidan?"

"I never stopped supporting him financially. His art didn't pay the rent on that penthouse apartment, believe me."

"You owed him more than that. You should have behaved like his father or told him the truth. Instead of leaving him to wonder why you hated him."

Errol had already stopped listening. "You're not going to make me feel guilty, Frank. I'm not the one who created this mess. I didn't bash in Dawn Taggart's skull. But your daughter is very much involved—so if you have concerns for her well-being, I suggest you follow my lawyer's advice. Gerry is very good at his job, and he'll work on your family's behalf, if you let him."

I knew he was right; I knew I'd have to stay on Gardner Standard Time a little while longer and agree with their official story. But I also knew that Maggie's ties to the family had been severed. The wedding was off, and she was now a free woman. She could go anywhere, do anything, leave Osprey Cove and never return.

Which was exactly what I planned to do.

7.

Two police officers listened to my story and recorded my statement, but neither asked a lot of questions. They seemed eager to confirm that my recollections aligned with the statements given by Errol and Gerry, and then they sent me on my way. The entire conversation took less than fifteen minutes.

By the time I started back to my cottage, the lawn was empty; the caterers had carried away every last trace of the reception. It was all gone, like no part of the weekend had ever happened. The door to Blackbird was locked and I had to use my phone to get inside. I called out for Tammy and Abigail but to my surprise the cottage was empty.

I went upstairs to my bedroom, changed out of my tuxedo, and carefully placed all its components back in the garment bag. Then I pulled on my chinos and a T-shirt and a light fleece sweatshirt because I knew I would be driving all night and I wanted to be comfortable.

My suitcase was still on the lower bunk bed and I unzipped the top. Inside the main pocket was an old manilla envelope containing ten one-hundred-dollar bills. I realized this had to be the gift that Aidan had mentioned, but I didn't understand the point of it. He promised the gift would keep me safe, but what kind of protection was $1,000 going to buy?

I studied the envelope for secret markings or some other clue but couldn't find anything. The money had the old musty scent of a used bookstore, and none of the bills were minted after 1953, so I suspected they were from a secret stash in the underground shelter. Maybe Aidan was so naive about money he thought $1,000 would make a real difference to a working-class schlub like myself. The thought made me angry, and I was tempted to leave the envelope in my cottage. But at the last second I tossed it back into my bag, then piled all my dirty clothes on top of it.

By half past four, I was carrying my suitcase up to Osprey Lodge. I entered through the kitchen, where a half dozen police officers were gathered around a buffet of sides and salads—all foods prepared for the reception and left behind by the caterers. Gerry was encouraging the officers to bring the trays home to their friends and families, so the meals wouldn't go to waste. But at my arrival, they abruptly stopped talking and averted their eyes, like they felt ashamed of benefiting from my misfortune.

I found Maggie and Tammy hidden away in the living room, sitting with the doors closed and the curtains drawn. And just like the police, they stopped their conversation as soon as I arrived. Maggie occupied nearly the entire sofa in her billowing white lace gown. She had tissues in her hand and a box of Kleenex at her side, but all her makeup was still intact. Her cheeks were dry.

"The police said we're free to go," I explained. "You two can say goodbye if you want, but I'll be waiting outside."

"You want to leave?" Tammy asked.

"It's over. Everyone's gone."

"The guests are gone. We're family. This is one of those occasions where we pull together and support one another."

"I don't support this at all, Tammy. Three people are dead, and the only reason I'm keeping quiet is because of her." I pointed at Maggie because I couldn't bring myself to address my daughter by name. "I'll wait twenty minutes so you can pack your things. But then I'm leaving whether you're ready or not."

Tammy understood I was serious and stood up. But Maggie didn't move.

"There's nothing here for you anymore," I told her. "It's over. No marriage means no prenup. You get nothing."

Maggie's expression suggested that these facts were still up for debate. "It's definitely a change of plans," she said, "but I still have a lot of things to discuss with Errol. You and Tammy should leave, but I'm going to stick around a little longer."

I worried that if I left Maggie in Osprey Cove, she would never get away—that she would be bound to the Gardner family forever. But I was too tired to fight anymore. I couldn't keep rehashing the same arguments over and over. I hadn't eaten anything all day and my back was killing me. I just wanted to lie down, close my eyes, and sleep.

Instead, I had to drive six hours to the small, sad, desperate world that my daughter used to call home.

Maggie gave us both hugs and promised to call the next day with an update. Then she announced that she was going upstairs to get changed. "I had this dress altered three times but it's just never fit me right." She hitched up her train and walked out to the foyer, and we watched her climb up the stairs until she was gone.

"Well," Tammy said quietly. "I'll get my things."

"Don't forget your stock shares."

She flinched like I'd slapped her, and I wished I could take back the words. "You know I already feel horrible," she said. "You don't need to make it any worse."

"I'm sorry, Tammy. I shouldn't have said that."

Was I angry that she took the shares and cheerfully suggested that we all just look the other way? Yes. But would I have done the exact same thing if our financial circumstances were switched? Almost definitely yes. Tammy had spent her whole life cleaning up after other people's messes; she'd always been undervalued, unappreciated, and underpaid. Five years of salary was life-changing money, and I wasn't going to judge her for taking it.

"I thought Aidan was okay with the situation," she said. "I thought the plan was his idea! If I had any inkling he was going to—to—"

I put my arm around her so she wouldn't feel obliged to finish the sentence. "No one's blaming you, Tammy. This camp just messed with your head. All the money here—it makes people say and believe crazy things. And we just need to get the hell away from it. Where's Abigail?"

"Back at our cottage."

I explained that I had just come from the cottage. "She wasn't there. When did you last see her?"

"Back at the Globe. When we all got the news. I told Abby to go to the cottage and I followed Maggie here."

"And that was the last time you saw her?"

"Time slipped away from me. I've been overwhelmed."

"Go pack your stuff," I said. "I'll find her."

I looked all over the camp. I checked the beach, the dock, and the boathouse. And then I walked up to Big Ben, the climbing tree, where Abigail had jumped onto my shoulders and injured my back.

Finally, in desperation, I went to the place where she was last seen—the Globe, where we'd all gathered for the ceremony. The stage was cleared and the string quartet was gone. The flower bouquets had been carried away and all the benches were empty save for a single person in the back row. The last one at the wedding was a little girl with a crown of summer daisies hanging crookedly around her head. In her lap was a tiny basket of flower petals. She sat facing the stage and appeared to be waiting. Like she was nurturing a small hope the ceremony might still begin.

I took the seat beside her. "Hey, Abby."

"Hello." Her voice was a sad little croak, and I realized she was crying. Of course she was crying. She'd been promised a fairy-tale wedding.

She'd been invited to witness the single greatest promise that any two people can make to each other—an extraordinary declaration of love and faith and commitment. And now Aidan was dead and everyone was gone and come Monday Abigail would leave Tammy's condo and go live with some unknown mystery caregiver who might or might not look after her.

I knew it had been a mistake to bring her.

I said, "We're going to drive back now," and Abigail rubbed a knuckle into her eye and nodded. "So we need to get going, is what I mean."

This just made her cry even more. Embarrassed, she put both hands over her face and turned away from me. "I'm so sorry, Mister Frank, I just—"

Her face was full of tears and snot and I couldn't make out the rest. I pulled off my sweatshirt and used the soft fleece lining to gently dry her cheeks. She leaned forward and blew her nose into the fabric and then apologized. I told her it was fine. I said, "Get it all out," and she honked her nose a couple more times and then took a deep breath and at last she was clear.

"Did Tammy tell you what happened?"

"She said there was an accident."

I nodded, because this was certainly all she needed to know. "I'm sorry it happened, Abigail."

"I feel so bad." She doubled over like she had stomach cramps and gritted her teeth. "I mean, it just hurts so much."

All the other wedding guests were already moving on with their lives. They were on their way home, heading back to reality, and here was the one person at Osprey Cove who shared all my pain and grief, who felt even worse than I did.

"I'm hurting, too," I said. "I'm sorry we put you through this, Abigail."

I put my hand on her knee and she sort of melted into my side, and we sat there without talking for a long time. Every so often, I felt my phone twitching—I was getting lots of text messages from my sister, who was looking all over for us—but I didn't bother to read any of them. I felt like Abigail deserved somebody's full attention, and right now that somebody was me.

I don't remember how long we sat there, but after a while I noticed the sun was dropping. Soon, it would be dusk. I thought maybe Abigail had fallen asleep, but then I cleared my throat and she stirred. "We have to get going. We'll both feel better if we leave."

"You really think so?"

"I'm sure of it. You'll feel a tiny bit better tomorrow morning. And a tiny bit better the day after that. Right now we just need to push through it."

Abigail nodded and pushed the fleece sweatshirt back into my lap. It was streaked with boogers and snot so I just turned it inside out and wrapped it around my waist. Then I stood up but she refused to budge.

"Come on," I told her. "We gotta go."

She raised her arms, asking me to carry her. I didn't think my back could handle it but I agreed to give it a try. I held her little hand while she climbed up onto the bench. Then I lifted her by the waist and swung her onto my hip. I was surprised to discover she didn't weigh very much at all. With my free hand I grabbed her basket of flower petals and we set off down the trail to Osprey Lodge. Abigail hooked an arm around my shoulders, then used her free hand to scratch the side of her head.

"Still itchy?"

She nodded.

"I thought Maggie called a doctor."

"She said she was gonna."

"But no one ever came?"

Abigail shook her head. Then scratched it some more before resting it on my shoulder, and together we walked back to the camp.

V.

PARTING GIFTS

1.

The next afternoon, I drove over to the Men's Wearhouse in Stroudsburg to return my tuxedo. The kid with the pink hair and pierced eyebrows—the same kid who sold me the expensive accessory package—was standing behind the register. "Hey, welcome back! How did everything work out?"

I mumbled something polite and got the hell out of there. The answer to his question was: I still had no idea. I'd spent the previous evening driving back from New Hampshire with Tammy and Abigail. I dropped them off around midnight and I was back in my own bed by twelve-thirty, completely exhausted but too wired to sleep. I kept waiting for my phone to ping with new information from Maggie, something to explain what was happening next. Despite her assurances, I couldn't stop worrying. At some point I must have drifted off, but I was up early the next morning and immediately reached for my phone: still no messages.

I tried to busy myself with chores. I went into Maggie's childhood bedroom and stripped the sheets off her bed and put them into the washing machine. I know she said she was never coming home, but I wanted to be ready in case she changed her mind. After returning my tuxedo, I drove over to ShopRite and filled a grocery cart with her favorite foods. And all the while I kept checking my phone, making sure I hadn't missed any calls. It was late in the afternoon before anyone reached out to me, and my stomach did a flip-flop when I checked the caller ID: it was Vicky, calling from Supercuts. I didn't want to answer but I knew this conversation was inevitable.

"I'm sorry to bother you, Frank. I hope I'm not interrupting?"

She said she'd heard what happened and she was calling to express her condolences. Apparently the story was all over the news and she'd read about it on Facebook. I guess anytime the son of a wealthy tech tycoon dies in a firearms accident just minutes before his wedding, you can count on algorithms and influencers to spread the word.

"How's Maggie coping?"

I didn't know how to answer that question. I wouldn't lie to Vicky, but I sure couldn't tell her the truth.

"She's very confused."

"Of course she is. She's probably in shock."

"I wish I could help her. I don't know what to do."

Vicky asked when I was driving back to Pennsylvania and I explained that I was already home, that I'd been home all day.

"Oh, Frank, why didn't you say so? Do you want to meet up tonight? Talk about this over dinner?"

"I don't think so."

"You're welcome to come here. I've got food in my kitchen. I can put something together."

God, I wanted that more than anything. I was so desperate to tell her what happened. But of course I could never tell anyone the truth. Especially her.

"I'm not good company right now."

"I understand if you don't want to talk about it. I can respect that, Frank. You've been through a very traumatic experience. But I think, you know, psychologically? You could use a little emotional support."

And I knew that if I didn't get off the phone I would agree; I would race to her house and tell her everything. So I pointed out that she wasn't a professional therapist.

"What's that have to do with anything?"

"I don't think you should be giving me advice. You don't have any training in this stuff. You're just the person who cuts my hair."

And I knew this hurt her. I could tell from her reaction—or rather her lack of reaction—and the long dead silence that followed.

"I am *not* just the person who cuts your hair, Frank. I would have come to the wedding if you'd asked me sooner. If you hadn't waited until the last possible minute. It's not my fault I had to work."

"I have to go, Vicky. I'm sorry."

I ended the call and went over to the refrigerator where I kept all her business cards posted with magnets. I pulled them all down and put them in my trash so I wouldn't be tempted to call her back. It would be at least another month before I needed to get my hair trimmed, and I knew I could just drive to the other Supercuts, the one that was two towns away in Mount Pocono.

2.

About an hour later, my supervisor at UPS called to express his condolences. He reminded me that I had a massive bank of paid sick days and he encouraged me to use them, so I could help my daughter with her bereavement. I assured him that Maggie was surrounded by friends and the best thing for me was getting back to work. I promised to report first thing in the morning and drive my usual Monday route.

Now, if I'd been paying any attention to the rest of the world, I might have noticed the heat wave in the forecast. The mayors of New York City and Philadelphia were already declaring states of emergency and encouraging residents to stay indoors, stay hydrated, and look after their elderly neighbors. Normally I prepare for these shifts by filling an Igloo cooler with ice packs and sliced watermelon and a couple of navel oranges, but Monday morning I left my house with my usual ham-and-cheese sandwich, an apple, and a thermos full of water.

I got my first inkling that it wasn't a normal day when I arrived at the package facility and found the managers passing out sun hats and cold sleeves and extra bottles of Poland Spring. Most UPS vehicles don't have air-conditioning, so we were all reminded to pace ourselves and take frequent breaks. The guy who loads my truck is a Korean kid named Jun, and as I did my usual walkaround he warned me to be careful. "You got a lot of dog food today, Frank." "Dog food" is warehouse slang for any absurdly heavy or irregularly shaped item that people buy online—mattresses, cartons of printer paper, flat-pack furniture, and (surprise!) giant sacks of dog food. I thanked Jun for his heads-up and tipped him a little extra, because loading all that dog food is hard work for him, too.

I left my center at eight-thirty, and by nine o'clock I was soaked in sweat. Outside my truck, the humidity was stifling—and inside my truck, a windowless metal box baking hotter and hotter under the rising sun—it was unbearable. Every time I went in back for a package, my pulse skyrocketed and sweat streamed down my forehead, stinging my eyes. And Jun was right: my deliveries included a shit-ton of dog food. Nine of my customers had purchased window-unit air conditioners to cope with the heat wave, and I had to hump these enormous boxes all the way up their long suburban driveways. My back was holding up okay, but after the third or fourth air conditioner I felt my hands and arms cramping up, a telltale symptom of heatstroke. So I stopped at McDonald's and rested in their air-conditioned dining room and drank a large orange Hi-C, a quick break to regulate my body temperature. It was not quite eleven o'clock in the morning, and I still had another 139 parcels to deliver.

I'd hoped that work would keep my thoughts off Maggie, but I couldn't stop worrying about her. Was she still in Osprey Cove? And where would she live, now that Aidan was gone? Catherine Gardner had been so quick to tell me the truth—but what would happen if she ever confessed her sins to someone outside the family? Tammy claimed that wealthy criminals always got off scot-free, but I could name a dozen recent examples to the contrary: Jeffrey Epstein. Harvey Weinstein. Bill Cosby. The Gardners may have seemed invincible, but I wasn't so sure. I drove through a four-way intersection and my travel computer beeped in error, warning me that I'd missed my turn and directing me to an alternate route. A tiny oversight that added six minutes to my workday.

By twelve-thirty my arms were cramping up again and my heart was revving like an engine stuck in neutral. I knew that I ought to stop and cool off, but there was no place to pull over. I was on a two-lane highway in a state forest with shallow ravines on both sides of the road. I had traveled this route many thousands of times, but that day the forest looked strange and unfamiliar. Like my windshield was filtering the view and saturating all the colors. I didn't realize it at the time, but this was probably the moment when I started to lose consciousness.

And then, in the distance, I saw a car parked on the side of the road, hazard lights flashing. A bright red Honda Civic. There wasn't much of a shoulder, so most of the vehicle was resting in my lane. A woman knelt at the back of the car, cranking a jack and raising the rear left wheel off the pavement. A man waited nearby, holding a spare tire, and my broiling brain recognized these people as Dawn Taggart and Aidan Gardner. (Wasn't this precisely how they met? Changing a tire on the side of the road?) I slowed my speed and drifted into the opposite lane to get around them. I craned my neck to take a better look at their faces, and my truck kept on drifting.

My left front tire went off the asphalt and into the grassy ravine and the soft earth immediately gave way. The steering wheel spun out of my hands and the truck pivoted sideways. Everything in my windshield turned clockwise, like the world was revolving around me. Then the glass exploded and I raised my hands to shield my face. The safety belt cut into my breastbone, pinning me to my seat. I clenched my hands into fists and braced myself for impact as all my parcels toppled from their shelves and tumbled around and around my truck like socks in the dryer.

3.

I woke up in a hospital bed with a broken arm, a broken nose, three cracked ribs, and symptoms of moderate heatstroke—but thankfully no one else was hurt. The biggest casualties of the crash were my vehicle and my twenty-six-year streak of accident-free driving. I was visited by a union rep who assured me I was at no risk of losing my job. Then I was visited by a suit from the corporate office who seemed a lot more ambivalent; I asked about my future with the company, and he simply answered, "Well, the investigation is still pending."

That same day I was visited by a reporter from the local newspaper in Scranton; she was writing a story about the appalling working conditions of delivery drivers. Her theory was that UPS management was somehow responsible for my accident, that the lack of air-conditioning in my truck had nearly killed me, but I told her she had it all wrong. I insisted that I'd been properly trained to work in extreme temperatures, that I caused the accident through my own carelessness, and I wasn't going to start blaming others for my own dumb mistakes.

The doctors kept me at Holy Redeemer for three nights, and plenty of people came to see me. Drivers, preloaders, and other assorted folks from the warehouse, but also Tammy (who brought me a phone and a charger) and even two of my favorite customers, who'd heard about the crash on the local news. But a full forty-eight hours passed before I heard anything from Maggie. I thought she might rush home to see me but instead she called from Boston, where she was helping the Gardners plan a memorial service for Aidan. She said it would be a small affair, immediate family only, and there was no reason for me or Tammy to attend. And maybe this was just the painkillers talking, but I told her I was fine. "It's just a couple scratches. Nothing to worry about."

The next day, I went home with my right arm in a sling and a heavy plaster cast, and for the first time in twenty-six years I found myself with absolutely nothing to do. I tried watching daytime television but, holy mother of God, what happened to daytime television? When I was a kid, it used to be silly sitcoms and *The Price Is Right*. Now it's just endless marathons of *Dr. Pimple Popper* and *FBoy Island*. The cable news was even worse, with all the patriots hating California and all the progressives hating Florida and everyone hating Congress. All these shows made my blood boil, and I clicked off the TV, convinced that the whole stupid world was going down the toilet.

I never heard another word from Armando Castado, but I suspect his thumb gently tipped the scales of my accident investigation. After a complete review of my vehicle's many sensors and computers and onboard cameras, the committee voted to put me on "paid leave through pension." Meaning that I would continue collecting my base salary for the next three years until I was eligible to retire—but I would never drive for UPS again. When I heard the news, I almost wept. I'd spent the last twenty-six years fantasizing about my last day on the job, but I never imagined it would end like this: in a windowless second-floor conference room with a half dozen lawyers, execs, and union reps sitting in hard-backed chairs while I signed my name to endless waivers and releases.

And after that happened, I had no reason to get out of bed in the morning. I had no reason to do much of anything, and I found myself falling into a pretty dark place. I stopped responding to texts and phone calls. I stopped looking after my house—and started spending way too much time looking at my stupid phone. I wasted entire afternoons obsessing over the accident, replaying the details beat by beat and trying to pinpoint the exact moment I'd lost control. I remembered thinking the man on the side of the road looked exactly like Aidan Gardner, and I'd wanted to stop and ask him questions: Did he know if my daughter was okay? And why in the world had he left me $1,000? I still had the envelope of hundred-dollar bills stashed inside my dresser, because I felt too guilty to deposit them in my bank account.

It was late in August, nine-thirty on a Tuesday morning, when my sister roused me from sleep with an unexpected phone call. She'd been offered a gig caring for an Alzheimer's patient in Pocono Pines, and she needed me to watch Abigail for a couple of days.

"A couple *days?*"

"Just until school starts. This job pays fifty dollars an hour, and I can't say no to that kind of money."

I hadn't seen Abigail since we'd left Osprey Cove, and the last I'd heard was that she'd gone back to live with her birth mother. Only there must have been some kind of problem, because a week later Abigail moved to an orchard in Kutztown, one of these family-farm operations where six or eight fosters bunk together and help with chores after school. That must not have worked out, either, because now Abigail was back in my sister's condo.

"I can't do it, Tammy."

"Why not? What are you doing today?"

The answer was nothing—but I was too groggy to dream up a decent excuse. "I'm still wearing my cast. How can I babysit with a broken arm?"

"You don't have to lift her. She's not an infant."

"I can't do it. I'm sorry."

She hung up, so I thought the matter was settled and fell back to sleep. But twenty minutes later I could hear Tammy unlocking my front door—and when I stumbled out to my living room, Abigail was standing there with a pencil case and a Sudoku magazine, wearing sneakers and shorts and a backpack like she'd just arrived for summer camp.

"Hey, Mister Frank."

"Where's Tammy?"

"She just left. She said she'd be back at seven-thirty."

"Seven-thirty *tonight?*"

"I think? Sorry."

Abigail looked different than I remembered. All the lice were gone and she was growing out her hair; now it was an awkward shaggy length between a buzz cut and a bob. She removed her backpack but stopped short of placing it on the floor. Like she wasn't sure where to put it, or herself.

"You can have the couch," I told her. "I'll take the recliner."

She moved to sit down and tripped on a plank of wood, part of the homemade coffee table that I still hadn't finished assembling. I apologized for the mess and opened the curtains to let more light into the room. And this just made everything look worse. I'd let my house-keeping slide, and there were little drips of coffee and Chinese food all over my furniture. I handed the TV remote to Abigail and told her we could watch anything she wanted. "Or you can go play outside but stay off the train tracks."

She took a walk to scope out the neighborhood and came back after twenty minutes, claiming there was no one around. You used to see lots of kids on my block riding dirt bikes or just farting around, but now I guess they all stay inside and look at the internet. Abigail turned on the TV and we spent the day watching shark documentaries on the Discovery Channel—hours of exclusive interviews with marine biologists and shark attack survivors. Sometimes Abigail would work on her puzzle book, and when she got bored of that I gave her a roll of paper towels to draw on. And when she got hungry, I sent her down the street to the Exxon Mobil with money for a hot dog and pretzel, because I couldn't motivate myself to cook anything.

The next day was more of the same, but sometime in the afternoon I fell asleep in my recliner—and when I opened my eyes, Abigail was gone. On my television screen, a shark was silently prowling through cloudy red water in search of its next meal. I wondered if maybe Abigail had walked to the gas station for another hot dog. Instead, I found her in Maggie's bedroom, going through my daughter's dresser and quietly inspecting all her things. I watched from the doorway as she touched the old sports trophies, then sifted through a drawer of neatly folded sweaters. Then she knelt beside a wicker basket full of stuffed animals and pulled out the Build-A-Bear that Maggie had designed some fifteen years ago, on our trip to the King of Prussia Mall near Philadelphia.

"You can have that, if you want," I said.

Abigail hadn't realized I was watching. She was so startled she dropped it. "Really?"

"Anything in that basket, you can take. You might as well. Maggie's never coming back here."

I didn't know it was true until I said it out loud. In the month since the wedding, my daughter's job had taken her all over the world—to Singapore and London and Los Angeles—but nothing was drawing her back to Stroudsburg, not even the accident that shattered my ribs and landed me in the hospital.

I opened the closet and gestured to all the colorful dresses on hangers. "This stuff is fair game, too. Help yourself."

Abigail had zero interest in the clothes, but she dragged the wicker basket out to the living room and began to inventory its contents: SpongeBob, Curious George, lots and lots of Beanie Babies. She marveled over every item before setting it on the couch. Shark Week was still playing on the television, but I switched it off and just watched Abigail play with the toys. I hadn't seen her this excited since Osprey Cove. I suddenly felt an overwhelming urge to escape the funk of my house and leave it all behind. I stood up and grabbed the keys to my Jeep.

"Come on," I told her.

"Where are we going?"

"I don't know. Anywhere."

That first afternoon we just drove around the neighborhood. I took her to the patch of highway where I crashed my UPS truck and showed her how I went off the road. And then we drove past St. Luke's, the church where Colleen and I were married, and Silvio's, the Italian restaurant where we'd had our wedding reception. I didn't expect Abigail to be interested, but she had scores of questions: How many guests did we invite? What was the song for our first dance? What *was* Italian food, anyway? This last question blew my mind. How do you get to be ten years old without tasting Italian food? So we went inside and I explained the situation to the waitress. She was happy to bring us little sample plates of all the house specialties: gnocchi, bruschetta, risotto, lasagna, chicken parm, broccoli rabe. We ate until we were stuffed and then Abigail said she'd never had tiramisu, she'd never even had gelato, so we had to order those, too. It made me happy to see her looking so happy. Honest to God, it felt like the first meaningful thing I'd accomplished all summer.

So the next day, I tried to do it again. We made a whole long list of things she'd never experienced, and then we spent the rest of the summer experiencing them. We toured Crystal Cave and the Hershey chocolate factory. We ate dinner at Shady Maple, the largest smorgasbord buffet in America, and at Shogun Palace, one of those Japanese places where they cook everything right in front of you. We even drove down to Philadelphia, so she could attend her first Major League Baseball game. It was a lot of traveling but it felt good to be back on the road, driving with the windows down and the music way up.

For the last day of summer vacation I wanted to do something really special, so I brought Abigail to Casey's Canoes on the Delaware Water Gap. I hadn't been there since Maggie was a kid, but the place was just like I remembered. They rented watercrafts and provided transportation up the river, and they even sold brown-bag lunches with sandwiches and apples and juice boxes. Within the hour, Abigail and I were riding on a big yellow school bus full of rowdy teenagers. With my arm still in a cast, everyone looked at me like I was crazy. The bus driver asked how I planned to make it down the river, and I explained that Abigail would do all the work.

The Delaware River is long and wide and most of the year it runs really slow; if you're looking for white-water action, it's a massive disappointment. But if you're a ten-year-old just getting started, it's the perfect place to learn. After thirty minutes of coaching, Abigail was paddling with confidence and steering us around boulders and bridge piles. For lunch we found a little island full of families and stopped there to eat our sandwiches. I found a nice seat in the shade of a weeping willow while Abigail splashed around in the water with some kids. And to my great surprise I found myself wishing that summer didn't have to end.

4 .

But the summer *did* end, so Tammy assured me I was off the hook
and my childcare services were no longer required. I kept helping out,
anyway, just to make things easier for my sister. If Abigail had math
club after school, I made sure she arrived on time. I brought her to
a pediatrician to get all her shots up-to-date. I found a good dentist
to fill her many cavities, and he referred us to an orthodontist, who
peered inside her mouth with wonder and awe, like he'd just been
presented with the greatest technical challenge of his career. "She's
going to need a lot of braces," he announced. And then I spent a week
on the phone with Pennsylvania Medicaid, begging them to cover
the costs. They kept trying to steer me to a cheaper provider, but I
wanted the job done right, so I ended up paying most of the bill myself. I wasn't going to let some jackass ruin her teeth.

By October, the three of us had settled into a nice daily routine.
One afternoon, my sister hit a snag at work and asked me if I could
get Abigail from school, so I picked her up in my Jeep and brought
her to Tammy's condo. I made tacos for dinner while Abigail sprawled
out on the living room floor with her homework. After we finished
the dishes, we watched a little Netflix together—one of these cooking shows where complete morons attempt to bake, with disastrous

results—and then I sent her upstairs to bed. I gave her a half hour to read, and then I stopped by her bedroom to say "Lights out."

"Five more minutes?" she asked. "Please?" She was reading a fantasy novel about Warrior Cats, and she swore she was ten pages from the end.

"Five minutes," I agreed. "But you better be asleep when Tammy gets home, or I'll catch all kinds of hell."

Abigail flashed me a thumbs-up and returned to her book—and as I turned to leave, I noticed a map pinned to her wall, just above her dresser.

She had recently gone on a decorating spree, papering her bedroom with mazes, crossword puzzles, Sudoku grids, Disney movie posters, and glossy advertisements cut from magazines—and the map was half-hidden amid the clutter. It was a small topographical drawing of Lake Wyndham, specifically the square mile or so fronting Osprey Cove, with wavy contour lines and numbers detailing the elevation of the land and the depths of the water.

"Abigail, what is this?"

"The summer camp."

"Where did you get it?"

"Aidan gave it to me."

"When?"

She shrugged. "When we got back from New Hampshire, I found it in my suitcase. In the side pocket. I think because Aidan knew I liked geography, so he wanted me to have it."

I looked more closely at the picture. It looked like a photocopy of a much larger map, the kind of navigational tool used by boaters and fishermen. Someone had used a pencil to sketch in some additional features: the boathouse, the L-shaped dock, and Osprey Lodge. But the most notable addition was a bright red X in the deepest section of the water, an irregularly shaped crater with a depth of fifty-two meters.

"How do you know it's from Aidan?"

"There's a note on the back," Abigail said. "You can take it off the wall if you want to read it."

I carefully unpinned the map and then turned it over to read the message: *This could be helpful someday. Don't be afraid to use it. —Aidan*

Abigail saw the confusion on my face and offered a theory. "I think it's a treasure map."

"You do?"

"One day, I'm going to go back to Osprey Cove and look for the X. I'll buy a scuba suit to see what's down there. You should come with me."

"Have you shown this to anyone? Has Tammy seen it?"

Abigail shook her head. "She says we're not supposed to talk about Osprey Cove. She says that if DHS knew what happened there, we would all get in trouble."

I felt like I was going to be sick. I knew I had to choose my next words very carefully. "Abigail, listen to me. I think you got this map by mistake. I don't think Aidan meant for you to have it." Her expression turned suspicious and I quickly explained: "I think Aidan wanted to give you money. I think he wanted to give you a thousand dollars."

She thought I was teasing her. "Very funny, Mister Frank."

"No, I'm serious." I proceeded to outline my theory. I told her that Aidan had left $1,000 in *my* suitcase because he didn't realize Abigail and I had switched bedrooms. "You were in the master suite and I was in the kids' room. So he put the money in my suitcase, and he put this map in yours."

"That's crazy! Are you kidding me? *One thousand dollars?*" By this point she had cast her book aside and was standing up on her mattress in her pajamas. "Do you still have it?"

"I do. I haven't spent a single penny."

"Then will you trade it with me?"

I don't think she ever imagined I would say yes, but I agreed it was the fair thing to do. I had eighty-four dollars in my wallet and I gave her all of it, with a promise to put the rest in a savings account. I told her I would try to get her a bankbook, if they still made them, so she could keep track of her wealth and grow it with future deposits. Abigail fanned the bills with an eye-popping grin, like the lottery winners in a Mega Millions commercial. But I could barely hold on to the map because my hands had started to shake.

5.

"Burn it," Tammy said.

This was later in the evening, after Abigail was asleep and my sister was home from work. We sat at her kitchen table with two cups of decaf and the map unfolded between us. The wavy topographic lines seemed to pulse and vibrate if I stared at them too long, like the document was radioactive.

"You can't keep it, Frankie. It's too dangerous. So you either burn it, or you turn it over to the FBI. And I know you're not turning it over to the FBI."

I thought back to Linda and Brody Taggart and their tidy little home on Alpine Creek. I liked to tell myself that Aidan's death had brought the family some measure of peace and closure. But I hated that they never had the chance to recover their daughter's body and give her a proper burial. It could really mess me up if I dwelled too long on it. I'd have to stop and remind myself that Maggie's well-being was still my primary concern.

So as soon as I got home, I went outside to my backyard and dumped a bag of charcoal briquettes into my hibachi grill. I soaked them in lighter fluid and struck a match, then waited until the coals were nice and hot before retrieving the map from my pocket. I wanted to make sure it was completely obliterated, that no forensic investigator would ever recover flecks of the thing from my grill. And just before I set the paper onto the flames, I wondered if I was throwing away an opportunity.

Here was one last chance to show my daughter how much I trusted her. To show her how much I'd learned from the mistakes of my past. If anyone was ever going to need leverage against the Gardners, it was Maggie. Not me. I refolded the map and put it back in my pocket. And then I replaced the lid on the grill. By this point it was nearly eleven o'clock but I tried dialing Maggie, anyway. I reached her at the penthouse apartment in Beacon Tower. She explained that she was still living there, that the Gardners had encouraged her to stay as long as she liked.

"What's going on?" she asked.

Her voice was bright and cheerful, like we were the sort of father and daughter who talked every day, and maybe I just needed to run over to borrow a cup of sugar.

I said that I needed to tell her something in confidence. Something that she could never pass along to Errol or Gerry or anyone else. "Can I trust you to keep this between us?"

"What are you talking about?"

"You have to promise first. Please."

"Fine, I promise. What is it?"

"Do you remember Abigail? Tammy's foster kid?"

"The one with the head lice? Sure."

"She found something in her suitcase. Right before Aidan died, he left her a map. Of Lake Wyndham. And there's an X on it. Marking a spot on the water. I think it's—"

"Wait, wait, wait." Suddenly she was very engaged in the conversation. "You need to back up. Why does Abigail have a map of Lake Wyndham?"

So I had to explain the whole story—how Aidan inadvertently left the map in Abigail's suitcase instead of mine. "He was trying to give me some protection. So I'd have leverage over the Gardners."

"And it's just been hanging in Abigail's bedroom? Where anyone can see it?"

"It's fine, Maggie. She's still new here. She hasn't made a lot of friends yet."

"What about social workers? Don't they visit the condo to check on her?"

"Trust me: I'm the only person who knows what it means. And I was going to burn it, just to get rid of it. But then I thought maybe you should have it. In case *you* ever need it. If you want to come home, I'll give it to you."

"Well, I would really like to see it but I'm flying to Madrid on Wednesday and I'll be gone for ten days."

I didn't want to sit on the map for ten days. I suggested that maybe I just burn it, after all.

"Or what if you came to Boston?" she suggested. "Are you doing anything tomorrow? We could meet here. I'll see if Lucia's free to make something. You liked her cooking, remember?"

6 .

I'd packed a small overnight bag with clothes and a toothbrush but I didn't bother finding a hotel; I wasn't sure if I'd need one. I remembered that the penthouse apartment had a guest bedroom and I hoped Maggie might invite me to stay over. Maybe we'd stay up the whole night talking. Maybe we'd find a Waffle House in the morning and go out for pancakes.

These were stupid thoughts. I know that now. There are no limits to how far parents will go to deceive themselves.

It was late Tuesday afternoon when I crossed the Zakim Bridge and followed the familiar road back to Beacon Tower. This time, I simply left my Jeep in a vast employee parking lot, then crossed the street to enter the lobby. Once again, the beautiful Olivia was working the front desk and she welcomed me back with a warm smile. "It's wonderful to see you, Mr. Szatowski," she said. "How was your drive?"

"Pretty good, Olivia. Thank you. Do you need to see my license?"

"Oh, no, sir, you're all set. Elevator D is right behind you. Enjoy your visit."

I entered the familiar black metal box without buttons, and once again the elevator seemed to move of its own free will. The small digital screen flickered to life and tallied the numbers of the passing floors:

2–3–5–10–20–30–PH1–PH2–PH3. Then at last the doors parted and I was back in the apartment and Maggie was waiting for me—all dressed up in a shiny sleeveless gown and diamond earrings. "Dad! You made it!"

Her hair was longer and two shades darker than I remembered—she must have colored it since the wedding. She wore tall spindly heels that lifted her face to my level. She greeted me with a gentle embrace, taking great care not to jostle my sling. I pulled her closer and assured her that my arm was already healed. The doctor was going to remove the cast at the end of the week, so she was free to hug me without the risk of breaking anything.

The apartment had been redecorated. It still had the same floor plan with the same big windows overlooking the city skyline. But all the furniture was new and the black-and-white paintings were gone. They'd been replaced by a couple of tasteful prints from Boston's Museum of Fine Arts. Sailboats and flowers in vases, that sort of thing.

"No more faces?"

She laughed. "Thank God, right? Those things always gave me the creeps." She shivered at the recollection. "I was glad to put them in storage."

I realized I was underdressed again. I'd worn a sweater and jeans because the bulky plaster cast made most other choices impossible, but Maggie looked like she was ready for the Academy Awards. "I didn't realize we were going out," I told her. "You said we would eat here."

"We are. You're totally fine. Everyone else is on the patio."

I followed her across the living room, and with a sinking feeling I realized Errol Gardner and Gerry Levinson were waiting outside on the balcony, leaning against the railing with tumblers of bourbon. Maggie opened the sliding door and they greeted me with fake smiles.

"Frank Szatowski!" Errol said. "How's the arm, my friend? We heard you took a real tumble."

I ignored him and turned to my daughter. "What are they doing here?"

"This concerns all of us, Dad. I think it's better if we work together. Just be transparent about everything."

I realized Hugo was there, too. Standing at the far end of the patio and pretending to ignore my arrival. He studied the skyline with a flat, neutral expression.

And on one of the sofas, Sierra was slumped face down with her eyes closed, gently snoring. She'd kicked off her heels and the hem of her dress was riding up, leaving parts of her thong exposed.

"What happened to her?" I asked.

"Too many cocktails," Gerry explained. With an affectionate smile, he reached for a blanket, shook it open, and carefully draped it across his wife's body. "When you only weigh ninety-eight pounds, you really have to pace yourself."

I couldn't resist turning to Errol and asking after his wife. "How's Catherine doing? Is she going to join us, too?"

He seemed disappointed with me, like I'd made a joke in poor taste. "It's been a difficult year for her, Frank. She's lost her only son."

"But instead of staying home to support her, you're here to see me. I'm flattered."

Because I just didn't care anymore. Or as the young Capaciti employees might say, I had zero fucks to give. Errol didn't seem troubled by my sarcasm but Hugo tensed up, like he was just waiting for a signal to throw me off the balcony.

"Frank, I came here to express my appreciation to you. The information you found has a lot of value to a lot of people, and I know you could have made a different choice."

"I brought it for Maggie. Not for you or anyone else. She's the only reason I'm here."

The glass door slid open and a smiling Lucia stepped outside, dressed in a white chef's coat, and I thought I recognized a flicker of sympathy in her eyes. I imagined that she'd overheard a lot of conversations while doing her invisible labors in the kitchen, that she was probably burdened with lots of ugly and unpleasant secrets. Maybe she'd always known the wedding was a farce, that my daughter had been lying to me from the start. Because she seemed to understand how much it hurt me to be there. "It's nice to see you again, Frank. Could I bring you something to drink? We have beer, or cocktails, or really anything you'd like."

Over on the sofa, Sierra flopped onto her side and her blanket slipped to the floor, exposing her thong and bare bottom to the entire city skyline. Lucia was unflappable and pretended not to notice.

"Thank you, Lucia, but I'm only staying for a minute. Just a quick hello and then I'll be out of your hair."

Maggie put up a small, polite protest. "Dad, are you sure? She's made her famous roast duck. It takes seventy-two hours to prepare and it's out of this world."

I said I was very sorry to miss it but insisted I needed to get back to Stroudsburg.

"Some other time," Lucia promised, and I think she knew the truth before I did: I was never coming back to the apartment; I would never sample Lucia's cooking again. I waited until she was inside with the door closed before reaching for the map and passing it to my daughter.

"Aidan called it protection. I think he was trying to give me some kind of leverage. But I'm never going to do anything with it, Maggie. I only want good things for you. So you might as well have it."

"Thank you, Dad. I appreciate it."

My daughter studied the map before passing it to Errol and Gerry, and then they signaled for Hugo to come take a look as well. They all seemed unafraid to handle it with their bare hands, and I understood why a moment later, when Errol brought it over to the firepit and carefully fed the map to the flames. It took a moment to catch—and then with a flash the fire engulfed it, reducing the paper to a few flecks of ash. Over on the sofa, Sierra rolled onto her back and softly whispered in her sleep: "Don't, don't, don't—"

Errol gently clapped his hands together, suggesting the problem had been resolved. "Frank, are you sure we can't get you a drink? The traffic's crazy right now. You may as well stay for a beer."

I didn't want to stay any longer than necessary. And I really didn't want to say goodbye to Maggie in front of all these assholes, but she hadn't left me with any choice. "Three years ago, you asked for my help and I let you down, and I've always felt bad about it. So I hope this makes up for it, Maggie. I only want the best for you." There were a million other thoughts going through my head—so many more things I wanted to say—but I realized there was only time to make one last point: "If you ever get tired of all this, if you don't want to be here anymore, you can always come home. Anytime you need a place to stay, I'll be waiting for you."

"I know, Dad. Thank you. Let me give you a hug."

She stepped forward and put her arms around me, and I sure hoped this wasn't the last time I'd ever see her but I realized it might be.

And I really couldn't make sense of it. Somewhere inside her was this kid who loved to read *Good Night, Gorilla*. A kid who loved to play Hug Monster, a kid who loved strawberry pancakes with extra whipped cream. A sweet little girl who ran laughing through lawn sprinklers on hot summer days. I didn't know what had happened to that kid. I didn't know where I went wrong or how I screwed up, but I knew I would always love her, despite everything that came after. I broke away because I felt myself starting to cry and I was not going to let Errol see that. *Come on, Frankie. Keep it together.* I said goodbye and my voice was barely a whisper: "I love you, Maggie. Be good, okay?"

"All right, Dad. Safe travels."

Then I turned and went for the patio door, and I heard Gerry clear his throat. "Frank, there's just one more thing," he said, reaching into his pocket for a small notebook. "Where's the girl staying now?"

The question hung in the air, and I was still too choked up to understand it. "What girl?"

"Abigail Grimm. The girl who found the map."

"She's with my sister."

Hugo brought his tablet computer over to Gerry and showed him the screen. "And your sister's still at Eighteen Conover Road, unit one-zero-six?"

"Yes, but why does it matter?"

Gerry dismissed my question with a wave of his hand. "Just checking."

"Checking for what?"

I looked from Errol to Maggie. Neither was willing to answer my question. "What's happening here?"

At which point Gerry finally spoke up: "Our understanding is that Aidan gave the map to Abigail. Possibly by mistake, as you suspect. Or perhaps it was intentional. Maybe he wanted Abigail to have it. Maybe he shared other information with her. The truth is, we don't know. And that's a problem."

"She's only ten years old," I reminded them.

"A very bright ten years old," Gerry said. "With an incredible memory for detail. Your sister thinks she should go on *Jeopardy!*"

"Little pitchers have big ears," Errol said. "She probably heard all kinds of rumors that weekend."

Maggie reminded me that Abigail had even met Brody Taggart, when we'd first arrived in New Hampshire. "Brody told you that Aidan killed Dawn Taggart and hid her body at the camp. Then three days later, Aidan gave Abigail a map of the camp with an X on it. Sooner or later, she's going to connect the dots."

"And do what? She's in fifth grade. She sleeps with stuffed animals."

Errol spoke in a calm, level voice that suggested everything would be fine. "We're just trying to stay ahead of the situation, Frank. The bottom line is: you're family and we trust you. We know you want the best for Margaret. And we trust Tammy for the same reason. But the girl is a wild card. An unknown variable. She'll piece together the puzzle, eventually. And one day when she's grown-up and home-less and pregnant and addicted to drugs, she might try to trade on this information. So our challenge is: How do we prevent that from happening?"

As Errol explained all this, I noticed Hugo typing a message into his phone. "What are you doing?"

He ignored me until he'd finished typing the message and sent it off. "You needn't concern yourself, Mr. Szatowski. You've already done the most important thing, which was bringing the problem to our attention. We can take care of the rest."

Over on the sofa, Sierra awakened from her nap, sat up, and smacked her lips together. She looked like she'd accidentally swallowed a bug. "Sorry," she murmured, before looking down at her legs and tugging her dress to a more modest length.

"No need to apologize," Gerry assured her. "You're just sleepy."

She pinched two fingers between her lips and then carefully extracted a long length of hair, then studied it through bleary eyes. "This is definitely *not* one of mine." Then she walked unsteadily to the edge of the balcony, tossed the hair over the railing, and watched the wind carry it away. Everyone seemed unconcerned, like this behavior was all perfectly normal.

"Maggie, I need you to translate this conversation. What are we actually talking about?"

She said a translation wasn't necessary. "I think you understand the conversation perfectly."

"And you're okay with it?"

"I'm not happy about it. None of us *want* this to happen. But I understand why it *needs* to happen."

And I suppose that's when I knew I'd completely lost her. Up until that point, I'd been willing to rationalize just about anything. But this? It was so monstrous, so barbaric, so immoral and evil—

"There's a silver lining we can all feel good about," Gerry continued. "Next week, the Capaciti Cares Foundation will make a generous donation to foster care charities in Abigail's name. Enough money to fund twenty-five college scholarships for disadvantaged young women. That's twenty-five little Abigails getting a boost out of poverty toward a brighter future."

At some point I stopped listening. I tried to imagine how it might happen. Every weekday, Abigail walked home from school through several busy intersections; there were multiple opportunities for a hit-and-run accident.

Or maybe it would happen at the condo. An attempted burglary gone wrong, an accidental house fire, maybe some glitch with the toaster oven.

Or maybe she would simply go missing. Maybe the police would discover her sweatshirt in the woods behind Tammy's condo.

"Dad?" Maggie snapped her fingers in front of my face. "Did you hear what Gerry just said? About the scholarships?"

"When would all this happen?"

Gerry promised me I had nothing to worry about. "By the time you get home, it will all be over."

He spoke with the confidence of an experienced attorney assuring his nervous client that everything was going to be fine. The plan was already in motion. Everything had been decided before I'd arrived. I checked the urge to reach for my phone and call Tammy, call the police, call anyone.

Errol leaned closer to me, interlacing his fingers and studying my expression. "Frank, are you okay? Is there anything we need to talk about?"

I forced myself to mirror his behavior. I knew I had to stay calm, to react in a way he would understand. Suddenly I wished I had asked Lucia for a drink, just so I could be holding a glass. A prop to draw attention away from my face.

"I didn't want to bring her to the wedding," I reminded him. "It was all Tammy's idea. I told her it was a mistake."

"I remember," Errol said. "As I recall, you seemed pretty unhappy about it."

"Exactly. She never should have been there in the first place. So I don't really care how you handle the problem."

Errol relaxed. "That's good, Frank. That's very understanding of you."

"But if you want me to be okay with it, I'm going to need five thousand shares."

For a moment, I worried that I hadn't asked for enough, that my figure was too low to be convincing. But then Gerry started to object, saying I was in no position to make demands, and I realized I'd hit the bull's-eye.

"You gave my sister a thousand shares just for coming to the wedding," I reminded him. "And I brought you the map tonight on good faith. I was happy to leave here with nothing. But if you want me to be okay with this last part, if you want me to live with it, I need five thousand shares. In a brokerage account. By end of day tomorrow." I turned to Maggie to finish making my case. "You know this is going to wreck your aunt Tammy. She'll be devastated."

"She'll be fine, Dad. There's a long line of kids waiting to take Abigail's place."

"No, Maggie. They'll never trust her with another foster placement. They'll take away her license and she'll never forgive herself. And I'll have to deal with the fallout. You know I will. Now tell them this is fair."

My daughter showed the slightest hint of a smile, and then I recognized something in her expression that I hadn't seen in a long time: respect. For the first time in years, I'd finally impressed her.

"I do think it's fair," she said. "But it's not my decision to make."

"You're damned right it's not," Gerry said.

"I can handle this," Errol told him. "Five thousand shares is a lot of money, Frank."

He was looking into my eyes again, trying to measure the depths of my conviction, and I didn't dare look away. I didn't even blink. This was it, the moment of truth, and the best thing working in my favor was that Errol Gardner had never bothered to get to know me.

So now I could pretend to be anyone.

Finally, he reached for his bourbon and shrugged. "I can't transfer that kind of stock overnight. There are certain precautions we take to avoid scrutiny. But give us seventy-two hours and you'll have it. Fair enough?"

In other words: he believed me. But then of course he believed me. To men like Errol Gardner, my response was perfectly rational. In his worldview, every relationship was transactional—and when you found yourself with the upper hand, it was natural to exploit your advantage for maximum gain. Cooperation was for chumps. Grace was for losers.

"Seventy-two hours is fine," I said.

He smiled. "Well, I guess this dinner is going to cost a little more than I expected. Are you sure you won't stay and join us?"

I pointed out that I still had a long drive back to Stroudsburg—and much to deal with upon my return. "But I will use the restroom before I go."

Maggie offered to show me the way but I told her I remembered how to find it. I left them on the balcony, crossed the living room, and followed the short hallway past the powder room and the closets and all the way back to the master bathroom. The door was ajar; I went inside and locked it. Someone must have recently showered, because there were traces of condensation on the mirror and wall tiles.

I immediately reached for my phone and called my sister. "Hey, Frankie, how's—"

"Tammy, listen: Abigail isn't safe."

"What?"

"Get her out of your condo. Right now. Go to a hotel and don't tell anyone where you're going. Do you understand?"

"No! Not at all! Why would I—"

"The map, Tammy. They know she saw the map. They're worried she'll talk. Someone is coming to your condo right now."

My sister called for Abigail, asking her to come downstairs and put on her sneakers. "We need to take a ride, kiddo." Suddenly I could hear her bustling around her kitchen, gathering her wallet, keys, and coat. "This is all my fault," she said in a low voice. "You were right, Frankie. I should have listened to you. What's going to happen?"

"Just get out," I told her. "I'll call you as soon as I can."

She had more questions but I didn't have time to explain. I ended the call and then reached for the lid of the toilet tank. It was awkward and clumsy work with just one hand; I used the front of my leg to keep the lid from sliding out of my grasp, then carefully knelt down and set it on the tiled floor. The black plastic pouch was still duct-taped to the bottom, and I opened the medicine cabinet in search of something sharp, hoping for scissors and settling for pointy tweezers. I scraped at the plastic until it ripped and then used a finger to gouge it open. Inside was a narrow metal box about the size and shape of my checkbook. One of those things people use to back up the data on their computers.

My first night in the apartment, I'd suspected Aidan was hiding secrets from my daughter. But on Maggie's wedding day, she'd made a confession to me. She said she'd recorded hours of conversation with the Gardners: *Errol, Catherine, Aidan, even Gerry. If they ever try something, I'll bring them all down with me.* All this time, the person hiding secrets in the apartment was Maggie. And I was taking her secrets with me.

I put the box in my pocket and then turned my attention back to the porcelain lid. I was tempted to rip off the rest of the plastic and duct tape to eliminate every last trace of the thing. But it was clumsy, difficult work with one hand and there wasn't enough time. I needed to hurry. So I lifted the lid with my good hand and in my rush to stand up I felt wet porcelain slip through my fingers.

It hit the floor and shattered into pieces.

I froze, too scared to move, and waited for footsteps to come rushing down the hallway—for the sounds of Maggie or Hugo or anyone hurrying to inquire about the crash. Surely, they all had heard it.

Unless they were still outside, on the balcony. Surrounded by the noise of the city. After a few more seconds of silence, I allowed myself to think that maybe I would be okay.

As long as I left immediately.

Cleaning the mess was impossible. There was simply too much of it, too many fragments and shards of porcelain, and a white powdery dust all over the floor. Instead I just opened the bathroom door and found Sierra standing in the hallway, rubbing a knuckle into her eye. "Do you got any saline?"

"I'm sorry?"

"For contacts. My lenses are so dry."

I opened the medicine cabinet and tried to direct her attention to the shelves, but she was already staring at the toilet tank and the mess on the floor. "What happened?"

I found a bottle of Bausch & Lomb moisture drops and pushed it into her hand. "You should try these. I'll close the door to give you some privacy."

I returned to the living room and found a smiling Maggie waiting at the door of the balcony. "All set?"

"I think so."

Errol and Gerry followed her inside the apartment and Maggie pressed the call button for the elevator. The four of us made awkward chitchat about late-afternoon traffic, and Errol observed there was still a chance of beating the rush if I left soon. I listened for movement in the elevator shaft, for the sounds of motors or gears or pulleys, but I couldn't hear anything. I gave the button another little push, even though it was already lit up, and smiled at my daughter.

"Where's my wife?" Gerry asked.

"In the bathroom. She's having trouble with her contacts."

As if on cue, Sierra emerged from the dark corridor, wobbling on high heels and bracing one hand on the wall to support herself.

"There she is," Errol said.

Somewhere down below, the elevator finally began its ascent, and soft mechanical sounds echoed up the shaft.

"My lenses are killing me," Sierra said. "I think I'm going to nap for a while."

"Take the guest room," Maggie offered. "The bed's all made up."

Sierra nodded. "I think I will. Thank you." She was turning to leave, ready to retreat down the hallway toward the back of the apartment, when she added a final thought: "Also, your dad broke your toilet."

Maggie, Errol, and Gerry all turned to study me, and I laughed, trying to suggest this was just another one of Sierra's bizarre proclamations. "Someone definitely needs a nap."

Sierra must have been more clearheaded than I realized, because she narrowed her eyes and scowled. "I'm serious, Margaret. Don't blame me for the mess because *I* didn't do it. He did. You see the dust on his clothes?"

Maggie looked at my pants. Across my knees was a dusting of white powder that looked like confectioners' sugar. "Dad? What is she talking about?" The elevator was still squealing and churning and groaning and still the doors did not open. "Did you do something to the toilet?"

Even after everything that had happened, I still couldn't bring myself to lie to her. Errol or Gerry, sure. But not Maggie. The most important thing we can give our kids is the truth. She must have seen it in my eyes, because she turned and hurried down the hall to investigate.

"Maggie, come on!" I called. "I'm leaving!"

But still the elevator doors wouldn't open. Errol observed that they were always busy around five o'clock, because it's when employees on the lower levels began leaving for the day. "The parking lot's going to be a zoo."

"If I ever get down there," I joked, while Sierra glowered at me from across the living room. She was sitting on the sofa and waiting for Maggie to return, convinced she would be vindicated.

With a gentle ding the elevator doors finally opened, just as Maggie called to me from the depths of the apartment. "Dad! Wait! Stop!"

I pretended not to hear her. "Good night, gentlemen."

"Don't let him leave!"

And I don't know where he came from, or how he moved so quickly, but suddenly Hugo was standing between me and the elevator. "Mr. Szatowski, your daughter's calling. Don't you hear?"

Maggie rushed into the living room, and her eyes were mad with panic. "Give it back."

Errol was confused. "Give what back?"

I realized I had put her in an impossible position. She couldn't ask for the recordings without admitting that the recordings existed— without admitting that she'd been secretly recording Errol and Gerry without their knowledge.

"He took something from me. A hard drive. With personal information." She looked to my waist and she could see the outline of the metal box through my pants. "And now it's in his pocket."

"*And* he broke your toilet," Sierra crowed. "I told you so! But none of you listened because nobody takes me seriously." She tipped back her head and closed her eyes. "So now you can all go fuck yourselves."

Hugo released his hold on the elevator and my heart sank as the doors slid closed. He said, "You can take the next one, Mr. Szatowski. Can you empty your pockets, please?"

I realized that all my hard-earned situational awareness skills had failed me, and I'd stupidly allowed myself to be trapped. Gerry stood to my left, Errol and Maggie were on my right, and Hugo stood in front of me, waiting for me to comply with his instructions. He'd reached inside his coat for a small black pistol but held the weapon casually at his side, simply making its presence known. An unnecessary gesture, in my opinion. I knew he could overpower me even without a weapon. I still remembered how he pinned me to the wall of the fallout shelter and forced me to listen to Aidan's last breaths. I reached into my pocket and removed the hard drive.

"That's it!" Maggie said.

She went to grab it but Hugo ordered her back. "Very slowly now, I want you to hand it to Mr. Gardner," he told me. "Then we'll all find a computer and together we'll see what's on it."

But I couldn't bring myself to turn it over. I knew this tiny metal box was my only hope of keeping Abigail safe. As long as I had their secrets, they wouldn't dare come after her. Hugo raised his gun, pointing it now, encouraging me to follow his instructions.

"Don't be stupid," Errol told me. "Whatever you're thinking, you're not smart enough to—"

He was interrupted by a shriek. Lucia had emerged from the kitchen with an enormous platter of roast duck—but at the sight of the gun, she'd screamed. The serving dish hit the floor with a spectacular crash, and I swung at Hugo with my right arm, connecting my thick plaster cast with the front of his face and mashing his nose like a ripe red strawberry. He dropped his gun and stumbled backward, clutching hands to his face as blood spurted between his fingers. I hesitated only long enough to exchange glances with Lucia—and I swear that woman knew exactly what she was doing, sacrificing her exquisite seventy-two-hour meal to give me a chance.

I ran down the hall, past closet doors and the powder room and the door to the master bedroom. I knew enough about fire codes to know there had to be a second way out of the apartment. And since there were no exits in the kitchen or living room, it had to be the door at the far end of the hall—the one with the metal crash bar across its center. I slammed through it and found myself at the top of a wide concrete stairwell. The letters PH3 were stenciled onto the wall next to a simple fire alarm T-bar. I pulled the lever and the alarm was instantaneous, an earsplitting klaxon in a concrete echo chamber. I ran down to the alarm on PH2 and pulled that lever, too.

By the time I made it to the fortieth floor, the building's employees were already filing into the stairwell while pulling on their jackets and complaining about another pointless fire drill. I pushed past them, trying to descend as quickly as possible but feeling safer with every step. We weren't in Osprey Cove anymore. We were back in the real world where actions had consequences, and I didn't think a wanted international fugitive like Hugo would start firing blindly into a stairwell full of people.

We all emerged into a lobby crowded with employees and unhappy tenants. Poor Olivia at the front desk was surrounded by angry faces and ringing telephones. Through the exterior glass walls, I saw a fire engine approaching with two police cars, lights flashing and sirens blaring. There were streaks of fresh blood on my cast and sweater. I was suddenly aware of a dull throbbing pain in my right forearm and wondered if it was broken again.

I pushed through the lobby and exited to an even larger crowd of people waiting outside on the plaza, some two or three hundred employees gathered in clusters for warmth and conversation. Some people were watching the upper floors for signs of smoke or fire; many more were staring mindlessly into their phones. Three firefighters in bright yellow coats rushed past me, their boots trampling up the plaza stairs. A second fire truck was already pulling into the lot, lights flashing and sirens pealing, and over the din I thought I heard Maggie calling for me.

"Dad! Dad! Dad!"

I might have imagined it. I wasn't sure. I didn't dare turn around to check. The sirens rang louder and people clapped their hands over their ears, swelling toward the building to escape the deafening noise.

"Dad! Dad! Dad!"

I walked alone against the crowd, the only person actively moving *toward* the sirens, until my ears were numb and I couldn't hear her voice anymore.

Don't turn around, Frankie.

Keep walking and don't look back.

7.

Supercuts closed at nine o'clock and I didn't make it back to Stroudsburg until ten-fifteen. My gas gauge was well past empty and my engine was running on vapors, but I'd been too scared to stop and fill up.
I knew I didn't have a moment to waste. I pulled into the strip mall
parking lot, left my Jeep in a loading zone, and ran past all the skateboarders in front of the Chipotle. There were a half dozen teenagers
doing tricks and flips off the wheelchair ramp. The sign in front of
Supercuts was flipped to CLOSED but thank God I could see Vicky
through the window, pushing around a broom and sweeping up the
hair clippings. She'd locked the door, so I rapped my knuckles on the
glass to get her attention. Without glancing up she called out, "We're
closed."

I knocked louder. "Vicky, it's Frank."

She paused for just a split second and then continued her sweeping, pretending this meant nothing to her. "You'll have to come back in
the morning. We have stylists on duty starting at seven-thirty."

"Vicky, please. I need to talk."

"Well, I can't imagine why. I'm just the person who cuts your hair."

"I didn't mean that. I'm sorry I said it. Can you please unlock this
door?"

"And I can't have customers in the salon after closing. It's against corporate policy."

Now she was arranging the fashion magazines on the table in the reception area, carefully fanning the latest issues of *Vogue* and *Elle* and *InStyle* for the next day's customers. Vicky was dressed in a black sweater with an orange jack-o'-lantern and letters spelling BOO! Her salon was all decked out for Halloween with paper cutouts of skulls and bats and Frankensteins.

"Maggie's done something terrible, Vicky. I didn't want to tell you, because I'm ashamed of it. But I didn't want to lie, so I've just been avoiding you. And now I'm really in trouble and I need your help. I can't even go home right now. I'm not safe there. Can you please, please open this door?"

With all my shouting, I'd attracted the attention of the skateboarders. They'd interrupted their ollies and kickflips to eavesdrop on our conversation. A girl with a metal rod through her nose offered me the use of her phone, suggesting that I might want to call 911. I waved her off with a polite "No, thank you." I didn't need the police just yet. I'd already called my sister from the highway, and she assured me that she and Abigail were safe inside a room at the Hampton Inn, waiting to hear from me about next steps.

"Vicky, please." I held up the hard drive so she could see it. "I want to play something for you, okay? On your computer? And when you hear it, I think you'll understand why I've been so weird lately. It's going to answer all your questions."

Now I had her attention. Vicky was a smart, inquisitive person. She'd once told me that all her favorite historical romances involved some kind of secret or mystery. She came over with a massive set of keys, unbolted the door, and opened it just far enough to let me slip inside. Then she locked it, lowered the blinds over the windows, and twisted them closed.

"Our computer's ten years old," she warned. "Last week it crashed and we lost all our October appointments, so don't expect any miracles."

We moved behind the reception desk where customers checked in and paid for their haircuts. Vicky found a USB cord connected to the back of the computer tower and I plugged it into the hard drive. A little window opened on the monitor, alerting us to the presence of a new device and asking us to wait. A tiny little hourglass spun around and around and around. Vicky was looking me over, and I realized I smelled awful. I was soaked with sweat after driving home in a mad panic, zig-zagging through traffic at eighty miles an hour. I was tired and severely dehydrated, and there were tiny dry bloodstains on my sweater. "Jeez, Frank, what happened to you?"

I realized Vicky was focused on my hair. I told her I'd started going to the other Supercuts, the one in Mount Pocono, and my new barber was a guy named Rooster who learned to cut hair in prison.

"The way he layers, you're better off cutting it yourself," she said. "Just put a bowl over your head and snip off the edges."

At last a file directory opened on the screen and I saw the disk contained some two dozen items. None of them had coherent names—just scrambles of letters, numbers, dates, and times—but Vicky seemed to recognize an order in them.

"Which one are you looking for?"

"I don't know."

She double-clicked on the first one, and a little audio player opened on the screen. The file was eight minutes and seven seconds, and as soon as it began to play I recognized the voices in the conversation:

AIDAN: So how long are we thinking?

MAGGIE: Two years.

AIDAN: Two *years*?

GERRY: Twelve months should suffice.

AIDAN: That's still too long.

ERROL: What are you thinking?

AIDAN: Thirty days. Like a Vegas wedding.

MAGGIE: No one's going to believe thirty days.

AIDAN: Well, I can't do a full year. I'm sorry. I'd rather go to prison.

GERRY: You won't be the only one going. Your decision has consequences for a lot of people.

ERROL: Son, this isn't what you're thinking. Maggie and I will spend most of the year traveling. Once or twice a month, you'll make a public appearance together. Otherwise, you'll be a free man.

AIDAN: Actually, I'll be a married man. Married to your girlfriend, Dad. Am I the only person who thinks that's fucked up?

"Wait, wait, hang on." Vicky reached out and paused the recording. "Who's marrying Dad's girlfriend? Is that Aidan?"

"Yes."

"Then who's the girlfriend?"

I hesitated just long enough for Vicky to put two and two together and her eyes went wide. Then I clicked open the next file, anxious to hear another conversation.

MAGGIE: . . . And then I called my father.

ERROL: And?

MAGGIE: It went okay. He was happy to hear from me. And he said he'd come to the wedding.

ERROL: Good. People will expect him to be there.

MAGGIE: But he wants to come to Boston this Friday. Meet his future son-in-law. And Aidan's being stubborn.

ERROL: Why?

MAGGIE: He says he already has plans.

ERROL: What kind of plans?

MAGGIE: I don't know. I tried to make it easy for him. I said we'd do it at the apartment and I'd hire Lucia to cook. Two or three hours tops. But he's giving me shit.

ERROL: Tell him it's essential.

MAGGIE: He says it's more than we agreed to.

ERROL: Come here, beautiful. It's going to be fine. I'll have
   Hugo talk to him.

MAGGIE: What's Hugo going to say?

ERROL: Don't worry about it. Just go ahead and plan your
   dinner. I guarantee Aidan will be there.

There was more after that but I lost my focus. I started remembering my first visit to the apartment, remembering Aidan's late arrival
and his general unhappiness at dinner. The way he'd seemed so reluc-
tant to speak with me.

And Maggie warning me not to ask about his bruises.

Vicky hit the space bar on the keyboard to pause the conversation.
She'd been keeping silent but she couldn't hold back anymore. "You
gotta help me, Frank. I need some context here. What are these people
talking about?"

"I'll tell you the whole story," I promised. "But first we need to call
your son."

8.

Seven months later, Abigail made her stage debut in her elementary school musical, *Beauty and the Beast*. She played a spoon (or rather, she played a castle servant who was magically transformed into a spoon). She had just one song and ten minutes of stage time, but she'd been rehearsing for weeks like she had the lead role. At seven o'clock on opening night, the curtain went up and I found myself backstage with a couple of other dads who volunteered to push around the heavy sets. I was surprised to find myself feeling nervous. I really wanted the show to be perfect. After a long week of rehearsals, I'd memorized the lyrics to every song, and I found myself whistling the melodies anytime I was stuck at a red light: *Be our guest, be our guest, our command is your request . . .*

Vicky and Tammy watched from the third row, with an extra seat reserved for Abigail's birth mother—but to no one's great surprise, the poor woman didn't show up. I know that sounds terrible, but I'd stopped blaming her a long time ago. Vicky's been teaching us all about the destructive powers of addiction, and I've learned how hard it is for anyone to make a full recovery. It's not clear if Abigail and her mother will ever have much of a future together. But after everything Tammy and I sacrificed for the kid, there was no way we could let her go back into the system, so my sister filed for adoption last year and signed all the paperwork on New Year's Eve.

I wanted to cosign the documents but Pennsylvania won't allow a brother and sister to share custody, so legally I had to settle for being Uncle Frank. But I still made a point of seeing Abigail every day. I put myself in charge of all her after-school and weekend childcare, so my sister can get a break now and then. And when Abigail's drama teacher needed volunteers with strong backs to help wheel the sets, I was the first person to raise my hand.

Opening night was a huge success. At the end of the show, the whole cast got a standing ovation, and everyone called for the stage crew to come out and take a bow. I was busy dragging a giant papier-mâché log into the wings, where none of the other kids would trip over it, so I missed the curtain call. But later I found Abigail backstage and together we went outside to the school parking lot, where the teachers and parents had organized a reception.

It was the first warm night of the year, and all the kids were reveling in the spring temperatures, running around the blacktop without jackets or gloves, fueled by sugar from all the homemade cookies and cupcakes and brownies. There was a very long line for hand-dipped ice-cream cones but Abigail and I resolved to wait in it, and she passed the time by sharing new jokes she'd learned at math club. Don't start a conversation with pi because it will just go on forever. The best way to keep warm in a freezer is to find a corner, because they're always ninety degrees. And you should never call someone average because it's actually mean. I couldn't even understand this last one, so Abigail had to stop and explain it to me.

As soon as she had her ice cream, she made the mistake of running away—and a large scoop of chocolate chip rolled off her cone and hit the asphalt with a sickening splat. I reached for her empty cone and said, "Take mine. Trade with me."

Abigail refused. She said it wouldn't be fair.

"Come on, I *want* to switch," I told her. "The cone's my favorite part, anyway."

It took a little more cajoling but I got her to swap, and then she carried my ice cream very carefully across the parking lot to join her friends.

Vicky saw what had happened and came walking over. "The cone's your favorite part? Seriously?"

I shrugged and showed her that Abigail's cone wasn't completely empty—there was still a fair amount of chocolate chip ice cream packed into the bottom. "This is plenty for me," I told her. "It's just the right amount."

We had a nice time talking to all the other parents and watching the kids celebrate. After Abigail finished her ice cream, she and the other spoons and forks treated the crowd to an encore performance of "Be Our Guest." They linked their arms and kicked their legs like Rockettes and shrieked the lyrics without a shred of self-consciousness.

Just before the reception ended, I was approached by the school's principal—the only man who'd come to the show dressed in a suit and tie. I knew a lot of the parents disliked him—some of these people were always finding flaws with the teachers and the curriculum and the facilities and even the quality of the hot lunches—but I thought he did a nice job.

"I want to thank you for volunteering tonight," he said. "You're Abigail's father, right?"

I've learned it's important to be clear with school administrators, in case there's ever some kind of medical emergency. "Actually, I'm her uncle."

"Aren't you Frank Szatowski?"

"Yes, but Tammy Szatowski is my sister. We're not married." Tammy was across the playground in conversation with a gaggle of moms, and I pointed her out. "She adopted Abigail last year."

He seemed embarrassed and apologized for the misunderstanding. I could tell he was used to dealing with parents who were a lot more sensitive, and I assured him it was fine. "Abigail loves your school. All her teachers have been fantastic."

I wasn't sure the principal heard my compliment. He still seemed hung up on his mistake. "Can I show you something?" he asked. "If you can spare a minute?"

Vicky and I followed him across the parking lot, inside the building, and up a flight of stairs to a darkened hallway full of classrooms. We stopped at a bulletin board that was covered with photographs and short essays about famous people. There was "#1 Songwriter Beyoncé" and "#1 Quarterback Jalen Hurts" and "#1 Magician Shin Lim." The principal explained that the fifth graders were writing biographies of their heroes and sheroes—men and women who inspire us to do great things. Then he directed my attention to a photo of myself posing in a canoe and an essay titled "#1 Dad Frank Szatowski."

"This is why I got confused," he explained.

I didn't have my reading glasses, so I had to squint to make out the text: *Here are some fun facts about my father: He was a soldier in the United States Army. He fought in the Gulf War. He worked for UPS and drove over ONE MILLION MILES to deliver the stuff you need. He is good at canoeing, making grilled cheese, and getting the bugs out of my room. And he is good at taking care of me.*

"If Abigail's confused about the relationship, we can schedule a sit-down with our head of counseling. She's very good at leading delicate conversations. Would you like her to give you a call?"

I didn't answer because I was afraid my voice might break. I tried to gesture that there was a tiny piece of cone stuck in my throat, and fortunately Vicky came to my rescue.

"Frank's okay with this," she said. "He can talk to Abigail himself and let her know it's all right."

The principal looked relieved—another crisis averted—and said he needed to return to the reception. But he encouraged us to stick around and read the entire essay. "It's one of the better ones. She got an A-plus."

9.

FCI Corbettsville is a minimum-security correctional facility near Bing-hamton, New York—about a two-hour drive from my house. It's a new facility, less than five years old, designed to house nonviolent offenders. Instead of cells with bars, the inmates share spaces that resemble college dorm rooms. Everyone gets a window with a view. There are various jobs that pay sixty cents an hour, plus weekly classes in gardening, baking, cosmetology, finance, web design, and creative writing. It's not nearly as nice as FPC Alderson in West Virginia—aka Camp Cupcake, where Martha Stewart famously served five months after lying to federal in-vestigators. But it's reportedly cleaner and safer than nearly any other federal prison in the United States, and this fact helps me sleep at night.

Visiting hours started at eight-thirty but by seven o'clock I was parked in a long line of cars outside the gates, because all the internet forums advised me to show up early. Once inside, I showed my driver's license to a pair of corrections officers, and then a beautiful black Lab came trotting over to sniff my Jeep for drugs. I greeted the dog with a friendly hello and an officer immediately reprimanded me. "Don't distract the animal," he said. "She's working."

Once inside the prison, I waited in more lines. An officer surveyed my clothes and decided they met the appropriate standards (no hats, no offensive T-shirts, and above all no orange, the color worn by inmates). Then I walked through a metal detector and raised my hands over my head so I could be lightly frisked. I was surprised by the professionalism of the staff; movies and TV shows had prepared me for the worst, but the officers were unfailingly polite; they said "yes, sir" and "no, sir" and "thank you, sir." I wondered if they recognized my name, if they knew the details of my daughter's story, and now they were giving me some kind of preferential treatment. But from what I could gather, they were offering the same courtesies to everyone.

After about an hour of waiting, I finally arrived at a desk marked REGISTRATION. I presented my driver's license and visitation slip to a pair of officers seated behind a plexiglass window. They were both about my age, and they had the easy, familiar rapport of an old married couple—or just two employees who had been working at the same job for a long, long time. The man keyed my information into his computer while his partner compared the photo on my license to my real-life face. Then she must have noticed my date of birth because she smiled and said, "Happy birthday."

"Thank you."

I expected her to follow the comment with some kind of snarky joke, but she was being sincere. She acted like visiting a prison on your birthday was a perfectly normal thing to do—and for many of the parents waiting in line with me, I suppose it was. I felt like I was back in Osprey Cove all over again—back in another strange new world filled with unfamiliar customs and social cues.

The man clicked a few buttons on his keyboard, then sighed and shook his head. "I'm sorry, Mr. Szatowski, but I don't see your name on her list."

I was prepared for this moment. I knew most prisons in the United States required inmates to draft a list of preapproved people for visitation days—family, friends, attorneys, clergy. You can't just wander in off the street and visit the inmate of your choice. Which is exactly what I was trying to do.

"I did the forms online," I told him.

"Right, I see your security clearances. But Margaret needs to add you to her list. So we know she actually wants to visit with you." He shrugged, suggesting that nothing else could be done. "You gotta straighten it out with her and come back. Mondays, Wednesdays, or Saturdays, eight-thirty to three."

He pushed my driver's license back across the counter but I refused to pick it up. I'd seen enough Reddit discussions on FCI Corbettsville to know the officers were considered "decent" and "flexible" and "sometimes acknowledge that you're an actual human being."

"I'm sorry for the mix-up. This is my first time."

"Rules are on the website."

"And I woke up at four-thirty to beat the traffic. I drove all the way from Stroudsburg."

"Tell Margaret she needs to visit the warden's office and add your name to her list. And then next time you won't have any problems, I guarantee it."

He was already looking over my shoulder to the next person in line, but I made one last push. "I understand, but I've been waiting here since seven o'clock. Is there anything we can do today?"

"No, sir."

"Could you call her room? Tell her I'm here?"

"The inmates don't have telephones. I'm sorry, but if you're not on her list, you're not on her list."

His partner seemed poised to disagree. She opened her mouth like she was about to offer a solution, so I shifted my focus to her. "There's no other family to visit. It's just me. Is there any way you can help?"

She checked her wristwatch. A digital Timex, almost exactly like mine. "At this hour, all the women are in the yard. For morning exercise. I'll see if I can find her." Then she pushed herself to a standing position and told her partner to seat me at a table.

He shook his head—he seemed amused by her willingness to do more than the bare minimum her job description required—then proceeded to read my instructions: "Walk directly to table eighteen and sit down. Do not attempt to sit at any other table. Do not converse or gesture to any of the other inmates or visitors. If you need to visit a restroom, raise your hand and ask the guard. If you want to make a purchase from the vending machines, raise your hand and ask the guard. You are allowed to respectfully embrace the inmate at the start and end of your visit, but all other physical contact is forbidden. Do you understand all the rules I've just outlined?"

"Yes, I do."

"Door's on your right. Have a nice day."

I stepped inside the visitation room, which had bright, cheerful colors and large windows admitting lots of natural light. It reminded me of the cafeteria at Holy Redeemer Hospital. There were vending machines dispensing everything from sodas and coffee to chips and even cold sandwiches. As I crossed the room to the table marked eighteen, I glanced at the other visitors, trying to discern all the various relationships on display: inmate and spouse, inmate and child, inmate and attorney. "Just seven more months, honey," I heard one woman saying. "In seven more months, all this will be over, and you'll be back home where you belong." Elsewhere in the room, a baby was crying, and a surprising number of people had bowed their heads to pray together—in English and Spanish and languages I didn't recognize.

I sat down at table eighteen. There was a large TV playing the *Today* show with the volume muted and the subtitles on. Al Roker was interviewing a Second World War veteran who had found late-in-life fame as a TikTok celebrity giving out life wisdom: "I don't think children are meant to be molded," he was saying. "I think they're people waiting to be unfolded." There were a couple of digital clocks spaced around the room, to help visitors keep track of the time, but none of the clocks were in sync. One said 10:05, another said 10:06, and another said 10:03—but according to the *Today* show, the actual time was 10:19.

As I waited, the broadcast cut to a commercial with Chris Pratt and Aubrey Plaza promoting the Chrysler Reactor with the new-and-improved Miracle Battery Infinity. Despite all the controversy of the past year, Capaciti was on track to have another year of record sales. Customers didn't seem to care that the FBI had launched four simultaneous raids of Osprey Cove, the apartment at Beacon Tower, the Gardners' home in Cambridge, and Capaciti's research headquarters. A team of special agents had arrested Errol, Catherine, Gerry, and Maggie, but of course my daughter was the only one serving any time—three to five years for conspiracy to obstruct justice and being an accessory to murder after the fact. Catherine Gardner was "receiving treatment" at a beachside rehab center in West Palm Beach while Errol and Gerry remained free on millions of dollars in bail, filing appeal after appeal and using every last loophole available to the 0.001 percent. I didn't expect they would ever be properly punished. But I took some comfort in knowing that Dawn Taggart's body had been recovered from the bottom of Lake Wyndham, so her mother and uncle could finally lay her to rest. Better still, Hugo was promptly apprehended and extradited back to Kinshasa, the capital of the Democratic Republic of the Congo, where he was awaiting trial for scores of human rights violations. Many speculated that he would be the first Congolese prisoner sentenced to death since 2007, but I was trying not to get my hopes up.

Eventually the woman from registration entered the visitation area to find me. Her face was somber—she looked like a surgeon emerging from the ER to deliver some bad news. "I found Margaret in the exercise yard, and I told her you were waiting here. But she's decided she isn't going to come see you."

I felt bad for putting her in the middle of an awkward situation. I stood up and said, "Thank you for trying."

"One thing you could do is write her a letter," she offered. "Tell her what you're feeling on paper. Let her know you're interested in supporting her." She was trying to be helpful, which I appreciated. So I didn't mention all the letters I'd already sent over the past few months.

Or the cards for her birthday and Christmas and just because. Always with a personal note but never any pocket money, because the prison wouldn't allow cash by mail.

"I've met a lot of parents in your situation," the woman continued. "So don't leave here feeling like you're alone, okay? Because you're not the only one."

I left the building and walked out into the sunshine. It was still early, a beautiful clear morning, and suddenly I had my whole day ahead of me. Vicky had planned a special dinner for later in the evening, and she'd invited a couple of my friends from UPS. Plus Tammy and Abigail would be there, and after dinner I was sure we'd play charades or Pictionary or some other party game, because that's how we always celebrated our birthdays together. I knew I was fortunate to have so many wonderful people in my life. But I also knew at some point I would look around the dinner table and remember who was missing.

I crossed the parking lot and unlocked the door to my Jeep, then turned to take one last look at the prison. It was an imposing concrete building with three levels of cells, and a window in a stairwell allowed a glimpse inside the facility. I could see dozens of female inmates in orange jumpsuits ascending the stairs, moving in an orderly single-file line. And I noticed something peculiar: nearly every single woman turned to glance outside, to steal a quick look at the world beyond their walls. They were all different ages and races, but they all shared that same impulse. Most looked to the horizon—toward Route 81 way off in the distance—but every so often, an inmate locked eyes with me. Checking to see if I was someone she knew.

"Excuse me, sir?"

A corrections officer was walking toward me. A young woman, about my daughter's age, dressed in a blue collared shirt, a black necktie, and a black hat.

"Have you finished your visit?"

"Yes."

"Then I need you to exit the parking lot. We have another group

THE LAST ONE AT THE WEDDING   335

of visitors coming at eleven, and they're going to need parking spaces. So they can go inside and see their loved ones."

My wristwatch said it was only 10:32, but evidently this kid was the law-and-order type. I liked that she took the extra time to explain the rules to me. She was tough but fair. Someone had raised her right. I apologized, opened the door to my Jeep, and got inside.

Then I looked back at the window. The inmates were still filing past. All returning to their cells, I guessed, after a session of morning exercise. I'd already counted some forty women, and there were only a hundred or so in the entire facility. I got out of my Jeep and called to the guard. "Excuse me? Officer? Could I ask a favor?"

She stopped and turned around.

"Can I stay five more minutes?"

ACKNOWLEDGMENTS

I'd like to thank everyone who helped me plan this wedding, especially Rick Chillot, Mike Russell, Doogie Horner, Grace Warrington, Jill Warrington, Steve Hockensmith, Ian Doescher, Kelly Chancey, Patrick Caulfield, Dave Murray, Grady Hendrix, and Michael Koryta.

No wedding would be complete without flowers, and the gruesome bouquets in this book are courtesy of Alweina Design and Will Staehle. Will also designed the wonderfully sinister cover of the North American edition.

When I found myself in desperate need of a quiet place to write, David Borgenicht gave me a key to his office building and refused to accept a dime in rent. I couldn't have finished this book without his kindness and generosity.

My UPS driver, Ian, took time out of his busy schedule to cheerfully answer all my questions, and I hope he'll forgive whatever creative liberties I've taken here.

Anytime I felt overwhelmed by this wedding, my editor, Zack Wagman, was a voice of calm and confidence. I'm grateful for his enthusiasm, his encouragement, and his many smart editorial suggestions. Thanks also to the rest of the Flatiron/Macmillan crew, especially Cat Kenney, Marlena Bittner, Katherine Turro, Maxine Charles, Megan Lynch, Bob Miller, Keith Hayes, Nancy Trypuc, Malati Chavali, Steve

Wagner, Brad Wood, Michelle McMillian, Morgan Mitchell, and all the talented people working behind the scenes in production, sales, and distribution. And to the entire team at Sphere/Little, Brown in the UK—especially deputy publisher Tilda Key, who identified many subtle and clever ways to improve this story.

I feel very lucky to have Doug Stewart as my literary agent. I can't imagine having a more knowledgeable or tireless advocate working on my behalf. Thanks also to his assistants, Tyler Monson and Maria Bell—and to Szilvia Molnar, Amanda Price, and Caspian Dennis for sharing my stories around the world. And to Rich Green, who is likely running another marathon instead of reading these acknowledgments.

Finally, here's a special wedding toast to my wife of twenty-four years, Julie Scott. And to our wonderful children, Sam and Anna. And to my parents and my brother and my entire extended family. They all supported the writing of this book but (thankfully) did not inspire it!

ABOUT THE AUTHOR

Jason Rekulak is the author of *Hidden Pictures*, a national bestseller and winner of the Goodreads Choice Award for Best Horror, and *The Impossible Fortress*, a finalist for the Edgar Award. He lives in Philadelphia with his family.